FATAL RACE

Diane Cobalt

Copyright 2019 by Diane Cobalt
All rights reserved.
ISBN: 9781795205283

Cover Image courtesy of Fotosin and Canstockphoto
Cover by Joleene Naylor

This is a work of fiction. All of the characters, organizations and incidents portrayed in this novel are products of the author's imagination and are used fictitiously.

Also by Diane Cobalt

Fatal Impact
Fatal Move

*To my volunteer publicist, editor
and marketing guru:
Pat Shaw*

*Thank you for your never-ending
support all these years!*

PROLOGUE

Two months earlier

The first thing she remembered was a jarring clank of metal, maybe a door? Or was it just the constant ringing in her ears getting louder? She tried desperately to open her eyes but her lids felt too heavy and swollen to obey her brain's command. Maybe she should call for help. But the only thing she was capable of tasting was the salt of blood overpowered by a mix of copper and aluminum. Had she been eating the change from the bottom of her purse? Why were there so many cobwebs in her head? She needed to think, get up and get back to the bar.

The bar! Geoffrey was waiting for her. He would be wondering what was taking her so long. Meredith Matthews attempted to sit up, but no part of her body seemed to be able to move. What was going on? Where was she? It started coming back to her in separate little chunks, like a thousand piece jigsaw puzzle. Her cell phone...she had been talking to her mom on her cell phone...but where? It had been noisy, lots of people talking loudly. Yes! She had been inside the little bar at a party. Ah, an edge piece found; Geoffrey had been across the room talking to one of their friends.

The sound of keys jangling intruded, momentarily crowding out the buzzing in her ears and halting her hunt for more puzzle pieces. A small poof of air passed over her face. Someone had just walked into the room. No, more than one person. She could hear their footsteps, smell their sweat.

"Che khabar?"

Meredith wasn't sure if the deep male voice was talking to her. Geoffrey? No, not his voice. The words were garbled and she couldn't comprehend what the man was saying. If only her hearing would clear.

"Khabari nist."

The second voice sounded female. Also not one she recognized.

Wait a minute! Another piece to the puzzle popped into Meredith's fuzzy brain. She was living in Frankfurt, Germany. They were probably conversing "auf Deutch"!

"Che khoob. Man bayad beravam. Ba'adan mibinamet," the male voice said. The metal banged again, indicating the man had departed.

Fatal Race

No, definitely not German. Meredith really needed to find one of the four corner pieces to this puzzle. If her brain was jumbling the words or her ears just weren't hearing them correctly, then why had she understood the exchange between the man and the woman?

"What's new?"

"Nothing much."

"That's good."

"I have to go. See you later."

Farsi! They were speaking Farsi! Yay, finally a corner piece! But she was stumped as to why she could identify that language, let alone comprehend it. Great, back to the puzzle.

Meredith felt a cool cloth swipe her forehead. She was fairly sure that she was not in a hospital. Her back was beginning to ache from the hard surface beneath her and the typical smell of institutional antiseptic eluded her. Something seemed to be holding her down, but it wasn't a bedsheet and she could only feel it at her wrists and ankles.

Oh God, no. She was tethered to something. Unsure whether the woman who wiped her brow was standing over her, she dared not try to move.

Meredith went back to the puzzle and the pieces she had locked into place. She knew she had been in Germany at a bar with her husband, Geoffrey, and that she had been talking to her mother on her cell phone. Was her mother in Germany? No. Meredith didn't think that felt right. In fact, she thought her mom lived far away, but nothing clear was coming to her.

Diane Cobalt

While Meredith concentrated on holding still, she circled back to details about herself. Her name was Meredith Baldwin Matthews. Good, at least she knew who she was! She was an American living in Germany doing...what? She was there with her husband who was doing...what? She somehow understood Farsi because...oh shit! Because she worked for the CIA. Maybe finding the ultimate corner piece wasn't such a good thing.

Meredith's clouded brain seemed to clear with a deluge of puzzle pieces now forming the entire outer frame. She and Geoffrey had lived in the Frankfurt area for several years and after searching for months, had finally found the key ISIS operatives the CIA had been looking for. They were close enough into the final parts of the operation that their bosses thought they needed to go underground until the men had been captured. Hence, the going away party with friends whom Geoffrey worked with at Exxon/Mobil, his cover assignment.

But wait, what was her cover assignment? She must have had one. Just being Geoffrey's wife wouldn't have filled her days. All of a sudden the puzzle pieces interlocked with each other filling in the picture. She and Geoffrey were parents to a five year old little boy, Ryan. Meredith had just returned from escorting Ryan back to the states for her parents to take care of until she and Geoffrey returned. Their assignment was just weeks from being complete and Meredith had felt they were in too much danger to have Ryan hanging around. She'd been talking to her mom on her cell phone, but had trouble hearing because of the noise in the bar. She had walked outside to call her back when...nothing. Her mind was blank, a big missing piece in the center of the puzzle.

Had she been taken prisoner? Had they hurt her? Where was Geoffrey? He must be looking for her.

Meredith heard something buzz, perhaps a vibration.

"Salam. Negaram nabashid. A'alan? Bateh."

The woman in the room had answered her phone. "Hi. Don't worry. Now? Yes," was what Meredith heard. A blast of warm air blew in and the door clanked shut. Meredith assumed she was alone in the room.

Carefully, in case anyone else was still there, Meredith twisted her hands from side to side. They were definitely tied down with some kind of thick rope. She rotated her right ankle, then her left. More rope. She needed to see. Slowly, Meredith lifted her eyelids enough for her to see a little light topped with black fringe. It took several seconds for her to realize the fringe was her eyelashes. *Open just a little more,* she commanded her eyelids. This time they obeyed. Meredith found herself on a cot in a room no larger than ten by ten feet constructed out of concrete block. About a foot from the ceiling on the wall to her left was a glass block window, the only source of light. She surveyed the room without sitting up. She was alone.

With a huge amount of effort, Meredith lifted her head off the cot and was able to prop herself up on her elbows. She scanned her body. Her chest was wrapped in bloodied strips of fabric. Her jeans were ripped from her thigh to her knees on her right leg but fine on the left. She still wore her loafers she'd had on in the bar.

Meredith plopped her head back down on the cot. So she had been injured, but not fatally. Once again keys rattled at the door. Meredith realized the best way to find her most important puzzle pieces, Ryan and Geoffrey, would be to appear to her captors that she had amnesia.

CHAPTER ONE

Jennifer Baldwin watched her handsome husband walk down the path in front of their new home. He was heading towards her car to retrieve her cell phone. Her heart was pounding with happiness. Realizing she couldn't wait one more second to throw her arms around him, Jennifer asked her friend Kate to watch the boys and bounded down their front walk.

Beau was reaching into her car, his back to her.

"Did you find it?" Jennifer could see she had startled him by the look on his face.

Beau turned to Jennifer. He held her cell phone in one hand and a second cell phone in a yellow case in the other. "What's this phone for, Jennifer?"

Jennifer froze. *Oh shit!* She'd forgotten that she had hidden the phone in her center console. Manuel Garcia had given her the phone in the yellow case to communicate with him when she found information on the terrorist cell the Eagle's Nest was pursuing. It was one of only a few secrets she had ever kept from her husband. But so far, they had not given her permission to reveal that she was helping members of the U.S. government track down a dangerous group of individuals residing in their community. Jennifer had come close to telling Beau so many times. But her fear of Beau's objections to her role in this case always overruled her decision to share the truth. Jennifer wanted to make a difference to society and this seemed like an excellent opportunity.

Was now the time to let him in on her secret? To admit that she left her job to work for a suspected terrorist? That she potentially was putting them all at risk? She had just seconds to decide.

"There it is! Thank God you found it, Beau," interrupted Kate. "I've been looking all over for that phone. Drew's mother left it at our house by accident yesterday. When I went to grab mine just now to take a picture of Chris and Ryan on the stairs, I thought I'd just dial her number and maybe I would hear it amongst all the boxes in case I'd put it down while unpacking. But no, there it is, right where I left it when we were out shopping in your car!" Kate Lange's shiny, chin length chestnut brown hair caught the setting sun's light.

Beau visibly relaxed. "Mystery solved. Here you go!"

Kate took the phone from Beau's outstretched hand. "Thank you so much! I'll just take a pic of those two sweet boys on this phone so my mother-in-law will have a surprise!"

Jennifer pasted a large enough smile on her face to let her bright, white teeth and dimples show. She watched her best friend go back inside. The one acting class she'd taken in high school was coming in handy. Crisis averted... at least for now. She knew she'd have some explaining to do with Kate. Her phone! If Beau had found it under all the papers in her console, then it must have been vibrating which meant Manuel was trying to reach her. Fortunately, the phone had been programmed so as not to show any "missed call" alerts. And Jennifer knew that voice mails were forbidden as were texts. She'd have to find a way to retrieve it from Kate as soon as possible. But for now, Jennifer needed to act normal.

"Actually, I followed you out here to give you this," Jennifer turned to face her husband and gave him a hug. "Thank you for doing all of this...it's just incredible that you could pull this off." *And nothing short of a miracle that I didn't get caught.* "I didn't even know this house was on the market."

Beau smiled down at his wife. "Technically, it hadn't been listed. I contacted Darcy Gibbons and told her we were looking for something in the neighborhood, but on a different street. She remembered showing us this house when we were looking for our last home and contacted the owner who just happened to have gotten transferred to California. They had already moved out and were eager to accept our offer. Darcy recommended a mover who specializes in complete moves from packing to unpacking. Kate supervised the movers this morning while we were at Ryan's guardianship hearing. Clearly they're not quite finished. There are still a lot of boxes to unpack and even a few things left at our old house. And I need to add your signature on all of the paperwork." Beau paused, surveying his front lawn. "I made an appointment at the title company for you for tomorrow at noon, but I can change it if you can't get away from work. They said it will take about half an hour."

Jennifer looked into Beau's hazel eyes. His bushy black eyebrows provided a beautiful frame. "Wow! You and Kate and Darcy are my heroes!" Jennifer kissed her husband. "My boss is out of town right now so I have some flexibility in my schedule. Tomorrow's a big day for Ryan...and I guess for the moms. The PTA sponsors a coffee for the kindergarten parents after they drop off their children." Jennifer looked down at the sidewalk. "I feel so bad for Ryan that his mother isn't here to take him to his first day of school. And I feel bad for Meredith too."

Ryan's father, Geoffrey Matthews, had been killed in Germany during the bombing at a local bar where he and Beau's sister, Meredith, had been attending a farewell party. They had flown Ryan back just a few weeks earlier ahead of their relocation back to the U.S. Meredith was still missing. So Beau and Jennifer had gone to court the day before to seek full guardianship of Ryan until Meredith was found.

"Should I go?" offered Beau.

"Let's get Kate's opinion on that. I'll see if Drew is going."

Beau nodded in agreement. He and Kate's husband, Drew Lange, had become almost as close of friends as Jennifer and Kate were. "Great idea! Let's go back inside and take some pictures."

"Yes, she'll want to get Chris home. He has a big day tomorrow too."

Beau took Jennifer's hand in his and walked her back inside. As they reached the double front doors, Beau halted. "Wait! We're going to do this right, Mrs. Baldwin."

Jennifer looked at him, puzzled. Beau swung open the massive door then scooped up Jennifer in his arms and carried her over the threshold.

Jennifer giggled. "Good thing I'm not further along in my pregnancy or you might not be able to lift me!"

Beau gently set her down on the marble tile of their new foyer. "Not to worry. I will just keep working out so that no matter how much weight you gain, I can still carry you!"

As Jennifer stood up, Ryan came running over. "Aunt Jennifer, can Chris spend the night in my new room?"

Jennifer looked over at Kate who was shaking her head. "That sounds like a great idea, but we'll have to save it for this weekend. You and Chris have a big day tomorrow."

Ryan hung his head. "But that's tomorrow."

Beau stooped down and tousled Ryan's curly blond hair. "Hey, Slugger, you and Chris need to get a good night's sleep. Kindergarten is a lot of fun."

Ryan's face lit up. "That's right. They have that big playground outside."

Chris walked up to his friend. "Don't forget all the blocks and paint in that...room. What did they call it again?"

"Classroom," answered Kate as she walked up to the group, purse in hand. "Shall we carpool together in the morning? Or do you want to go separately, Jen?"

"I was going to ask, do you think Beau should go too?"

Kate shrugged and tilted her head, narrowing her big brown eyes. "Hmm. I would say probably not. I don't think Drew plans on going. Sometimes you don't want too big of an audience, if you know what I mean."

Beau laughed. "Got it. You two take the boys. I'll be waiting to hear all about it."

Kate smiled. "Sounds like a plan. I'll pick you two up about seven thirty. Come on, Chris. The sooner we get home, the sooner tomorrow comes."

When the door closed behind Kate and Chris, Jennifer looked at her guys. "Ryan, I haven't had time to really look around this house. How about you show me around while Uncle Beau orders takeout for dinner?"

"Yes!" shouted Ryan. "Let's go upstairs first so you can see my room."

His room. The thought of that made Jennifer smile. He was assimilating into their family so well. But a moment later, she wanted to cry. Hopefully, Ryan wasn't forgetting he had a mother or that his father had died. And hopefully, Ryan's mother was still alive.

It had taken over half an hour to get Ryan settled into his bed in his new room. He had crept down the stairs twice, first asking for a drink of water and then just saying he couldn't sleep. Jennifer felt sorry for him. He'd had a busy day and the thought of starting something new could be weighing heavily on his mind. It took Beau reading his favorite childhood story, "Put Me in the Zoo," before Ryan finally nodded off.

The Baldwins' new home came complete with an amazing backyard. The pool was about twenty yards long and in the shape of a figure eight. Large rocks outlined a huge waterfall on one side. A separate hot tub was situated between the doors to the master bedroom and a gazebo. On the other side of the yard was a covered outdoor kitchen with a flat panel TV hung over the bar area.

Jennifer sipped a glass of Topo Chico as she sat on the "mermaid's ledge" of the pool. Her shoulder length, wavy brunette hair was pulled back into a ponytail. Her golden brown eyes watched Beau come out of the door that led to their new family room.

"He's finally asleep," Beau pronounced.

"Come join me," Jennifer patted a spot next to her. "This is an incredible property. I couldn't have designed a better backyard. I don't remember this from when we looked at it."

Beau sat down next to his wife. "The owners added most of this since we first looked at it. I can't imagine ever wanting to move from this property."

"It will be a wonderful place to raise our kids," Jennifer smiled and laid her head on Beau's shoulder. She had completely forgotten that Manuel Garcia was trying to reach her.

CHAPTER TWO

Jennifer sat up with a start and looked around the darkened bedroom, at first not realizing where she was. Then it sank in...their new home. She glanced at the neon blue light from the clock next to her bed: six a.m. At least she had slept well for most of the night.

Rolling over, Jennifer watched her sweet husband sleeping peacefully. *Sweet and unsuspecting.* She couldn't shake the guilt that plagued her on a daily basis. How would she feel if Beau were working for a government agency without her knowledge? Maybe he would never have to find out? Ha! And when he did, would he forgive her?

She moved onto her back and felt the precious little life stir within her belly. Jennifer smiled, treasuring the moment. *If only it were all this simple.*

Fatal Race

Jennifer started making a mental list of what she needed to accomplish that day: get Ryan ready for school after a hot breakfast; attend the back-to-school tea for kindergarten moms with Kate—ugh, explain to Kate about her yellow phone. The phone! She had forgotten to get in touch with Manuel! Add that to the growing list: call Manuel; go to work; sign the mortgage documents at the title company; pick up Ryan from school; fix dinner... Jennifer squeezed her eyes closed, exhausted before the day had even begun.

There was a soft knock on their bedroom door which opened before Jennifer could put her feet on the floor.

"I'm ready for school," whispered Ryan.

Beau bolted up. "What? What's wrong?"

Jennifer laughed and made her way across the dark room to her nephew, giving him a big hug. "It sure looks like you're ready, Ryan. You even have your backpack on."

"Hey Buddy. It's not quite time to get up yet," Beau yawned. "How about you go and watch some TV while your aunt and I get dressed?"

"Ok," Ryan replied somewhat dejectedly. "I can't tell time yet, you know."

Beau nodded in the dark. "True and I forgot to put a digital clock in your room. I'll do that tonight."

Ryan left their bedroom and Beau took Jennifer in his arms. "Sorry about that wake-up call. I guess we're lucky he slept most of the night."

"It's okay. I was already awake. I guess I'm excited for the first day of kindergarten too!"

After she had showered and dressed, Jennifer came out to her new kitchen, hoping she could find the necessary equipment to make Ryan scrambled eggs. He was diligently sitting on their black leather sofa watching cartoons. Jennifer marveled at how adaptable children were. Fortunately, they had plenty of time before Kate was due to pick them up. She was now wishing that she hadn't agreed to go with them to school so that she could drive directly to the Eagle's Nest headquarters on her way to work. Kate would have to drop her off afterwards and Jennifer didn't want too much time alone with her best friend, giving Kate additional time to ask further questions about the phone. Yet she didn't want to vary from the plan and risk upsetting Ryan.

Beau entered the kitchen and came up behind Jennifer, wrapping his arms around her growing belly. "And how's our little nugget this morning?" He kissed her neck.

"The nugget seems to be sleeping now that I'm not!"

Beau laughed, grabbing plates and silverware and setting the island area for breakfast. "Do you think Ryan can handle sitting up here to eat?"

At the sound of his name, Ryan bolted to Beau's side. "Yes! I can sit in those tall chairs?!"

"Well why couldn't you?" Jennifer responded. "After all, you're a big kindergartener now!"

The family of three thoroughly enjoyed eating breakfast on their new kitchen island. Jennifer was surprised that Ryan ate all of his eggs, sausage and toast with strawberry jam. As soon as he finished, he grabbed his backpack and headed towards the front door. "I'm ready!"

Beau and Jennifer laughed. "We've still got a little time before Kate and Chris get here to pick us up."

"What have you got going on today?" Jennifer asked Beau as she poured him a cup of coffee.

"Well, I'm scheduled to have lunch at Winding Trails with Clay Hirsch to find out how he likes working for Callaway. He said there might be some opportunities for me." Beau ran his fingers through his black, straight hair. "I sure don't feel right about not working now, especially with a little one on the way. This is too much pressure on you."

Jennifer sat down opposite her husband and stared into his eyes. "Our marriage is a partnership. You did the right thing leaving Cardio Technologies. And I want you to be happy with this next position. Take your time finding something you really want to do."

Beau nodded and looked down at his plate. His wife was not only working full time, but was also pregnant and playing mom to his nephew…for how long, no one could say. Beau hoped Clay would have some great suggestions. "I can pick up Ryan if that would help your day."

"Actually, that would be a big help. I'll find out how the system works for picking up when I talk to the other moms at the coffee this morning."

"System for picking up? Don't I just pull up and he comes out to the car?"

Jennifer laughed. "Maybe. I don't know. There might be a carpool line or the moms might park and walk up to the front door. And it may vary for the kindergarteners since they're so little."

"I'm not little," yelled Ryan from his post at the front window.

Beau grinned and then lowered his voice. "Today's going to be a huge learning experience for him."

Jennifer nodded. "Shoot! I forgot to pack his lunch!" She glanced at the oven clock. "I've got fifteen minutes before Kate gets here. That should be enough time."

When Kate and Chris arrived ten minutes early, Jennifer and Ryan were waiting for them in front of their house. Beau had taken the requisite "first day of school" pictures and Jennifer promised to get at least one of Ryan in front of his school. And as fun and exciting as this day was, Jennifer hoped that Ryan's mom would be snapping the pic on her phone for Ryan's first day of first grade.

After strapping Ryan into the car booster seat in Kate's Volvo SUV, Jennifer climbed into the front passenger seat. "Good morning, Darling!" Kate greeted her college friend.

"Yes, it is a good morning, isn't it?" Jennifer responded. Ryan and Chris were talking nonstop in the backseat as if they hadn't just seen each other the night before.

"Did you remember to pack a lunch for Ryan?" Kate asked Jennifer.

Jennifer smiled and nodded. "Yes, I'm not a complete idiot, you know."

Fatal Race

"I know. I know. It's just that you became an instant mother and you're not used to doing all these things. Motherhood can wear you out. I'm pooped today!"

"Probably because you did so much unpacking for me."

Kate shrugged. "Not really! The movers did most of it. I just directed where things should go...kind of like I was queen! I hope everything is at least close to where you'd want it to be."

"After living together in that apartment in college, you know me very well. I even found all of the pans and utensils I needed to make breakfast this morning and they were right where I would have put them." Jennifer smiled.

Kate pulled down the small street lined with maple trees leading to Grandview Elementary School. The street itself ended just past the front of the red brick building and became a one-way drive that circled back behind the school and its playground and emptied onto another dead-end street. She moaned at the line of cars. "Do you think it will be like this every morning?"

Jennifer shook her head. "I doubt it. The first day of school is a really big deal. I'll bet by Friday we'll be wondering where everyone is."

Kate expertly maneuvered her SUV into a snug space between two vans.

"Impressive," commented Jennifer.

"We're here! We're here!" shouted Chris as he unbuckled his car seat and helped Ryan do the same.

"Let us open your doors," cautioned Kate. "There's a lot of traffic around here."

"In fact, why don't you both get out on Ryan's side of the car? That way you won't be stepping into the street," suggested Jennifer.

Chris nodded and obediently slid over to his friend's side of the backseat. Jennifer slowly opened their door and both boys jumped onto the sidewalk.

Kate and Jennifer each grabbed their kindergartener's hand and carefully crossed the line of cars circling the front of the school.

"Before we go in, I want to take your pictures by the school's sign," Jennifer said.

"Looks like there might be a bit of a line to do that," Kate commented.

When it got to be their turn, Jennifer took a picture of both boys, then one of Ryan alone. Kate followed up by taking one of Chris alone. "We've got to have one for your scrapbook," she said to Chris.

Scrapbook? Jennifer hadn't thought of that. She'd be sure to keep all of the mementos for her sister-in-law. Jennifer said another silent prayer that Meredith was still alive.

Jennifer and Kate were still in the classroom when the bell rang. Mrs. Williamson shooed them out along with most of the other moms. Reluctantly, they headed towards the library where the PTA was holding a special coffee for the kindergarten parents.

Fatal Race

The library was practically overflowing with moms. "Do we have to go to this?" Jennifer asked her friend as they walked through the double doors. "We won't know anyone."

Kate laughed as she surveyed the situation from her five foot nine inch vantage point. She was three inches taller than Jennifer. "You still haven't changed a bit from college, have you? Always looking for a way out of that uncomfortable social setting."

Jennifer looked up at Kate. "This is hardly a fraternity party."

"Exactly! This is safe. You don't have to worry about them spiking the trash can punch in the school library. However, you might want to look at this as Open House Day during sorority rush. We're here to make some new friends and make a mental list of those we'd prefer to avoid."

Jennifer let out a deep breath. "What if they don't like *us*?"

"Then clearly there is something wrong with them. Come on!" Kate literally pulled Jennifer into the room and headed to a long table decorated with blue and yellow tablecloths. "I see some donuts and muffins and for once I am starving."

"Welcome to Grandview Elementary, ladies! My name is Isabelle and I'm president of the PTA. Please help yourself to some coffee or tea and a treat and then peruse the volunteer sign-up sheets." Isabelle rattled off her spiel quite perkily even though she must have said it a thousand times. The PTA president's name badge was pinned to her sleeveless shift. Jennifer hoped all the moms weren't this perfectly coiffed and dressed. She wanted to like Isabelle but didn't quite have the energy

"Why thank you, Isabelle! I'm Kate and this is my best friend, Jennifer. We are moms of kindergarteners. Can you point us in the direction of those volunteer lists?"

Isabelle practically beamed. "We are so glad that you're a part of Grandview Elementary! There are name tags to fill out at the end of the table and the kindergarten sign-up sheets are right next to them. Please let me know if you have any questions. I know you'll love it here."

"How could we not?" Kate smiled back and gently nudged Jennifer towards the end of the table. When they were safely out of earshot, Kate whispered to her friend. "Oh my God, I really hope they aren't all as plastic as Isabelle! She may be one of the original Stepford wives."

Jennifer almost laughed out loud. "I was trying to decide if she's just super friendly and nice, or a fake." She looked down at the sheets listing various volunteer opportunities, most of which were already filled. "What do you think we should go for?"

"Hmm. The only list that has two spots open is Room Moms."

"That sounds like a big job."

"Which is probably why no one has signed up for it." Kate paused, pushing her chestnut brown hair behind her left ear. "What the hell, we handled sorority responsibilities that probably would make room mother duties pale in comparison. Let's go for it!"

Jennifer hesitated. She really didn't feel like signing up for anything.

Kate looked at her friend. "I know you have a lot on your plate. I'll do the lion's share of the work if you will just be my assistant."

"Okay, but I'm just the assistant. Deal?"

"Deal!"

Jennifer looked at her watch. "I really need to get to work pretty soon."

But before Kate could respond, they were interrupted. "Hi Moms and Dads of kindergarteners and welcome back to our PTA members." It was Isabelle in front of a microphone at the far end of the library. "I'm Isabelle Humphrey, President of the Grandview Elementary PTA. We are so glad to have you as part of our community and know that this is a momentous day for you. Some of you are dropping off your oldest or only child so all of this is brand new. And others of you are dropping off a younger sibling of current students here. And for some of you, this is your last kindergarten tea because your youngest is finally school age! Whatever category you fall into, our precious kindergarten teachers have a little parting gift for you: a bag of tea and a cute poem to assure you that you can relax and know that your little one is in excellent hands. I won't take any more of your time today. I know many of you are heading to work or appointments. But please take time to join the PTA and sign up to volunteer on a committee. Again, welcome!"

"Okay, let's split!" Kate said to Jennifer as they slowly moved with the crowd of mostly women to the double doors of the library. Another PTA volunteer was passing out blue and yellow pouches made of netting which held the promised tea bag along with a note.

Jennifer breathed a sigh of relief when they got into Kate's SUV.

"See that wasn't so bad, was it?" Kate asked her.

"No, I guess not. You know me. I'm not one who is good in a crowd."

Kate laughed as she punched up the fan on her A/C and pulled out of her parking space. "And evidently you're not good at hiding secret cell phones from your husband."

Boom! That was typical Kate. She was always direct and to the point and had a memory like an elephant.

"Thanks for bailing me out of what could have been a tricky situation. I owe you one."

Kate glanced over at her friend. "What you owe me is an explanation. And by the way, the phone is in the glove box there in front of you."

Jennifer pushed the button and the box hinged open. She removed the yellow phone.

"Please tell me you're not using that phone to communicate with Alex Hart!"

"What? Gosh no!" Jennifer couldn't believe Kate had come up with that idea. "It's a work phone."

"Then why didn't Beau know about it? He seemed pretty confused."

Jennifer took a deep breath and blew it out. "Because my boss gave this to me so he could reach me when he's traveling internationally. I decided not to mention it to Beau because he already feels bad that I am working so hard and taking care of Ryan all while I am pregnant."

Kate nodded, not quite believing her friend. "Okay, makes sense."

"Why did you think I was communicating with Alex?" *He's the only man who's ever broken my heart.*

"Because he's communicated with me! Unzip the outside pocket on my purse. There's a letter in there for you... from Alex."

Jennifer was stunned. "What?"

"Just open it. I'm dying to know what he has to say!"

Jennifer slowly unzipped the side pocket of Kate's brown leather Coach bag and extracted a folded envelope. Her name was written on the outside. It was definitely Alex's handwriting. "Kate, you have to know that nothing has gone on between us. I love Beau. In fact, the last time I talked to Alex was at dinner the night that...the night of the accident in our pool. I don't even know where Alex is."

"I do. He's in Germany."

"Germany? Why? And how do you know?" For some reason, Jennifer felt as if she'd been kicked in the stomach. Why would Alex tell her best friend his whereabouts and not her?

"He's opening health clubs over there...mostly because he needed to get away and try to forget you."

"For heaven's sake. That's ridiculous. He knows he had no chance with me. Zero."

Kate shrugged as she pulled into Jennifer's driveway. "He's not a man who gives up easily it would seem."

Jennifer felt as if she were going to cry. "Thanks for the ride. Beau will pick up Ryan and Chris after school. And thanks for covering for me about the phone." She opened her car door and got out still clutching the unopened envelope from Alex in her hand.

CHAPTER THREE

Jennifer watched Kate pull away and headed to the garage. She wasn't sure what to do first: call Manuel or open Alex's letter which was still in her shaking hand. Why did Alex have this effect on her? And why was he still trying to interfere in her life when she had been so clear that night at the restaurant...their last dinner together...that Beau was her life? And that she was expecting their first child...there was no room for him in her life...anymore.

It had been twelve years since that horrible, dark day during Jennifer's junior year in college. Now it seemed like a whole lifetime had fit into that time span. Yet she could recall it as if it had happened yesterday.

Hot tears had surged down Jennifer Monroe's cheeks as she had tightly squeezed her long lashes together, hoping that when she opened them, the handwritten letter she held in her shaking hand would carry a different message. The tears raced across her jawbone and splashed onto her chest like the first few raindrops falling from a dark cloud. She glanced down at the familiar handwriting, but it still conveyed the same, startling message: Alex Hart, her boyfriend for more than two years, was marrying someone else.

Jennifer shook her head as if to clear the unwanted image in her brain. Just last year when she had run into Alex at his health club, Alex had explained that he'd been tricked into marrying his high school sweetheart who claimed she had a fatal cancer. It turned out Alex was the one who had been duped and eventually got a divorce. But Jennifer had made it clear that she was deeply in love with her husband and there was no chance of any reconciliation. Too late!

This letter would have to wait. Manuel Garcia, a U.S. Border Patrol agent who had helped Jennifer rescue Beau just last year, might think she had gone AWOL. Manuel was the reason Jennifer had agreed to assist a group that called themselves "Eagle's Nest" in finding information on a potential terrorist cell in her community. At first, Jennifer thought she'd just be their eyes and ears...if you see something, say something...no big deal. But then a job had opened up, working with two former coworkers who had "retired." It was a job the Eagle's Nest insisted on her taking. They were quietly investigating the owner of this company, Alan Smith, as the likely leader of the terrorist cell.

Fatal Race

Jennifer hoped Manuel was calling with some news about Meredith's whereabouts. She pulled out the phone from inside her purse where she had stashed it and punched the only autodial number programmed into it.

"Jennifer," Manuel stated in the same tone of voice he always answered his phone with: serious. "I was concerned when you didn't call back and I tracked the phone to someone else's address, your friend Kate's I believe."

Jennifer checked her rearview mirror before backing out of her driveway, the yellow phone to her ear. "When you called yesterday, my husband heard the phone buzzing in my car and wanted to know whose phone it was. Fortunately my best friend, Kate, covered for me because she thought I might be having an affair with a former...flame."

Manuel actually laughed, something he did not do often. "You? Cheat on your husband? Highly unlikely. But at least she saved you from an explanation."

Am I really that boring? Jennifer rolled her eyes. "Do you have any information on Meredith?"

"Not yet. But we are still hopeful."

"If she had been blown up in that incident, wouldn't there be some kind of...remains? Or would she have been totally disintegrated? I hate to ask, but I keep wondering."

"That's a great question. It is likely that there would be some kind of DNA producing evidence, but that's not a guarantee in an event like that. Because our agents have found absolutely no proof, we feel she may have escaped somehow. But that's not why I was calling you."

"Right. Sorry. Go on."

"Our sources have told us that your boss is on the move organizing some kind of prototype event."

"What does that mean?"

"It means that they want to test something on a smaller scale that would have a detrimental impact on your community. Just keep your eyes and ears open. Anything that doesn't seem logical to you let me know as soon as it is safe to do so."

"Okay. I will. He's supposed to be out of town today and I'm not sure when he'll be back."

"He's in town. In fact, he's at the office right now."

Jennifer shook her head, always amazed at how much Manuel knew. "Then I better get in there." *And now I might not have time to sign the mortgage documents!* Her yellow phone went dead before she could end the call. She made a mental note to find a new hiding place for it. But for now, she'd have to leave it in her car. It was too dangerous taking it into the office.

Five minutes later, Jennifer swung into her parking space at Data Shield. She grabbed her purse and saw the crumpled envelope from Alex underneath it. She shoved it into the side pocket and headed inside. It would be lunchtime before she had a chance to open it.

Beau's meeting with his friend Clay Hirsch had been informative, but unfortunately the best Clay could offer Beau at the current time was a part-time position as a golf club fitter. Beau wasn't too sure taking that position would be a good idea since it involved a lot of weekend work, but he did agree to at least try out some Callaway clubs over the next few days to see how he liked them.

Clay had calls to make and left Beau in the pro shop at the local course close to his house. In fact, he could walk home if it weren't so blasted hot. Beau paid for a large bucket of balls and headed to the driving range to begin testing the clubs. He hadn't been there more than a few minutes when the head pro, Nick Alderson, who'd played with Beau at SMU walked up to him.

"Hey Beau! Good to see you."

"Well hey there, Nick. How've you been doing?"

The two shook hands. "Say, we've got a big tourney going on today and one of the teams is short a player. Would you be interested in joining us? Your entrance fee is already covered."

"Now that sounds like an offer too good to pass up. What's the tee time? I have to pick up my nephew from his first day of kindergarten at three."

"Five after ten. You should be off the course by two. Lunch is included afterwards. You may have to duck out of that early..."

"Perfect. I want to try out these new Callaway clubs. I may take some part-time work being a fitter for them."

"Those are some nice clubs. Come on in to the clubhouse after you're finished warming-up and I'll introduce you to your team."

Diane Cobalt

Beau couldn't wait. He hadn't played in a tournament in several years. He hoped he hadn't lost his swing.

The tournament was sponsored by several local real estate brokers who were welcoming new clients to the area. The company paired the newcomers with local businessmen as an introduction to their new communities.

Beau's foursome included an insurance agent from his town and two men who had just moved into a neighborhood in an adjacent suburb a few months ago. Beau was filling in for a local businessman.

The man with whom Beau was partnered stuck out his hand. "Hi, I'm Dr. Mark Hunnicutt."

Dr. Hunnicutt was tall and thin, his light brown hair was balding. Beau guessed he was probably in his mid-forties.

"Beau Baldwin. It's nice to meet you! Welcome to the area. Where did you move from?"

"I had a practice out in West Texas and business got a little slow when the oil prices dropped so I moved my family here. What do you do?"

Beau wasn't sure how to answer that question. He felt uncomfortable. "Right now I'm taking some time off. I was in medical equipment sales, but my brother-in-law was recently killed and my sister is missing so my wife and I are responsible in the interim for my nephew who's only five. I just thought it was better to provide a stable environment for him and not be on the road so much."

Dr. Hunnicutt and Beau secured their bags onto the cart. Beau got in the driver's seat and headed to the first tee.

"If you don't mind my asking, what happened?"

"My sister and brother-in-law and their son were living in Germany. They were getting ready to move back. In fact, my nephew had already returned and was living with my folks out East. But they were in that bar that exploded. My brother-in-law was killed."

"Oh no! They were in that bombing? I followed that story on the news."

Beau nodded. "Yes. I'm still hoping my sister is alive."

Dr. Hunnicutt was silent. "I'm sorry to hear about that."

"Not a good situation for sure." Beau pressed the parking brake as they approached the tee. "Looks like we'll be up after this foursome. So what kind of medicine do you practice?"

"I'm a cardiothoracic surgeon."

"Wow, that's impressive! Do you worry that playing golf will mess up your hands?"

The doctor laughed. "Nope. That's why I've insured them. What kind of medical equipment did you sell?"

"Actually, I've sold mostly cardio equipment, but no products used in surgery."

Dr. Hunnicutt nodded. "Looks like we're up."

After the first six holes, Beau loved the new clubs. He'd even given Dr. Hunnicutt a few to try and probably had made his first sale. And by the end of the round, Beau had not only wrapped up the sale, but also had made a new friend.

As the two walked into the building where lunch was being served, Dr. Hunnicutt put his hand on Beau's arm to stop him. "As much as I can't wait to get my own set of these clubs, I think your talent will be totally wasted working for this company. It's something I just can't allow."

"That's very kind of you, but..."

"No buts. I am in the final stages of developing a new product for cardiac surgeons. Can you handle being in surgery?"

Beau almost jumped up and down just as his nephew had this morning. "Handle it? I'd love it!"

"Then here's my card. Let's get together soon and talk details about you coming to work for me."

Beau took the card and put it safely in his wallet. "Thank you! I'll give you a call tomorrow. I'd hang around but I've got just enough time to get to the school to pick up my nephew."

Dr. Hunnicutt smiled. "I'll go check the results of the tournament."

Beau practically skipped with joy back to his car. Finally, his luck was changing.

CHAPTER FOUR

The small circular driveway in front of Dallas's exclusive Mansion Hotel was filled with exotic cars, everything from a Ferrari to an Aston Martin. Walter Simms almost felt poor pulling up in his black Mercedes AMG. But the valet who opened his door treated him as if he were driving the most expensive vehicle he'd ever seen.

"Welcome, sir. Will you be staying with us?"

"No. I'm just here for a meeting."

"Very good, then. Here's your claim ticket. Where can I direct you?"

"The lobby please."

"Through those double doors behind you. Enjoy your afternoon."

Walter walked into The Mansion's opulent lobby and appreciated the coolness of the air conditioning. He needed to get out of town and this oppressive heat. But he couldn't do that until he had tried talking some sense into his cousin. And that task could prove more difficult than staying cool in the heat of summer in Dallas, Texas.

Rachel Hayden had flown back into town two days ago ostensibly to avenge her sister's death. When Walter had called to notify her of Christina's death, he had cautioned his cousin that returning to the U.S. was highly risky due to the fact that she was still considered a fugitive.

Rachel had laughed. "You can't possibly think that I'd return using my former identity as that murderous lab tech, Bridget Colter, do you?"

Walter hadn't known how to respond to that. He really had no idea how similar Rachel was to Christina until just now. Neither had any sense of ethics or morals. But one was a survivor and the other was now six feet under. "Look, the purpose of my call was not to have you come back for the service. I just thought you should know that your sister has died."

"I believe you said earlier that she had been murdered. That alone makes a huge difference to me."

"Technically, she died from being electrocuted by the lightning when it hit the pool. But the woman involved was only trying to protect herself. Your sister had been stalking her to seek revenge for something that had happened to her in college." Walter protested.

"You mean the gang rape?" Rachel's tone was oozing hate. "You knew then."

"Of course I knew. I helped her through it...drove her to many reconstructive surgeries. Does this woman have a name and how was she involved in a rape? This makes no sense to me."

"Her name is Jennifer Baldwin and her husband, Beau, was a member of the fraternity whose members committed that heinous crime. As it turned out, Beau himself did nothing to your sister. I have proof of that," explained Walter.

Rachel was silent.

"Rachel? Are you there? Hello?"

Rachel cleared her voice. "I'm sorry. For a minute I thought I heard you say her husband's name is Beau."

"That's right."

"Beau Baldwin?"

Walter was getting irritated. He felt as if he were playing some kind of game without knowing the rules. "Yes! Beau Baldwin!"

"And just how did Sis know Beau Baldwin?"

"He worked for her. She'd just started another job, once again, with a different company because she'd been fired from the last one. Beau, whom I've met by the way, had recently started working for this company. He had left his previous company..."

"Coro-Med," Rachel interrupted.

"How did you know that?" Walter questioned. The game seemed to be getting more twisted.

"That's right. You don't know all of the details of my situation because you were out of the country at the time. Beau Baldwin was a sales rep at Coro-Med. Coro-Pharm, Coro-Med's parent company, had developed a life-saving new drug and needed to expedite its testing to get it to market faster. So I was hired to inject the drug directly into a patient's heart if that patient

happened to have a heart attack while having a stress test on Coro-Med's equipment. The only problem was that Beau started catching on to these 'under the radar' trials. He's definitely a Goody Two-shoes; so it doesn't surprise me that he was not a participant in Christina's rape." Rachel paused. *"So why was she so vindictive?"*

"Partly because she was Christina, a woman who got off on stirring up trouble. And partly because Beau knew what happened and didn't say anything."

"Yeah. I agree with my dearly departed sister. He should have had to pay for that in some way. And so now you're telling me his pretty little wife killed Christina?"

"From what I've read in the police report, Christina showed up at the Baldwins' with a gun and attempted to shoot Beau's wife. There was a struggle and the wife and your sister ended up in the pool. The wife hit Christina in the head with a pool skimmer and then lightning struck the pool. Again, Christina was electrocuted."

"I'll be on the next available flight to Dallas. Don't worry, Walter, I have several passports I can fly under. My husband won't be with me. That would make it too dangerous. Mrs. Baldwin has to pay for killing Christina. I'll be in touch with my itinerary. You can pick me up at DFW, can't you?"

Walter had gained no ground trying to convince Rachel on the drive in from the airport that Christina's death was an accident. She was hell-bent on destroying the Baldwins. That in and of itself was upsetting to Walter. Should he tell the authorities? Could he be an accessory to a crime if Rachel did something drastic? Yes and yes, he answered himself silently. But Walter also had a sneaking suspicion that Rachel, once known as Bridget Colter, had something else up her sleeve. He was taking her today to go look at apartments which puzzled him. Why would she need to be here that long? He'd actually been surprised when Rachel hadn't asked to stay with him. He shrugged as he pressed the up arrow for the elevator. He guessed if she had enough money to stay at The Mansion, then she could afford a short-term apartment rental.

Rachel opened the door to her suite as soon as she heard Walter knock. At first, Walter thought he had the wrong room...the woman on the other side was a blond. But then he remembered that Rachel had bleached her auburn hair which looked quite stunning against her island tan.

"Let's go," she said, making sure the door was locked behind her.

"Just how long are you planning on staying in Dallas?" Walter trailed behind her back to the elevator.

"As long as it takes."

Walter sighed. "As long as what takes? You've got to give up the revenge idea!" He lowered his voice although no one appeared to be in the hallway. "Do you want to end up in jail this time?"

The elevator doors slid open revealing an empty compartment. Walter and Rachel got in. "I have no intention of ever going to jail, Cousin. Now quit acting like my dad! Pierce and I have some unfinished business and a new client. Mrs. Baldwin is no longer my first priority."

Walter pursed his lips together. Pierce Hayden, aka Culver Nance, was Rachel's current husband. He was the research scientist who had been working on the drug that Rachel had assisted in illegally testing. Pierce had almost perfected the formula when he and Rachel had fled the country. That had been almost two years ago now. Maybe the couple had run out of money and Rachel's revenge against Jennifer Baldwin was just an excuse for her to return to stockpile some more cash. Or maybe she just wanted to mislead her dear cousin! Walter would have to keep his eye on her.

CHAPTER FIVE

A yellow sticky note from Alan Smith with the words "come to my office ASAP" was waiting for Jennifer on her computer monitor. Jennifer's stomach plummeted as she put her purse in her desk drawer. *Great! Can this day get any worse?* She plastered a smile on her face and walked to the end of the hall, knocking lightly on his open office door.

"You wanted to see me? I'm sorry I'm late...it's the..."

"First day of school! I know! I just got in myself. Please, be seated."

Jennifer nodded and relaxed. Good, she wasn't in trouble.

Jennifer's first impression of Alan Smith had been that he was trying too hard to look like someone named Alan Smith: generic. What stood out the most was that his bushy dark eyebrows didn't match the very bad blond toupee he sported. Mr. Smith's wire rim glasses were barely capable of handling his thick lenses. Jennifer had made mental notes of anything unusual in the room. His desk and matching credenza were fairly standard, pressed composite "fake" wood. There were no pictures on the wall and only one on the credenza behind him. As she had studied the photo, Jennifer determined the family in the frame was the same one pictured in every frame carried by that brand. In other words, Alan had no idea who those people were. Jennifer had also detected a Middle Eastern accent, but it sounded like Alan may have had some speech lessons in order to sound a little more American.

"I have a few more companies for you to work on. They take priority over all your other assignments." Alan reached back to his credenza and pulled off a half dozen legal sized accordion files. "All of the info you need to set up these companies in QuickBooks is right here. If you have any questions, come directly to me. Jack and Gordon are working on some other projects and I really don't need any of their expertise on this...just yours. And as always, this is confidential. I'm quite pleased with your work so far, Jennifer. You are quick, thorough and above all else, you know how to keep your mouth shut."

Jennifer looked as innocent as she knew how. "Thank you, Alan. And I appreciate your flexibility with my work hours. Taking care of our nephew is requiring more time than I had anticipated." She reached for the files and stood up.

"And where is it he goes to school?"

Why did Jennifer feel strange about telling him? She couldn't very well say she didn't know. "We enrolled him in Grandview Elementary for the time being. I'm sure his mom will be returning shortly."

Alan merely nodded. "I've heard it's a fairly good school. I have a dinner meeting this evening. Would you please prepare the file marked "BWP" for me before you leave today?"

"Of course. I should have it done in just a few hours. Is there any order for the other files?"

Alan shook his head. "No. That will suffice. Thank you."

Jennifer headed back to her office wondering why he was starting so many businesses.

As she had promised, Jennifer delivered the BWP file back to Alan within two hours. She had set up the company under the three initials as there was no further information as to the company's complete name anywhere in the file. In fact, after quickly perusing the other five files Alan had given her, Jennifer could find no names, just initials. They might be shell companies that Alan hadn't yet set up any corporate structure for. But some already had invoices to be sent out and a check for seventy-five hundred dollars to open a bank account was paper clipped to each folder. Jennifer glanced at her watch. If she hurried, she'd be able to stop by the bank and set up these accounts before her meeting at the title company. She opened the bottom desk drawer and grabbed her purse as she raced out of the office.

Diane Cobalt

An hour later, she finished signing the last of the documents required by the title company for the purchase of their new home. Jennifer was surprised how streamlined the process had become in just a few short years. Now she had time to grab a quick bite of lunch before returning to the office and working on the remaining five files. Jennifer was deciding whether to pick up something to take back to her desk or to give herself a much needed break when she spotted the corner of an envelope peeking out of the side pocket of her purse. Alex's letter! How could she have forgotten?

That solved her dilemma. She pulled into the parking lot at Café Max, ordered a salad sampler and then headed to a quiet table in the corner of the restaurant. Jennifer took a few bites of her favorite, the seafood salad, before extracting the envelope from her purse. Carefully, she unfolded the piece of paper inside and stared down at Alex's handwriting.

Dear Jennifer,

I was really hoping to never have to write another letter to you. Foolishly I thought I could win you back...that I am somehow better for you than your husband is. But even without my rose-colored glasses on, I can see that you are happy. And at the end of the day, if I can't have you, then I at least want you to be happy.

Fatal Race

I hope you understand that's it's too difficult for me to be in the same town and not contact you. So I've decided to go international with my health clubs. I'm not sure how long I'll be out of the country. But I do know that I will never stop loving you.

If you ever need me, Kate knows how to get in touch with me.

Be well, sweet Jennifer.

Love,
Alex

Jennifer realized her cheeks were wet with tears. She wiped them away feeling sad for the loss of Alex's friendship, but relieved that he had moved on. That was one less thing she had to deal with. Jennifer read through the letter one last time before tearing it up into tiny pieces. After she had finished eating, she put the torn pieces into her napkin and dropped them into the trash can on her way out.

It was after five when Jennifer arrived home. Beau and Ryan were happily playing in their new pool and didn't even notice when she stepped out onto the deck.

"Uh, hello?" she called.

Beau had Ryan on his shoulders. "I'm on top of the world, Aunt Jennifer!"

"I'd say so! How was school?"

"It was so much fun. I can't wait to go back tomorrow. I think they're gonna teach us how to read and write then."

Jennifer laughed. "Probably."

Beau dumped Ryan off his shoulders and onto the steps in the shallow end.

"I can't believe he has all that energy after a full day of kindergarten!" Jennifer commented. "Did you give him a sugary snack or something?"

"No, I didn't." Beau pretended to be offended then lowered his voice. "He fell asleep in the car on the way home! So I let him take a nap on the couch. He slept for about an hour."

"Yeah I had a dog nap!" Ryan added.

"It's a cat nap, Buddy," Beau reminded him.

"Cat, dog, how do you know which kind? I'm not either one of those."

"Maybe we should call it a growing school boy's nap," suggested Jennifer.

Ryan shrugged. "Can you come and swim with us? Please?"

"Just let me go get my suit on and I'll join you."

Swimming with Ryan and Beau was a good stress reliever for Jennifer. Ryan told her all about his big day at "the kindergarten!" Despite his having a "dog nap" she was sure he would sleep well tonight.

Fatal Race

After their swim, Beau cooked chicken on the grill while Jennifer made macaroni and cheese, one of Ryan's favorites. By eight, the sun was still up, but Ryan was not. Finally, Beau and Jennifer had some time to themselves.

"How did your meeting go with Clay Hirsch?" Jennifer asked as she curled up next to Beau on their leather sofa.

"Well they don't really have any openings right now, but he wanted me to try out some of their clubs so that maybe I can be a golf club fitter. The problem with being a fitter is that work is mostly on the weekends and that's a deal breaker for us. But I didn't tell him that because I wanted to try out the clubs!" Beau smiled slyly. "So while I was hitting with the clubs on the driving range, Nick Alderson walked up and said they had an opening in the tournament going on today and I could play for free if I wanted...so that's what I did!"

"You did all that before three?"

Beau chuckled. "Wait! There's more! This tournament was held by a local real estate company who pairs newcomers with the community business people. My partner was a cardiothoracic surgeon who just moved here from West Texas."

Jennifer sat up. "No way!"

"Oh yes. And after finishing eighteen holes and winning the tournament, he wants me to work for him."

"Well congrats on the tournament, dear, but I hate to break it to you that you're not a doctor or a nurse or even proficient in being an office manager so why would he want to hire you?"

Beau beamed. "He's developed a new product for cardiac surgeons and he wants me to sell it!"

"As in head of sales, ground floor opportunity?"

"I don't know the details yet, but maybe."

"Beau, this is just perfect for you! What a great day you had!"

"Yes, you could say that! And Drew called and asked me to coach the boys' soccer team with him. I hope you don't mind, but I said yes."

Jennifer threw her arms around her husband. "That's terrific! And just to let you know, you're sleeping with one of Ryan's room mothers."

Beau looked around pretending to be frantic. "What? Where is she?"

"Right here, Mr. Soccer Coach."

CHAPTER SIX

Rachel Hayden, aka Bridget Colter and currently using the alias of Paige Walker, pulled her shoulder length blond hair into a ponytail. She studied her face in the bathroom mirror and noticed slight crow's feet edging her green eyes. The result, no doubt, of spending too much time squinting in the bright sunshine of Grand Cayman. She'd have to remember to wear her sunglasses more often.

Walter had been such a drag yesterday afternoon as they traipsed through one small, dreary house after the other with the real estate agent. She really had no intention of moving out of The Mansion, but she knew she'd have to take action in order to keep Walter from insisting she move in with him. And her husband kept reminding her that their "stash" from the development of the heart attack reversing wonder drug, Cardiovax, was running low.

Ah, but that was about to change! Halfway through the "tour of homes", as the agent kept saying, Rachel's phone vibrated. It was Pierce and her husband rarely called due to the cost of calling internationally. "Excuse me a minute, Gentlemen. I need to take this call. I won't be long." Walter and the agent continued their discussion in the dismal master bedroom while Rachel went into the weedy backyard.

"What's up?" she whispered. "I'm right in the middle of looking at rental properties."

"For the lab?"

"No, homes to live in since you say we can't afford my staying at The Mansion much longer."

"Well you might want to accelerate your lab finding efforts because we have another potential job. He wants to meet with you tonight…for dinner if possible. Hence the reason I called." Pierce was talking rapidly which he tended to do when he was excited.

"Who is he?"

"His name is Alan Smith. He works for a company in Richardson called Data Shield. Mr. Smith got my name from some friend of a friend who knew about our efforts for Coro-Pharm. He is interested in having me develop another drug. I told him I was still out of the country but that you might be able to get the details from him and pass them along to me."

"And you told him my name is…?" Rachel held her breath, hoping her husband remembered the alias she was using on this trip.

"Paige Walker...that's correct, isn't it?"

Rachel let out a sigh. "Yes. Good job, Pierce. When and where? And most importantly, how much?"

Pierce laughed. "I'm letting you negotiate with Mr. Smith since you'll be better at judging how deep his pockets are once you meet him. He did say it's a big job. I thought it would be better if you are not seen at your hotel with him, just in case this isn't on the up and up. So he suggested you meet him at a restaurant called Taverna. It's on a street called Knox in Dallas, not too far from where you are. He'll be at an outside table at seven tonight. Just ask the hostess for Mr. Smith."

Rachel nodded. "Do you think his name is really Smith?"

"Not in a million years. He has a fake sounding British accent."

"Okay I'll be there. What's the minimum I need to accept?"

"See if you can get a down payment in the mid six figures. That will really bolster our cash and make up for the time this will take me away from finishing our other project. And see if you can find those two buffoons to transfer it to me again. What were their names?"

"Something like Jack and Gordon. I'll look them up in my contacts."

"That sounds right. Once you get the details of what it is that Mr. Smith wants, I'll be able to judge how much testing we'll have to do and how long that may take. But he did say he needs this completed in the next several weeks if possible."

"Weeks? Is he nuts? You can't get any kind of FDA approval in months let alone weeks."

Pierce paused for a moment. "He's not seeking any kind of FDA approval for this drug."

A bead of sweat raced down the side of Rachel's temple. She wasn't sure if it was from the Texas heat or from the unspoken fact that this was an underground job obviously of an illicit nature. "I'm on it. Tell him I'll be there. You can give him this number. I have it registered under Paige Walker. I'll text you after the dinner."

Rachel pressed the red circle disconnecting the call just as Walter and the real estate agent slid open the patio door and came outside.

A few minutes after seven that night, Rachel had gotten out of one of The Mansion's Mercedes in front of Taverna. It was a nice service her hotel offered and preferable to having to chat with an Uber driver. The restaurant offered two outside seating areas, one in front facing the street which had a canopy that had been rolled back. The other was straight ahead between two buildings. The hostess took her to the second area where Alan Smith was seated at a table in the far corner.

He stood as Rachel approached the table. "Ms. Walker I presume?"

Alan Smith was about five foot nine inches tall with bushy dark eyebrows and a very fake looking blond toupee.

He wore wire rim glasses. "Yes, please call me Paige." Rachel stuck out her hand and noticed Alan wore no jewelry, only an iWatch. This man was certainly no Dick Murphy, the man she had worked for, slept with and murdered the last time she was in the U.S. —when she had been known as Bridget Colter. Alan Smith's picture could be next to the word "nerd" in the dictionary. Well, she took that back, Middle Eastern nerd. She hoped that sex would not be something necessary to make this job a success.

"Please, be seated."

Rachel sat down and took the menu the hostess offered her. She looked back towards the entrance to the restaurant and noticed several people were waiting for a table, yet at least four tables adjacent to theirs that sat empty. Had Mr. Smith paid for those to insure privacy?

Over a delicious dinner of shrimp risotto and Italian wine, Rachel had learned two things: Alan Smith's British accent was a cover for his decidedly Middle Eastern nationality and what he wanted them to do was highly illegal.

"So do you think you can get this accomplished for me in a few weeks?"

Rachel had almost choked on her dinner. "Mr. Smith..."

"Please, call me Alan."

"Alan. Unless my partner already has something similar to this drug in the works, the testing time on mice would at least necessitate a month, maybe more." Rachel smiled and took another sip from her wine glass. "But we can certainly try."

Alan returned her smile. "Ah, I knew I'd found the right people for this job. Of course, it's highly confidential. Only you, your partner and I can know about it. I will own the rights and once you have completed your assignment, you will be required to leave the country."

"That sounds perfect."

"By the way, where are you living?"

Rachel continued chewing her dinner while she decided if she wanted Alan to know that information. "Well, that's an interesting question. I'm currently staying at a very nice hotel. But since this may take several weeks, I might feel a little confined there."

Alan nodded. "Hotels are no good. There are too many people in and out of your room. I don't want you staying there." Rachel was caught off guard by Alan's abrupt tone. "A friend of mine has a lovely home. It's quite large and located in a beautiful suburban neighborhood. She often rents out her extra bedrooms on Airbnb. I will contact her and make arrangements for you to stay there."

Rachel smiled. Alan's tone had reverted to cordialness. "How much does she charge?"

"I will be happy to cover it. As you young people say: 'no worries'."

The offer would save Rachel not only money, but also time. "Thank you, Alan. I'll take you up on that."

Alan seemed pleased. "You should be able to move in within a day or two. I will let you know."

Following their after dinner drinks Rachel was anxious to end the meeting. She did not want the awkward situation of having to turn Alan down should he invite her to his place. "If I am to keep my promise of developing this formula within a few weeks, I need to get an early start tomorrow morning." Rachel stood, lifting her purse from the back of the chair. "Thank you for dinner. I look forward to working for you."

Alan stood, extending his hand. "Yes. I'll be in touch."

After shaking Alan's hand, Rachel walked to the street and out of Alan's view. She pulled out her phone to summon an Uber driver, relieved that Alan had not offered to drive her home.

The moment that Rachel disappeared from view, Alan grabbed his phone from his pocket. He scrolled through his contacts and pressed the call button. "A woman named Paige will be contacting you about staying in one of the rooms you rent...Yes, I am aware you don't rent rooms. It's the story I gave her. She is working on our project and I need you to keep an eye on her. As soon as her part is complete, she will be eliminated."

CHAPTER SEVEN

At forty years of age, Alex Hart felt like a failure. Sure, he owned a booming health club chain in Texas. He came from a wealthy family and had an MBA from the Cox School of Business at SMU. He was blond, blue-eyed and his five foot ten inch frame was obviously very fit. In his college days he had been quite the player, even cocky. But now he couldn't find anyone who truly made him happy. Well that wasn't true, he had to admit. Jennifer Monroe, now Jennifer Baldwin thanks to his screw up, made him unendingly happy. Problem was he'd seemingly lost her forever thanks to his trying to be the knight in shining armor by marrying his high school girlfriend when she claimed to be dying of cancer. That decision cost him the love of his life, Jennifer Monroe.

Fatal Race

He thought he'd been on track to win her back until the night she told him face-to-face that there was no room for him in her life. She adored her husband, blah, blah, blah and by the way, she was pregnant with their first child. That was the nail in his proverbial coffin.

So Alex did the only logical thing: he left the country. He put his assistant temporarily in charge of operations at his string of ten health clubs and headed for Italy. One day he ended up at a small café across a very narrow street from his hotel.

While eating lunch at a table next to the window and working on polishing off a bottle of the café's best Brunello, he started counting the unending stream of tourists and locals walking by. To his surprise, only about twenty percent were overweight, almost the opposite of what seemed to be a very dangerous trend in the U.S.: obesity. Alex must have counted three hundred people walk by in thirty minutes. The percent of fat people remained consistent in each group of one hundred. But by the third group, Alex made another observation: most of those who were overweight appeared to be Americans or Germans.

Alex drained the last drop from his wine glass and paid his bill. He had found the perfect distraction for his romantic woes: expand his health club to Germany.

Alex put his plan into action. He found the perfect site, got his attorneys to negotiate a lease, hired local help and within three months had opened his first Hart Health Club in Munich, Hart's Guter Gesundheit.

Diane Cobalt

He'd found, while researching his competition, that Germans enjoyed outdoor activities like hiking, rock climbing, and soccer. They liked to play games and they liked to win. The local health clubs Alex had visited offered none of these things. In fact, they did not have a lot of members. Many had closed. It almost seemed to Alex that the Germans had given up on being fit and healthy and headed to the local pub every night after work instead of the gym.

Hart's Guter Gesundheit (good health) provided lots of activities, many of which were outside in the wooded area next to the facility. Germans could take guided hikes or play soccer on an outdoor field which would have a retractable cover by fall. They could even learn how to log roll or stand-up paddle board in the small pond adjacent to the woods. There were leagues to encourage competition and a small restaurant that served healthy foods and protein shakes. He wanted Guter Gesundheit to be a place for its members to hang out, not just work out.

His membership coordinator had signed up two hundred in their first week with more stopping by daily for a tour. Alex had just finished walking through the locker room when he noticed a group of women waiting in the lobby area. They didn't appear to be Germans.

"Sprechen Sie Deutsch?" asked one of the ladies who was dressed in black jeans and a black t-shirt. Her accent didn't sound natural.

"Ah, nein, nur English. Ein moment, bitte." Alex had only picked up a few phrases during his time in Germany.

Fatal Race

He paused a second in case one of them recognized the word "English", then paged Dieter to the front. The women started conversing with each other in a language Alex did not recognize. He was surprised. Most people in Munich spoke English as well as they spoke German. And many spoke other European languages.

Dieter appeared almost out of nowhere. "Yes, Boss?"

"I need someone who can speak German to this group of ladies. Thanks for your assistance."

Alex walked away after noting the serious expressions on the women's faces. They seemed very uptight, not typical fun-loving Munich residents.

By the end of HGG's second week, Alex had installed some weight resistance machines along with several sets of free weights. After all, he still needed to work out. And it wasn't long until that area got so popular that he added a second one.

After another exhausting day, Alex headed to his office on the second floor. From his vantage point, he could see every station indoors and out of his floor to ceiling window he could see the pond and soccer fields. He was reviewing some other possible locations for future HGG's when his cell phone chimed. It was a text message from Kate Lange.

"Thought you might want to know. I gave Jennifer your letter yesterday. Don't know if she's read it or not. You did the right thing by leaving. She's happy."

"You just now gave her my letter?" Alex spoke out loud to no one. "I wrote that over four months ago!" He stood up and started pacing his office. What had she thought about it? Would Jennifer try to reach out to him? Would she at least tell him to come back to the U.S.?

Why did Kate think it was important to text him? Maybe Jennifer wasn't okay. Maybe she'd lost the baby. Was there something Kate was trying to surreptitiously tell him? Should he respond to Kate's text?

Alex reread the text. He shook his head. The sentence "You did the right thing" jumped out at him. That should be enough to make him feel better. Kate wouldn't have said that if Jennifer needed him. But that made him feel worse... that Jennifer didn't need him, would never need him again.

But what was frustrating most of all was that *he* still needed *her*. Alex decided not to respond to Kate.

CHAPTER EIGHT

Beau toweled off his black hair, added a little gel and smoothed it back into place. He couldn't wait for his meeting with Dr. Hunnicutt. Jennifer had just left the house with Ryan to pick up Chris and take them to school for their second big day of kindergarten. Kate would bring them home after three. Beau promised Jennifer he would be home waiting for Ryan and would make sure he had a healthy snack before soccer practice at five. Beau and Drew would be coaching this new little team and Beau was almost as excited about that as he was about his meeting in an hour.

He grabbed a long sleeved white shirt out of his closet and buttoned it to the top. Tie or no tie? It was still really hot out. Hmm...jacket or no jacket? Jacket with tie or without? Beau sat down on his bed and took a deep breath.

He needed to relax, just take one step at a time. Pants! Yes, pants would be a good idea. Beau chuckled and went back into his closet. He chose khaki dress slacks, his navy blazer and a blue and gold tie. It was always better to be overdressed than underdressed, right? And always dress for the position you want, not the position you have. Then no golf shirt for sure!

Glancing at his watch, Beau realized he only had an hour before his interview with Dr. Hunnicutt whose office was about thirty minutes away if there was no traffic. That meant he had time to finish dressing and go over his resume one more time.

In reality, it took Beau just over twenty minutes to arrive at Dr. Hunnicutt's office. He had one of the new office suites across the street from the Heart Hospital in Plano. Parking was just outside the door and if needed, Dr. Hunnicutt could walk to the hospital. Beau noted the only name on the door was Dr. Hunnicutt's. He wondered if there would be more doctors joining the practice.

Beau got out of his car and walked in. "Good morning! Can I help you?" asked the young woman sitting at the front desk.

"Yes. I'm Beau Baldwin here to see Dr. Hunnicutt."

The woman frowned. "I don't see you on the schedule. Did you have..."

"Beau! Come on back," Dr. Hunnicutt said as he walked into the empty waiting room. He shook Beau's hand. "How do you like my office?"

Fatal Race

"Looks brand new!" Beau was a little taken aback by Dr. Hunnicutt's appearance away from the golf course. Without his visor on, his thin lanky frame now looked a little nerdy in the white lab coat. And a pair of bifocal glasses now graced his face instead of the Ray Bans he wore the other day.

"It is! My wife still has a little decorating to do. But it's workable for now. Let me give you the tour before we sit down to chat. I have six exam rooms," he said walking by each one. Then he stopped and opened a seventh door. "This is my test slash procedure room."

Beau nodded, noticing a top of the line exam table and what appeared to be built-in cabinets above a counter. A small stool that matched the color of the cabinets sat under the counter.

The doctor returned to the hallway and took a left down another hall. "And this back here is my lab."

"You do your own patient's lab work here?"

"No. I mean *my* lab. This is where I conduct my research for new medical products." Dr. Hunnicutt practically beamed. "Come. Right across the hall is my office. Let me show you my invention."

Beau noticed two other closed doors and wondered what was behind them. Dr. Hunnicutt saw him looking towards the doors. "Those are two empty offices...in case I add some other physicians...or management for my cardio products company. And I have an option on the space next door if I need to expand. Please, have a seat. Can I get you anything to drink?"

Beau shook his head as he sat down in a leather chair across the desk from the doctor. "This is all very exciting."

"I think so! Don't get me wrong, I love surgery and that will always be a part of my practice. But the creativity of designing and implementing new surgical equipment is equally as exciting to me."

Beau sat back in his chair and smiled. "The suspense is killing me. Uh, probably not the wisest choice of words."

Dr. Hunnicutt pulled open his top desk drawer and extracted a folder. "Before I show you my product and research, I have to ask you to sign this nondisclosure agreement. It just says that you will not release any information about this product to anyone until I give you authority to do so."

Beau looked at the form and signed it. "Sure. No problem."

"Great! Thanks! My new product is sitting on this desk."

Beau scanned the top of the desk and spotted their golf trophy. "Nice trophy!"

"Ah yes! I almost forgot! This belongs to you!"

"Thanks for the offer, but I think the new kid on the block should keep it. So I take it, the trophy is not the new medical device?" Beau joked.

"Not quite. Look again."

There was a phone, a laptop, a picture frame, a pencil holder and some papers held down with a small paperweight. His heart dropped. This guy was a Looney Tune! Beau started sweating. He had to find a way to kindly get out of here. He looked around the office and noticed the

Fatal Race

doctor's medical school diplomas: Sloan Kettering, UT Southwestern, both top-notch schools.

Dr. Hunnicutt started to laugh. "Beau, you look very worried. I know! You don't see it! But it's right in front of you…the paperweight! Pick it up!"

The guy had designed a paperweight? Beau gently picked up a round disc about the size of a quarter and turned it over. "This is no paperweight, Dr."

Dr. Hunnicutt grinned from ear to ear. "Of course it's not! It's the RPPMD which stands for rechargeable, programmable pacemaker defibrillator. Sweet, huh?"

Beau frowned. "It's rechargeable? How?"

The doctor continued smiling. "I'm so glad that's the word in the acronym you focused on because it's what truly makes this product, well, revolutionary." He stood and opened a cabinet behind his desk and pulled out the top half of a mannequin. The mannequin wore a tight tank shirt. "See this circle, right here?" he said pointing to the upper left chest area of the shirt. "This is the recharger. It can be worn by the patient at night or during the day when needed to recharge the device."

Beau stood up and touched the shirt while holding the RPPMD in his hand. "I can hardly feel it."

"Exactly. So it won't be uncomfortable."

"Wow! Tell me how the device works."

"As you may know, in the past, we implant either a pacemaker or a defibrillator in a patient. After a certain number of years, the battery begins to go bad and a second surgery is required to replace the battery. There are always risks to surgical procedures: infections, etc.

The RPPMD eliminates the need for subsequent surgeries and the programmable portion allows the doctor to implant one device and program it to be a pacemaker, defibrillator or both."

Beau whistled. "This is genius! Has it been..."

"FDA approved last week. I hold the patents."

"Well, I can already see a problem."

The doctor frowned. "What's that?"

Beau smiled. "You're going to need more office space and a much bigger staff."

Dr. Hunnicutt laughed. "You had me worried for a second there. I hope you don't mind, but I've already researched your background."

Beau's smile faded.

"You've had a tough few years working for some unethical folks. It's time you start working for a good person with a great product. I'd like you to start by selling the RPPMD in Dallas. Then as it takes off, head to a few major cities. After that, you'll need to start hiring sales reps for me in those areas...do whatever you need to build your sales team."

Beau was speechless. He'd anticipated a sales job with a hard to sell product. In no way had he dreamed that he would be on the ground floor level selling the next new technology in cardiothoracic surgery. And the ability to build his own sales team...head of sales...at his age?

"That would be phenomenal."

"So you accept?"

"Yes, of course! This is the most exciting device! It's logical, practical and obviously needed. And you did this all by yourself?"

The doctor nodded. "Yes, in my spare time."

"Which I'm sure you don't have a lot of. When do you want me to start?"

The two shook hands. "Follow me." Dr. Hunnicutt walked out of his office and opened the door to the room next to his. "How about starting today? Here's your office."

Beau's new office was a carbon copy of the doctor's. The top of his desk had a phone, a laptop, a picture frame, a pencil holder and some papers held down with the RPPMD.

"I want you to help me with the marketing literature, how we would structure a sales organization, who we should target first, etc. Heck, I don't even have a name for the company! It's okay with me if you eventually work from home when you are in town, but for now, I'd like you to office here. How does that sound?"

Beau nodded. "That sounds fine. I do have an obligation at three today, but until then, I'm all yours!"

"Excellent! I will have my attorney draft an employment contract for you. We need to discuss what you think is a fair compensation program. Of course given the fact that I have not sold a single unit yet because it was just approved, I will give you a generous guarantee."

Beau was giddy. He would have worked on commission only because he knew that this product would make it big.

Diane Cobalt

Revolutionary was an understatement. "I can't wait to get started," he said sitting behind his new desk and already thinking of names for this new company.

CHAPTER NINE

By ten o'clock, Jennifer was ready for a break. The baby seemed to be lying on her bladder again, so she got up from her desk and headed to the bathroom. She walked by Alan's office and noticed it was still dark. She frowned. He hadn't said anything to her yesterday about not being in today. Hmm, maybe that's why he'd wanted those two files finished so quickly.

When she came out of the bathroom, she could hear her co-workers, Gordon and Jack having a heated discussion in their office which was one, double-sized room. Jennifer had worked with the two men at their previous employer, SDS, a high-tech company. The pair had gone to work for Alan Smith at Data Shield last year after their so called "retirement" from SDS. When Alan needed a CFO, both men had recommended Jennifer for the job. The only similarity between Jack and Gordon was their age. They were both in their early sixties. Jack's oily dark hair framed his round face which usually needed shaving. He was overweight and grouchy. Gordon was bald except for a fringe of dark hair going from ear to ear. He loved working out and was a sharp dresser. Jack and Gordon reminded Jennifer of Felix Unger and Oscar Madison.

She decided to go see if she needed to referee. "Guys! What's the trouble? You sound like a couple of little boys who can't get their way."

Jack immediately looked at the floor as if he'd been scolded. Gordon flashed Jennifer a smile. "Well it seems our expert programmer here is not such an ace when it comes to creating apps."

Jennifer took a seat across from Gordon's desk. "What kind of app?"

"An impossible one, that's what kind," grumbled Jack.

"Now, now, Mr. Crabby," cajoled Gordon. "We'll figure this out. It's really a cool idea after all. In fact, you might be interested in being one of our test people, Jennifer."

"Why? She doesn't have teenagers."

"No but she will someday, even if it's a long time from now. Alan asked us to develop an app to help parents prevent other kids from bullying their children."

"That is pretty cool. How does it work?"

"It doesn't," snapped Jack.

"Jack, let me tell her how it is supposed to work, would ya? The parents have the control app on their phone which can send a message to the child's phone disrupting any kind of communications including texts and phone calls and Facebook notifications from everyone but the parent."

"How do the parents know their child is being bullied?" Jennifer wanted to know.

"Well if little Bobby wears glasses and is six inches shorter than everyone else in his class, they might have a good idea," Jack answered sarcastically.

Gordon turned his back on his coworker. "Good question, Jennifer. This app also has a feature that enables the parent to read all incoming texts, emails and social media without being detected."

"So this is a way to spy on their kids?"

"Exactly!" Gordon beamed.

"Well, I guess that must be necessary in today's world."

"Unfortunately, yes."

"So why are you two at each other's throats over this?"

"You mean why does Jack have his panties in a wad?" Gordon joked.

"Oh. Shut. Up."

Jennifer smiled, waiting for Gordon's response.

"We're just having a disagreement on some of the programming. And we have a little side job to take care of that I think takes precedent. Jack does not."

Jennifer arched her eyebrows. "Interesting. Well don't let me detain you two."

"Don't worry," said Jack grudgingly. "Alan won't be back until next week so we probably have time to get both jobs done."

"Next week? He didn't say anything to me yesterday when he dumped all these new companies on my desk," Jennifer replied. "Where'd he go?"

"I don't remember. I wasn't paying any attention. I'm just glad when that fake isn't around," Jack offered.

"Hey," Gordon whispered. "Be careful what you say. He could have this office bugged."

Jack folded his arms across his chest and leaned back in his chair. He whispered back, "Okay, Mr. Paranoid. Mum's the word."

Jennifer laughed, but wondered to herself if she should ask Manuel to have someone check for any recording devices.

"To answer your question, Jennifer," Gordon said in a normal voice, "I think he went somewhere in Europe."

"Deutschland," muttered Jack.

"What? Speak up!"

"You just told me to pipe down. Make up your mind!" Jack snarled.

Gordon rolled his eyes.

"I said Deutschland."

"Germany," affirmed Jennifer. "Interesting. I haven't seen any paperwork for any companies over there. Well, I better get back to work. I have an after school meeting today at three thirty."

Fatal Race

Jennifer was seated in a gray metal folding chair towards the back of the cafeteria at Ryan's elementary school. She had arrived about five minutes before the meeting was to begin hoping that Kate was saving her a seat, but Kate was nowhere to be found. Fortunately, the PTA president, Isabelle, had not yet started speaking. Jennifer carefully extracted her phone from her purse and was about to text Kate when her friend came in, plopping down in the chair next to hers. "Sorry I'm late. Have I missed anything?"

Jennifer shook her head. "Nope. They haven't started yet."

"You know how I hate to be late. But this time I am." Kate grinned.

Jennifer was busy putting her phone on vibrate and did not see Kate's face. "It's okay. No worries!"

Kate put her hand on Jennifer's arm and whispered. "I'm late because I'm late."

Jennifer's head instantly swiveled to face her best friend. Her eyes got as big as saucers. "You're..."

Kate nodded. "With child. Yes I am!"

"That's great news!" Jennifer hugged Kate. "When? How far along are you?"

The room started quieting down as Isabelle took the podium.

"I'll tell you when this is over," whispered Kate. Jennifer merely nodded.

Isabelle cleared her voice. "May I have your attention please? Thank you. Welcome to the annual Room Parent kick off meeting. We so appreciate your dedication of time to your child's classroom. Since most classes have two parents sharing this responsibility, I have two folders for each teacher. After the meeting adjourns, please be sure to pick up your folder. It will have grade level specific info in it. So if you've been a room parent before, do not assume you know everything. For example, sixth grade moms and dads...well you have a lot of extra activities, especially at the end of the year." Isabelle stopped to laugh. Kate rolled her eyes.

"Okay first up on our calendars is the carnival which is our fall fundraiser. It's very important that each grade level participate in their booth activity to raise money as well as the school's activity. This year instead of selling wrapping paper we will be selling water!"

A buzz of conversation instantly spread across the room.

Someone raised her hand. "Water? Last I checked that was free for all!"

Everyone chuckled.

Isabelle put up her hand to silence the room. "I meant to say bottled water." She reached into her purse and held up a bottle of water with the school mascot on its label. "Everyone needs to have their bottle of water handy ... at PTA meetings, school events, soccer games, dance recitals, etc.! And aren't these labels just the cutest things ever?!" All the parents around Kate and Jennifer seemed to be nodding.

"Really? They couldn't come up with something more original as a fundraiser than water?" Kate whispered to Jennifer. Jennifer shrugged.

Fatal Race

"I know, I know. This seems very...well elementary!" Isabelle laughed at her own joke. "But just think about how many activities you attend with your children and why not drink out of something with our cute little Gator on it? We've partnered with a local company who's given us a great price. Usually a twenty-four pack of sixteen point nine ounce bottles runs anywhere from four to six dollars at the grocery store. Our partner will sell them to us for five dollars with our labels on them. However, we are going to sell them for a dollar each or a six pack for three dollars! Our diligent treasurer has done the math and we anticipate making a profit at the end of the fundraiser... drum roll please, somebody...ten thousand dollars!" Cheers went up. "We will be asking each student to be responsible for selling four six packs. That's not a lot and we realize not everyone will participate but we anticipate selling a lot of them at the carnival to the general public who comes. And don't forget family members too! I'll let you all meet now with your grade level coordinators. Thank you in advance for your enthusiasm for our fall fundraiser!"

Kate leaned over to Jennifer. "Well if I weren't already tired, I would be after listening to that!"

Jennifer smiled at her friend. "How are you feeling?"

"Just tired so far. I'm not even far enough along to go to the doctor yet. I'm only about a week late, but the test this morning was positive!"

Jennifer stood up. "That's so great! I'm so happy for you! When are you telling Chris?"

"Not until after the first trimester. There's no point in getting his hopes up if it's not going to ..."

Jennifer put up her hand. "Stop! Don't even say it. You're going to be just fine. Come on, let's go get our folders and see what's going on in kindergarten land!"

Kate nodded. "We'll have to see when this water will be available so we can pass it out at soccer games!"

"That's a great idea!"

While Jennifer was happy for her friend she realized that Kate's pregnancy may cause her to not be able to be as active, at least for this fall, as she had promised Jennifer. And Jennifer would have to try to find more time to devote to this volunteer position. Maybe Meredith would show up...soon?

CHAPTER TEN

From her best estimate, it had been over two months since Meredith had awakened, tethered to a dirty cot in what had appeared to be a cell. Since that time, her captors had moved her twice, blindfolding her each time. When they spoke Farsi to her, she acted as if she didn't understand them. In fact, she made sure to take her time speaking at all which made them think she had suffered some kind of brain damage during the bombing and justified her current state of amnesia.

Meredith had decided not to appear to be an American. Under no circumstances did she want them thinking she was the missing woman from the incident in Frankfurt. Yet she couldn't help but wonder if anyone was even looking for her. They may have assumed that she was dead. But Geoffrey would know to look for her, wouldn't he? Without any proof she had been killed in the blast, he would never give up searching for her.

The van ride had lasted about an hour. With nothing to see, Meredith counted to herself to determine the time. Most of the way had been at a high speed, meaning they had been on the autobahn. But the direction they had been going had been a mystery.

Her latest home away from home seemed to be a youth hostel. This surprised Meredith. With all of the remote cottages in the German countryside, why would they risk someone spotting her? And why would they want to be around young people? Perhaps they were looking for more candidates for their team? It didn't matter. Meredith couldn't talk to anyone. She was still confined to her room and only allowed out in the hallways when accompanied by one of her handlers.

Meredith had chosen German as her main language a few weeks ago when she decided to speak a few garbled words. But every few sentences she would switch to English and then jumble a whole sentence by alternating words. Her strategy worked: her captors were perplexed as to which nationality she might be.

And that was the perfect thing they were looking for...a human with no history whom they could shape and mold into one of them. They wouldn't need to radicalize her because she would be indoctrinated from the beginning.

Training had started a week ago when they took her to a modified gun range in the German countryside. While most of Meredith's injuries had healed, she still seemed weak due to her lack of food and exercise so handling the assault weapons had been a struggle, or at least she made it appear that way to them. Fumbling through the loading of the ammo, being confused as to how the weapon worked, missing the target completely the first time she took aim, all were tactics Meredith used to ensure her cover. She was a hundred percent sure they had no idea that she was an American CIA agent.

A lot of good that did her now. Yes, the training was coming in handy, but communicating back to her base seemed impossible. Until today.

Daria, the only woman who had been with Meredith almost every day, unlocked the door to her room and entered with a breakfast tray. "Guten Morgan," Daria said slowly and distinctly; clearly she was uncomfortable with the language.

"Good Morgan," replied Meredith in her "German/English". "Danke."

Daria placed the tray on the tiny desk in the corner of the room. "Schnell, wir gehen." *Quick we are going.*

Meredith looked down at the plate. There was a soft boiled egg, thick cut bacon and a hard roll. Always "eating for the hunger to come", she devoured the entire breakfast while wondering where they were going and what the hurry was about.

Daria hustled Meredith into the backseat of an old rickety BMW. The inside door handles had been removed so the passenger could only exit the vehicle by someone else opening the door from the outside. Or, they could climb between the front seats and exit via the front doors, but Meredith didn't want to escape quite yet.

Daria climbed in behind the wheel and roared off down the side streets in what appeared to be a quaint southern German village. After several turns, she pulled to an abrupt stop in front of a Schönheitssalon, beauty salon. How odd. Meredith could understand them taking her to the gun range, but a salon?

Daria parked, got out and opened Meredith's door. "Kommst mit mir." *Come with me.*

Meredith obeyed and climbed out of the car and into the bright sunlight. She wished she'd had a pair of sunglasses. Maybe they would be willing to get her some. It was strange not having any cash or credit cards or cell phone. God how she missed her phone, but not nearly as much as she missed Ryan and Geoffrey. It must be late August by now, she thought. Ryan should be going to kindergarten. How ironic, a German name for his first level of school. Her heart ached at the thought of missing his first day.

The two women entered the shop and were immediately escorted back to one of the stations. Daria motioned for Meredith to sit in the stylist's seat. A large, blond German woman came up and greeted them in English. "How are we today?"

"Gut, fine," answered Meredith.

"And what do you want...color, a cut...?"

"Beides, bitte," answered Daria.

"I'm sorry. For you, Miss?"

"Nein, für das Mädchen."

Fatal Race

While the two went back and forth about what to do to Meredith's hair, she examined herself in the mirror. It was the first time she'd been in front of one in over two months. Her jet black hair was a tangled mess and she had dark shadows under her blue eyes. But apart from that, she had weathered the storm pretty well.

The hair stylist flung a cape around her and snapped it closed around her neck. She turned her around in the chair so that she no longer could see her reflection and began applying hair color. Two hours later after a shampoo and a drastic haircut, the stylist turned her back around so she could see herself in the mirror. Meredith was now a blond! Her shoulder length hair had been chopped into a pixie cut. It was all Meredith could do to keep from groaning. She looked nothing like the woman she was when she came in. They must be getting ready to move me, she thought.

Daria escorted Meredith back to the shabby BMW and pushed her inside. Without saying a word, she revved the engine and sped down the street towards the autobahn. Meredith could see the speedometer from her vantage point in the backseat: one hundred kilometers per hour. She didn't bother doing the math...too damn fast! One exit flew by after the other as they raced down the highway. Without putting her indicator on, Daria veered right down an exit ramp marked "München". They were going to Munich.

Meredith noted how familiar Daria seemed with the city. How long had Daria lived in this area? Munich seemed to be in the opposite direction from where they had been staying. Maybe they were going clothes shopping? No, that would be too good to be true.

Instead, Daria parked on the street in front of what looked to be a health club. The logo looked like a monogram with a big H in the middle and two G's on either side. As they approached the front double glass doors, Meredith could see the name Hart's Guter Gesundheit in back of the lobby. As they passed through the front area, Daria motioned for Meredith to follow her. The pair went down a short hallway and turned left. Daria pushed open a swinging door which led to the ladies locker room.

Meredith wanted to shake her head. *First she has me get my hair done and now I'm going to a locker room to change into what? And then we're going to work out?*

Daria pulled out two keys from her backpack and handed one to Meredith. Meredith eyed the tag on the key: 335. She found the corresponding locker and swung open its door. There, inside, was a pair of athletic shorts, t-shirt, socks and shoes all in her size. How thoughtful! At least she'd have another change of clothes.

Once the women had changed, they headed onto the gym floor. Meredith was amazed at all they had to offer. HGG was similar to fitness centers back in the states: there were free weights, stationary bikes, treadmills and a few rowing machines. But here there was also a climbing wall and signs that pointed outside to a soccer field and a pond with stand-up paddle boards and log rolling. The only thing missing was a pool.

Before they could start using any of the equipment, a blond man approached them. "Hi, Ladies, I'm glad you decided to join us." He spoke English with a definite drawl. Meredith's face lit up. Then she remembered that she couldn't be an American.

Daria practically glared at the man. "Danke."

Meredith realized the man was waiting for her to say something. "Thank you."

Alex Hart extended his hand to her. "Are you an American?"

Shit! She hadn't added the British clip to her two words.

"Nein," she replied as she shook his hand.

"Sorry! My mistake," Alex said. "Let me know if you all need any help with any of our activities. I'm the owner, Alex Hart."

Daria grabbed Meredith's wrist and led her over to the free weights.

Meredith's mind was racing. She not only had the opportunity to get stronger again, but she also had an opening to speak to an American. Maybe there would be a way to get Mr. Hart to convey a message back to Geoffrey. But she'd have to play things cool. Meredith knew they would have to be coming here at least for a few weeks if they wanted to get her strength up. She'd have plenty of time to concoct her plan for escape.

Daria stayed close to Meredith's side the entire hour they were in the gym. That would have to change if Meredith hoped to communicate with Alex Hart.

CHAPTER ELEVEN

Jennifer checked her rearview mirror as she approached the Grandview Elementary circle driveway. Her golden brown eyes once again spied the gray Toyota sedan that had been behind her ever since she had pulled out of their subdivision. It seemed a little coincidental that a woman would just happen to be going to the school at the exact same time. Or would it? Maybe she was just getting paranoid. Jennifer craned her neck to see if she could spot a child in the back seat, but the sun's reflection off the Toyota's windshield blocked her view. She also thought it was odd to see a sedan in a land of SUV's and mini vans. Jennifer shrugged.

"What's the matter, Aunt Jen?" Ryan asked from his spot in the car booster chair on the passenger side.

"Nothing, why do you ask?"

Fatal Race

"So you were just lifting your shoulders like you were talking to yourself again without saying any words."

Jennifer smiled. Kids seemed to have no filter. Maybe that was a good thing. She looked at him, this time, using the rearview mirror. "You're right, Sweetie. I've been thinking about all the things I have to do today." She slowly made the last turn and pulled up in front, waiting until it was their turn to get out of the car. One of the teachers who had been assigned to car pool duty that morning opened Ryan's door. Both boys hopped out.

"Bye!" they called to her.

"Have a good day, boys!" Jennifer's purse buzzed. It must be Manuel. Her regular cell would have come through her car radio via Bluetooth. She'd have to wait until she was out of the school zone to check it, meaning she'd have to call Manuel back. In her hurry to exit the school area, Jennifer missed seeing the driver of the Toyota sedan parking on a side street and exiting her car alone.

Several minutes later, Jennifer pulled into a vacant office's parking lot. She opened her purse and retrieved the yellow phone from its new hiding place: the zippered compartment of her purse where she kept her tampons. Beau wouldn't ever go looking in that section of her purse, even if she asked him to!

Jennifer hit the dial button and was instantly connected to Manuel. "I saw that you called."

"Yes. We need to see you ASAP. And by that I mean sometime today. Are you available over your lunch hour?" Manuel sounded more tense than normal.

"Sure. Alan's gone again. But you probably knew that."

"Uh huh. If you can, research recent major cash transactions for his various companies. We'd like to see them in a spreadsheet format if possible...by noon."

"No problem. By major you mean...?"

"Over seventy-five hundred dollars."

"Ok," Jennifer replied thinking that amount was a little low. There could be a lot of them to trace. "I'll be there at noon."

The line went dead. Jennifer put her hands on the steering wheel and rested her forehead on it. She was overwhelmed with all of her responsibilities. It seemed they just kept multiplying.

She needed to tell Beau. He was the only one who could lighten her load just by listening. Jennifer thought about the lively conversation with Ryan at the dinner table last night after soccer practice. Ryan had been so excited with the new skills Beau had taught him and his team. Beau seemed to revel in his role as soccer coach. It was like he was a kid all over again and Jennifer adored seeing that side of her husband.

Later, after Ryan was in bed, Beau told her about his new job. He'd actually started working that day and was bombarding her with possible names for this new company. Jennifer had smiled on the outside but was crying on the inside. Beau had yet to work for a company without encountering major drama so she had been relieved when he had decided to take a break from the medical equipment sales world. Maybe the third time would be a charm.

Fatal Race

With another major challenge on Beau's plate, Jennifer didn't want to burden him with the knowledge of her association with the Eagle's Nest. Besides, what if he demanded she quit? Or worse, what if he never forgave her for not telling him about it from the beginning? No, she was in too deep to say anything.

"Okay, Jennifer, develop a plan," she said to herself in the car. "Half the battle is what to do next." Having a to-do list always calmed her nerves. First on her list was to get back to the Data Shield office and put together the spreadsheet Manuel had requested. That would likely take up most of the morning. Second, she would meet with Manuel. Then she had the rest of the day to figure out what was going on with all these companies Alan had asked her to set up.

Feeling slightly more relaxed, Jennifer picked up her head off the steering wheel and headed to her office.

Five minutes later, she yanked open the glass outside office door and walked in. "Hey, Jennifer! Do you have a second to look at this app?" Gordon called to her as she headed toward her office.

No, not really, but I will make the time. "For you, Gordon, sure!"

Jennifer sat down in the chair opposite Gordon's desk. "Say, where's Jack?"

Gordon rolled his eyes and lowered his voice. "Well, you know what they say. When the cat's away…"

"He's not happy working here, is he?"

Gordon shook his head. "He likes the money all right. He just doesn't like having to work this hard...which believe me is not all that hard. Plus you know how prejudiced he can be. I think he might, and I stress the word might, be happier if our boss weren't foreign."

Jennifer nodded in agreement and made a mental note to ask Manuel how to find out if Alan had bugged the office. "Show me what you've got so far on the app."

Fortunately, Gordon had quickly walked her through how to use the app. Jennifer had been frantically researching the cash transfers for the past two hours. The problem was many times the cash had been transferred to companies Jennifer had no paperwork for. When she came across those companies, she'd hit a dead-end. While that didn't sit well with her, she had no proof of anything illegal...yet. The total, however, was staggering: half a million dollars had been transferred in the past two days.

It wasn't until an hour before she was to meet with Manuel that she hit pay dirt. Jennifer had gone back to the initial deposit of seventy-five hundred dollars for BWP. The check had been drawn on a company named Richardson Shopkeepers, Inc. Jennifer looked them up online and found nothing. They weren't one of Alan's companies either. The check had been drawn on a credit union but was not one Jennifer had heard of. She frantically researched the credit union...it didn't exist! Jennifer had hit a roadblock. Maybe Manuel would be able to help her.

She printed out her spreadsheet, put it in her briefcase and headed out the door. "I'll be back after lunch, Gordon."

"Okay. Have a good one."

Manuel met Jennifer at the front door to the office space Eagle's Nest occupied. He escorted her back to their secret conference room behind a hidden panel. Jennifer always got a little thrill when the 'invisible door" raised into the ceiling.

This time several of the other members of the group were already sitting at the conference table. Their leader, Vincent O'Donley, sat at the end. Jennifer grew serious. Vincent was employed by the Department of Homeland Security. There must be some major news either about the cell or about Meredith.

"Jennifer, please be seated," Vincent greeted her. "Manuel, please get her some water." Manuel poured Jennifer a glass of water from a pitcher.

Jennifer sat down and pulled out the spreadsheet. "Here's the spreadsheet Manuel asked for," she said sliding it down the table to Vincent.

Vincent looked at Manuel. He seemed confused.

"I thought it would be a good idea to have Jennifer do a little forensic accounting...get her feet wet in that area. She tracked all money transfers seventy-five hundred and above."

"What's interesting is I found that dollar amount being transferred over and over again," Jennifer commented. "You'll want to take note of the total."

Manuel looked at the bottom line and raised his eyebrows. "That's a lot of zeros, but I can't say that I am surprised."

"Thank you, Jennifer. I appreciate your hard work." Vincent slid the paper into his briefcase. Jennifer was a little disappointed that she couldn't go over it in detail at least with Manuel.

"The reason we requested your attendance here today is we want you to be on the lookout for this woman." Vincent pointed to a video screen. An image of a redheaded woman with green eyes and lots of freckles flashed up. "This is Amineh Al-Yacoub. She has used many aliases so there's no point in our even guessing what name she is using now. Our intel confirms that she recently located to the area, perhaps with a child. Amineh has been on the Most Wanted list for about a decade."

"But she looks like an American," Jennifer interjected.

Vincent smiled. "You can't judge a book by its cover. In fact, few women who wear the traditional Burka are dangerous. Amineh has had extensive skin grafts and other surgeries to "Americanize" her. Memorize this picture and her name and let us know if you see her."

"Okay. What else?"

"Manuel has your new phone. You can exchange your old one for it."

Manuel pulled out a new green phone and Jennifer gave him the yellow one. "This phone has all the current bells and whistles on it. We can track it, of course, like any iPhone. But this one will allow you to send us computer data without any evidence you've done it. For example, the next time you make a spreadsheet, you can do it on your laptop, save it, but it won't actually save to your laptop. It will be on your phone. Here's a special zip drive to erase any evidence of the spreadsheet you made for us this morning. Alan's on a plane right now so he can't see what you've been up to on your computer today."

Jennifer felt her heart plummet. "I didn't even think about not making the spreadsheet on my work computer. I'm sorry."

"No worries," said Manuel. "I should have advised you to use your personal laptop."

"Do you have any other questions?" Vincent asked.

"Yes. Have you found anything relating to Meredith Matthews?"

Vincent shook his head. "Not yet. We remain hopeful."

Jennifer nodded. "I have one more question. Would it be possible to know if Alan Smith has bugged our office?"

"Hmm. Not without us going in there and we don't want to risk that. Just assume he has for now," Manuel answered the question.

Great! Jennifer would have to warn Gordon and Jack without revealing her source! She zipped up the green phone and special zip drive in the interior liner of her purse and headed out to her car with Manuel at her side.

CHAPTER TWELVE

Jennifer had spent the remainder of the afternoon erasing any evidence of the spreadsheet she had built for Manuel and then trying to make sense of the transfers. Most of the money ended up going to various banks in the Caribbean. But from there, the path ended. Frustrated, she had begun working on the stack of remaining companies that Alan had asked her to set up. He wasn't due back until later that week, so at least she had some breathing room.

Gordon had knocked off work early which would have given Jennifer time to snoop around, but she had been too concerned that Alan might have secret cameras hidden in Jack and Gordon's office, so she elected to finish several files and then head home herself. The baby had been unusually active, making her unusually uncomfortable.

Fatal Race

At four thirty, Jennifer had had enough for today. She stopped by Starbucks and got a Venti size of her favorite peach tea, then swung by the soccer field at the park behind Grandview Elementary. Beau and Drew were holding practice. Kate was talking to a group of moms under a big shade tree. She grabbed her drink and made her way across the grass to Kate.

"Hey there, Jennifer!" Kate greeted her with a hug. "I wasn't expecting you to make it to practice."

Jennifer smiled. "I wasn't either, but I'm glad to be here."

"Hey everybody," Kate said to the group of moms. "This is Jennifer Baldwin, the other coach's wife and aunt to Ryan Matthews."

Each mom, in turn, introduced herself to Jennifer. She noted there was not a red-head in the bunch.

"Are you all in Mrs. Williamson's class?" Jennifer asked the group of six. They all nodded.

"Yes, in fact, we were just telling Kate before you walked up that we've all had her before! I mean we've had an older child have her before!" laughed a blond named Kim. "She's just wonderful! Ryan and Chris are lucky to have her." Then she lowered her voice, "Mrs. Williamson is much better than the other kindergarten teacher. In fact, we all requested her."

The other moms were nodding like bobble head dolls. "I didn't know you could do that," Kate chimed in.

"Well, you're not supposed to," commented one of the other moms, "but we all do!"

Diane Cobalt

The group giggled. "Good to know for the future," Kate responded. "I'll have to get your recommendations for first grade."

"They're both good," commented Kim, who seemed to be the ringleader of this group. "You just need to choose who you want Chris to be in class with and find out who they're requesting."

The politics of Grandview Elementary was giving Jennifer a headache. She wished she had stayed at work longer and avoided this clique. Kate was looking at her like maybe she should say something.

"Say, while we're here and since you've had so much experience at the school, do you have any suggestions for what our room's game should be at this year's carnival?" Jennifer felt like this would be a safe topic.

"Well, for years it's been musical chairs," piped in Susie, another blond. Jennifer was wondering if they all went to the same hair stylist. Five of the six were blonds and of those five, all wore their hair pulled back into ponytails. The sixth, a brunette, seemed more reserved and thoughtful. Jennifer could get to like her.

"Yes, but last year there was a lot of fighting when the music stopped, don't you remember?" Kim added. "I think it would be a great time to start something new."

Jennifer thought she saw a brief flash of a smug look cross Kim's face. Was she setting them up for failure?

"We're open for any and all ideas," Kate said.

"Did they give you the list of games for all the other grade levels? That way you know not to pick any of those," the brunette wanted to know.

Kate stooped down and opened the lid on her Yeti cooler. "Would anyone like a bottle of water?" She held up a bottle with the school mascot on it.

"Where did you get that?" Kim practically screeched.

Kate beamed. "They just came in today. I got an email this morning and decided to start getting the word out."

"They're so cute!" said Susie who looked like she might be pregnant or maybe was just bloated. Jennifer wasn't sure. "I'll take one!"

Kim took one as well. "I've got to hand it to you, Kate. You're diving in head first into all this school hoopla. You're husband's the soccer coach and you're the room mom..."

Kate put her arm around Jennifer. "We're the room moms. And Beau's coaching too. I wouldn't do any of this without my best friend." Kate tilted her bottle of water and toasted it with Jennifer's Starbucks cup.

Jennifer just wanted to go home. She was glad that it would be another five years before she had her own child and would have to be part of this covey of moms. It was just their luck that they were in class with so many "returning" moms.

"So back to the carnival game," Jennifer reminded them.

"Yes," added the brunette. "I think we need to keep it grade appropriate, yet fun for older siblings. How about a fishing game? We inflate a few mini pools, put those plastic fish in and get the rods with the magnets on the ends of the lines? There's a number on the bottom of each fish that corresponds to a prize."

"I think *you* get the prize," said Kate. "That's a great idea."

Jennifer waited for someone to object, but the group was silent. "Perfect! We've found our game. Now we just need to decide on the prizes."

"Watch out!" yelled Beau. Jennifer and Kate turned just in time to see a soccer ball headed their way. They ducked successfully.

Kim kicked it back onto the field.

"One more thing while we have you here, ladies." Kate said. "We need everyone to sign up to bring snacks to the games. You can pick which game is best for you and just initial it on the schedule which Drew has posted on Google sheets."

"You are organized, girl," said Kim.

Kate smiled. "Well, it is just kindergarten."

"Hey, I'm going to head home and start dinner," Jennifer said to Kate.

"I'll walk you to the car."

When the two best friends were out of earshot from the group, Kate said, "Whew. We've gotten ourselves into a tough group of moms. I'm so glad I didn't give them my idea for a carnival game."

"Which was...?"

"Pin the tail on the pregnant woman! Four of those moms are with child...just a few weeks further along than I am. It must be something in the water." Kate and Jennifer laughed.

CHAPTER THIRTEEN

Rachel sat on the balcony of her suite at The Mansion and enjoyed her last drop of coffee as she appreciated the downtown Dallas skyline in the distance. She was frustrated. Alan Smith had blown her off today. They were to meet, discuss the details of this project so she could find a lab that would be adequate for testing. Instead, she woke to a text message from him that he had been called out of the country and his return date was TBD. Just two nights ago he had been in a hurry for this drug and now they were on hold.

Oh well. That gave her today to look for more lab space. Yesterday she had looked at an old high school's unused lab that smelled so bad it was all she could do not to be violently ill. She peered at her list. Her first stop was at a doctor's office. At least that shouldn't smell. And once she found her new "office", she'd have to put an order in for some lab rats. And she had almost forgotten that she needed to get back in touch with Jack and Gordon so they could verify Alan's wire transfer to their account in Grand Cayman.

Rachel's international phone vibrated. It was Pierce. "I hope you have good news. Because Alan Smith has blown me off today," she answered.

Pierce chuckled. "Ah, my Love, you have such little faith in me. Of course I have good news."

"Well...don't make me wait. You know how I am when I am frustrated."

"Okay, okay. Mr. Smith contacted me. I know exactly what he wants and I already have a drug that shouldn't take much work to get it to accomplish Mr. Smith's goal."

"Which is what?"

"Well, that's kind of the bad news," Pierce's tone of voice grew serious.

Rachel remained silent. She knew by the amount of money they were being paid that Alan Smith wasn't having them develop a cure for cancer.

"He wants to destroy the United States from within."

"And he's going to do that by having *us* develop a drug?"

"Yes and no. Please don't think for a minute that we are going to develop a drug that will kill off our fellow citizens. In fact, he's not even asking for that. He just wants something that might slow down the population growth."

"Ah, an infertility drug!"

"Something along those lines."

"Then I have nothing to be worried about, do I?"

"No you don't...that is unless we don't perform on this contract. So let's get started! We probably will need to eventually do some testing on humans. So be on the lookout for a confined group that we can reach through some means."

"Well that's as clear as mud," Rachel twisted her hair around her finger as she waited for more instructions.

"For now, you'll need some mice."

"Males? Females?"

"Some of both. Let me know once you get the lab."

"Will do, Pierce."

"Perfect, Love! Kiss kiss!"

Rachel disconnected. Sometimes Pierce could be downright irritating. She rolled her eyes as she removed her fluffy white Mansion robe and got in the shower.

Two hours and two lab tours later, Rachel gave her Uber driver a ten dollar bill and exited the car. She was in front of a one-story brick professional building in a northern Dallas suburb. There was a hospital about three blocks away. The building looked fairly new and still had space available. Ok, she thought, let's be positive...look at the pluses not the negatives because after this lab, she had exhausted her list and the options she had just seen would not work. The first one had been close to the airport... great for quick getaways...but the landlord had been way too nosy with his endless questions. The second lab she had looked at would have given her lots of privacy, there was nothing even remotely nearby, but that was the deal breaker...there was nothing nearby. It would have taken eons to get lab tools to and from that lab and she was a long way from Alan Smith.

Rachel opened the door into a lobby area of a doctor's office. No perky attendant was at the front desk and no patients were waiting on the upholstered chairs which lined the wall. "Hello?" she called. Nobody responded. Should she venture down the hallway? Or wait? Maybe this doctor had texted her that he had an emergency to attend to. Rachel opened her large Louis Vuitton bag and extracted her iPhone 10.

"Ms. Walker, I presume?"

The man's voice startled Rachel causing her to jump.

"Dr. Hunnicutt?" Rachel replied as she stuck out her hand.

"I'm sorry, Ms. Walker. I didn't hear you come in. Please, follow me." Dr. Hunnicutt looked like a highly intellectual surgeon, balding with bifocal glasses. He reminded her a little of Pierce.

Rachel followed him down a long hallway. The doctor turned left down a shorter hallway. At the end of the hall, he came to a stop in front of a solid door with a code punch lock. "Obviously you would have complete control over this lock and change the combination so that you and only you will have access to your laboratory," Dr. Hunnicutt explained as he punched in a several numbers and held the door open for Rachel.

A pristine lab complete with every modern convenience Rachel would need, lay before her. She slowly walked between the rows of counters. "How much do you want per month?"

"That depends on how long of a lease you want to sign."

"I'm thinking I might need it three months, but just in case, let's say six months."

"How does $2,000 a month sound?"

"If I prepay, would you take $10,000 and call it a day?" Rachel smiled at the doctor.

The doctor smiled back. "We have a deal Ms. Walker."

"Please, call me Paige," Rachel said. "When would I be able to start using the facility?"

"Why, today if you can make a payment."

Rachel went back into her Luis Vuitton purse and extracted a wad of hundreds. "Here you go," she said.

Dr. Hunnicutt raised his eyebrows, surprised that she would have so much cash with her. "Well, cash always works for me. Let me get the contract for you to sign and the code to reset the combination lock on the door."

While the doctor went to his office, Rachel looked around. She loved the fact that there was no glass in the door to the hallway, so no patients or nosy nurses would be able to see her. It would have been nice to have a separate entrance so she could come and go unnoticed, but she had to relax. With her new hair color and a few little plastic surgeries, she looked nothing like Bridget Colter. Who was going to recognize her? Besides that little snafu happened years ago. Paige Walker wasn't a lab tech, she was a scientist.

"Ah, here we go," said Dr. Hunnicutt as he handed Rachel a one-page contract. If you would just sign and date at the bottom, then we have a deal."

Rachel scanned the document and seeing that all the amounts and dates were correct, signed it "Paige Walker".

"By the way. Can I see some I.D.?" the doctor asked.

Rachel almost froze. "Of course. Here's my passport." She pulled it from her purse.

"Thanks. I just thought that was the right thing to do. You could be anyone I suppose," he laughed.

Rachel laughed with him. She liked the way he crinkled his eyes when he smiled. His hands were smooth, yet strong. And yes he had on a wedding band. That had never stopped her before.

"Is there anything else I can do for you?" the doctor asked. "I am expecting some patients in a little bit."

"Uh, yes. I have a few questions," Rachel responded. "Just so that I don't get in your way, what days do you have office hours?"

"I see patients on Wednesday afternoons and all day Thursdays unless I get called in for an emergency operation."

"Great! And last question, from whom do you get your lab supplies?"

"Well, the standard disposable gear I get from a McKesson rep. But if you are looking for true laboratory supplies, I use a company called Lab Rats."

"Really? It's actually called Lab Rats?" Rachel laughed.

"Yes, Labrats.com is their website. They even deliver."

"So you've done some research I take it?"

"You could say that," answered Dr. Hunnicutt. He looked at his digital watch. "I've got a consult in a few minutes. Here's the code to change the lock on the door," he said handing her an index card. "It will be nice having you around, Paige."

Rachel stuck out her hand. "Thank you, Dr. Hunnicutt. I appreciate all of your help and suggestions. Please let me know if there's anything I can do for you."

The doctor merely nodded as he turned and exited the lab. Rachel read the instructions on resetting the lock's keypad numbers on the door to the lab and entered in her new code and then pushed the button on her phone to summon Uber. She would have all afternoon to order supplies which she would do poolside at The Mansion.

As Rachel's Uber driver pulled up in front of the doctor's office, she noticed a black Nissan Maxima pull into a parking spot. But she didn't see the driver exit his vehicle. The driver was Beau Baldwin.

CHAPTER FOURTEEN

The walls of the tiny room in the youth hostel seemed to be closing in around her. It was almost midday and Meredith was sitting cross-legged on the lower level bunk bed. Daria left over two hours ago, locking Meredith inside. She was starting to get hungry since breakfast had consisted only of a hard roll and some coffee. Meredith needed to get out and get some exercise. Maybe they would go to the gym this afternoon since they hadn't gone yesterday. Or maybe they'd take a trip to the gun range...but probably not since they'd just been.

Meredith scanned the room for what seemed liked the thousandth time. At the end of the room were a built-in desk and a small wooden chair. In the middle of the room sat a table with two dilapidated metal folding chairs. And right next to the door was a sink. On the wall opposite the two bunk beds was a small window, maybe three feet tall by two feet wide. It had a screen so on nice days, Meredith could open it and get some fresh air. There was no doubt in her mind that she could squeeze through it, but the room was on the third floor of the hostel. At a minimum, she'd break a leg trying to jump to the street below. She considered making a rope from her bed sheets, like everyone sees people doing on TV shows, but that also seemed risky since it would take a little time and she never knew when her captors were going to return.

Her best bet for escape was the guy at the gym. Meredith knew she needed to be patient, but not wait too long in case they moved her again. Maybe today would be the day she would be able to get her hands on a piece of paper and pencil.

The door rattled briefly before the lock slid open. Daria came in followed by two of her teammates; the last one carried a plate with a cupcake on it.

"Herzlichen Glückwunsch zum Geburtstag, Gretchen," sang Daria.

Happy Birthday? And who the hell is Gretchen? Since Meredith "couldn't remember her name", she'd lived the last months without one. It was very strange not to have an identity.

Daria handed Meredith a package. "For me?"

The three women nodded. They were actually smiling.

Meredith removed the tied yarn ribbon and carefully removed the newspaper they had used in place of wrapping paper. There was a small box. She opened it to find a

German passport. The name on the passport was Gretchen Bruckmann and Meredith's picture was next to that name. She flipped through the pages of the passport. Apparently, Gretchen had traveled quite a bit. There were stamps from several European countries and the U.S. Clearly, they had plans to take her to another country.

"Ich heiße Gretchen Bruckmann?" *My name is Gretchen Bruckmann?*

Daria nodded, smiling. One of the other women snatched the cupcake off the plate and handed it to Meredith.

"Danke," Meredith replied. It was good to be someone again even if she was now a German. Meredith took the newspaper she had removed from the box and smoothed it out. Maybe she'd be able to find an open space on the margin to write a message to the gym owner. Of course a pen or pencil might be helpful.

Meredith scanned the paper as unobtrusively as she could, searching for that tiny space she could use. She stopped. Fortunately the three women were busy discussing plans for the day in their native tongue and didn't notice that Meredith had turned pale. The paper was in German so chances are the women hadn't bothered to read it. Plus it was old news. On the underneath side of the paper Meredith read the headline: Ten Die in Bar Explosion outside of Frankfurt. Two paragraphs below that Meredith saw Geoffrey's name listed as one of the dead.

It had to be wrong. Meredith sat up straighter in order to help her breathe. Geoffrey had to be hiding. The CIA just wanted everyone to think he was dead. She needed to be able to read the entire article, but the way the paper had been folded, she could only see those two paragraphs. Somehow, she'd find a way to hide the paper so the next time she was left alone, she could read it.

Suddenly remembering that she held a cupcake in her hand, Meredith took a bite. "Sehr gut!" Very good. One thing was certain; there was no lack of excellent bakeries in this part of the country.

Daria and the other two were engaged in a heated argument about what to do the rest of the day. None of the three wanted to babysit Meredith and Daria insisted they "stay on plan" with Meredith's training. While the three began talking louder, trying to get their way, Meredith seized the opportunity to stow the newspaper in her pillowcase and then finished her cupcake. She washed her hands in the sink. The women, none the wiser.

Finally, Daria turned to her. "Kommst Du!" *Come!* She grabbed Meredith's arm and opened the door.

Daria had won the argument. They were heading to the gym. Meredith's only goal was to confiscate a pen or pencil.

Middle afternoons on weekdays were the slowest times at HGG. Alex usually used the time to meet with vendors, interview prospective employees or work on identifying sites for his next health club. But today he was antsy and didn't know why. Things were running smoothly at the gym. The outdoor construction on the removable cover for the soccer field was on schedule. There really was nothing for him to do. Maybe that was it...he didn't have enough to do and when that happened, he started wondering if Jennifer was okay.

Alex decided to take a stroll through the club and make sure everything was up to his standards. He grabbed a pad of sticky notes off his desk, in case something needed attention, and headed downstairs.

It was quiet...almost too quiet even for the middle of an afternoon. Alex made a note to himself to work on a marketing plan to attract more members. In fact, he came up with the idea to survey those who were using the club this afternoon to see what their professions were and why they chose this time to work out.

Alex crossed the floor and headed to the trainer's desk. He grabbed a clipboard and a pen and headed to the treadmill section. In his best German, he asked the man closest to him if he would mind answering a few questions. The man brushed him off. Great, Alex thought to himself, this wasn't going to be an easy task. Maybe he needed to start with some women.

He spotted a group he'd seen just a few days ago, the blond with the short hair who he thought was an American. They were once again working with the free weights.

"Guten Nachtmittag, Fräuleins." Alex gave them his best winning smile. Three of the women simply ignored him. The blond smiled back.

"Tag," she responded.

Fatal Race

Hi? That's all he could get out of her was "hi?" His charm needed some work!

"Ah, wie geht es Ihnen?" *How are you?*

"Gut."

Now one of the other ladies looked up and glared at him. Alex put his palms up. "Sorry to bother you." The blond acted as if she understood him while her friends clearly did not. Maybe they didn't speak German. Alex shrugged and turned to head back to his office when someone bumped into him causing him to drop his clipboard and pen.

It was the blond. "Entschuldigen Sie bitte!" *I'm so sorry.*

"No problem," Alex responded picking up his clipboard, but not noticing his pen had rolled under the weight bench.

Meredith waited for Alex to leave. She quickly glanced over her shoulder making sure Daria and friends weren't looking. She then sat down on the bench, picked up the pen and slid it under her shorts.

CHAPTER FIFTEEN

It was finally Saturday. But Jennifer and Beau discovered that what used to be a day of rest and doing a few errands turned into accompanying Ryan to his extracurricular activities and buying needed school supplies for various upcoming projects.

Today was the first soccer game for the Prairie Dogs. Jennifer wasn't sure who had come up with that name. It certainly set low expectations.

"Jen, have you seen my roster?" Beau was very nervous and untypically disorganized.

"Didn't you put it on your phone?"

"Oh yeah. That's what I did with it. And do you know where my whistle is?"

"Try your car. You might have left it there after practice. I'll go upstairs and see if Ryan needs help putting on his shin guards."

"Great idea. Thanks, Sweetheart," Beau said as he kissed Jennifer's forehead. "I couldn't do this without you!"

Jennifer smiled and headed to Ryan's room where she found him crying. She took a deep breath. "What's the matter?"

Ryan looked at the floor. "I want my daddy to be here today."

Jennifer squatted down and put her arm around him. "I'm pretty sure he's watching you from heaven. We just can't see him."

Ryan took the back of his hand and wiped his nose. "Are you sure?"

"I'm sure. He'll be so excited when you score your first goal." Jennifer wished she hadn't said that. What if he didn't score a goal today?

"Then that's what I'll do. I'll score a goal for my dad."

"Okay, but before you can do that, you have to put on your shin guards. Uncle Beau sent me up here to see if you needed help with them."

Ryan rolled down his knee socks showing her that he had already put them on.

Jennifer ruffled his hair. "Excellent job!" She reached for his hand. "Let's go!"

But Ryan stood planted to the floor. "Please don't tell Uncle Beau that I want my dad," he sniffed.

Jennifer smiled. "It will be our secret. When I point to the sky after you score that goal, you'll know what I mean!"

Ryan moved toward the door. "Good idea!" And his tears seemed to evaporate.

Traffic moved at a snail's pace along the road that encircled fifteen soccer fields in east Richardson. "I'm glad we left in plenty of time," Beau announced as he inched forward.

"We can change drivers and you and Ryan can head to the field if you're worried about the time," Jennifer suggested.

Beau checked his watch. "I think I'll take you up on that. We're on field number seven. Look! It's right there. So as soon as you find a parking spot, grab it."

Jennifer nodded as she took her place behind the wheel and Beau grabbed Ryan's hand. It wasn't long before Jennifer found someone who was leaving and was able to park. As she shut and locked her door, a woman came towards her. It was Kate.

"Darling, there you are! Isn't this quite the mess? I can't imagine having to negotiate this every Saturday for the next two months!"

Jennifer smiled as she hugged her friend. "At least you're not quite as big as I am. This heat is a killer for pregnant women!"

"I know and there's not a tree in sight. Maybe we should have brought our umbrellas to provide a little shade." Jennifer wasn't sure if Kate was serious or if she was poking fun at some of the other parents who were standing under umbrellas. "I'm kidding!" she exclaimed. "I don't want to look like a nerd."

Jennifer shrugged. "Well at least they'll be cool nerds!"

"Now that's funny! Let's go find the team."

The pair zigged and zagged through the maze of soccer fields until they finally reached field seven which was right in the middle of the mayhem. Beau and Drew had the Prairie Dogs warming up on half the field while their opponents ran around on the other half.

Jennifer surveyed the group of parents sitting on the bleachers. None looked suspicious or even out of the ordinary. And there were no redheads. "How do we know which side to sit on?" whispered Kate.

"I'm not sure. I just assumed that we would sit on the same side Beau and Drew will be standing on. That's Beau's duffle bag lying on this sideline," Jennifer whispered back.

Kate nodded. "Good catch! There's Kim and Susie!" Kate waved to a group of five moms sitting on the top tier.

"Goody goody," Jennifer muttered under her breath.

Kate looked at her friend with disdain. "Come on. It will be fine."

Jennifer pasted a smile on her face as the two sat down on the front row.

"Drew brought a cooler of water. Let me know if you want some." Kate reached down and extracted a bottle with the school gator on it.

"You are shameless!" Jennifer said.

"No, I just want our room to win the top fundraising prize."

"Which is?"

"A pizza party for the class and a weekend for four at The Mansion."

Jennifer perked up. "Now that's a worthy prize."

The referee, a kid who looked to be about fifteen years old, blew his whistle indicating the start of the game. The teams seemed to take turns kicking the ball and running after it in clumps. The ball never even came close to the goal. This was going to be a long game.

Jennifer turned to the mom next to her and introduced herself. "Hi, I'm Jennifer Baldwin, Beau's wife."

The petite woman with long black hair smiled and shook her hand. "I'm Leslie Woodward, Luke's mom. Who's your son?"

"Ryan, number twelve." Jennifer decided not to get into the fact that Ryan was their nephew. The fewer parents who knew, the better.

After cheering for the Prairie Dogs for what seemed like an eternity, it was finally halftime. The little boys were dripping with sweat in their blue and gold uniforms. Beau and Drew were giving them instructions for the upcoming half, but most of the boys were not paying attention.

Once again the referee blew his whistle. The Prairie Dogs took the field. Ryan seemed to be standing away from the other boys. Jennifer hoped he was okay. She couldn't get his attention to see why he was standing there. Then, suddenly, Chris kicked the ball to him. Ryan ran towards the goal and kicked it right past the goalie who was picking a dandelion off the grass.

Fatal Race

"Yay! Great job, Ryan!" Jennifer yelled as she stood up and pointed to the sky. Ryan looked over, saw her and pointed up too, a huge smile on his face. "Nice assist, Chris!"

"Way to go boys!" shouted Kate. Drew and Beau were trying to stay calm but it was hard to miss the grins on their faces.

The Prairie Dogs ended up winning the game two to nothing. Chris had scored the other goal. It appeared that the best friends were the best players on the team, at least so far. The Baldwins and the Langes took the boys to Chick-fil-A to celebrate and then to Dairy Queen after that.

By eight o'clock that night, Ryan was fast asleep on the couch. Beau carefully scooped him up and deposited him into his bed upstairs.

When he got back downstairs, he noticed Jennifer was sound asleep as well. He laughed. Saturdays were turning out to be the hardest day of the week.

A little after two in the morning, Ryan burst into Beau and Jennifer's bedroom. "I can't find him. He's gone!"

Beau sat up and reached for Ryan. "Who's gone, Buddy?"

"My dad is. I saw him. He was real proud of my soccer goal." Ryan was crying so hard, Beau had difficulty understanding him.

Jennifer sat up. "Your dad saw that goal from heaven. Remember how we talked about that?"

Ryan shook his head vigorously. "No. He was in my room. Just now. And then he was gone."

Beau wrapped his arms around Ryan. "Let's go get a drink of water and we'll go up and look for him." Jennifer got out of bed and followed. While she waited for them to get some water from the kitchen, Jennifer looked out the front window. She noticed several expensive cars in the driveway of the house catty corner and across the street from theirs. She hadn't seen them earlier. They must be having a late party, but no lights were on.

Beau and Ryan headed up the stairs and Jennifer followed. After about thirty minutes, they finally had convinced Ryan that his dad couldn't be in his room because he was living in heaven. Jennifer rubbed his back for a while and Ryan succumbed to sleep.

As Jennifer and Beau headed down the stairs they heard a slam. "What's that?" asked Beau.

"It sounded like a car door." They heard another slam as they reached the bottom step.

Two couples across the street had gotten in their cars and left. "That's weird," Jennifer whispered.

"What is?"

"Well, I've never seen those cars over there before. And there aren't any lights on like they were having a party. Plus Bentleys and Ferraris in this neighborhood?"

"Yeah, I'm not sure who lives there. Maybe you should take them some of your world famous chocolate chip cookies and find out," Beau teased.

Jennifer thought she might have to do just that.

CHAPTER SIXTEEN

Rachel decided to check the mice one last time before calling it a day. Fortunately, Pierce seemed to be on track with his formula and they were just waiting a little longer to test the drug on the mice. Rachel extracted a vile of clear liquid from the small refrigerator in the lab. Carefully, she set it down on the counter. It was important that the drug be colorless, odorless and able to exist at room temperature without losing its potency. Once they were able to determine that it worked under those conditions, Rachel thought they should test it in warmer temperatures.

The mouse motel, as she liked to think of it, was located on a lab counter across the room from Rachel's desk. Both males and females occupied the three by five foot glass container. It appeared that they had plenty of food and water for the evening, so Rachel grabbed her phone and ordered an Uber. She then removed her white lab coat, hung it up and headed to the door.

"Good night little rats," she said out loud before flipping off the light switch. Just as she was about to open the door she heard voices in the hallway. Thank heavens she heard them or she would have forgotten to crack the door open first to make sure no one would see her exit. Peering out the window, she saw Dr. Hunnicutt and his nurse discussing a file. They then moved into the doctor's office. Rachel waited a few seconds and walked out of her lab, carefully locking the door behind her. She couldn't imagine that anyone would recognize her especially with her new hairstyle, but better safe than sorry.

The Uber driver pulled up in front of the office just as she walked out into the oppressive Texas heat. How anyone survived a summer here was unimaginable.

"Mansion?" the Uber driver confirmed.

"Yes, please." She couldn't wait to take a dip in The Mansion's pool.

An hour later Rachel toweled off, gathered her things off the chaise and headed to her room. As important as this assignment from Alan Smith was for financial reasons, it paled in comparison to the main reason that she had returned: to avenge her sister's death.

She swiped her key card over the door lock to her suite and entered. The room felt too cold on her still damp skin. Rachel grabbed a bottle of Perrier from her fridge and headed to the balcony to finish drying off.

Fatal Race

It was time to begin crafting her plan. The high rise glass buildings dotted the downtown Dallas skyline. Rachel could see the heat emanating off them like the rage she felt building inside her. How dare Jennifer Baldwin drown her sister! No one deserved to die that way. Christina might have interfered in the Baldwin's marriage, but she certainly shouldn't have had to pay for that indiscretion with her life. What kind of monster was Beau's wife anyway?

Rachel looked at the Perrier bottle she held in her hand and decided she'd need a little more fortification than sparkling water to develop her plan of revenge. She headed back into her suite and retrieved an airplane sized bottle of Scotch from the minibar. Rachel deposited several ice cubes from the ice bucket into a glass. She watched as the amber liquid invitingly splashed over each cube and took a sip. Ah, now she was ready.

Where to start? How much did she actually know about this Baldwin woman? Not much. Her husband was a Goody Two-shoes who had gotten in her way of testing a miracle drug. Rachel grabbed her iPad and propped her feet up on the balcony's railing.

"Hmm, let's see if I can find her on LinkedIn," Rachel said to herself as she logged into her fake LinkedIn account. "Ah, there she is. Jennifer Baldwin works for SDS. Wait, no, she worked there. Past tense. So where does she work now? Or is she staying at home? Do they have kids?" After a half hour of scouring the internet, Rachel came up with nothing. She'd have to rely on her cousin. Maybe he'd be available for dinner tonight. She brought up his number on her cell phone and pressed the dial button.

"Rachel?" Walter answered immediately. "How are things going? I've been meaning to call you. I'm about to go out of town on business."

"Well, then my timing couldn't be better. How about dinner tonight, Cuz?"

"Tonight? I guess I could swing that, but I need to be home by ten. I have an early flight in the morning."

"That's not a problem," Rachel cooed. "I can be ready in an hour. Where do you want to meet?"

"I'll just come there. I heard The Mansion has a new chef and I've been dying to try out their new menu."

"Well, that works for me. I'll call down and make a reservation. See you at seven?"

"See you at seven," Walter confirmed before disconnecting.

Walter arrived fifteen minutes early, a bad habit of his. He would have to be alert tonight. His intuition told him that Rachel didn't just want to have dinner with him tonight because she was lonely. No, she needed something from him, but what?

"Can I help you, sir?" the hostess standing behind the podium at the entrance to the restaurant interrupted his thoughts.

"Ah, yes. I'm here for a reservation under the name…" Walter paused, trying to remember the alias Rachel was using. "Um, Paige Walker."

The petite hostess smiled and checked her tablet. "Yes, I have a party of two for seven. Would you like to be seated?"

Walter nodded. "That would be wonderful."

The hostess, wearing a black dress and heels, pulled two more tablets from her podium. "Right this way, please." She led Walter to a quiet booth in the corner of the room. "Will this be okay?"

"Fine, thank you."

The hostess placed the tablets on the linen covered table. "You will find our wine list, cocktail suggestions and menu on this. Robert will be taking care of you."

Walter smiled and again thanked the hostess. He surveyed the main dining room, noting several waiters rushing to prepare the private dining room. It was not uncommon to spot celebrities here. Walter wondered who might be showing up tonight.

Robert approached the table. "Hello, my name is Robert and I'll be taking care of you this evening. Can I get you a cocktail while you wait for Ms. Walker?"

"Yes. I'll have Crown on the rocks and a glass of water."

"Still or sparkling?"

"Still will be fine."

The waiter nodded and left to get Walter's drink.

Walter searched the wine list on his tablet menu while he waited for Rachel. It seemed to be an extensive list with several great selections by the glass. But Walter's mind kept wandering from the wine list to his list of potential things Rachel might want from him. They ranged from borrowing his car, to moving in with him, to somehow manipulating him into doing some of her dirty work. Was she still after Jennifer and Beau Baldwin? He'd expected more questions from her by now. He turned his attention back to the wine list. A cab versus a blend? Now that was a better conundrum to ponder.

"Hello there," Rachel said as she slid into the booth opposite him.

"You startled me. I didn't see you approach." Walter put down the tablet.

"You looked deep in thought," Rachel commented.

"Yes, you could say that. This wine list is very comprehensive to say the least."

Robert arrived at the table with Walter's Crown on the rocks and a glass of still water on a silver tray. "Good evening," he said to Rachel. "I'm Robert and I'll be taking care of you tonight. Can I bring you something from the bar?"

Rachel flashed her dazzling smile at Robert. "I'd love a dirty martini and a glass of sparkling water, please."

Robert nodded. "Very good."

"Very high-tech menus," Walter commented to Rachel.

"Yes, I haven't seen these in the Caymans yet. I suppose they are quite handy as far as updating. But I am a bit surprised. I would think this place would have something a little more formal."

There was a buzz coming from across the room as a group of eight entered the main dining room before turning left into the private party room. Walter subtly scanned the group for celebrities. "There's Owen Wilson," he said to Rachel.

Rachel looked up from her tablet. "What's he doing in town?"

"He's from here."

"That's right. Maybe that's his parents with him?"

Walter shrugged. "Could be."

Robert arrived with Rachel's martini and Perrier. "I'll give you some time to enjoy your cocktails and will return to tell you about this evening's specials."

Walter smiled at him. "Thank you." Then he directed his attention to Rachel. "So what have you been up to?"

Rachel tilted her head to the side and grinned. "I've always liked that about you, Cousin; you're direct. Well, you'll be relieved to know that I've found a job working at a lab."

Walter almost swallowed the ice cube he had in his mouth. "A job? How long are you planning on staying?"

Rachel shrugged. "I don't know. Pierce needs me to do some research for him stateside and my employer has agreed to let me use the lab after work hours."

Walter raised his bushy eyebrows. "Interesting. Does that mean you would need a place to stay? You're always welc..."

Rachel put her hand up indicating Walter should stop talking. "I appreciate the offer. I really do. But I've already found a place."

Walter set down his drink. "Really? Where?"

"In one of the suburbs. I haven't been by to see it. I found it through Airbnb."

"Excellent," Walter replied, knowing that Rachel still wanted something from him.

"I was wondering if I offer to take you to the airport in the morning, would you let me borrow your car while you're away?"

That was it? "Certainly, but you don't need to take me to the airport. I can Uber."

"Oh no. It's the least I can do. How long will you be out of town?"

"A week."

Rachel smiled. "Perfect! That gives me time to find a rental car."

Walter didn't like this. Rachel had something up her sleeve. And he'd bet that it wasn't something good.

CHAPTER SEVENTEEN

The house was finally quiet. Jennifer had taken Ryan to school a few minutes ago. All three were exhausted after a tumultuous night with Ryan crying for his mother. Beau poured himself another cup of coffee and stared out the front bay window at the house across the street. There were no cars in their driveway this morning. Their newspaper sat out on the front walk. What the hell had been going on last night? It seemed that every time he and Jennifer had gone upstairs to check on Ryan, there was a different car coming or going across the street. Beau hadn't been able to get back to sleep because he was racking his brain trying to decide if there were drug deals taking place or if it was some kind of party for swingers or upscale prostitutes. Neither was an acceptable answer.

Ryan's crying was another issue entirely. The poor kid had lost his father and didn't know where his mother was. Beau glanced at his watch. He was to meet with Dr. Hunnicutt for lunch, but until then he could work from home by researching the best market to test Dr. Hunnicutt's product. But that could wait a few more minutes. Beau needed to make a call to his fraternity brother.

It had been over two months since Beau had heard from Preston Hightower. He wished like hell that he didn't have to keep contacting him, especially after what Hightower and his class of pledges had done to Christina LaRue. Preston's words "ancient history, Bro", still rang in Beau's ears. How had someone with those ethics become active in federal government? Beau laughed at himself. His own naiveté was shocking.

Beau found Preston's number in his contacts and pressed the button on his cell phone to connect. "Mr. Hightower's office," answered a female voice.

"This is Beau Baldwin. Is he in? I need to speak with him."

"And you are with...?"

"I'm an old frat brother of his. He'll speak to me."

"One moment, sir. I'll see if he's available."

Beau waited on hold for almost a minute before Preston answered.

"Beau, my man! How are you?"

Beau grit his teeth wishing he could slap Preston's smug face. "I'd be better if I knew where the hell my sister is."

"That's right." Preston lowered his voice. "I'm afraid we still don't have any news about Meredith. The bar's been totally cleared and no remains have gone unidentified. I wish I could say we'd found her. Is it possible she might just be laying low? But don't worry. I'm sure the intelligence community is still looking for her. They don't give up on family members of their own."

Beau froze. Was Preston speaking in a foreign language? Maybe he had Meredith and Geoffrey confused with someone else. "I'm sorry. I think you're confused. We're talking about my sister, Meredith Matthews. Her husband was Geoffrey Matthews. The bombing was thought to be an act of terrorism so I'm sure the CIA and FBI were looking into it. Is that what you're referring to?"

Preston was silent. How could Beau not know? "That's right, Beau. The bombing outside of Frankfurt was deemed a terrorist act."

Beau waited for Preston to continue, but he remained quiet. "Preston, did you just say that Geoffrey was in the CIA?"

"Um, look. I didn't say that."

Shit! My brother-in-law was a CIA agent! How much danger is my sister in? Is my family safe? Beau thought back to Geoffrey's obituary. His family hadn't included a picture. Had it said that he worked for Exxon? Would they have printed something that wasn't true? Or didn't they know either?

"Beau? Are you still there?"

"Yep, I'm still here. And I heard exactly what you said. Thanks for the info."

Preston wasn't sure what to say. "I'll keep my ears open for any word on your sister."

"Thanks." Beau disconnected. If the terrorists were after Geoffrey, did they have his sister now? Would they be coming after Ryan? What should he do with this information? Should he tell his folks? Or Jennifer?

Beau ran his hand through his black hair. He'd sit on this info for a bit. No sense in alarming Jennifer. She had enough on her plate. He'd get back to researching which groups of doctors would be the best candidates for trying Dr. Hunnicutt's device.

But after fifteen minutes, Beau gave up. He was totally unable to focus on the task at hand. Quickly he pulled up Geoffrey's obituary online. No picture. And no mention of where his brother-in-law worked. Was that by request? Maybe he should call the Matthews? And say what? "Hi was your son in the CIA?" Not a good idea. It was better not to stir up the hornets' nest.

Unfortunately, Beau had no contacts in the CIA or FBI. But then not many people did. Did his sister know what her husband was really doing? *She must have. That's why she brought Ryan back to the states...to make sure he was safe!*

Beau decided he might be able to concentrate better in his new office. He packed up his laptop and headed to his car.

Fortunately, Beau's office was only a quick twenty minute drive from his house this time of day. He swung into the parking garage behind the one-story office building complex. It was also a benefit that his car was under cover during the heat of the day.

Undercover. Geoffrey had been working undercover. His sister had been married to a CIA agent. How had that happened? Beau grabbed his laptop off the passenger seat and exited his car, carefully locking the door behind him. His head swiveled from side to side. No one seemed to be following him. He laughed. This was no time to get paranoid. There was nothing he had or knew that would help the terrorists or the CIA. *Just relax! There are enough real things for you to worry about!* Maybe he should share this with Jennifer. She'd laugh at how silly he was being. After all, what were spouses for? For better, for worse, for richer, for poorer, for keeping you sane!

Feeling more at ease, Beau pushed through the revolving door and into the cool lobby before entering the back door into Dr. Hunnicutt's office suite. The doctor was in surgery this morning which is why he wasn't meeting with Beau until lunch. Beau closed his office door behind him so he would have peace and quiet. He deposited his laptop on his massive desk and got to work.

CHAPTER EIGHTEEN

The parking lot had been empty when Jennifer had pulled in shortly after eight this morning. At first she had been confused, but then quickly remembered that Alan was still out of town and both Jack and Gordon were attending a seminar about creating apps. The other tenants in the adjacent offices rarely got to work before nine which meant Jennifer was always guaranteed a close parking space.

It was the first time, however, that Jennifer had been alone in the office and she had to admit that it was a little creepy. Once or twice throughout the morning she had gotten up from her desk just to double check that she had locked the front door. Her office had no windows. In fact, only Jack and Gordon's office space had windows that overlooked the parking lot. Even Alan's large office, in the back, was windowless.

Without Jack and Gordon interrupting her, Jennifer had been able to complete the backlog of accounting entries for the string of companies her boss had started. Some were linked together while others seemed to be stand-alone entities. Alan had developed an elaborate numbering system for each corporation, none of which were labeled with anything other than initials. And so far, Jennifer had not received any payroll information for any of them. Surely Alan couldn't be running these all by himself. It seemed a reasonable question for her to ask him once he returned.

In the meantime, Jennifer had some extra time to start researching some of the invoices to see if they were legitimate expenses. She made sure to use the computer the Eagle's Nest had given her which ensured she had safe access to the internet.

At two o'clock, Jennifer's stomach growled. She had postponed going to lunch, using it as a reward once she found some solid information on at least one of the vendors. So far it seemed that none of the invoices were from legitimate companies. Most of the addresses were to P.O. boxes. Any street addresses listed on the invoices belonged in foreign countries. Maybe tomorrow she'd try going at it from the accounts receivable side...see where the money she was depositing was coming from.

Since she negotiated with Alan a schedule that would allow her to pick up Ryan twice a week at three, Jennifer powered down her personal computer and headed for the door. There was an afterschool room mom's meeting to once again discuss the upcoming carnival. She had about forty minutes to grab a bite to eat before meeting Kate at the school.

Jennifer got in her car and yawned. What she really needed was a nap! But maybe once she got a little food in her, she'd wake up. Between her pregnancy and Ryan crying on and off all night, she was beat.

The lunchroom was packed with moms and their kids who had just gotten out of school and were anxious to get home. Kate was saving her a seat towards the back of the room. Ryan and Chris were happily drinking out of their juice boxes that Kate must have brought them. Jennifer marveled at how quickly Kate had gotten being a mom down perfectly.

"Hey! I hope you don't mind my giving Ryan a juice box," Kate greeted her friend.

Jennifer gave her a hug then hugged the boys. "Not at all. Thank you for thinking of bringing an extra."

Kate's chestnut colored hair seemed extra shiny under the fluorescent lights of the lunch room. She sat down at the picnic style tables with individual plastic swivel seats attached. She patted the seat next to hers. "Have a seat." Kate leaned over to Jennifer once she sat down. "I would have brought us an adult beverage, but A. I don't think they allow it and B. our unborn children definitely wouldn't allow it."

Jennifer sighed. "I should have been a thoughtful friend and brought you an iced tea."

"No worries. I would have just had to go to the bathroom again. I'm getting a little tired of these meetings."

Jennifer yawned. "Me too. Did anyone from our committee show up?"

Kate scanned the room. "Not that I have seen. There's supposedly someone new who wanted to be on the committee, but I have no idea what she looks like."

No idea what she looks like? Wait! I'm supposed to be looking for that redhead. I'd almost forgotten! Way to go, Jennifer!

"I said, who are you looking for, Jen?" Kate tapped her on the shoulder.

"Oh, no one in particular. I'm just trying to get to know all these new faces."

The ever perky Isabelle called the meeting to order. "Ladies, thank you for coming this afternoon. This should be a fairly quick meeting. First, our water bottles have arrived!" The moms started clapping. "Aren't they adorable?" Isabelle beamed holding one up for all to see.

"For heaven's sake, they're just water bottles," said Jennifer.

"I agree. You'd think they were the latest tech invention."

The applause died down somewhat. "On Saturday, we have a few dads who have volunteered to distribute pallets of these cuties to each family. So bring your vans and stock up! Money for the ones you take will be due in two weeks.

That's really all I have for today. You can now break out by grade level and work on your carnival game. If you've already decided what that game is and have it coordinated, you're free to go!"

"That's the best news I've heard all day," Jennifer said to Kate. "I'm so glad we've gotten all of that taken care of."

Kate nodded. "I am too. You look exhausted, Jen. Are you feeling okay?"

Jennifer patted her stomach. "We were up with Ryan several times during the night. He was calling out for his mom."

"Poor baby. That's got to be tough. Any news?"

Jennifer shook her head. "Hopefully tonight he will sleep better."

Kate stood up and motioned for the boys to come over. "At least there's no soccer practice tonight."

"Yes, I think we'll go home and go for a swim."

"Mommy, can Ryan come play. Please?!" Chris was tugging on Kate's purse.

Kate looked at Jennifer for permission. "It might let you take a nap?"

Jennifer smiled. "That's fine if it's okay with you."

"Okay boys! Let's go!" Kate announced. "I'll bring him home by five thirty if that's okay."

Jennifer nodded. "That's perfect." She couldn't wait to get home to take a quick nap.

Fifteen minutes later, when Jennifer opened the door to their garage, Beau's car was already there. So much for the nap, she thought. But at least they'd have some time alone. Jennifer pulled her car in next to his and went inside.

Beau was sitting at the kitchen table. "Hey, hon. Where's Ryan? Was I supposed to pick him up?"

Jennifer came up and kissed her husband on the neck. "No. He's playing over at Chris's house. Kate said she'd bring him home before dinner. I thought it might be a good idea for him to have some fun. Who knows, maybe he'll be less focused on his mom tonight."

Beau fidgeted with the pen he was holding. "Jen, sit down. We need to talk."

Jennifer frowned. Beau was rarely this serious. "Oh my God, did something happen to Meredith?"

Beau shook his head. "Not that I know of. I called Preston Hightower this morning to check on her. He made an interesting comment. One that he shouldn't have made."

"What's that?"

"He said that all the remains from the bombing had been accounted for. But that I shouldn't worry because the intelligence community doesn't give up on family members of their own."

Jennifer's stomach dropped. Did Beau find out that they were in the CIA? What should she do? She'd have to pretend she didn't know anything. "What is that supposed to mean?"

"I take it to mean that Geoffrey was a CIA agent."

"Did you ask Preston if that's what he meant?"

"Yes. He hemmed and hawed, but didn't deny it."

"But he worked for Exxon…"

"His cover, I'm sure. I did some research. His obituary didn't say anything about his working for Exxon and there was no picture."

Okay, good. Beau does not have any proof that Geoff was in the CIA. Jennifer smiled. "I think that's a bit of a stretch to make the assumption that a few omissions from his obituary make him a spy."

"But doesn't it make sense that Meredith brought Ryan back to the U.S. to protect him? She must have known who her husband really worked for."

Jennifer reached across the table and grabbed her husband's hands. "Sweetheart, do you think if she knew that she would have gone back over there and risked her own life? People in that world don't usually have families."

Beau shrugged. "What about 'The Americans'?" he asked referring to the TV series.

"Fiction. That's not a documentary. I think you're a little sleep-deprived and your imagination is running wild." *I am such a liar. How can I do this to my husband?*

"Really?"

"Really. His parents were in shock when they wrote his obituary. You can't put stock in those facts."

Beau blew out some air. "I was hoping you'd say that. I almost didn't tell you because we have so much on our plates. But then I knew you'd be the logical one and tell me I'm being silly."

Jennifer gave Beau her best smile but said nothing.

"You *are* going to tell me I'm being silly, aren't you?" Beau was practically begging.

Fatal Race

Jennifer looked down at his hands being held in hers. "You're being silly." *And I can't go on keeping information about Meredith from my husband. What kind of wife am I? I'm going to call Manuel first thing tomorrow.*

CHAPTER NINETEEN

Daylight was barely sneaking in around the dilapidated shade of the small youth hostel window. There was a slight rattle of the room's doorknob. Meredith, who'd always been a light sleeper, sat up on her cot. Since there was no clock in the room, she had no idea of what the exact time was. But judging by the predawn light, she'd guess it was around six. A clinking sound now ricocheted into the room from the keyhole. Meredith lay back down, pretending to be asleep.

In an instant, the room was bathed in light as one of her captors switched on the florescent bulb overhead. Meredith stirred, squinting. It was the one with the dark hair and pale complexion. Meredith liked her best and in her mind had named her Vicki after one of her college friends. She was thankful that the ringleader, Daria, was not in tow. Vicki was less observant.

"Get dressed, *Gretchen*," Vicki instructed in German using the name on Meredith's new passport. "We're going to the gym." Meredith was surprised that they weren't teaching her more Farsi. They had started down that path, and then abruptly stopped which Meredith took as a bad sign.

"Gretchen" swung her legs over the side of the bunk bed and nodded. Now she just needed Vicki to give her a few minutes of privacy so she could retrieve the note she'd written from her pillowcase. Vicki unknowingly complied. "Fünf Minuten!" Five minutes, Vicki announced before walking back into the hallway and closing the door behind her.

Meredith sprang into action. She grabbed the tiny piece of paper, folding it, making it even smaller. She held it tightly in her hand while she dressed, just in case Vicki came back in. But she didn't. And Meredith tucked the note into her sock. She was ready to work out.

It was a nice morning so Vicki and Meredith walked to the gym. During the twenty minute hike, Meredith wondered if the American she met the other day, Alex Hart, would be there. She was fairly sure that he was the owner. This would probably be her last chance to communicate with him now that she was Gretchen Bruckmann with a German passport. There was no way her captors didn't have imminent plans to move her across the German border. The question was where? In the moonlight last night,

Meredith had been able to add to the note the details of her new passport.

As the pair arrived in front of the health club, Meredith had to keep herself from laughing at the name, Hart Guter Gesundheit. It made her want to sneeze! But she knew from her command of the German language that Gesundheit translated to "good health". It was actually a fairly clever name. Vicki pushed open the front glass door to the gym and Meredith followed her inside. The clock over the front desk read six thirty. This was definitely the earliest time they had ever arrived at the gym. Maybe there were big plans for the day.

Meredith unobtrusively looked around the gym. Alex Hart was nowhere in sight. Vicki led her to the bikes where they both warmed up for a bit. The gym was busy this time of day and the free weights section, where they usually spent most of their time, was packed. They'd have to wait their turn.

Meredith hopped onto a bike and started peddling. There was a bank of four flat-screen TV's on the wall in front of them, each tuned to a different station. Two were local and the others were set to the BBC and to ABC. She smiled. Maybe she'd learn what was going on back home. However, she reminded herself not to seem too interested in any of the broadcasts in case Vicki was observing. Meredith glanced over at Vicki who had climbed on the bike next to hers. Vicki had earbuds on and seemed to be engrossed in listening to her music or whatever might be playing on her headset. She paid no attention to Meredith.

Fatal Race

Due to the seven hour time change, Meredith had missed the evening news broadcast from home so she turned her attention to the BBC channel with the news of the day. Nothing seemed particularly earth shattering. Most of the stories revolved around Harry and Meghan, the current darlings of the Royal Family. After several minutes, Meredith determined that the world stage was quiet at the moment. She reminded herself that terrorists were very patient and planned meticulously for their next attack.

With each rotation of the bike pedals, Meredith could feel the folded note against her ankle. She needed to think of a Plan B in case Mr. Hart was a no-show.

Alex pounded his fist on his desk. Why were memberships down at his health clubs back in the U.S.? Across the board? He looked up at his computer monitor again thinking he had somehow misinterpreted the month-end numbers. He'd felt confident putting Nate Daniels in charge of operations before he left. Nate had been working for him the longest of anyone on his staff and had been successful at running his gym in Plano, Texas. Alex looked up flights online. Maybe he needed to head back to straighten things out. *That's just an excuse, isn't it? An excuse to check on Jennifer.* Ever since Kate quit responding to his texts and emails, he was going crazy with worry about Jennifer's safety.

Diane Cobalt

Abruptly, Alex stood up and paced the floor. Right now was a crucial time for the success of not only this health club, but also for the others he was planning on opening across Europe. This afternoon a delegation of businessmen from Austria was coming to tour his facility. If they liked what they saw, Alex was hopeful they would become investors in several gyms in their country.

No, he needed to stay here. He would talk to Nate later this afternoon to find out why membership was down and what needed to be done to fix it. It would also help Alex to put Jennifer Baldwin out of his mind.

Alex grabbed his clipboard in preparation for a final walk through the club to make sure everything was perfect for the Austrians. He opened his door and proceeded to the gym and noticed that almost every station was busy. He pulled his cell phone out of his pocket and took a sweeping video of the area. He'd add that to his marketing packet for his presentation this afternoon. The two-for-one promotion he was running seemed to be working. Based on the theory that it's always more fun to work out with a friend, Alex had launched "Hart's Pairs" a week ago and watched as his membership numbers doubled. He passed the treadmills and bikes on his way to the trainers' station which was positioned in the middle of the gym. The station was empty because all of his trainers were currently on the floor working with clients. One by one, he assessed each workout area, looking for anything that might need improvement. He watched as two women got off the bikes and headed to the free weights area. It appeared they were waiting for some of the weights and a bench to open up. Maybe I need to expand that area, Alex thought. It must be frustrating to wait for weights. Alex laughed out loud at his own pun.

One of the two women waiting heard his laugh and turned around. It was the woman Alex had mistaken for an American last week. She quickly glanced away when her friend said something to her. The friend sat down on a bench that had just been vacated while the American-looking woman reached for some barbells to hand to her friend. After doing so, the American woman turned and stared directly at Alex. She almost seemed to be inviting him over with her eyes. He tilted his head and started to exit the trainers' station when his cell phone vibrated. He looked down at the number. It was one of the Austrians. Alex answered and immediately headed back to his office.

Oh no, thought Meredith. Don't leave! How was she going to get the note to him now? She'd have to find a way to get closer to him. She looked over at Vicki who was totally engrossed in completing a set of nose crushers.

Seizing the opportunity, Meredith walked quickly after Alex who was deep in discussion with someone on his cell phone. That would actually work to her advantage. The distraction would keep him from acknowledging her slipping the note in the back pocket of his athletic shorts. Meredith took one more look over her shoulder at Vicki who was oblivious that Meredith had even walked away. She bent down as if tying her shoe and retrieved the folded square of paper from her sock. Alex paused for a moment, becoming more engrossed in his phone conversation. Quickly, Meredith walked up behind him and gently placed the note in his pocket. Turning immediately, she congratulated herself. Neither Mr. Hart nor Vicki had realized what she had done.

It was midnight before Alex returned to his apartment which was located only a few blocks from his club. The meeting with the Austrians had gone much better than he'd expected, despite the last minute cancellation from an investor from Salzburg. Alex had fixed that by Face Timing him into the tour.

Alex sat down on the edge of his bed, removed his shoes, socks and shorts. He couldn't wait to hit the shower. As he picked up his shoes and shorts off the floor, he noticed a small, folded piece of paper.

"What's this?" he said aloud. Carefully he unfolded the note. The printing was so small that he had to grab his readers off his nightstand.

> Please call CIA. Tell them Meredith Matthews
> is being held against her will. Has German
> Passport number D5679325 under the name
> Gretchen Bruckmann.

Meredith Matthews? Why did that name sound familiar? And how did that note get in his back pocket? Alex threw up his hands. And how in the hell does one contact the CIA? It's not like he had them on speed dial.

CHAPTER TWENTY

The temperature in the stark conference room had to be below seventy degrees. Jennifer shivered, pulling her sweater tighter around her shoulders. She sat on the far side of the massive table, opposite the secret door marked "Storage" in the hall which rolled up into the ceiling instead of swinging open each time someone entered the room. Fortunately, Alan Smith wasn't supposed to be in the office until this afternoon. Manuel had answered immediately when she called him this morning and told her to head on over to the Eagle's Nest headquarters.

As was typical for her, Jennifer had arrived early. Julie, the receptionist had greeted her professionally and escorted her to the room. Because of the room's frosty temperature, Julie left a pot of coffee on the center of the table. Jennifer was currently using it to warm her hands when the door rolled open. Manuel entered the room followed by Charles Connor, Richardson's Chief of Police and her other handler. Vincent O'Donley joined them before the door slid back down.

It had been awhile since Jennifer had seen Vincent. She was confused why he would be here when she had been the one to call for a meeting.

"Ah, Julie's coffee!" Charles proclaimed, his bald head reflecting the overhead fluorescent light. "There's nothing quite as good in the entire city and I should know!"

Manuel walked over to Jennifer's side of the table and sat down next to her. He removed the coffee pot from her frozen hands and poured a cup for each of them. Vincent sat down in his usual place at the end of the table.

"I didn't mean for you to come, Mr. O'Donley," Jennifer said.

Vincent smiled as he opened his briefcase and extracted a manila folder. "Please, it's Vincent and I had already planned to be here this morning." He opened the folder. "Gentlemen, shall we get started?"

Jennifer felt the baby kick. She didn't belong here. Maybe they would let her resign. But then how would she get any information about Meredith? No. She needed to suck it up and stick this out.

Manuel cleared his throat. "Jennifer called me a little after eight this morning and asked to meet with me. I asked Charles, as her other handler, to join us."

Vincent looked down the table at Jennifer. He arched his brows. "What would you like to discuss?"

Jennifer clasped her hands under the table. "I thought you should know that my husband has a fraternity brother in D.C. who is helping him investigate his sister's disappearance. Beau told me yesterday that Preston, that's his frat brother, indicated that Geoffrey Matthews worked for the CIA."

Vincent looked at his notes. "Is this Preston Hightower?"

How did he know? Were there no secrets from this organization? Jennifer continued. "Yes. That's correct."

"And do you know exactly what Mr. Hightower said to your husband?" Vincent asked.

Jennifer shook her head. "I wasn't at home when he spoke with Preston on the phone. But Beau said that Preston mentioned all of the remains from the explosion in Frankfurt had been accounted for and that Meredith's were not among them. He also said for Beau not to worry that that the intelligence community doesn't give up on family members of their own."

"And your husband took that to mean...?"

"He thinks that Geoffrey was in the CIA."

"But not Meredith?"

"No, not Meredith." Jennifer brought her hands out of her lap and placed them on the marble conference table. "Look, guys, I can't keep lying to my husband. At least not about his sister."

The three men exchanged glances. Jennifer got nervous.

"What? Do you know something? Is she dead?"

"She's not dead," Manuel confirmed.

"That's great news! Where is she? When did you find her?"

Vincent took a deep breath. "We haven't exactly located her yet."

Jennifer frowned. "I don't understand. Then how do you know she's alive?"

Charles stirred his coffee. He clearly came as an observer and to offer Jennifer support. Manuel and Vincent were the ones in the know.

"Jennifer, what we are about to tell you is classified information," Manuel warned her. "I have to have your word that you will not share it with anyone, including your husband. Otherwise, our meeting will come to an end."

Jennifer's shoulders slumped. She had been certain that she'd get them to agree to tell Beau that she knew Geoff had been an agent and maybe even that his sister was one too. She really had no choice but to agree to remain silent. If she didn't, who knew how long it would be before they would know if Meredith was really okay. If Ryan was getting his mother back.

"Your confidentiality is required to help ensure Meredith's safe return," Vincent added.

Jennifer nodded. "Okay, then. I won't share this information with anyone outside of this room."

Manuel smiled. "Good choice. Vincent, go ahead and share the report with her."

Vincent leaned back in his ergonomic black chair. "We just received word this morning that Meredith Matthews is indeed alive. However, it is believed that she is being held captive by a terrorist group overseas. We do not know how she is nor have we had any direct communication with her."

"But that's still good news, right? You guys can get her back…safely."

Vincent rested his chin on his fingertips and looked directly at Jennifer. "That's always the goal. However, we are potentially dealing with some very nasty people. We don't know if they have discovered who she is. We hope they don't. I can tell you that Meredith has had extensive training on what to do in this situation."

Jennifer swallowed hard. "You mean they might be torturing her?" She barely got the words out.

Vincent shrugged. "Only if they know she's an agent. If she's just some random woman they came across…she wouldn't have any intel they would want. There's a possibility they might even release her. It's hard to say and we don't have enough details at this point."

"What did you say to Beau when he mentioned that Geoff might have been in the CIA?" Manuel asked.

It took a minute for Jennifer to answer. She was stunned that her sister-in-law was actually alive. Tears welled in her eyes. "Um he took what Preston said and then noted that Geoff's obituary didn't have a picture or state that he worked for Exxon. And that made him surer that Geoff worked for the CIA. I tried to tell him that was just circumstantial and that usually CIA agents don't have families. Do they?"

Vincent smiled. "I can't really say. But how did he respond to that?"

"He said what about 'The Americans,' meaning the TV show. And I told him that was fiction and that his imagination was just running wild. He seemed relieved and accepted that explanation."

"Good work, Jennifer. For now, you just have to let your husband believe that Geoffrey and Meredith were in the wrong place at the wrong time so that we can do our jobs securing Meredith's safe return. Does that make sense?" Vincent said.

Jennifer nodded. "Yes. It's not what I wanted to hear, but I do understand. How long do you think this will take? We are still taking care of Meredith's son and recently he's been asking for her. It breaks my heart."

"Well, I wish I had an answer. Unfortunately, I can't even give you a rough estimate. It could be weeks, days, or even months."

Jennifer sighed. "I guess the important part is that she's alive...and hopefully well."

Vincent stood. "We will inform you the minute we know anything. I've got to run to another meeting. I think Manuel and Charles may have some further questions for you." Vincent walked over to Jennifer and stuck out his right hand. "Thank you for all you are doing to ensure not only your sister-in-law's safe return, but also the safety of your community."

Jennifer shook Vincent's hand while staying seated. "You're welcome. Just please get her back as fast as you can."

Vincent nodded before exiting the conference room. As the door slid back down behind him, Manuel pulled out a pad of paper. "How's the research on the fund transfers going?"

Jennifer pulled a zip drive out of her purse. "Here's the latest on what I've been able to track. The funds go all over the place, but all end in Grand Cayman. While that seems logical with their numbered accounts, it seems too obvious. It would be easy for you all to send someone down there and find out who owns those accounts or who is trying to access them, right?"

"Well, you'd think. But there are a lot of laws that protect those folks."

"But isn't that what tax evaders do? Send money to a numbered Swiss account or in the Grand Caymans? I kind of thought I'd be able to see money going back to Iran or Afghanistan."

"It probably is. We just haven't found the path yet. Someone's probably written a computer program that is hiding the route."

Jennifer froze. Jack and Gordon knew how to write computer programs. But there's no way they would do something so illegal, would they? Maybe there would be a way she could innocently ask them how one would go about doing that. But not ask them in the office where their conversations may be recorded. She'd put that on her to-do list.

"I'll keep researching the companies Alan Smith is having me set up to see if any are real. Maybe I'll suggest we need to take inventory or something like that."

Manuel smiled. "As long as you feel it won't put you in danger or reveal what you are working on for us."

"And remember, we've got a few staff members that can help you," added Charles.

"Last time you asked us if we knew if your office was bugged. It is," Manuel warned.

"How did you find out?"

"The landlord has a standing order for pest control."

At first, Jennifer didn't understand. Then it became clear. What a clever ruse. "Thanks for letting me know," she said standing to leave. "If we're done here, I better get back to work."

Both Manuel and Charles rose. "We are. Call us if you need us."

Jennifer nodded, not feeling any better than when she'd arrived.

CHAPTER TWENTY-ONE

Contacting the CIA while living in a foreign country was not easy. And for all Alex Hart knew, it may not be an easy task stateside. The first thing he did was look up CIA on the internet. He got sidetracked by reading the article on the website titled "Myths and Facts." Down at the very bottom of the home page, Alex found the words "Contact CIA." He hesitated for just a moment before pressing it. "Submit questions or comments online" popped up in a blue bar on the page. Damn! He didn't want to have this kind of information traceable. He thought the CIA would realize that. Alex had been expecting some kind of hotline. Then he read down to the last bullet point which stated that if you have information the CIA might be interested in "pursuit of the CIA's foreign intelligence mission" to once again use the email form and they would be careful to protect all info provided including your identity.

Of course they would! Alex spent thirty minutes pacing his bedroom before plopping back down on his bed. He looked at the top of the screen and saw the lock icon indicating the site was secure. What other choices did he have? He'd racked his brain trying to think of anyone he might even casually know in the FBI or TSA or CIA. Nothing! For someone who considered himself to be well connected, he certainly was missing friends in this area.

For the life of him, he couldn't figure out who had slipped the note into his pocket. Shoot, it probably had her fingerprints on it and he'd touched it! But he didn't know what it would say. The club had been packed today. There had been plenty of women he'd walked by.

Alex glanced back down at his laptop. He'd just have to bite the bullet and fill out the damn form. What to say? He decided not to type the contents of the note into the email. It was too risky. All of a sudden he felt very protective of this woman. "I have been given information from someone claiming to be one of your agents..." he started typing. Then he deleted it and started over. "Please contact me for information regarding one of your employees..." Alex shook his head. No, that sounded like he was trying to get someone in trouble. He needed to convey the urgency of the matter. "Please have someone call me regarding information I don't feel comfortable revealing online." Alex nodded. He liked that and then finished by adding his cell phone number. Yes, that was good. He didn't reveal his name or location or the woman's identity. He wondered how long it would take for them to contact him.

Instantly his phone rang. The caller ID said unknown. "Alex Hart," he answered.

"Mr. Hart? This is Agent Brown with the CIA. I'm responding to an email you just sent us."

"Yes, thanks for your very prompt reply."

"How can I assist you?"

"Is it safe for me to talk to you on this line or do we need to meet in person?"

"Our conversation is scrambled. I can have someone meet you, but if this is urgent, it's best to get started right away. Your call."

Alex liked Agent Brown, if that's really what his name was. And he appreciated the option of meeting in person. "Well, I'm overseas in Germany."

"We have officers everywhere, sir."

"Of course you do. I received a note surreptitiously in my back pocket today from a woman claiming to be one of your agents. Should I go ahead and give you the details?"

" No. I will send an agent to see you. Please go to a convenient location in the next thirty minutes, and then call me back at this number from that location. We suggest you do not use your home or business for the rendezvous point. A coffee shop or bar or even a restaurant would work best."

"Okay. I will call you back in thirty minutes."

Agent Brown disconnected.

Diane Cobalt

=+=

Alex sat in an overnight coffee shop waiting for the final five minutes of the allotted time to pass. He'd wished he'd waited until morning to start this endeavor. He held the note in his right hand, fearful that he might lose it. Finally the timer on his cell phone beeped. Alex brought up the last call and hit the number to redial it.

"Agent Brown. To whom am I speaking?"

"Alex Hart."

"Perfect. Agent White is just a few minutes from your location. His badge number is CW642QX. Please stay on the phone with me until he arrives."

"How will he know who I am?"

"He'll find your phone."

Alex sat in a booth facing the door to the coffee shop. A man with dark hair wearing sweats entered. Probably not an agent. Alex looked at the badge number he'd written down on a napkin.

"That's my number," said the man in the sweats who was now standing right next to him holding out his CIA badge.

"He's here," Alex told Agent Brown.

"Very good. Thanks for contacting us." And Alex's cell went dark.

Agent White slid into the booth opposite Alex. The waitress came over and took his order. Once she returned with his coffee and Danish, Agent White looked at Alex. "Before we start, do you have any ID? A passport or driver's license?"

Alex reached into his pocket and pulled out his passport. Agent White flipped through it and then nodded. "What do you have for me?"

Alex opened his hand that was grasping the note. "When I got home tonight from the health club that I own, I found this note in my pocket." He pushed the note across the table, hoping no coffee spilled on it. "I'm sorry I touched it. I had no idea it was in my pocket."

Agent White slowly unfolded the note and read it. He nodded slowly then put some Euros on the table to pay for his coffee. "Thank you for your help. We appreciate it." He started to stand but Alex stopped him.

"Wait a minute. Aren't you going to tell me what's going on?"

The agent tilted his head to the side as if to say "Really?"

Alex nodded. "I get it. It's just that I'd like to help if I can."

Agent White looked at him. "We'll be in touch if there's anything further you can do to assist us. Again, thank you for passing on this information." And with that, Agent White left the coffee shop.

Alex tried to replay the brief conversation in his mind. Did the agent know this woman? Why wouldn't he have questioned him as to exactly where his gym was or did they already know? He took a sip of his own coffee realizing it would take a long time for him to fall asleep tonight. He might as well enjoy Agent White's Danish too. As he took a bite, his phone vibrated. Alex looked at the number. It was Agent Brown.

"Alex Hart."

"Mr. Hart, Agent White conveyed the contents of the note to me. It is critical that we meet you tomorrow. First thing. At your health club."

Alex smiled. He might actually get to help this woman. "That's fine. We open at six. Do you need the address?"

"No. Agent White and possibly another agent will be there shortly after you open. Again, thank you for your help."

"You are quite welcome," Alex replied and quickly realized Agent Brown had already disconnected.

At five a.m., Alex gave up trying to sleep and headed to his gym. He couldn't wait to discover how he might help this woman. He unlocked the glass front door, entered, and then immediately locked it behind him. Munich was a fairly safe city, but he didn't want to deal with early arrivals until more of his staff had reported to work.

The health club was eerily, but not unusually, quiet for being empty. Alex always relished the peaceful time he had every morning before the hum of the cycles and whir of the treadmills interrupted it. Reaching his office, he unlocked his door and flipped on the lights.

Carefully, Alex removed his laptop from his backpack, placed it on his desk and fired it up. He wondered again what questions Agent White might ask him. If only he could remember details about the women in the gym yesterday.

At a quarter to six, Alex exited his office and headed to the juice bar area of the club where Max, his most loyal employee, was busy making a smoothie. "Hey there, Boss. I've just about got your protein shake ready."

Alex smiled as he took the cup from Max. "Thanks Max. You always make exactly what I need."

"I added a little kiwi this morning. If you like it, I may feature it today."

Alex took a swig. "Not bad. See how it sells." Alex noticed a pair of men crossing the street and heading to the club. Both were wearing sweat suits. He was fairly sure one of the two was Agent White.

The men tried the door, but it was still locked. Alex made his way over and let them in. "Good morning," he greeted them. "Welcome to Hart's Guter Gesundheit."

Both men nodded and shook Alex's hand. "Would you mind giving us a tour of your facility?"

Max frowned at the odd request for this time of day, but Alex waved him off indicating he knew they were planning to come. "Of course. Follow me."

Alex guided them through each of the work stations, showed them the rock climbing area and pointed to the outdoor facilities through the windows.

"Okay. I think we've seen enough. Is there somewhere we can meet privately?" Agent White asked.

Alex nodded and escorted the pair to his office, closing the door behind him.

"Please, have a seat. Can I get you a smoothie, tea?"

Both men shook their heads. "No, thanks. This is Agent Jones. He'll be working with me on this case."

Agent Jones smiled briefly. "Nice to meet you Mr. Hart."

"Please, call me Alex."

Agent Jones cleared his throat. "Alex, then. We have a few questions for you. First, do you have any video tape from yesterday?"

Alex took a seat behind his desk. "For privacy purposes, we do not have our security cameras on during hours of operation. So no."

"Can you think of any women who might have gotten close enough to you to place the note in your back pocket? Were you training any of them?" This time Agent White asked the question.

Alex shook his head. "I've been over and over this in my mind and I just can't come up with a visual of any specific woman. We were slammed for a while yesterday, so busy in fact that some members were waiting to move on to another..." Instantly Alex could see the two women on the bikes, in particular the one who finally went over to the free weights area and stared at him. "Hold on a second! I do remember two women yesterday, but then there were many other women in the gym. I'm not sure I can give you a real good description of her." Alex snapped his fingers. "Yes!" He reached for his cell phone. "I was so happy that the club was virtually at capacity that I took a quick video to show some potential investors who were coming by in the afternoon, which is usually our quietest time."

Fatal Race

Alex brought up the video and looked at it. The second time he viewed it, he pressed pause. "Here...right here. These two women on the bikes are the ones I remember most. I'd seen the one that is further right before and had mistaken her for an American." He handed the phone to Agent Jones.

Both agents looked at the picture. "Uh, do you have a shot, perhaps of their faces?" Agent Jones handed the phone back to Alex.

"Yeah. I guess their backsides don't help a whole lot." Alex reviewed the video again, but realized it didn't catch their faces. "Sorry."

"No, that's good thinking," Agent White said. "Do you think you might recognize her from a picture?"

Alex shrugged. "Probably."

Agent Jones reached into his backpack and extracted a portfolio. He opened it to a page that had been earmarked. "Do any of these women look familiar? Keep in mind they may have a different hair style or color of hair."

It only took Alex a few seconds to identify the mystery woman. "It's this one. She's got blond hair that is cut really short now."

"You're sure?" Agent Jones confirmed.

"One hundred percent sure. I talked to her several weeks ago, when she was in with a couple of other women."

"And were these women with her yesterday?"

Alex thought. "One of them was."

"And do you see a picture of that woman on this page?" Agent White asked.

"No."

"You're sure?"

"No, I mean yes, I'm sure neither woman was with her."

Agent Jones nodded, putting the portfolio away. "Thank you for your time, Mr. Hart...I mean Alex. You've been very helpful."

Alex stood up as the men prepared to leave his office. "Wait! You mean that's all? You're not going to tell me who she is?"

Agent White gave Alex a sad smile. "I wish we could. But for her safety and yours, we can't do that. However, if she comes back in, we need you to give her this." The agent handed Alex a small cell phone. "And make sure that no one, including the women who might be with her, sees you give it to her."

"And it goes without saying that you will contact us immediately after you see her," added Agent Jones handing Alex his card.

Alex took the phone and the card. "I will. But what if she doesn't return?"

"Let's hope that she does," Agent Jones said.

CHAPTER TWENTY-TWO

The sun was shining brightly and the air had a crisp feeling. Fall was definitely trying to crowd out summer, at least in Germany. Despite a mostly sleepless night, Meredith felt refreshed and hopeful. Her handlers were most likely moving her to a different country today. And that meant someone might identify her from her passport; that is if Alex Hart had discovered her cryptic note in his back pocket.

It was her best chance for being extradited by the agency from her current predicament. However, Daria's and Vicki's constant arguing might also attract some unwanted attention from the authorities. They had been mostly silent during the past two hours as they zipped along the autobahn.

Diane Cobalt

Daria had exploded into Meredith's room looking for Vicki shortly before midnight. "Wo ist sie?" she demanded from Meredith. *Where is she?*

"Vicki? Ich weis nicht." Meredith really didn't know where Vicki had gone, but she suspected she had gone to meet her new lover at a bar. She had spotted Vicki talking to some man wearing sweats and a hooded sweatshirt on the street below her window after they had returned from the gym yesterday. The man had put his arm around her shoulders and they walked away, disappearing from her view. How odd that Daria wouldn't have some hi-tech way of keeping tabs on her compatriot.

Daria had fumed, pacing the tiny room and checking her watch every few minutes. Meredith simply ignored her which seemed to infuriate Daria even more. At one in the morning, Daria seemingly gave up and stormed out of the room, locking the door behind her.

For the next four hours or so, Meredith had been able to get some sleep which had been a wise decision on her part. Because before dawn, Daria unlocked the door and entered the room dragging Vicki behind her.

Vicki looked disheveled. Perhaps she was drunk. Her usual piercing violet-colored eyes were droopy and her brunette hair was sticking out at crazy angles to her head. Meredith wondered where Daria had found her.

The two had returned to speaking Farsi, thinking Meredith couldn't understand them. But to Meredith, it was as easy to understand as English.

Fatal Race

"Why did you take her to the gym again?" Daria had wanted to know.

Vicki seemed totally disinterested and tried to disengage from the argument. "It was something to pass the time. You know, waiting around for directions from above is boring."

Daria glared at her and lowered her voice. "That's part of our devotion to the goal or have you forgotten?"

"No. I haven't forgotten. So what's with dragging me back here?"

"I finally have orders. We leave in two hours." Daria glanced at Meredith to make sure she did not comprehend what they were saying. "They want her to teach...in one of our compounds."

"Teach what?"

"German."

Vicki shrugged. "I'll get her ready to go."

"You're going too."

Vicki looked confused. "Why?"

"They need more women teachers. Where we are going, women do the teaching. So pack your things. I'll be back for both of you in an hour."

Meredith had no idea where they wanted her to teach German, but clearly it wouldn't be in Germany or one of its neighboring German-speaking countries. The older model BMW they were now riding in didn't seem sturdy enough for a long trip. Meredith reviewed the countries who were Germany's next door neighbors as they continued along. France didn't seem likely, nor did the Netherlands. Where would they have a compound? The two most likely countries would be Poland or the Czech Republic. Both were east of Munich and they were heading south.

Daria, who was driving, steered the BMW to an exit indicating the direction towards Prague. That must be their destination then. Meredith decided to get a little shut eye and leaned her head back against the worn leather of the backseat. She didn't notice when the car slowed to a stop.

A pounding on her window startled Meredith. The man motioned for her to get out of the car. Vicki opened her door from the outside and told her to grab her passport.

Meredith pulled it out of the holder she had on a cord around her neck and handed it to the border patrol agent. It appeared they had made it to the Czech border. Would this be her moment of freedom?

The agent looked at the outside of her passport and peered into the car. "Gehen." *Go.*

He wasn't even going to open her passport and look at her picture? Freedom would have to wait a little longer.

Daria smiled at the agent while getting back into the driver's seat. "Danke."

The trio sped off down the highway. Meredith tried to determine where they were. A compound would most likely be in a rural area, but it appeared that they were heading for Prague.

"Let's stop to eat," Vicki suggested, speaking Farsi.

"No time. Our flight leaves in two hours," Daria replied back.

Flight? Where were they going? Meredith was once again hopeful. They'd have to check her passport at the airport. And by now, surely Alex Hart had contacted the CIA. They would have bulletins set up at every customs point worldwide.

As they approached the airport exit, Daria said something to Vicki under her breath. Vicki reached into her backpack and extracted a red curly-hair wig. She passed it back to Meredith and told her to put it on.

Meredith had a bad feeling that got worse when Vicki handed her a new passport. It was from Great Britain. She was now Sally Davies. Her picture inside had an authentic looking photo of her in the red wig which had to have been photo shopped.

These people were crafty and smart; she'd give them that. But careful? Not so much. Neither Daria nor Vicki asked her to return Gretchen Bruckmann's passport. That should get her stopped for questioning when they went through security.

There were two main terminals in the Prague airport. Terminal One was used for commercial flights. Terminal Two was used for private flights. Each terminal had its own security check points. So far so good, Meredith thought. This would be her best chance at freedom. When asked for her ID, she'd simply hand them the German passport.

The trio approached what appeared to be a check-in counter for private flights. Daria turned to her. "Give me your passport," she commanded in German.

Diane Cobalt

Meredith handed her Sally Davies' passport. Daria, in turn, handed it to the woman behind the counter who opened it, casually looked at the women, and then returned the passports. She instructed them they would be leaving out of gate three in approximately thirty minutes and pointed to the security check point.

Good, thought Meredith. I still have a chance to run. She followed Daria with Vicki behind her. Damn! She wanted to go through last so the others wouldn't have a chance to stop her. There was no line at security. Daria plopped her backpack on the conveyer belt and waited for the guard to motion her through the x-ray machine.

This was Meredith's chance. She stooped, pretending to retie her shoe, motioning Vicki to go around her. Vicki did, depositing her bag onto the belt. But she stood, waiting for Meredith to pass through the x-ray first. Her escape would have to wait.

CHAPTER TWENTY-THREE

It was early afternoon and Jennifer had just finished completing the setup for the fifteenth of Alan Smith's companies when she heard the office door open. "Hey, Alan!" Gordon greeted his boss. "Welcome back to the good ole U.S. of A."

"Yeah. Ditto what he said," Jack chimed in gruffly.

"Thank you gentlemen," Alan said, using his pseudo British accent.

"How was your trip?" Gordon asked.

"Quite busy, actually. Look, I have a lot to catch up on as you would say. But I do want to talk to both of you this afternoon about the App. Let's meet in my office around four."

"You got it!" Gordon said. Jennifer thought she heard a "harrumph" from Jack. He had probably been planning on cutting out early.

Jennifer was about to greet her boss, but he walked on by her office without saying a word. That was fine with her. She could use a little extra time to get things organized.

The pager on her desk phone beeped. "Yes, Alan?"

"Please come to my office as soon as you have a minute, Jennifer."

"Right away, sir." Jennifer always smiled at the way he pronounced her name: Jen-E-fur.

She grabbed a pad of paper and pen off her desk and headed towards his office at the end of the long, narrow hallway.

"That was quite fast!" Alan greeted her. "Please, sit."

Jennifer did as she was told. "I finished setting up the last of your companies."

Alan sat down behind his massive desk. A puzzled look crossed his face. Jennifer tried hard not to stare at his blond wig which currently sat catawampus on his head. He must have put it on hurriedly. To keep from chuckling, Jennifer stared at her blank notepad.

"The companies! Yes, yes. I apologize. I have been so busy conducting business overseas that I forgot that I had dumped all that work on you before I left. Thank you for finishing it so promptly."

Jennifer looked up at him, but focused at a spot on the wall directly behind him. "You're welcome. The companies are all open and ready for business."

"Good, good. And I like that you only ask necessary questions." Jennifer looked at him long enough to see a smile cross his face.

"Well you are very busy."

Alan's gaze was momentarily directed to his computer monitor. Jennifer wished she could see what he was looking at. She waited patiently while he read...something. "Yes, and I seemingly will remain that way." He forced a laugh. "But along with your continuing to do the accounting and financial work for my companies...and there will be lots of activity coming up on those...I need you to work with Jack and Gordon on their App."

"But I don't know how to program, Alan. I'm just a 'bean counter' as they call me."

Alan tilted his head to the side and Jennifer was afraid his toupee might fall off. "Is that a nice term? Bean Counter?"

Jennifer used the moment to laugh. "Hardly. It's similar to my calling them 'Code Toads.' It's an insulting term."

"Then I shall tell them to stop that immediately."

Jennifer put her hand up. "It's okay...really. I know they're just poking fun at me."

"Well, if you say so." Alan took a deep breath. Jennifer thought he seemed a little tired, maybe from the jetlag. "I want them to test the app on your phone."

Jennifer thought it might be best if she not tell Alan that she already had it on her phone. "Sure, no problem. I'm happy to help."

"Thank you. I..." Alan's cell phone rang. He answered it instantly. Jennifer waited for him to motion for her leave the room, but instead, Alan merely swiveled his chair so that his back was to her. Jennifer wasn't sure if she should leave or not; so she stayed.

"Yes, yes. I understand your concern," he said to the caller. "You must not waste any more time on this matter. Do *you* understand? It never should have gotten to this point. Take care of it...today!" Alan actually barked out the last sentence. Jennifer was about to stand when he twirled back around in his chair. Alan disconnected the call.

"I'm sorry. I should have left when your phone rang," Jennifer apologized.

There was something about Alan's smile that sent a shiver down her spine. "I'm sorry I showed my emotions. I rarely do that."

Jennifer stood. "If that's all you have for me, I'll get with Gordon and Jack about the app."

"You might want to wait until after I meet with them this afternoon. I have a few changes I want to discuss with them."

"Sure. No problem."

"Please close the door behind you, Jennifer."

Jennifer did as she was told and headed to her office. She could hear Alan already speaking in a foreign language to someone. If only she knew what he was saying. One thing she definitely understood from the tone of his voice, Alan was pissed off.

Gordon was standing in the hall outside of his office, a cup of coffee in hand. Jennifer decided to let him know that Alan wanted her to be a tester for the app.

"Hey, Gordon, FYI, Alan wants me to help you and Jack with the app by being a guinea pig for it. I didn't think I should tell him I already am."

"That's fine. We'll let him think it's his idea." Gordon winked at her.

"What was up with all that hollering in there? He wasn't mad at you, was he?" Jack popped his head out of the doorway to their office.

"Oh look, it's Mr. Nosy," Gordon teased.

"I'm not nosy!" Jack snapped back. "Just making sure Jennifer wasn't in some kind of trouble in there. He may be our boss, but he needs to be nice."

Jennifer smiled. "He was talking to someone on the phone, not to me. No worries, Jack."

"Okay." Jack went back inside his office.

Gordon took a swig of coffee. "Who's he talking to now? He sounds like he's growling at someone," Gordon said in a soft voice.

Jennifer shrugged. "Beats me. I just work here."

Gordon laughed. "True. We have a meeting with him a little later, so we'll get together after that. If you need to pick up the little guy from school, we can discuss the app in the morning."

"Thanks! You read my mind!"

As Jennifer turned to enter her office, Alan swung open his office door. "Jack! Gordon! In my office now...please!"

Gordon raised his brows and looked at Jennifer who quickly exited the hallway. "Right away. Come on, Jack!"

The two men filed by Jennifer's office and entered Alan's, closing the door behind them.

Jennifer plopped down into her desk chair. The baby kicked her. That reminded her of the upcoming sonogram next week. She'd need to remind Beau.

Jennifer stared at her computer screen. She wished she could learn Farsi or whatever language Alan Smith had been speaking earlier. What a laugh! She barely had time to breathe. There was no way she had time to learn another language. But maybe she could learn a few words or phrases. She could do it online. Maybe even Manuel could suggest a site for her to go to...just not while she was at work.

Right now, she strained to hear what Alan was saying to Jack and Gordon. It was unusual for them to be in there with the door closed. Occasionally, Jennifer could hear a word here or there, but nothing that was giving her any clue as to what was going on.

Less than ten minutes later, both men trudged back down the long hall to their office, not even acknowledging Jennifer as they passed her office doorway. Jennifer surmised that whatever their meeting was about, they weren't happy.

Alan suddenly appeared in her office. "I've been unexpectedly called out of town. As soon as you have time, get with Jack and Gordon." Alan walked to the office's front door and disappeared into the parking lot.

It took Jack and Gordon less than a minute to park themselves in Jennifer's office.

"What was all that about? You two look very unhappy," she commented. Gordon who was normally jovial looked as if he'd seen a ghost. "Did he fire you?"

Jack shook his head. "Nope. But I'm beginning to wish he had."

Gordon swatted him with the rolled up piece of paper he held in his hand. "Would you shut up?" Gordon pointed to his ear, indicating Alan might have the office bugged.

"Right. Right."

"So Jennifer, we need to add this app to your phone. And then we'll need to update it once we make the 'tweaks' Alan has requested." Gordon made air commas when he said the word "tweaks".

"Okay. Fine. That's no big deal," Jennifer assured them.

"Hey did you remember to bring me that file from our old boss? You said you had it at home." Gordon said as if he were speaking in code. He motioned his head toward the front office door. At first Jennifer was confused. Then she realized he wanted her to go outside.

"Yes, I did. I left it in my car. Do you want me to run out and get it now?"

Gordon smiled. "That would be great. I'll go with you so I can just put it in my car. That way I won't forget it here. Jack, you get to work on what Alan asked us to do."

Jack stood and saluted Gordon. "Yes, sir!"

Gordon sighed as he followed Jennifer to her car, making sure Alan was not in the parking lot. Jennifer opened her car door. "What's the matter?"

"I'll tell you what the matter is. We all are working for a criminal and I don't know what to do about it."

"What did he ask you to do?" Jennifer had a sinking feeling in her stomach that was not caused by the baby.

"As you know, we designed an app that would allow parents to be able to control communications from others with their kids."

Jennifer nodded. "Yep. And?"

"And Alan was so impressed that he wanted us to add an additional function."

"Which is...?"

"The ability to jam all communications with the phone, including the parents'."

Jennifer frowned. "But why would anyone want to do that?"

Gordon just stared at her. "Well not for any good reason that I can think of."

The sick feeling in the pit of her stomach was growing. She didn't know what to say.

"So, since he is adamant about our adding that to your phone, I'd suggest you get a second phone within the next few days and make this your secondary line."

Jennifer stood with her mouth open. "Do you and Jack even know how to come up with something like that?"

"I'm sure we can figure it out. But it ain't legal."

"Then don't do it!"

"We have families, just like you, Jennifer."

"He's threatened you, then."

"Not in so many words...but I can't take that chance. Would you? I think he's got some powerful connections."

Jennifer could only nod. She knew she'd be contacting Manuel to find out what they should do.

CHAPTER TWENTY-FOUR

Jennifer sat by herself in the Eagle's Nest conference room waiting for Manuel to arrive. Gordon and Jack had been so upset by Alan's latest request that they had decided to take the rest of the afternoon off. Jennifer had texted Kate asking her if she could pick up the boys from school. Fortunately, Kate was already at the school helping stuff the Friday Folders that went home from school with each student at the end of the week.

Manuel had been in Fort Worth at a meeting and was on his way. When Jennifer arrived at the Eagle's Nest office, Julie, the receptionist, advised Jennifer to wait in the conference room. Pacing the room helped pass the time and seemed to lull the baby back to sleep. He or she had been very active today. Jennifer wondered if the stress was upsetting their child.

Fatal Race

It was time to get out of this situation. Jennifer had to think not only about her baby, but also about Ryan. What good would it do for them to find Meredith only for her to come home and find her son was missing...or dead? Jennifer only had herself to blame. If she would just mind her own business, she'd be in a lot less trouble.

The door rolled up and Manuel entered the room. He was alone. "Jennifer," he greeted her, "what's so urgent?"

"Alan Smith asked Gordon and Jack to develop an app for parents, so they could intercept any calls and messages from friends they didn't like," she began.

"And?"

"And today, he asked them to modify the app to allow the user to jam all communications."

Manuel sat down next to her. "That's not good. Are they capable of writing that kind of code?"

Jennifer nodded. "I asked and Gordon said yes. He actually told me in the parking lot in case the place is bugged. He and Jack are spooked. They don't want to do anything illegal, but are afraid for their families if they refuse."

Manuel took a deep breath. "So what are they going to do?"

"They don't know. Of course they don't know anything about what I am doing. The reason they even told me about this assignment is because Alan wants it tested on my phone."

Manuel didn't respond immediately.

"What do you want me to do?" Jennifer asked.

Diane Cobalt

"I need to contact Vincent so that we can craft a plan that will keep the three of you safe, but allows us to continue with our surveillance of Mr. Smith. It may take twenty-four hours before I can get back to you. In the meantime, though, have Gordon and Jack drag their heels. Maybe they hit a snag when they test it for the first time and have to go back to the drawing board. Be creative."

Jennifer nodded. "Um, Manuel, I hate to say this, but maybe it's time for me to get out of this position."

Manuel looked hard at Jennifer. "Really? You've never struck me as being a quitter. We're getting closer."

"I know. It's just that I have to think about my family."

"Which now includes your nephew. And with his mother being alive, we don't dare rock the boat by making any drastic changes. Meredith's best chance at reuniting with her son lies with you, Jennifer. Not to mention that we can't take this group of terrorists down without you."

Well isn't that great! Becoming a hero isn't what it's cracked up to be! "Okay. I'll suggest they take their time with the app. Anyway, Alan may be out of the office for a few days. He left suddenly after receiving a phone call this afternoon. He was speaking quietly with his office door closed in a language I've never heard before."

"It was probably Farsi."

"That's what I was thinking. Is there any way I could at least learn a few words or phrases?"

Manuel smiled. "Yes, but only use the laptop we gave you. I'll send you a link to an excellent website."

Jennifer stood. "Thanks."

Fatal Race

Manuel also stood and put his hand on her shoulder. "Relax. We've got your back. This will all work out just fine."

With tears threatening to spill onto her cheeks, Jennifer nodded.

Beau checked his watch for the tenth time. He could still hear Dr. Hunnicutt talking on the phone to another doctor about a patient. He needed to talk to him before leaving for soccer practice which was in less than an hour. If he had to be a little late it would be okay because Drew would be there. But Beau didn't want Ryan thinking that he wasn't important to him.

"Agreed. Thanks for the consult," Beau overheard Dr. Hunnicutt say. Great! Now was his chance! Beau stepped into the hallway. Glancing to his right, he saw a light coming from underneath the door to the lab. He wondered who was using it if Dr. Hunnicutt was in his office. The door to the doctor's office swung open.

"Beau! How did your day go?"

"Awesome! If you have a few minutes, I'd like to bring you up to speed."

"Of course. I'm going to grab some coffee, down the hall. Can I get you some?"

Beau shook his head. "No, I'm fine."

"Take a seat. I'll be back in a second."

Beau sat down in a chair facing the doctor's desk, his back to the hallway. He was going over his notes when he heard Dr. Hunnicutt down the hall talking to someone. That was strange since he thought the office staff had left for the day. Maybe he was on his phone again. He hoped not. Beau didn't want to get waylaid. Then Beau noticed the doctor's cell phone on his desk.

Dr. Hunnicutt walked back into his office, coffee in hand. "I was just talking to the woman I rented my lab to," he commented. "Nice looking, but most unfriendly. I'd tell you her name, but she demanded confidentiality when she signed the lease."

Although Beau thought it *w*as interesting, he didn't need to spend extra time discussing the tenant. "I think you're going to be exceptionally happy with what I've been able to accomplish today."

The doctor took a seat next to Beau instead of behind his desk. "Go on. I'm intrigued."

"First, there's a large cardiology group in Houston who is very interested in being pioneers of your product. They want you to come down and make a presentation next week, if possible. That group alone implants over fifty pacemakers a month."

Dr. Hunnicutt beamed. "That's excellent, Beau. I may have to move a few things around on my schedule, but I'll make it work."

"Great! I'd suggest we fly down for the presentation. Or just you can go..."

"Absolutely not. I want you there with me." The doctor picked his phone up off the desk and looked at his calendar. "See if they can meet with us next Wednesday or Thursday afternoon."

Beau made a note. "Will do. The other thing I want to discuss is the upcoming National Cardiovascular Surgeons Conference. As you may know, it's being held in D.C. early next month. I was able to reserve a small booth at their vendor fair."

"Yes, yes. I already have plans to go. I had forgotten about the vendors they have there."

"Thanks," Beau said sarcastically.

"I didn't mean to come across in a degrading manner. Quite the opposite. I should have thought of that as a marketing tool."

"That's why you hired me! Should I go ahead and send payment in to secure our booth?"

"Payment? How much? I never realized those companies paid to be there." The doctor frowned.

"That's how the costs of the conference are defrayed! Fortunately this isn't as pricey as some that I've seen. I can get us a booth for as little as five hundred dollars, but I'd rather go for a corner spot which sees a little more foot traffic. That will probably be a grand."

The doctor nodded. "That's fine. Whatever you think will give us the most visibility."

"This is one of the best shows for your product. I also think you need to see if you can give a seminar."

"It's too late for that. I'm sure they already have their participants lined up."

"Maybe. Let me do some checking. I have a contact or two within that organization. If it's not too late, are you interested?"

Dr. Hunnicutt grinned. "Of course! I love talking about my product."

"I'll get to work on that. The last thing is that we will need some marketing tools to take to that conference like signs for the booth and some giveaways."

"Giveaways?"

"Yes, like pens or maybe even batteries. I'll come up with a few ideas and run them by you tomorrow. I'll need to get them ordered as soon as possible so they're ready."

"And book your flight and hotel, Beau. I'll forward my itinerary to you so we can be on the same flight and stay at the same hotel."

"I'll likely need to go out a day ahead of you to set things up."

"I really like you! You're doing an outstanding job."

Beau smiled again. "I'm excited about this product. It's going to make a lot of money." He stood up. "I need to get to Ryan's soccer practice."

Dr. Hunnicutt stood and shook Beau's hand. "Keep up the good work!"

Beau couldn't wait until this product was actually being used. It would revolutionize the pacemaker world.

CHAPTER TWENTY-FIVE

Rachel knew she had to be more careful entering and exiting her lab. She had patiently waited for over an hour for Dr. Hunnicutt to get off his phone and leave for the night. As soon as he had finished his conversation, she started to leave, but then had to duck back in as the new sales associate he'd hired stepped into the hall. The new guy's back had been to her, but something about him looked familiar. When the doctor had made his way to the makeshift kitchen at the end of the hall, Rachel made her dash to leave.

Ordinarily she wouldn't have minded spending another hour or two in the lab. The more trials she could complete, the closer she and Pierce were to finalizing the drug. But she had an appointment at five to meet her new landlord.

Diane Cobalt

Rachel's research had finally uncovered where the Baldwins had lived and the address where they had recently moved. Alan's friend's home was convenient to work and more importantly just down the street from Jennifer Baldwin's new home. Rachel would now be able to keep an eye on her target.

A few minutes after five, Rachel entered the Baldwin's subdivision. The main street into the neighborhood was lined with beautiful maple and oak trees. Rachel took a few extra minutes to drive down several of the side roads. She noticed there were many types of homes, everything from zero lot line houses to large two-story brick houses. But when she turned onto the street where she would be living, the houses got even larger and more opulent. Rachel pulled up in Walter's Mercedes in front of the address Alan had provided. Not too shabby, she thought before collecting her purse and walking up the steep driveway towards the double front doors. She paused, surveying the quiet street, and then pushed the doorbell. Rachel noted it was a "Ring" doorbell so the owner probably had already been alerted to her presence.

A woman in her early thirties with red hair and freckles answered the door. "Hi! My name is Amy! You must be Paige. Come on in!"

Other than being a little too perky, Rachel was pleased. "Thank you. It's nice to meet you."

The entryway was more like a stepping stone on the edge of a massive living area. There were two separate seating areas, one facing a gigantic flat panel TV and the other facing a fireplace. Rachel thought the room could have easily been in *Southern Living* magazine. In fact, she wondered if anyone used it or if Amy had just picked it up to look nice for her.

"I thought I'd give you the tour and show you the room you'd be renting."

Rachel nodded. "Sounds great. Show me the way."

Amy walked through the living area and into a large kitchen which overlooked a beautiful swimming pool. "Of course, you are welcome to use the kitchen. All I ask is that you clean up after yourself."

"Of course," agreed Rachel. "And can I use the pool?"

"Yes. We have a sign-up sheet in the laundry room. That way, if you want to have the pool to yourself, you can pick a time when no one else has signed up."

"That makes sense. How many other tenants do you have?"

Amy continued walking through the kitchen and opened the door to a laundry room so Rachel could see the pool schedule. It was on a dry erase board. "Well, it depends. Right now we just have one besides you. We use the same sign up system for the laundry room. You have to provide your own detergent and please only use HE detergent in this washer."

"What's this door?" Rachel asked pointing to a locked door just outside the laundry room.

Amy frowned. "That goes to the basement. You will not have access to that. It's used mostly for storage anyway."

Diane Cobalt

So far so good, thought Rachel. Amy closed the door to the laundry room and headed back to the front of the house. "There are two bedrooms down here, mine and one other. Let's head upstairs so I can show you yours."

The stairway was just to the left of the front door. There were eight steps straight up and then the stairway made a jog to the right with another eight steps. Again, everything was well maintained. All the floors were hardwood and the walls appeared to have been freshly painted a gray taupe color. Amy passed a door on either side of the hall and walked to the door at the end of the hallway. She produced a key from her pocket and unlocked it. "This would be your room."

Rachel followed Amy into the bright corner room. The room was minimally furnished with a queen bed, single nightstand with a lamp, a dresser with four drawers and a small chair. Amy opened a door to show Rachel a walk-in closet and then a second door that led to a small bathroom. Rachel looked out the window and realized she had a great view of Beau Baldwin's home. "It's perfect! When can I move in?"

Amy seemed a little taken aback with Rachel's quick decision. "Well, I guess tomorrow? How long are you planning on staying here? I rent by the week or by the month."

"I'm not sure. Can I start with a month and then go week by week if I need to extend my stay?"

"That works for me," said Amy. "I have a no smoking and no pets policy."

Fatal Race

"That's fine. What do you need from me?" Rachel asked knowing that Alan was paying the rent.

Amy smiled. "I have a simple one-page lease for you to sign. I keep them in the kitchen." Rachel nodded and followed Amy back downstairs to the kitchen. Amy pulled a form from a drawer in the built-in desk.

Rachel perused the page and signed her name as Paige Walker.

"Welcome home!" Amy exclaimed. "I'll make a copy for you."

"One question. Where should I park?"

"Anywhere on the street is fine. I ask that the tenants keep the driveway clear so I can get in and out of the garage. This is a very safe neighborhood, but I always recommend not leaving anything of value in your car overnight."

Rachel nodded. "Fine. I'll probably move in sometime early afternoon tomorrow."

"That's perfect."

Rachel got in Walter's car. She'd have to park around the corner so the Baldwins wouldn't see her coming and going, but that was not a big deal. Plus, she reminded herself, they would never recognize her. Too bad they couldn't say the same thing for themselves.

Jennifer decided she needed some fresh air to clear her head. Kate had texted her that she would take the boys to practice and then Beau could bring Ryan home. So no one would be expecting her to show up. The practice field they used was located behind Grandview Elementary. There was no parking right next to it which made it safer. No one was chasing balls into an area where there were cars moving around. Jennifer pulled up behind the line of other parents' cars. She got out and grabbed the peach tea she'd bought at Starbucks on the way over. Walking by each car, Jennifer noted that Kate wasn't here. She must have gone back home to fix dinner. In a way, Jennifer was relieved that her best friend wasn't around. It would give her more time to "scout out" the other parents. She had yet to find the red-haired woman Vincent had asked her to look for.

Slowly, so as not to alert any of the other parents she was there, Jennifer approached the soccer field. A narrow, three tiered row of bleacher seats held several moms. Unfortunately, their backs were to Jennifer. Beau blew his whistle and waved the players over to give them some instruction.

"Hi, I'm Jennifer Baldwin," she said as she sat down next to a mom on the first row of the bleachers.

"Hi! I'm Kenna. You must be the coach's wife!" Kenna held out her perfectly manicured hand, a ring decorated almost every finger. "I'm Carson's mom."

Jennifer shook her hand and smiled. Kenna had straight, jet black hair. Her skin was olive colored. Jennifer guessed she might be Native American. "Nice to meet you, Kenna."

"This is Mari. Mari just moved here," Kenna added, leaning back so Jennifer could see the red-haired woman sitting on the other side of her.

"Hi, Mari. I'm Jennifer," Jennifer said as she shook hands with her and noted her freckles. "Where did you move from?"

Mari smiled. "We moved here a few days ago from overseas."

Okay. Can you be more specific? "Well, it's nice to have you. What's your son's name?"

"It's Reuben." Mari turned her attention back to practice. Kenna looked at Jennifer as if to say she wasn't too sure about her.

Jennifer raised her eyebrows and shrugged. Was this the woman Manuel was looking for? She had the same hair color and freckles, but Jennifer wasn't sure about the structure of her face. Of the two, Kenna looked more foreign.

Maybe she could get a picture of her. That way Manuel could have someone run it through their database. But taking a picture of the parents just watching practice didn't seem plausible. She'd have to wait until the soccer game on Saturday. She'd bring her camera and pretend to take pictures of the team. Beau's folks would be in town. His dad loved taking pictures. Between the two of them, surely she could get one of Mari.

In the meantime, Jennifer decided to get to know her. She motioned for Kenna to trade places with her on the bleachers. "Mari, we have an online sign-up sheet for parents who want to provide drinks or snacks for the players after the game. If you give me your email address, I'll send you the link."

Mari looked at Jennifer as if she had three heads. "Is that your custom here?"

Jennifer nodded. "Especially during the first half of the season, the boys really look forward to juice boxes and a cookie or fruit bar after the game."

"Our email isn't set up yet. Can you just put me down for the last game of the season? That way I'll have time to get settled."

This wasn't going the way Jennifer had planned. "Sure. I can do that. Beau will need some contact information for you in case he has to reschedule practice or cancel a game due to weather."

"It's on our registration card." Mari seemed put out by Jennifer's questions.

"Great! Then we're all set." Jennifer would get her info from Beau and pass it along to Manuel. Part of her hoped this was the woman they were looking for. It would explain her chilly attitude to strangers. But the other part of Jennifer hoped she'd never come across the terrorist living amongst them.

CHAPTER TWENTY-SIX

By eight fifteen the next morning, the breakfast rush at Panera Bread in Richardson had slowed down. Jennifer, Jack and Gordon sat at a round table in the corner near the secondary exit. Gordon looked over at Jack's plate as the server set it down. "Wow, Jack. Are you on a diet or something?" The plate held a breakfast sandwich and a toasted Cinnamon Crunch bagel.

Jack rolled up his newspaper and hit Gordon on the head. "Would you shut up, Smart Ass?"

Gordon recoiled, laughing. "Seriously, that doesn't look like enough for a growing boy such as you!"

"Whatever," Jack muttered under his breath.

Jennifer never tired of the banter between these two. Jack meticulously slathered his bagel with butter and then dug into his sandwich.

"At least Jennifer would have an excuse to eat that much since she's eating for two," Gordon continued.

Jennifer laughed. "You two are so funny."

"Funny as in ha-ha or funny as in strange?" Jack wanted to know.

"Why are you asking her questions you already know the answer to?" Gordon chimed in.

Jennifer held up her hand to stop the arguing. "Enough! Funny as in ha-ha. I asked you two to meet me here so we could discuss the changes to the app that Alan requested."

Both men quieted down. Their expressions instantly went from jocular to somber.

"Yeah. About that. I thought about it all last night and I ain't doing it," said Gordon.

"Yeah. Me either," agreed Jack.

"If that rat bastard starts threatening me, I'll go to the police. Simple as that," said Gordon.

"Rat bastard? Did you just call our boss a rat bastard?" Jack wanted to know.

"Yeah I did. What's it to you?"

"Nothing. I agree. Just shocked Mr. Goody Two-shoes even knew that term!"

It was nice to have a little comic relief, but Jennifer knew that she had to keep them in the game at least until Manuel gave her further instructions. "Let's not get carried away with this, gentlemen. I think it might be wise to 'play along' for a little while."

"Why's that?" Jack growled.

"Well, if he's up to something that's really...criminal in nature, the farther along he is, the easier for the police or federal officials to apprehend him, right?"

"Feds? As in FBI?" Gordon asked.

Jennifer shrugged. "I don't know. Perhaps. Doesn't it sound like something that could totally destroy an area?"

"Shit! She's right," Jack said. "We can take our time with this. He can't make us write the app so that it works."

Gordon nodded. "Agreed."

"And it's also critical, I think, that we not discuss any of this in the office. You two, and I hate to say this, may be correct in thinking the office is bugged. He may even have tapped our cell phones."

"Aw, crap. I didn't think about that," said Gordon.

"That's okay. We haven't called or texted anything of importance. So let's each get a prepaid phone today and exchange numbers. That way if we want to set up a breakfast meeting, Alan Smith will be no more the wiser," Jennifer suggested.

Both men nodded. "I'll stop and get all three on the way back to work," said Gordon. "I'll distribute them along with their numbers at happy hour today. Let's say five at Mena's."

"She can't go to happy hour," Jack complained.

"Sure I can. I'll just have iced tea," Jennifer responded.

"Sorry about that, Jennifer. I didn't think about you being pregnant," Gordon apologized.

"No worries. Let's get to work."

Diane Cobalt

By dinner time, Rachel had moved and unpacked all of her clothes. It had been hard leaving the luxury of The Mansion, but it was time for her to get to work on her second project: eliminating Jennifer Baldwin. The binoculars she bought at Best Buy would come in handy. Rachel extracted them from their case and headed over to the window which provided the best view of the Baldwins' new home. She could definitely see their front door and part of their driveway, but actually seeing in any of their windows might be a challenge due to their trees.

Pierce was still trying, unsuccessfully, to dissuade her from taking any action against Jennifer. He reminded her that she owed her sister nothing. In his opinion, her best revenge would be in making a ton of money from their new project and living in the lap of luxury for the rest of their lives. But Rachel thought that was Pierce's goal, not hers. Unfortunately, she did not have the appetite for blood and guts that her dearly departed sister had. So shooting Mrs. Baldwin and stabbing her were not options. Even running her over in a car was too grisly for Rachel. She'd have to think of something "cleaner" yet personal.

All evening the house had been eerily quiet. Amy appeared to be out and there had been no sign of the other tenant. About eleven, Rachel turned off the big screen TV and headed upstairs to her room. She had just made the turn on the stairway when she heard voices outside the front door. It must be the other tenant she thought, continuing her climb up the second flight of stairs.

Fatal Race

But an hour later when she couldn't sleep, Rachel tiptoed to the top of the stairway. Below, she could see one of the sitting areas of the living room. There were at least eight Middle Eastern looking men speaking to each other in a foreign language. Rachel sniffed. Was that a hookah she smelled? What about Amy's no smoking policy?

There was a knock at the front door. Rachel backed up a few stairs so as not to be seen. An African American man and woman came through the doorway. The group of men instantly began speaking in English. What the hell was going on? Carefully, Rachel crept back down to her hiding place on the stairs. Soon, another black couple entered the room. The group of eight handed them cash...wads of it. There were too many conversations going on for Rachel to discern what was being said or why these couples had arrived. Amy hadn't mentioned anything about the possibility of late night parties. Maybe she should just go down and join them...see what was going on.

But something told Rachel not to. Maybe it was the man who was posted by the front door with a gun holstered on his hip. Or maybe it was the uncomfortable look on the women's faces. Or maybe it was the fact that a lot of money was exchanging hands for seemingly nothing in return.

What had she gotten herself into? What kind of crazy neighbors did the Baldwins have?

Rachel decided the safest place for her to be was locked in her room.

CHAPTER TWENTY-SEVEN

Rachel was exhausted. The "party" downstairs had lasted well into the wee hours of the morning. Car doors slamming off and on had kept her awake more than the murmur of voices drifting up from the first floor. She hoped this would be a one-time event. If not, she'd have to talk to Amy about it. Rachel was almost certain that Amy wasn't there at all last night.

Thankful for the brief commute to her lab, Rachel pulled Walter's Mercedes into a spot behind the doctor's office. That was another thing she had to put on her to-do list today: get a rental car. Walter was due back in a few days.

Rachel grabbed her backpack from the passenger seat, locked Walter's car and headed into work. She used her key to unlock the back door and then quickly relocked it behind her. The staff wasn't due in for at least another hour. All the lights were off, indicating that neither Dr. Hunnicutt nor his new salesman had arrived yet. Awesome. She wouldn't have to sneak around.

Efficiently, Rachel punched in her code to unlock the door to her lab. She flicked on the overhead fluorescent lights and set her backpack down on the counter. The first thing she did each morning, now that she had started trials on the mice, was to check on them. The mice's quarters were located on the far side of the lab. Rachel crossed the room, prepared to meet her half dozen furry friends. "What the...?" Rachel gasped. Two mice were clearly dead. A third one was bleeding, indicating she was miscarrying. The others were running around ignoring the other three.

Great, thought Rachel. Now I'll have to order some more mice. As if on cue, her phone lit up. It was Pierce.

"How's it going?" Pierce got right to the point not wanting to waste their international minutes.

"Good news and bad news," Rachel replied. "The good news is one of the mice is miscarrying."

"And the bad news?"

"Two are dead."

"I was afraid of that," Pierce commented. He did not sound surprised.

"Why? Is there something wrong with the formula?"

"Yes. While reviewing the chemical compounds I'm using, I suspected that I need to reduce one of the components. It should be an easy fix. The only tricky part is that this element helped to reduce the taste of the other components. I may have to add a non-active ingredient to accomplish that goal."

"Have you actually tasted your formula?"

"Of course I have. I'm not pregnant. Nothing is going to happen to me."

Rachel nodded. "True. But your brilliant compound has killed two mice."

Pierce laughed. "I would have to ingest several hundred doses in order to expire. No worries. But we do need to get this perfected soon. Alan Smith is chomping at the bit to get this done and won't give us any more money until it is."

"Okay. Just give me the new formula and I will call in an order to Lab Rats."

"That's the name of your supplier...Lab Rats?"

"Yes. Clever, huh?"

"Quite. By the way, how's your new abode?"

Rachel stifled a yawn. "Just splendid, except for the wild party that went on all night."

"A wild party? I thought you had moved to the quiet suburbs of Dallas."

"So I thought. Listen, I'll fill you in later. I've got to place this order and get some more mice."

Pierce dictated to Rachel the components and their amounts for his new formula. They had agreed not to have any of it in writing on the internet or on their phones. Rachel repeated the elements and their amounts back to Pierce and then ended the call.

Fatal Race

Jennifer lay on the exam table while Dr. Morrison squeezed the sonogram jelly onto her growing belly. "We should be able to determine the baby's sex today. Do you want to know?" he asked Beau and Jennifer.

Beau and Jennifer had spent quite a bit of time last night deciding the answer to this question. Beau wanted to know and Jennifer didn't. Ultimately, Beau had given in. After all, he wasn't carrying their child, she was.

"We do not want to know." Jennifer said adamantly.

"Okay then," Dr. Morrison replied. "I'll turn the monitor away during that part of the sono."

"Just for the record, Dr. Morrison, I'd like to know. Maybe I could just come over to your side and take a peek?" Beau interjected.

Dr. Morrison looked at Beau over the top of his classes as he gently placed the sonogram wand on Jennifer's belly. "That's rarely a good choice...to have one parent know and not the other."

"You'll just have to wait, Beau," Jennifer cautioned. Dr. Morrison smiled and continued the sonogram, pointing out the head, fingers, legs, toes and of course the beating heart. "Fortunately, the baby is not cooperating in its position. I can't tell for sure if it's a boy or girl. I will make a DVD for you, though."

"Ha!" Jennifer said to Beau. "Whether it's a boy or a girl, it's on my side!"

Beau pretended to be disgusted with his child. "Already playing favorites, are you little one? You must be a mama's boy."

Jennifer rolled her eyes and sat up, using the paper gown to wipe off the remaining jelly.

"Okay. Baby looks great and is on track for your due date. I'll see you back in four weeks." Dr. Morrison shook Beau's hand and exited the exam room.

Beau checked his watch. "Do you have time for lunch?"

"Yes, if we can make it a quick one. I have a project to finish before Alan gets back in town and I'm not sure when that will be."

Beau and Jennifer ate lunch at New York Subs, one of their favorite eating spots while they were in college. They slid into a booth that was marked by a picture of New York City, pre 9-11.

"You know, it's amazing that the smell of this place brings me instantly back to the year I met you," Jennifer said taking a bite of her roast beef sandwich.

"Well, that's better than the moldy smell of my fraternity house," Beau responded.

"Yes. I wonder if the new house still has that smell."

"We could pop in after lunch and see," Beau suggested, grinning.

"Uh no, I think I'll pass on that offer." Jennifer smiled back at her husband.

"Say, I have to go to Houston for the day with Dr. Hunnicutt next Wednesday. I'm thinking about asking Mom and Dad to stay a day longer so you won't be by yourself."

"I'm a big girl, you know. And I won't be alone. I have Ryan to keep me company."

"Ryan is not on my list of protectors for you." Beau was alluding to the last time he had been out of town when his crazy boss had tried to kill Jennifer at their former house.

"I realize that I have not stayed by myself since then. But, Beau, I'm going to have to do that sometime. And anyway, you won't be gone overnight, will you?"

Beau studied his ham and cheese sandwich. "Not this time. But there's a cardiology conference coming up in D.C. that I really need to go to. And if Meredith hasn't turned up by then, I may make a quick trip to Frankfurt." There, he'd said it. He didn't want to leave his wife alone again, but he at least had to go to that conference.

"When is the conference?"

"In two weeks. I'll have to leave the day after the carnival."

Jennifer took a deep breath. "Well, that works well on two accounts. You'll be at the carnival. I know Ryan's been looking forward to that and it is the first family event at the school."

Beau nodded. "And the second account?"

"My folks will be back from their trip to the Orient. They can stay with Ryan and me." Jennifer smiled at her husband. "All things being equal, I'd rather you not go to Frankfurt though. We've already lost one family member over there. And if the authorities can't find your sister, what makes you think you can?"

"It's not so much as my being able to find her, Jen. It's about closure. Maybe I can make peace with all of this if I just visit the site where she was last seen."

Diane Cobalt

Jennifer took a deep breath. She knew Meredith was alive, but not where she was. If only she could just share that tidbit of information with her husband, he'd drop the need to go over to Germany. On the other hand, knowing that she was alive, might spur him to go over there sooner. "I just can't lose you, Beau Baldwin. Our baby needs its father."

"Maybe Meredith will resurface by then," Beau said, relieved that Jennifer would not be alone in their house and hoping he wouldn't have to go visit the site where his sister may have taken her last breath.

CHAPTER TWENTY-EIGHT

It was Friday afternoon. Beau and Ryan waited patiently at the luggage carousel at DFW International Airport for Beau's parents to walk through the revolving door that prevented non-passengers from entering the secure area.

Ryan jumped when the buzzer sounded on the luggage conveyor belt. "What's that?"

Beau laughed. "That's just a noise they use to let you know that your bags are coming."

"Oh." Ryan seemed confused. "Will Grandma and Grandpa's bags get here before they do?"

"I doubt it. Those are probably from another flight."

"How much longer, Uncle Beau? Can I have something to drink maybe?"

Beau glanced up at the monitor which showed his parents' flight had arrived at the gate. "I think they'll be coming through that door within the next five minutes. Let's wait to get something to drink until they do. They'll probably be thirsty too, don't you think?"

Ryan nodded as he hopped from one floor tile square to another. Jennifer had warned Beau that he would have some pent up energy from being in school all day and she was right. Beau was used to seeing him spend his energy in soccer practice. It must be brutal on the days when Ryan just went home from school.

Ryan wandered over closer to the baggage carousel. He started counting the pieces of luggage as they plopped down onto the belt. "I bet they get here before I count to one hundred," he called to Beau. "We're practicing our counting so that we can count to one hundred by the one hundredth day of school. But I already can!"

As Ryan reached forty-one, Beau's parents pushed through the revolving door. "Time to stop counting, Buddy," Beau called to Ryan.

Ryan looked up and spotted his grandparents. "Grandma!" he yelled as he raced over to Beau's mother and jumped into her outstretched arms.

"Ryan! You have gotten so much taller since I last saw you," Martha Baldwin said as she kissed the top of Ryan's head.

Beau's dad stooped down and gave his grandson a hug. "Hi, Grandpa! What did you bring me?"

"Ryan! That's not nice," Beau cautioned.

"Please, Son. Ryan knows I always have a little something for him." Beau's dad reached into his carry-on and pulled out a snow globe. "Do you know what this is?"

Ryan studied the snow globe for a minute and then shook his head. "Does it do anything?"

Beau's dad laughed. "Of course it does. It snows!"

Ryan wrinkled up his nose. "It can't snow in there, Grandpa!"

"Oh yeah! Just watch!" He shook the globe vigorously and watched Ryan's eyes grow wide.

"Cool! Let me try now!"

While Ryan played with the snow globe, Beau greeted his parents. "I'm glad you could come, Mom and Dad."

"We've wanted to all summer, but we were afraid to leave home in case there was any news about..." Martha Baldwin stopped before mentioning her daughter's name in front of Ryan.

"Yeah. We left our contact information with the authorities," Robert Baldwin added. "At this point, we're no longer holding our breaths."

Beau nodded. "I think your bags are up."

Beau and his dad walked over to the carousel while Ryan stood next to his grandmother. "Are you thirsty, Grandma?"

"You know, Ryan, I am. Is there a place around here where we can get something to drink like maybe lemonade?"

"Or maybe a milkshake?" Ryan countered with a sly grin on his face.

"We'll have to get Uncle Beau to approve that one. It may be too close to dinnertime."

"But if he says it's okay, we can have a milkshake?" Ryan was devising his plan.

"Yes we can," agreed Martha.

"Goody!" Ryan raced off to ask his uncle who was out of earshot from his grandmother. "Uncle Beau, Grandma is thirsty and she wants a milkshake. Do you know where we can get one?"

Beau glanced over his shoulder at his mother who was smiling. It would be at least an hour before they got home and they likely wouldn't eat right away. Besides, if his mom wanted a milkshake, he could hardly say no. "Sure, Buddy. Just as soon as Grandpa and I get their luggage we can go get a milkshake."

"Yay!" yelled Ryan who raced back to his grandmother. "Uncle Beau says yes."

"Well that was easy," commented Martha.

Ryan shrugged. "I just told him you wanted a milkshake."

Martha Baldwin rolled her eyes as she laughed at her clever grandson.

The Baldwin household was up early on Saturday morning. Jennifer was busy making her famous pancakes when Martha and Robert came downstairs escorted by Ryan. "We're having chocolate chip pancakes this morning! Yay!" he shouted.

"I've heard all about these from your uncle. I can't wait to try them!" said Beau's dad.

Jennifer smiled. "I hope they're not overrated. Did you sleep well?"

Robert Baldwin frowned. "Well, not really. The bed was great, but the noise from across the street went on and on and on."

"What noise, Dad?" asked Beau who was busy microwaving the bacon.

"Car doors slamming. It was about three in the morning. Way too late for a party to be ending. So I finally got up and looked out the window. There must have been a dozen cars parked on your street."

"Great. Not again!" Beau responded.

"Again? It's happened before?" asked Martha.

Beau nodded. "Last week. Ryan was having some...bad dreams. Jennifer and I were up and down the stairs all night long. We noticed the same thing."

"They were nice cars too. And there seemed to be couples getting in them." Robert lowered his voice. "Do you suppose there's some kind of swingers' club going on over there?"

"Dad! No! This is a nice neighborhood."

"Well, maybe there are some nice swingers!" Beau's dad laughed. Martha glared at her husband to cut him off.

"Well, hopefully tonight there will be no parties," Beau added.

"Time to eat," called Jennifer who was holding a platter of pancakes.

"What time's the soccer game today, Beau? Do you want me to take some pictures? I brought my camera," offered Robert Baldwin.

Jennifer smiled. Her father-in-law was a real shutterbug.

"The game's at two. We'll need to leave here about one thirty," Beau answered.

"You're going to watch me play, Grandpa?" Ryan asked with a mouthful of pancake.

"Remember what we said about talking with our mouth full of food?" Beau reprimanded.

Ryan nodded. He swallowed. "Uh huh. You said not to. I forgot."

Robert Baldwin smiled. "Both your grandma and I can't wait to watch you and your friends play. Why you know back in his day, your uncle was a pretty darn good soccer player."

"I thought he played golf," Ryan responded.

"He played golf too," Martha chimed in. "But before that he played a lot of soccer. I'll bet he's a good coach."

"Chris's dad is our coach too."

"Chris is my best friend's son," Jennifer added.

"That's right. Kate! I met her last time I was here," said Martha. "She's a doll. You'll love her, Robert."

Ryan frowned. "She's not a doll, Grandma. She's a mom."

The room erupted in laughter. "It's a just a phrase that means she's cute and nice," said Jennifer.

Ryan had already helped himself to another pancake.

"These pancakes really are delicious," said Martha.

Fatal Race

Robert nodded in agreement, pointing to his mouth to indicate it was full.

Ryan smiled.

"Say, Robert, would you mind getting some candid shots of the parents for me?" Jennifer asked.

Robert finished chewing his pancake before responding. "I'd be happy to do that. I'll also include a few of the coaches if that's okay with you, Son."

Beau got up from the table to get some more coffee. "Take whatever pictures you want. I know better than to try to put any limits on you."

"After the game, I'll download them on to your computer, Jennifer. That way you can sift through and use whatever you like."

"Thanks. That would be great!" Jennifer hoped that Mari would be at the game. There was no way she could single out that parent without raising some eyebrows. But Manuel's sources were pretty good at identifying people from some lousy pictures.

Several hours later, after Ryan had scored the winning goal for his team, the Baldwins headed to Baskin Robbins with Chris and his family to celebrate. By the time they got home, Ryan had recovered from the game and was ready to swim with his grandparents in the pool.

Robert was excited about some of his action shots. He downloaded them onto Jennifer's laptop before heading to the pool. With the Baldwins busy splashing around outside, Jennifer had time to peruse the pictures for a good shot of Mari. It didn't take her too long to find one. The only criticism of the picture was that Mari was wearing sunglasses...as were the other parents. Jennifer emailed the picture to herself and then forwarded it onto the phone Manuel had given her. From there she texted it to him hoping they could identify Mari as the woman they were looking for.

CHAPTER TWENTY-NINE

If Americans knew how many terrorist compounds there were in the U.S., they wouldn't be able to sleep at night. During Meredith's training years ago at Quantico, she learned that there were at least two thousand of them scattered across the country. Two thousand meant an average of forty per state. And the number had probably grown exponentially since then.

She'd seen reconnaissance pictures of a few, but of course, had never visited the inside of one…until now. Some of the compounds were run by Al Qaeda, but that number had been reduced in recent years. However their progeny had become their focus, primarily the Islamic State of Iraq and the Levant or ISIL. ISIL looks for "the inspired youth" through social media. Other compounds were formed by ISIS and used to conduct surveillance for an ultimate attack on the United States. However, Meredith was now residing in a compound formed by the MOA, Muslims of America. Although she had been blindfolded on the car ride from Houston's Hobby airport to the compound, she was fairly sure from her training that this was the compound located on about twenty-five acres near Sweeny, Texas. The MOA had started it about a decade ago and used it mostly to recruit African Americans who converted to Islam while in prison.

For some reason, the MOA was not on the U.S. State Department's watch list. But they were a dangerous group who were prepared to pursue jihad on any enemies of Islam including the U.S. government.

Meredith had arrived two days ago. Once she was "processed" into the compound, Daria had left. But her other handler, Vicki, remained at her side. There were three buildings on the property. The main building housed the essentials: cafeteria, training rooms, rooms for staff and even a clinic. The second building housed the "residents" in dorm style rooms with no doors and no windows. Guards constantly patrolled the hallways so there was absolutely no privacy. The third building was solely used for training. The MOA trained its residents on everything from Farsi to bomb building to surveillance techniques to the use of automatic weapons. In the basement of the building was the compound's prison. If any staff member determined that a "resident" was resisting radicalization, the "resident" spent time in the basement where other residents were trained in interrogation techniques that made Guantanamo Bay look like a spa.

Today, Meredith attended her first Leadership in Education class. During the past few years, the MOA had established several of their own schools in Texas where the concept of charter schools had opened the pathway for almost anyone with enough funding to open a school and receive accreditation. Meredith found out the purpose of the MOA's schools were to continue the education primarily of the African Americans they had radicalized in order to launch multiple attacks on the U.S. The purposes of these attacks were three-fold: to reduce the non-Islamic population, to hurt Americans through their children and to destroy the current American system of educating its citizens. The MOA schools also served an additional purpose of providing a safe place to educate the Islamic population.

The words protect, train and radicalize were used over and over in the class Meredith had to take. Her class was taught in English. And in fact, her second class of the day was an ESL class. Her captors were convinced that Meredith was a German who had, no doubt, learned English in school. But her injuries from the bombing in Frankfurt had jumbled her brain enough that they thought a refresher course would be wise.

By dinnertime, Meredith was worn out from the constant dumbing down of the topics she was supposed to learn. She attempted to make small talk with the mostly African American men at her table in the cafeteria where they ate chicken fried steak, powdered mashed potatoes, corn, green Jell-O and rolls. But the men were angry and only sneered at her. Vicki nudged her indicating she should shut up and eat the slop in front of her. When dinner was over, Vicki escorted her to her dorm room where she too resided. Meredith couldn't figure out why her captor needed to watch her that closely. There was no way she could escape. The building had armed guards and she knew from her training years ago that the land surrounding the buildings would be riddled with snakes, bears and even mountain lions.

Meredith waited for Vicki to begin quizzing her on the material she'd learned that day. Her instructors had indicated she would be expected to study with her comrade. But Vicki sat quietly on her bunk reading a magazine.

A week ago when Meredith got to the Prague airport, she had no clue as to where they were headed. Surprisingly, they had flown straight to JFK Airport in New York. There she had spent two miserable nights knowing how close she was to her parents and potentially to Ryan. Again, she had been hopeful that the U.S. Border Customs agent would recognize her. But once again, they barely looked at her passport when she passed through the booth. Meredith wondered if somehow Daria had been able to orchestrate which lane to enter at the customs window allowing an "insider" to overlook her. She knew Daria's passport was a fake. There was no way she was a U.S. citizen.

Two days later, Meredith and Vicki boarded a bus to Long Island's MacArthur Airport where they boarded a flight to Dallas Love Field and then connected to a flight to Houston Hobby Airport. She had heard Daria tell Vicki in New York that she wouldn't be going with them. Daria had been called back to Munich.

Meredith was grateful to be back in the United States. She felt safer here and at some point she knew she would escape...just not while she was in this compound.

"How long?" she whispered to Vicki.

Vicki looked up from her magazine. "How long what?"

"How long does our training last?" Meredith made sure to speak slowly as if she was trying to remember her English.

Vicki shrugged. "Depends on how long it takes you to learn what you need to learn."

Well that was helpful! "I can learn much faster than they are teaching me."

Vicki seemed to perk up. "Maybe I can ask them to give you a test tomorrow."

"I can study tonight if you can get me the materials," Meredith offered.

The guard walking down the hall stopped at their doorway. "Quiet!" he barked before moving on.

Vicki waited several minutes before pulling a paper napkin out of her bra. She extracted a pen from her sock and wrote five words on the napkin before handing it to Meredith. "Convince them you are radicalized," were the words.

Meredith nodded. She could hear the jangling of the guard's keys as he turned at the end of the hall and headed back their way. "Eat it," commanded Vicki.

Meredith stuck the napkin in her mouth, let her saliva dissolve the thin ply of the paper and swallowed.

CHAPTER THIRTY

Now Jennifer had two secret phones to check: the green one from Manuel and the one she now used to communicate with Gordon and Jack. Fortunately, Beau was distracted with his new job and with entertaining his parents which made it less tempting for Jennifer to confide in the love of her life. She reminded herself daily that this subterfuge was necessary to safely get back Beau's sister and more importantly, Ryan's mother. Beau would have to forgive her, wouldn't he?

It was Monday morning. Beau and his parents took Ryan to school so that they knew how to get there. Tomorrow was a grandparents' day lunch and they were looking forward to being there for Ryan. It also gave Jennifer a little more time to herself before she headed in to work.

Diane Cobalt

After folding a load of laundry, Jennifer grabbed the backpack she used for work and grabbed the phone she had hidden in an interior zipped pocket. There was a text from Gordon. "Just pulled into the parking lot. Alan's here."

Great! He was back much sooner than Jennifer had anticipated which meant he might start pressuring Jack and Gordon about completing the app. Jennifer texted Gordon indicating she got his message and would be there in fifteen minutes.

She decided it would be a good idea to touch base with Manuel and let him know Alan was back in town. Her green phone was in the inside zippered compartment of her purse. "What's up?" Manuel always answered her calls without any identification of who had answered.

"Alan's back. I thought you would want to know. And Jack and Gordon are totally on board with stalling the completion of the changes Alan requested on the app. We now have secret phones so that we can communicate with each other. Jack and Gordon are extremely nervous, to say the least," Jennifer reported.

"Good. Vincent wants them to cooperate without actually developing the app."

"But for how long?"

"I don't know."

Jennifer remained silent.

"We do have a piece of good news."

"And that is?"

"Your sister-in-law has entered the U.S."

"That's wonderful! When can we see her? I'm sure she's anxious to see Ryan!"

"I said a piece of good news, not lots of good news. She entered using a fake passport and now has dropped off our radar. We feel certain she is still with her captors."

"But finding her when she's in the U.S. has to be easier than overseas."

"It's still a lot of geography to cover. I promise to let you know the moment I hear anything."

Jennifer felt a little dejected, but remained hopeful. Maybe Meredith would resurface in time for the school carnival and Beau wouldn't have to go to Frankfurt.

"Thanks."

Manuel disconnected the call.

Jennifer placed the green phone back in its hiding spot and drove to work. She was not looking forward to seeing Alan.

Rachel had gotten a good night's sleep. There had been no middle of the night visitors to the house or if there had been, she hadn't heard them. So when her alarm beeped at six this morning, she was ready to get her day started. This time of year the sun was just beginning to rise at seven fifteen which made it the perfect time for Rachel to enter the office. All was quiet; her identity was protected.

She clicked on the lights in the lab, locking the door behind her. All of the mice were alive and healthy. There were now a dozen of them. The Lab Rats had delivered six more pregnant mice yesterday afternoon. Rachel had made the "tweaks" to Pierce's formula and refilled the mice's water supply with the new concoction. It would take a few more days to see if the formula worked, but at least they were all alive. Pierce would be happy with the news.

As Rachel retrieved her phone from her purse, she noticed she had a voice mail from an unknown caller.

"Ms. Walker, this is Mr. Smith. I tried contacting your husband, but he has not returned my call," said the man with a strange British accent. "Please call me as soon as you get this message. It's urgent."

Mr. Smith was their client. Pierce always took his calls. She hadn't spoken with Pierce since yesterday when she got his new formula. Was he okay?

Before returning Mr. Smith's call, Rachel punched in Pierce's number. "Hello, the person you are dialing is not available. At the beep, please leave your name and number."

"Pierce! Where are you? Alan Smith called me saying you hadn't returned his call. He sounded upset and wants me to call him ASAP. It's seven thirty central daylight time. I will wait half an hour for you to contact me. If I haven't heard from you by then, I will call him back."

Rachel ended the call. Maybe Pierce was in the shower or was running on the beach. She felt sure she wouldn't have to wait the entire thirty minutes.

But she did. And Pierce didn't return her call. Now she was forced to call Mr. Smith.

"Alan Smith," he answered gruffly and without the British accent. Strange.

Rachel swallowed. "Mr. Smith, this is Paige Walker. I'm returning your call."

"Yes. Your husband still hasn't returned my call." He was back using the British accent.

"I'm sorry about that. I just tried him myself and he didn't answer. Is there something I can help you with?"

"Maybe. I wanted to alert him that I need a favor and in return can do one for him."

"And what do you need him to do?"

"I need him to finalize the formula he is working on and mass produce it for me."

"We're getting very close to perfecting the formula. We just need to run a few more trials on the mice and..."

"Sadly, I no longer have time for you to run more trials. I need you to mass produce what you have and get it to my bottled water company by the end of this week."

Rachel felt sick. "We should be able to do that, but..."

"There are no buts. My agent will be contacting you as to a location. Once we receive your liquid, I will do a favor for you."

"And that would be?"

"I will obtain FDA approval on Cardiovax for you."

That was terrific news! Rachel couldn't wait to tell Pierce. Cardiovax was Pierce's wonder drug that could actually stop a heart attack and reverse its effects. They had been in the midst of testing it, albeit illegally, for their investor, Dick Murphy, when Beau Baldwin had interfered. Rachel had been considering conducting new trials of Cardiovax "under the radar" on some of Dr. Hunnicutt's patients. But this would be so much faster...and final. Financially, they would finally be set for life. "That's wonderful. When do you want the formula for our current project?"

"I don't want the formula. I will need you to continue to produce it for me as long as is necessary."

Rachel almost dropped the phone. She wanted to be finished working for Alan Smith. She and Pierce would just have to figure out a way to be free of him once Cardiovax was approved.

Jennifer arrived at her office to find a stack of paperwork on her desk. She set her backpack and purse on the credenza behind her chair and then proceeded to open the first of over a dozen accordion style file folders. Inside she found a conglomeration of invoices that needed paying, checks and a list of customers to bill for one of the companies she had already set up. It would take some time, but Jennifer categorized it as easy. She moved the folder to the left and picked up the next one. This was a new company Alan wanted her to set up. She'd need to open another bank account with the check included in the folder. Prior to that though, she'd have to set up the company on QuickBooks. Again, none of this was difficult, just time consuming.

An hour later, Jennifer had finished going through fourteen folders. She hoped Alan didn't expect her to accomplish all of this today. In fact, she probably wouldn't get to the bank until tomorrow. The amount of work was almost overwhelming. But Jennifer tackled it as she tackled all huge projects, one step at a time.

When Jennifer first came in, Alan's office door had been closed. Occasionally, she'd hear him say something so she concluded he must be on a conference call. Jack and Gordon had been seemingly hard at work in their office and had not stuck their heads in her office to say hi. That was quite unusual for them.

It was almost one o'clock. Jennifer and the baby needed some food. She stretched, grabbed her purse and backpack and headed to the parking lot.

"Hey there!" Gordon called to her from his office. "Want to grab some lunch with us?"

Jennifer paused at their doorway. "I'd love to."

"Great! Jack, are you coming or are you just waiting for a personal invitation?"

"Yeah, I'm coming. I've got to eat too."

"Of course you do," cajoled Gordon. "It's probably been, what, two hours since anything's been digested into that belly of yours."

"Hey! Stop that," Jack snarled.

Alan's office door opened. "Where are you all going?"

The trio froze. Gordon responded. "Lunch! Want to join us, Boss?"

For a moment Alan seemed to consider it. "No. Thank you. Not today. I do need to see you men in my office when you get back, though."

"Sure. No problem," said Gordon knowing he'd have heartburn no matter what they ate.

The trio spent their lunch hour strategizing on how to put the brakes on the app project. Gordon and Jack were adamant that they would never develop a final product that actually worked. They even thought of ways to make it seem like it was working. Jennifer agreed that was their best route to take.

By the time Gordon and Jack met with Alan, they were so prepared for putting Alan off that they appeared relaxed.

"Did you have a good lunch?" Alan wanted to know.

"Oh yeah. Eating's one of my favorite pastimes," Jack joked, rubbing his large belly.

Alan didn't seem amused. "Yes, I noticed. Anyway, I have a rather urgent project for the two of you. It takes precedent over everything else you're working on. This is confidential. And by that I mean it stays within these four walls."

Gordon had to work hard from breathing a sigh of relief. The app project was officially on hold. "What can we help you with?"

"Close the door," Alan instructed.

Jack frowned. The only other person in the office was Jennifer and as his CFO, she should know everything. He closed the door.

"I want you two to set up transfer points for money. They need to be untraceable by any entity, foreign or domestic. This system must be complex, but yet accomplish the goal."

Fatal Race

Gordon fidgeted in his seat. "What's that, Boss?"

"I am starting some companies overseas and I need to transfer large sums of capital on an ongoing basis. I will fund these companies from a single point once the money gets out of the U.S."

"And that destination is?" asked Jack.

"Syria."

CHAPTER THIRTY-ONE

It had been a long, busy week for Rachel. It was Friday afternoon and Pierce was AWOL. But she couldn't allow herself the luxury of worrying about him while trying to comply with Mr. Smith's demands. And to top it off, Walter was back in town and wanted to see her. She had told him it would have to wait until next week and he'd taken Uber to her new abode to retrieve his Mercedes. Rachel was hoping that once she turned the liquid compound over to Alan's "people" she could at least book a flight to Grand Cayman to search for her missing husband. She couldn't come up with a single excuse as to why he wasn't answering his phone. Unless...unless he lost it or it was stolen. He'd never bothered to memorize her number either. Yes, that had to be it!

Fatal Race

The doctor's staff and the doctor had left around five forty-five. Rachel had told Mr. Smith that it would be ready for pick up at six thirty just to be on the safe side that the office would be empty. The product was contained in two plastic water cooler bottles which were sitting on top of the lab counter. The ratio of the compound to water was point nine to sixteen ounces making it fit perfectly into the sixteen point nine ounce commercial plastic water bottles.

The knock on the door startled Rachel. She unlocked it, opening it slowly to see a petite, red-haired woman with freckles who looked startling similar to her new landlord. The woman removed her sunglasses. It *was* Amy, her landlord!

"Amy! What are you doing here?"

Amy smiled. "Paige, hi! My client said you'd be expecting me?"

Rachel's eyes widened. Had Mr. Smith himself contacted Amy? Surely not. She did her best to act normal in front of her landlord. "Of course. Here it is. It's a little heavy. I can help you carry it to your car." Maybe Amy wasn't aware what the bottles really contained. She could be totally unaware of what Mr. Smith was up to.

"Don't be ridiculous. I've got one of my co-workers with me who will carry them out." As she said that, a stocky guy who looked like a weight lifter showed up at the door. "Both of those?" she asked Rachel pointing to the bottles.

Rachel nodded.

"Great. Sam, would you please, carefully, take those water cooler bottles and put them in my car?"

Sam nodded and picked up one bottle in each hand.

"He's such a big help if you get my drift," Amy added after Sam left the lab.

Rachel wasn't really sure she did, but she nodded anyway. Maybe now would be a good time to ask Amy about the parties. Or maybe not. Rachel just wanted to go home and end this week. "Well, I guess that's it. I don't know about you, but I'm ready for the weekend."

Amy put her sunglasses back on. "I hear ya on that one. I'll see you back at my house."

Rachel made one last inspection of the mice before turning off the lights and locking the door to the lab.

Jennifer woke up Saturday morning with a headache. She had spent most of the night tossing and turning, trying to figure out why Gordon and Jack had acted so strangely the rest of the week. They had worked quietly in their office, staring into their computer monitors. They hadn't joked with her and Jack had even acted uncharacteristically nice to Gordon. Had they changed their minds about stalling on the app? Had Alan threatened them? What the hell had gone on when Jack closed the door to Alan's office?

Saturdays meant soccer games. The summer heat continued even though they were more than halfway through September. Fortunately, Jennifer didn't have to go sit in the heat at Ryan's game today. Unfortunately, she did have to sit through a final fall carnival planning meeting. She wasn't sure which was more brutal. At least Kate would be there.

The carnival was next Friday, which meant that a week from today Beau would be leaving for that convention in D.C. And that meant that in a little over a week he would be heading to Frankfurt.

Come on, Meredith. Find your way back to us! Jennifer had heard nothing from Manuel for the remainder of the week. She'd check her green phone again as soon as Beau left with Ryan for the game. And of course, she'd check her other phone for any word from Jack or Gordon. Maybe they would want to meet with her over the weekend to explain what, as Jack would say, "had their panties in a wad".

But neither phone contained any messages. Jennifer decided to treat herself to a shaken peach white iced tea from Starbucks on her way to the meeting. It probably wouldn't be much longer before they had completed their change over to their fall menu and would no longer offer her favorite beverage. Kate was meeting her at school so she could watch the first half of the game. Beau had told Jennifer he wanted her to stay out of this heat, especially since she couldn't shake this headache.

The street in front of the school was already filling up with cars. Jennifer shook her head. This carnival was a huge deal. She'd never been to so many meetings for a single event. You'd think they were hosting the Olympics. On her way up the steps to the front door, she caught up with Mari.

"Hi, Mari. I'm Jennifer Baldwin. I met you the other day at soccer practice."

Mari looked through her, not at her. "I remember. Why aren't you at the game?"

"Because I have to be at this meeting," Jennifer smiled, having decided that she didn't like Mari and wondering if Manuel had found anything out from the picture her father-in-law had covertly taken of Mari last Saturday.

"Yeah. Me too."

"Well, it's a good way to meet people," said Jennifer who held the door open for Mari.

"If that's your goal," Mari muttered.

"Beats sitting out in this heat," Jennifer countered and followed Mari to the lunchroom where the meeting was being called to order.

For the next half hour, each grade level, one by one, presented their game for the carnival and what prizes they would be giving out. Jennifer wondered if it would be rude to leave after her presentation since Kindergarten went first. But she decided to stay so she could see Kate.

Right before the fifth grade moms made their presentation, Kate scooted into the seat next to Jennifer. "I hope I don't smell too sweaty," she whispered to Jennifer.

"With all the different perfumes in this room, it would be hard to tell," Jennifer commented. "How's the game going?"

"They were ahead four to one when I left. Both Chris and Ryan had scored goals and the coaches had decided to let them sit out and let some of the others play since they were ahead."

Jennifer nodded. "Smart."

"Have I missed anything?" Kate wanted to know.

"Oh yeah. They've mapped a plan for world peace," Jennifer said sarcastically. "Seriously, no. It's just a review about the games per grade level. Then we get to hear what's for the picnic dinner and a review of the fundraiser. Then I think we can split."

Kate opened a bottle of the "fundraising water" with the school label. "Did you want one of these? They had them in a cute bucket of ice out in the hall. And I'm so thirsty."

Jennifer lifted her venti cup of tea. "I'm good, thanks."

"It sounds like we are going to have a lot of fun at the carnival," said Isabelle, the always bubbly PTA president. "Our food committee head couldn't be here today, but left me her report. As some of you know, our picnic dinner will be catered by Sonny Bryan's. There will be BBQ and chicken fingers along with baked beans and French fries. We are leaving the desserts up to our bake sale table. I know you all are getting tired and want to get out of here, so I'll end our meeting today with a fundraising update. So far, we have raised over six thousand dollars from our bottled water sales. In fact, we had to place a rush order for a second batch which was just delivered this morning." Everyone clapped. "That's right, everyone. We are at sixty percent of our goal and we haven't even had the carnival yet. So thanks for your hard work and have fun on Friday!"

Diane Cobalt

Kate leaned over to Jennifer. "I don't know about you, but I think my life will be so much easier after this blasted carnival. No more stupid meetings. No more stupid fundraising. Just soccer practice, soccer games and school."

Jennifer nodded, but felt the exact opposite.

CHAPTER THIRTY-TWO

After hearing uncharacteristic panic in his cousin's voice, Walter cancelled his plans to go to a fundraiser for the Dallas Opera at the Winspear and picked up Rachel for dinner. Rachel had suggested they meet halfway since Walter lived close to Uptown and she was out in the suburbs. But Walter didn't want Rachel driving while she was so upset. He made reservations at a nearby Thai restaurant for eight o'clock and picked up his cousin fifteen minutes prior to that.

Rachel, dressed in jeans, slid into the passenger side of Walter's Mercedes as soon as he pulled up in front of Amy's house. "Thanks for dropping everything and meeting with me, Walter," she greeted him with tears welling in her eyes. Walter had never seen her like this before. Rachel was always extremely confident and rarely exhibited any emotions except for anger and haughtiness.

"Of course. You sounded stressed out on the phone which is very unlike you." Walter checked his rearview mirror before pulling out onto the quiet street. "What's going on? And how can I help?"

Rachel snapped on her seatbelt and looked straight ahead at the setting sun in the distance. "It's Pierce. He's not answering my calls."

A domestic dispute, thought Walter. "And? Did you two have a little tiff?"

Rachel looked at her cousin. "No! Of course not! Everything was going great. We'd just perfected a formula for a big client of ours."

"When was the last time you spoke with him?"

"About a week ago."

"A week ago? Why so long?"

"We're trying not to spend a fortune on international calls." The old Rachel's caustic manner had returned.

Walter rolled his eyes. "Okay...maybe he lost his phone or a cell tower went down. You know that's not that unusual of an occurrence in the Caribbean."

"I called our bank today and they answered." Rachel countered.

"What about friends? Do you have any who might be able to check on him? Maybe he's sick or hurt?"

Rachel just stared ahead.

"Okay, so no friends."

Fatal Race

"Need I remind you that we're fugitives? We can't risk anyone realizing who we really are."

Walter nodded while turning into the restaurant's parking lot. He expertly maneuvered into a spot right in front. "Let's go in, get a drink and some food and figure out what to do."

Rachel nodded, relieved that Walter would determine what her next step should be.

The restaurant was packed. Fortunately, Walter had thought to make a reservation. The Asian hostess led them to a table for four located next to the window. "Hey, there's no bar here," Walter commented.

The hostess handed them their menus. "It's BYOB."

Walter took a deep breath. "Terrific," he commented sarcastically. "You might want to tell people that when they call to reserve a table."

"So sorry, sir."

Walter immediately brightened. "No problem."

The hostess walked away.

"It's okay. I can do without," offered Rachel.

"There's a restaurant across the parking lot. They have a bar and I know the owner. I'll go over and buy a bottle of whatever you want. What sounds good?"

Rachel actually smiled as she sat down. "A bottle of red. Your pick."

"Perfect. Order some appetizers. I'll be back in a flash."

Walter the Fixer, thought Rachel, too bad he couldn't have fixed my sister. The waitress approached the table. Rachel ordered two glasses of water and an order of crab rolls. She looked across the parking lot to see her cousin walking back, bottle in hand.

"Hopefully this place has a corkscrew," said Walter as he sat the bottle down on the table.

Rachel laughed. "I'm sure they do. Freemark Abbey Cabernet. Nice choice."

"Yeah. My friend, the owner, was actually there so I felt I had to make a statement. He wanted me to just dine there. Fortunately, I had you as my excuse. I told him you'd already ordered."

"And I have. I ordered our appetizer. Next time we can eat at your friend's restaurant."

By the time their dinners arrived, Walter had agreed to make a quick trip to the Cayman Islands to look for Pierce with one caveat: if Pierce contacted her between now and the time his flight left, he was going anyway.

After a stellar bottle of wine and a hard work week, Rachel couldn't wait to go to bed. She now could relax, knowing that Walter would find Pierce and a logical explanation for why she couldn't reach him. Before climbing into bed, Rachel decided to conduct the "find my iPhone search" again. When she'd tried it before, she'd gotten no signal indicating that his phone was off or his battery was low. After pressing the correct button, she sat down on the edge of her bed and yawned. It typically took a few minutes before she got a response. But there, blinking at her, was a signal from Pierce's phone! She put on her readers to view his location more clearly. It was definitely coming from somewhere close to their condo in Grand Cayman! Rachel wasted no time calling Pierce's number. It went straight to voice mail. "Pierce! What the hell is going on with you? I've been trying all week to reach you and I've been scared that something has happened to you. Please call me ASAP!" She punched the red button to disconnect and stared at her phone, willing it to ring. Why would the call have gone straight to voice mail? That usually meant the phone was off. Ah! Maybe it was, but was still transmitting some kind of signal? Or maybe he was on another call and made the selection to send the call to voice mail? Maybe his voice mail was messed up and he hadn't gotten her messages? That had happened to Rachel several times. She'd see the missed call, but the voice mail never came through. But usually they didn't go this long without touching base with each other.

Sometime after midnight, Rachel gave up trying to stay awake, waiting for Pierce's call. She turned out the light, but kept the phone next to her pillow.

It wasn't her phone that disturbed her sleep several hours later; it was the sound of distant laughter and muffled voices. Rachel sat up. What the hell? She was groggy... had been right in the middle of a dream. What was going on? She peered out her window and saw several expensive cars lining the street. Not again. Another party?

Grabbing her robe, Rachel quietly opened her door and padded down the hallway to the same spot on the stairs where she had been able to spy on the party goers last week. Once again there was a mix of African American couples and Middle Eastern looking men. They were speaking English, but she couldn't hone in on any one conversation. The couples were drinking and most, but not all, looked relaxed. She scanned the room looking for Amy. There was a knock at the door so faint that no one would have heard it except that a large man, who was obviously playing the role of bouncer, stood right next to it. He opened the door and another couple walked in. The bouncer motioned to another man who walked over and greeted the couple, but not by name. They followed the second man across the living area and out of Rachel's view. The bouncer resumed his post.

Rachel considered getting dressed and joining the party. After all, she'd mentioned it to Amy so it couldn't be much of a secret. The bouncer turned and acted like he was going to come up the stairway. Rachel quietly backed up and turned the corner. Then she heard the voices of another couple whom she assumed was entering through the front door.

"We have a bottle of wine," said a male voice.

"Yes. The meeting is in the wine cellar," said the bouncer.

Wine cellar? Hadn't Amy told her it was just a basement used for storage? Rachel quickly tiptoed to her room in case the bouncer headed up the stairway. She looked out her window in time to see two men putting something shaped like a cylinder in the trunk of their Tesla before driving away down the dark street.

Damn! If she'd been a few seconds quicker, she might have gotten a better view of what they had stowed in their trunk. It took both men to lift it. Maybe it was heavy? Rachel shook her head. She wasn't sure if she could stay awake to watch the next couple leave. What could she do to keep herself awake? Getting a cup of coffee was out of the question.

Rachel checked her phone. Nothing from Pierce. She didn't use social media and she really couldn't focus on playing any of the games she had downloaded. She looked out the window again, this time seeing the Baldwins' house in the distance. That's what she could do! By the time she planned Jennifer Baldwin's demise, the last couple would be leaving.

The only problem was that Rachel came up with most of her plan within a few minutes. It was simple and she could thank her dear husband for it if she was ever able to get in touch with him. She flashed back to the day she'd discussed the formula with Pierce. He had told her about the element that caused the mice to die and said she needed to decrease the percentage in the test formula. Therefore, Rachel had quite a bit of that agent leftover. It was colorless and tasteless and she could easily "customize" a bottle of water just for sweet, but not so innocent, Jennifer Baldwin. And her new landlord, Amy, seemed to be in the water distribution business on some level. There were a few details Rachel needed to iron out, most important of which was the timing, but this would be a piece of cake. She glanced over at the Baldwin house one more time before deciding sleep was more important than figuring out what was going on downstairs. As long as they didn't bother her, why should she care? Her main purpose for returning to the states, avenging her sister's death, was about to become a reality.

CHAPTER THIRTY-THREE

Although it was late September, the weather was still warm and sticky. Even though the air-conditioning was on, the air in the school felt thick. Kate Lange huffed and puffed and finally finished inflating the kiddie pool. Wiping the sweat off her forehead, she plopped the blue plastic pool on the floor in the hallway outside of the kindergarten classrooms. "Woof! That was not easy! I'm thinking my idea for a carnival game would have been way easier to put together."

Beau walked up carrying several gallon jugs of tap water. Drew followed with two more. "And what was your idea, Kate?"

"You probably don't want to know," answered Drew.

Kate put her hands on her hips pretending to be disgusted. "It was Pin-the-Tail on the ...she paused making sure Chris and Ryan were out of earshot...pregnant woman."

Beau laughed.

Drew did not. "See, I told you that you didn't want to know."

"Sounds like an easy game in this school."

Kate watched as the two men filled the kiddie pool with water. "Not that we would have done that, of course. But actually it's a good thing we didn't. Several moms have miscarried in the past week."

Jennifer, who had been using a Sharpie to write numbers on the bottoms of plastic fish, stood up and walked toward her best friend. "Like who?"

Kate wrinkled up her nose. "Well, you met one. Soccer Mom Susie? And I heard there was one in the other kindergarten class and a first grade mom."

Jennifer frowned. "Really? That does seem like a lot."

Kate nodded and patted her belly. "But all is safe in here!"

Jennifer smiled and touched Kate's stomach which had barely started to swell.

Ryan and Chris came running up. "Why is there a baby pool out here?" Ryan wanted to know.

"Yeah are we going to try to swim in that dinky little thing?" Chris added.

Kate laughed. "No. We're going to fish in it!"

The boys looked at each other and frowned. Ryan cupped his hand over his mouth and leaned over to whisper something in Chris's ear. Chris nodded.

"Um, we think we should tell you, Mom, that there aren't any fish in there."

Kate played along. "There aren't? Jen, where'd they go?"

"They're right here," Jennifer said pointing to a school of plastic fish at her feet.

"Those aren't real fish, you know," said Ryan.

"It's for a game," Jennifer explained. "When you catch one of these, there's a number on the bottom of it and that matches a prize shown on the prize board over here."

"That sounds fun," said Chris. "Can we try?"

Ryan elbowed his friend. "Uh there aren't any fish in the pool. So how would we catch anything?"

Kate took a few of the plastic fish in her hands. "Why don't you two help us put the fish in the pond and then you can be the first to try out the game?"

"Yes!" both boys claimed in unison as they jumped up and down.

Beau grabbed the toy fishing rod and handed it to Chris. "You go first."

Chris patiently dangled the magnetic hook over a bright red fish which attached quickly to the pole. "I got it! I got it!"

"Look at the number on the bottom of it," Jennifer instructed.

"It's a five."

"Very good. Now look at our poster on the wall. What prize is next to the number five?"

"A Kit Kat bar!" Chris shouted. "Do I get one?"

Jennifer reached in the prize bag and handed him the candy bar.

"Chris, you have to wait until after dinner to eat that," said Kate who tousled his hair.

"Okay," Chris said dejectedly. "Hey Ryan, you try now."

Ryan repeated the process and pulled out a yellow fish. "It's a number six, no wait maybe it's a nine."

Jennifer looked at the fish. "It's a nine. The line helps you know which way to look at the number so you know if it's a six or a nine. What prize does a nine get?"

Ryan looked at the chart. "Sour Patch...my favorite!"

Kate smiled and handed him his prize.

"Well, if you girls don't need us for any more heavy lifting, we'll take the boys and get some dinner," offered Beau.

"Are you sure you don't need us to work a shift?" Drew offered.

Jennifer shook her head. "Not unless someone doesn't show up for their time slot. I think we're covered."

Kate smiled. "You will be a big help just by getting the boys fed and taking them around to play the games."

"Done and done," Drew said leaning in to give his wife a kiss.

"Ryan can't wait to show you around," added Jennifer.

"When will you two get to eat?" Beau wanted to know.

Jennifer looked at her watch. "We need to make sure the first shift shows up, then we'll head your way. Save us a seat!"

Kate took a swig of water from her stash of the fundraising bottles. "Great idea! I'm hungry already." She offered a

Fatal Race

bottle to Jennifer who waved it away pointing to the plastic cup of Starbucks tea she was drinking.

The first shift of parents who'd signed up to work the fishing game showed up ahead of schedule so Jennifer and Kate were able to join their guys for some BBQ in the school lunchroom. Because they had been there early to set up, they were able to beat the crowd for the food line.

"This is a decent meal for a school carnival," Beau commented.

"Yeah at my grade school, we had hot dogs," Drew added.

"Was that the school that was way up the hill?" Kate teased.

Drew nodded. "Yes and it snowed a lot where I grew up."

"In Florida?" asked Chris, frowning.

"He's teasing," Kate prompted.

It seemed like it took Ryan and Chris about five minutes to wolf down their dinners and then rip into their candy.

"What games are we going to first?" Ryan wanted to know.

Both Drew and Beau looked at their wives for suggestions.

"Maybe you should start down at first grade and work your way up towards sixth. I think the games might become more...challenging as the grade level increases."

"We'll be good at all of them. I'm sure," said Chris solemnly.

"No doubt," said Drew. "Is it cool if the parents play too?"

"Actually, I think there are a few "parent" game rooms," answered Kate. "But I think you're a bit old for the kids' games."

"She's always a party pooper, isn't she?" Drew commented.

Beau wiped the BBQ off his mouth. "I'm ready when you guys are. Just lead the way."

"There's a bake sale table outside the cafeteria if you want some dessert later," Jennifer said as the boys stood up. "Have fun!"

"Where and when should we meet up with you ladies?"

"The games end at eight thirty and we can start disassembling them then," said Kate. "So if we don't run into you before then, would you meet us at the fish pond around that time?"

"Sure thing," said Drew as Chris pulled on his wrist to get him to leave.

Jennifer looked at Kate. "They're going to have a ball tonight. We'll have two tired boys on our hands."

"Yeah and I bet Chris and Ryan will be tired too!" Kate laughed. "Is it hot in here to you? I'm sweating like a pig."

Jennifer didn't feel too warm which was unusual for her. "Maybe a little bit. It's probably your hormones."

Kate stood up. "I'll get another bottle of water. They were smart to put some on ice."

"I'm ready to walk around and check out the other games so we know what awaits us in future grades," said Jennifer.

"Good idea. Say did we have anyone back out of helping tonight?"

"Yes," Jennifer answered on their way out of the lunchroom. "Two different women who signed up for different shifts. But I replaced them. Why do you ask?"

Kate handed a carnival ticket to the volunteer to pay for another bottle of water. "I overheard our favorite PTA president talking to a sixth grade and a fifth grade mom about several families who had left the school."

Jennifer shrugged. "Maybe they moved."

"No. It was a local transfer to some international school. Isabelle was concerned that maybe we aren't being welcoming enough to minorities, specifically the Middle Easterners."

"That's ridiculous. At least I can say that you and I have been friendly to everyone. Maybe some of those in the upper grade levels aren't quite as open-minded as we are." But Jennifer filed that information away to tell Manuel. "Have we lost any off the soccer team because of that?"

Kate nodded. "Mari's kid."

"Mari? She's not Middle Eastern." But she did match the description Manuel had given her. Now she'd definitely have to let him know and find out if Mari was who they'd been looking for.

"It's just an interesting observation. I'm all for smaller class sizes so if a few people want their children to go elsewhere to school it's no skin off my teeth."

Jennifer nodded in agreement.

Fortunately, Jennifer and Kate swung by the fishing pond on a regular basis to make sure the volunteers were in place. About ten after eight, the eight o'clock volunteers hadn't shown so Kate and Jennifer worked the last shift.

Jennifer noticed that Kate was sweating a lot. The halls were crowded with families but there seemed to be plenty of air movement. With ten minutes to go, the hall cleared out. "Hey are you feeling okay?" Jennifer asked Kate.

Kate looked pale and she was no longer smiling. "Not really. Maybe I've just overdone it today." But then she grabbed her lower abdomen and bent over.

"Here, sit down," Jennifer said grabbing one of the little kindergarten chairs.

Kate sat down. "I'm cramping," she whispered.

"Okay. Take a deep breath. Maybe that BBQ didn't agree with you and the baby."

Kate took several deep breaths. "You're right. That's probably it. I feel better already." Kate stood up and then immediately sat back down, holding on to her stomach. "Can you watch the booth? I need to go to the ladies' room."

"Go! I'll text Beau and have him come finish this so I can check on you."

Before Jennifer could finish her text, Beau and Drew came up with the boys.

"Where's my mommy?" Chris asked.

Jennifer did her best to look normal. "She had to use the ladies' room. And I need to head that way myself. Would you boys mind putting this stuff away?" Jennifer looked at Beau, her eyes widened indicating there was something wrong.

"Sure thing," said Drew who was unaware that Kate wasn't feeling well.

Beau casually walked part way down the hall with his wife. "Is Kate okay?"

Jennifer shook her head. "I don't think so."

CHAPTER THIRTY-FOUR

Jennifer found Kate on the bathroom floor writhing in agony. "I think I need to go to the hospital," she gasped. "Can you get Drew?"

"I think I should call an ambulance, Kate. You're bleeding."

Kate started crying. "I don't want to lose the baby! Please help me!"

Jennifer stooped down and held her friend. "Maybe you won't." She texted Beau that she suspected Kate was miscarrying and that she needed to call an ambulance. She also suggested that Beau take Ryan and Chris home immediately so they wouldn't see the drama that was about to unfold. But before Jennifer had time to dial 911, Drew burst into the bathroom.

"I'll take her," he shouted. "There's no need to have an ambulance pulling up while everyone's leaving."

Jennifer nodded in agreement. "I hadn't thought of that. I'll stay with her while you go get the car. We're closest to the door that opens out to that side street."

Kate wasn't paying attention to their conversation. She was breathing through another contraction.

"I'll be at that door in three minutes, tops," Drew promised.

"We'll make our way down the hall. Go!" Jennifer looked at him and mouthed the word "hurry." Drew left. Jennifer looked down at her friend whom she still held in her arms. "Do you think you can walk a little ways?"

Kate nodded. The cramping had seemed to subside. "But I'm bleeding."

"Don't worry about that. There's hardly anyone left out there and we need to get you to the hospital so the doctors can save your baby." That sounded wrong to Jennifer the moment she said it. It sounded like a promise that they would save her baby and Jennifer thought that was doubtful.

"Okay. I can get up on my own." Kate stood shakily. She put her arm across Jennifer's shoulder and the two headed out into the school hallway. The lights were still on and Jennifer spotted a janitor at the end of the hall, but other than that, the hall really was empty. They made it to the door just as Drew was pulling the car up. He jumped out, leaving the engine running and literally scooped up his wife. Jennifer opened the back car door so he could lay Kate down.

Less than fifteen minutes later, Drew pulled up to the hospital's emergency entrance. Jennifer had called Kate's OB/GYN en route. Drew's parents were on their way to the Baldwins' house to pick up Chris and take him home.

By the time the triage nurse had assessed Kate and processed her into the ER, Kate's doctor had arrived. Jennifer elected to stay in the waiting room to give Kate and Drew some time together.

It was less than a half hour later when Drew came out to get her. She knew instantly from the sad look in his eyes that Kate had lost the baby. Drew came up to Jennifer. She hugged him, saying nothing while he cried on her shoulder.

"How's she doing?" Jennifer whispered, fighting through her own tears.

Drew shrugged. "They gave her something to kind of knock her out. She's far enough along that the doctor needs to perform a D and C. They're taking her back in a few minutes. The doctor doesn't want to wait."

Jennifer nodded. "What can I do?"

Drew pulled out of her embrace. "Would you mind waiting with me? She'll probably appreciate seeing your face when she comes out of the anesthesia."

"Of course. Just let me give Beau a quick call."

Diane Cobalt

On the way home, Beau explained to Chris that his mother wasn't feeling well and that his dad was going to help her get better. Chris was coming off a major sugar buzz as was Ryan. Both boys had hit the proverbial wall.

By the time they walked into the Baldwin home, Beau had crafted a plan. He would get the boys ready for bed. Chris could probably squeeze into a pair of Ryan's P.J.'s and if he couldn't, Beau would just find him a large t-shirt. He knew Jennifer kept spare toothbrushes and with all the sugar Chris had had tonight, he'd need to brush his teeth!

The boys filed quietly into the Baldwins' kitchen. "Can Chris spend the night?" Ryan asked his uncle.

"I think that might be a good idea," Beau answered. "Let's get you two ready for bed and while you're brushing your teeth, I'll check in with Chris's daddy."

"You can wear my *Incredibles* pajamas, Chris." Ryan was excited to share his favorite pair with his friend.

"Cool!" said Chris.

"Come on. I'll get them for you."

Beau checked his phone and saw a voice mail from Jennifer and a text from Drew, but before he could finish reading it, the doorbell rang. He looked out the window and recognized Drew's parents' car which he had seen when they attended soccer games.

Beau opened the door. "Hi Mr. and Mrs. Lange. Come on in."

"We got here as fast as we could," said Mrs. Lange.

"I can see by the look on your face that you weren't expecting us," said Mr. Lange.

Fatal Race

"I'm sorry. I just walked in with the boys. I haven't had time to check messages. Ryan and Chris are getting ready for bed. Have you heard anything?"

Doris Lange's phone vibrated at the very second Beau asked the question. She looked down at her cell and realized she was looking at the neon green print which was on the phone's cover. She flipped it over and slid the bar to answer. It was her son.

Beau watched Mrs. Lange's face crumble. He knew without hearing the rest of the conversation that Kate had lost the baby. He focused on her phone to ward off the tears building in his eyes. It hadn't been that long ago that he and Jennifer had gone through a miscarriage themselves.

Realizing the Langes might want a few moments alone, Beau headed to Ryan's room to check on the boys. He found them, wearing their pajamas, seated on the floor building with Ryan's new Lego set.

Ryan looked up when Beau walked in. "Is Chris's mommy okay?"

Beau saw real concern in his nephew's eyes. He was probably thinking of his own mom.

"The doctors are taking extra good care of her," Beau replied. "Chris, your grandparents are here to pick you up."

"No! I want to stay here!" Chris pouted.

"Please, Uncle Beau, can't Chris just stay the night? There's no school tomorrow."

Beau thought about it. His flight didn't leave until noon tomorrow so he could cover for Jennifer and Drew at least until midmorning. "Let me go see if I can talk them into it. But no promises, okay?"

Both boys nodded. "He's a good talker-into-things kind of guy," Ryan reassured his friend.

It didn't take much of Beau's "good talking" skills to convince the Langes to let Chris spend the night. They were eager to get to the hospital to check on their daughter-in-law. As Doris Lange opened the front door to follow her husband to the car, she waved her neon green phone at Beau. "We're just a phone call away, Beau. We can come collect Chris on a moment's notice."

Beau smiled. "I'm sure that won't be necessary. The boys are thrilled to have a spur of the moment sleepover. Your son needs you right now."

Doris returned Beau's smile. "Thank you. We really appreciate it and I know how much my son values your friendship."

Beau quietly locked the front door behind them. He could see where Drew got his strong sense of family and caring attitude. But something bothered Beau about Doris. He just couldn't put his finger on it. Oh well, whatever it was, it must not be important. It was now time to deliver the good news to the boys.

Several hours later, Jennifer climbed into bed after checking on the boys. Like Beau, they were fast asleep. Beau woke up long enough to kiss her on the back of her neck and wrap his arms around her.

Shortly before dawn, Beau woke from a dream. He couldn't remember what the dream was about, but he suddenly remembered what had bothered him about Doris. It was her phone! Beau clearly remembered the day he had first shown Jennifer this house. He'd walked to her car to retrieve her cell phone and found another one vibrating. Kate had appeared claiming the phone belonged to her mother-in-law, Doris. Doris had been helping her unpack boxes to surprise Jennifer and had inadvertently left it there. She'd been looking all over for it, according to Kate. There was just one problem with that story: the phone he found in Jennifer's car was in a yellow case. Tonight Doris's phone was in a neon green one.

CHAPTER THIRTY-FIVE

Beau was nervous, not only about exhibiting his new product for the first time at the conference in D.C., but also his impending trip to Frankfurt. He was conflicted about leaving Jennifer alone that long. And worried that he wouldn't find any hints about Meredith over there – that he would not get the closure he and his parents so desperately needed. Fulfilling his role to Ryan as Uncle Beau was a lot of fun. But with every passing day, Beau feared he would also become his father.

That's why his dinner tonight with his fraternity brother, Preston, was so vital. If Preston still hadn't found any news out about Meredith, maybe he would have some tips on where and what to look for while in Frankfurt.

But this morning, he would enjoy Jennifer's world famous pancakes before she and Ryan took him to the airport. His mom was coming in on a flight that arrived an hour before his left so it made sense when Jennifer offered to take him to the airport.

The delicious pancakes and even better camaraderie at the breakfast table was just what everyone needed that morning.

"Yum! I had these once before at your old house. Do you remember that?" Chris said to Ryan.

Ryan had a mouthful of chocolate chip pancake. Jennifer arched her eyebrows and pointed to her mouth indicating he needed to chew and swallow before answering. Ryan got the message.

"Yeah. That was the first time I met you. I like this house better."

Chris laughed. "I do too! Your pool is awesome! Can we go swimming after breakfast?"

Beau smiled. "I'm afraid not today, Chris."

"We have to take him to the airport and then pick up my grandma again," Ryan practically beamed. He adored his grandmother. "And why isn't Grandpa coming again?"

Jennifer waited for Beau to answer. "Grandpa had some meetings to go to. He's super disappointed not to get to come this time," Beau replied, not wanting to reveal that his dad now refused to leave home until there was some word on Meredith.

"Besides, Chris, your mom is home waiting for you!" Jennifer announced. Drew had texted her just as she was starting breakfast that Kate was being released from the hospital any minute.

Chris's face lit up. "She is? Is she better now?"

How to answer that question, Jennifer thought. "She'll be much better after you give her a hug!"

"Did she have too much sugar at the carnival?" Ryan wanted to know.

Jennifer tilted her head to the side. Kids asked the darndest things. "I don't think so. Anyway, the most important thing is that she feels better. She may need to rest some today, though."

Beau took his plate over to the sink. "We need to leave here in about an hour."

Jennifer nodded. "That's fine. Doris is coming to pick up Chris."

Doris. The neon green cell phone. Beau knew he had to say something to Jennifer, just to appease his overactive imagination. "Funny thing about her cell phone."

Jennifer brought the boys' plates over to the sink. "Doris's cell phone? There's something funny about it?" Jennifer had totally forgotten about Kate's excuse for her yellow phone.

Beau finished rinsing the plates and putting them in the dishwasher. "Yeah. Remember when I first brought you to the house and I found that yellow phone in your car? Kate said her mother-in-law had accidentally left it here when she was unpacking some boxes."

Jennifer suddenly felt sick. She was not a good liar and was even worse at keeping secrets. "Yes? What about it?"

"Well, last night when she was here, she was talking to Drew on her phone and it was a neon green print."

Jennifer just stared at Beau. "So?"

"So that phone I found was yellow."

"Women change phone cases all the time, Sweetheart." And that was true.

"You don't."

"Because I don't have the time. I know women who change their phone covers to match their outfits."

Although he was pretty sure Doris didn't have on a neon green outfit last night, Beau couldn't argue with that. He felt relieved. That was one less thing on his plate to think about.

The airport was relatively quiet for a Saturday morning. Beau had breezed through security and actually made his way to the gate where his mom's flight was due to come in. It had been delayed which meant Ryan would be getting antsy. Beau was surprised that the bad weather on the East Coast hadn't delayed his flight out as well.

As he approached the gate, passengers were already streaming out of the Jetway from his mom's flight. Beau looked around frantically as they walked by, hoping he hadn't missed her. She didn't know he would be meeting her at the gate.

Within a few minutes, he saw her sweet, round face framed with her perfectly coiffed white hair heading in his direction. She didn't see him.

"Mom!" She didn't respond. "Martha Baldwin," Beau called.

That got her attention. "Beau! What a lovely surprise! What are you doing all the way out at my gate?"

"Your flight was delayed enough so that I had time to catch you before I leave." Beau kissed his mom's cheek.

"About that, Mr. I-Have-to-Save-the-World Baldwin…" Beau knew she was about to launch into one of her soap box speeches.

Beau reverted to the only defense he knew…pull a Colombo and play dumb. "About what?"

"I understand you have to go to this conference. But you do not need to go over to Frankfurt. If the authorities can't find your sister, what makes you think you can?" Martha had set down her carry-on bag and put her hand on her hip.

Beau put his arm around his mother's shoulder. "I probably can't. But it might give me some closure."

"And it might get you killed too." There. She'd said it. Martha Baldwin didn't need her other child to go missing or worse, be murdered.

"Is that what you're worried about?"

She nodded.

"It's a lot more likely that I'll get killed in a plane crash or a car accident, than get blown up in Germany. They're not after me."

"Who are they?"

Didn't his mom know Geoff was in the CIA?

"Whoever planted the bomb that blew up that bar." Beau congratulated himself on his quick thinking.

"Well at least consider changing your decision."

Beau smiled at his mom. "I will. And maybe Meredith will turn up in the next few days and I won't have to go."

"From your mouth to God's ears," Martha said.

"Hey, as much as I'd like to spend more time with you, there is one eager little grandson waiting on the other side of security for you! And that means his aunt is also eager for your arrival."

Martha beamed. "Yes. Even though I just saw him a few weeks ago, I can't wait to spend more time with him. He gives the best hugs."

"Okay. I probably should get to my gate. Have fun."

Martha hugged her son. "Be safe."

"I will. Don't worry."

"Oh, but I will," Martha assured him as she headed to the revolving doors that led to the baggage claim area.

Washington, D.C., our nation's capital, Beau thought as his plane descended slowly giving him a glimpse of several treasured monuments. The land of the free and home of the brave. His brother-in-law's death served as a reminder of the cost of freedom. Had his sister died too? Or had she escaped?

Beau looked at his watch. It was four o'clock. Vendor setup for the cardiology convention was from one to six p.m. with an opening cocktail party for attendees from six to eight. Beau knew that it would only take him an hour, if that, to set up the Hunnicutt Surgical Devices booth. The signage and brochures he'd ordered should have been delivered to their booth and he had the product with him. All he really had to do was to drape the two tables he'd ordered and put out the brochures. He would keep the devices with him...they were too costly to leave lying out on the table. Dr. Hunnicutt would be arriving late tonight. The show began at seven tomorrow morning.

Fortunately, he was staying at the hotel where the conference was being held. With any luck, he'd be there within the hour, finish the setup and have a little time to check into his room before the cocktail hour. As soon as the plane touched down, Beau's phone lit up with several texts from Preston Hightower. Preston had made dinner reservations for them at eight o'clock at a "great little restaurant" less than a "five minute cab ride" from Beau's hotel, the Westin Georgetown. Perfect! Preston also noted the dress code was business casual. Beau chuckled. Preston had always been concerned with appearances. Tonight, Beau was too. He wanted his fraternity brother to know how concerned he was with his sister's disappearance.

The booth setup and cocktail party had gone well. Beau had run into several doctors from Dallas who had promised they would stop by the booth. They were eager to speak directly with Dr. Hunnicutt.

Promptly at eight, Beau approached the maître'd at La Perla. "Yes, I'm Beau Baldwin. The reservation is under Preston Hightower."

The petite brunette with large brown eyes typed Beau's information into her tablet. "Ah, yes. Mr. Baldwin, please follow me. Mr. Hightower is already seated."

Preston spotted Beau before they reached the table. He stood and gave Beau the secret handshake. "Beau, my man! So great to see you! Have a seat."

"Good to see you too, Preston. I appreciate your making time to see me. I know you must be very busy."

Preston's sandy color hair and chubby face made him look much younger than he was. His green eyes still glimmered and his smile was just a tad crooked. "Brothers always make time for each other, right?"

Beau nodded as he took his seat across from Preston. A cocktail waitress approached the table. Beau noted that Preston already had a highball glass with some kind of amber alcohol halfway filled to the top. Beau really wanted a glass of wine, but decided to order a cocktail instead. "I'll have an Old Fashioned."

The waitress nodded. "Very good, sir."

It wasn't until the main course was served that Beau had been able to end the chit chat and get down to the purpose of their meeting. After taking a few bites of his veal Marsala, Beau decided to bring up Meredith. "So, Preston, I have booked a flight to Frankfurt for this coming Tuesday."

Preston was in the middle of chewing a bite of filet mignon. He arched his eyebrows while he swallowed. "Is there a medical conference over there?"

"No. I'm going to look for my sister." Had Preston forgotten about her?

"Right, right." Preston looked down at his steak, calmly cutting another piece before looking Beau straight in the eye. He lowered his voice. "My sources think she's alive."

Beau laid down his fork. "And you've waited this long to tell me?"

"Take it easy," Preston almost whispered. "This has to remain on the down low or we both could get in a lot of trouble. I couldn't risk telling you this over the phone. In fact, I picked this restaurant so no one could overhear us talking."

Beau looked around. Their table was fairly far away from other tables and those tables were currently unoccupied. "Okay," Beau said calmly. "Where do they think she is?"

"Well that's the rub. No one seems to know. And they don't know for sure that the woman they've spotted is Meredith."

"Okay, where was this woman, who might be Meredith, spotted?"

Preston took a swig of the Merlot he had switched to drinking. "Munich."

"Munich?"

Preston nodded. "And that's all that I have, Bro. I realize it's nothing solid, but I do think it's worth your while to head to Germany."

Beau wished he could leave tomorrow, but there was no way he could bag out on Dr. Hunnicutt. "Thanks for the tip, Preston."

CHAPTER THIRTY-SIX

The unmarked dilapidated bus rattled down the dusty back roads of Texas. What was once a vehicle used for schools was now used as transportation by the compound. The weather was still beastly hot so the air blowing in through the tops of the pull-down windows served as the only circulation device and a gritty one at that. Meredith wondered if the current Texas school buses were air-conditioned. Surely they must be. Maybe even this one had been at one point in time. Maintenance didn't seem to be high on the MOA's list at the compound either.

Vicki was stretched out taking a nap in the seat across the aisle from Meredith. There were a dozen others scattered throughout the bus. Vicki and Jennifer were the only Caucasians. There were six African American men and four other men of unknown ethnicity whom Meredith had seen working as guards at the compound. When the group had boarded the bus at dawn this morning, each rider had been given a boxed lunch and two bottles of water. They had been warned the bus was not making any stops along the way.

But no one would say where they were going. Meredith did the math and figured out the bus wouldn't be able to travel more than three hundred miles without refueling. That information along with the single meal meant that maybe the ride would only last four hours at most. Meredith looked out the window to see if she could figure out what direction they were heading. The sun was to her right so they must be heading north. Maybe once they got far enough away from the compound they would get on a highway and there would be some signs. She had no watch, so she wasn't sure how long they'd been traveling. Nor did she know if they were just being moved to another compound.

Over the past several weeks, Meredith had taken a wide variety of classes. Most of them had involved how to teach and how to plan curriculum. However, every day she had been required to take seminars which indoctrinated her into the Islamic way. Vicki had coached her to go along with their way sooner rather than later. It would not only be Meredith's ticket out of there, but she'd save herself some physical pain.

Meredith's training at Quantico had taught her how to withstand the very tactics they had used on her. She was now considered to be one of them. She worshiped only Allah. Her only concern now was to accomplish the goals of Islam. But the one thing her captors couldn't do was to highjack her soul. And right now her soul wanted to find her son.

Several hours later, as a symbol of hope, the Dallas skyline glistened outside Meredith's window. Dallas! Her brother and sister-in-law lived here! It took Meredith a few minutes to recall which suburb they lived in. She remembered they'd moved recently after Beau's disastrous last job, but they'd stayed in the same neighborhood. If only the bus would stop for gas, she could tell Vicki she had to use the restroom and escape through a window. Or she could give someone a note to dial 911. Or maybe it was better to just ride this out and help the agency bring down this cell. The information she'd gleaned at the compound should be enough to elevate the MOA on the watch list.

They were on a crowded highway now skirting downtown Dallas and heading north. The air wasn't as dusty, but it was still very hot.

"Are you going to eat your lunch?" Vicki asked, waking from her nap.

Meredith shrugged. "I didn't know how long I needed to make this last."

Vicki looked out her window. "We've already passed Dallas?"

"Looks like it."

"Then you better eat now. We're almost there."

"There" turned out to be Garland, Texas. More specifically, an International Academy School in Garland. The faded bus pulled into the parking lot in back of the school where four brightly painted buses with the IAS logo sat waiting for school to get out.

The compound's driver brought the bus to literally a screeching halt at the very back part of the lot. The head guard stood blocking the front door. "We have arrived. Please follow me quietly. I will escort you to your living quarters."

Living quarters, at a school? This must be some fancy boarding school, thought Meredith as she stood in the aisle waiting for those ahead of her to walk down the steps. Vicki followed her. Behind the school and across a soccer field were three identical buildings, each two stories tall. Meredith's best description of them would be they looked like low income housing. Not exactly a luxurious dorm for spoiled rich kids. She was trying to think what her brother had told her about the Dallas suburbs. Maybe he hadn't commented. But because he and his wife had gone house hunting, Meredith felt he must have some "pulse" on suburbia.

The four guards escorted the men to a building marked with the number one. It ran perpendicular to a road but like the other two buildings was surrounded by a fence on three sides. There was a parking lot around the buildings, but no cars filled them. The only ingress and egress to their new compound was through the gated lot associated with the school. Vicki led Meredith to the third building and the one furthest away from the school. She mounted the steps leading to a corner apartment, farthest away from the road.

Diane Cobalt

"Welcome home," she said to Meredith as she unlocked the door with the key the head guard had handed to her as she disembarked the bus.

Home was a studio style apartment, one big room. There was a refrigerator, oven, stove, microwave and sink against one wall. A bunk bed, small dresser, sofa and coffee table flanked the opposite wall. There was a bathroom and small walk-in closet at one end of the room and nice sized window at the other end. Meredith took inventory of what wasn't in the apartment: a TV, clock, dishwasher, washing machine and dryer. She walked over to the kitchen and opened the refrigerator, placing her second bottle of water inside. The refrigerator was empty, but cold. It looked brand new as did the other appliances. There were plates, cups, spoons and forks in the cupboard, but no knives.

"Looks like we need to go to the store," she said to Vicki.

"Yes. There's one across the street we can walk to later. But first you need to go to orientation."

Meredith plopped down on the less than comfortable sofa. "Why am I here?"

"You'll see at orientation." Vicki remained standing. "Go ahead and use the bathroom. Your orientation begins in fifteen minutes."

"About that..."

"About what?"

Meredith pointed to her wrist. "I don't have a watch. How can I be on time without one?"

"Good point. I'll get you one."

Fatal Race

Meredith was pleased. Too bad it wouldn't be an iWatch. She headed into the small, but clean bathroom to freshen up before her meeting.

As the pair headed back across the parking lot to the school, Meredith surveyed her situation. The first thing she noticed was that the faded bus was gone. Her eyes scanned the perimeter of the property. It was entirely fenced in. The fence did not appear to have any barbed wire.

"It's not just a chain-link fence," Vicki said as if reading Meredith's mind. "It's also got a powerful voltage. Don't even try to climb it. If you do, it will deliver so much current to your body that you will wish you would die."

"Thanks for the warning," Meredith replied. The school building was three stories tall and ran parallel to their apartment building. "How many students go to school here?"

"They'll go over that with you in orientation."

My, wasn't Vicki just a fountain of information, Meredith thought. They approached the back door to the school. Vicki punched in a code unlocking it. The cool air hit Meredith like a fresh breeze. She followed Vicki to a conference room located toward the front of the school. Vicki waved her inside.

"Have a seat. I'll go get your trainer."

Meredith took a seat at the conference room table. There was a blank dry-erase board and flat panel monitor at the end of the room. Before long the door to the conference room swung open. A red-haired woman with lots of freckles walked in.

"Hi! I'm Amy!" the woman said extending her hand to Meredith like she was a parent.

"Hi," Meredith replied shaking Amy's hand. Meredith wasn't prepared to meet such a high energy person. And she'd forgotten to ask Vicki if she was going by Sally or Gretchen here.

"I told Vicki she could have a break. I think she's going to the grocery store so if you need anything, just let me know and I'll text her."

Meredith saw an opportunity to get some information. "Well that might depend on how long I'm going to be here."

Amy kept on smiling. "Vicki didn't tell you?"

Meredith shook her head. "Vicki hasn't told me much of anything."

Smiling, Amy tried to look sad for Meredith. "That's too bad. I'm so sorry she hasn't been more communicative. She needs to work on that."

"So…how long will I be here?"

"Yes, Gretchen, you're here for the duration."

"The duration of what?" Meredith was quickly getting tired of these games.

Amy kept smiling. "You must not have been paying attention in your Islam class." She let a worried look creep across her face. "Don't let that bit of news get out of this room. The higher ups frown on us not knowing our Islam faith inside and out. I'll give you extra time later today to bone up on that…just in case. The duration is the amount of time before we are called to serve Allah and be with him in his realm. That could be today or tomorrow or decades from now. We aren't the ones who decide when we will be called to duty."

Splendid, thought Meredith. "Well then I guess you can text Vicki and tell her that along with a watch, I'll need a cell phone, some additional clothes, cosmetics, and some feminine hygiene products."

Meredith got a kick out of watching the expression on Amy's face when she dropped that last item for the grocery list.

"I'm afraid you're not allowed to have a cell phone," Amy announced as she texted Vicki. "Cell phones are earned by time and deeds. We'll go over that in your ongoing training. But today, I want to give you an overview of the school and a tour. How's that sound?"

Like I have a choice, Meredith thought. "Could you start with perhaps answering another simple question I have?"

"I'll try," Amy answered perkily.

"What am I doing here?"

"Well that's an easy question to answer. We need a German teacher here at the International Academy."

"And why do you need a German teacher in Garland, Texas?"

Amy looked dumbfounded. "Because we are creating world leaders here. And as you know, Germany is part of that world. According to your paperwork, you grew up there. And what better way for our students to learn German than from a native German?"

"Okay. I can do that." And good to know my name is Gretchen again.

"Great! I'm so glad you're on board with our philosophy. You see, the world needs more leaders of the Islamic faith." Amy paused, still smiling. "And we need them to speak in all kinds of languages as they go out in the world on behalf of Allah."

Islam isn't a religion. It's an ideal, you half-wit. "I can't wait to be part of our mission," Meredith replied doing her best to smile back at Amy.

CHAPTER THIRTY-SEVEN

Walter walked out on his lanai at the Ritz-Carlton Grand Cayman. He took a sip of his coffee. The view was spectacular! The ocean was a gorgeous clear aqua blue and he could see for miles. Walter was lucky that the weather was perfect as well. This was the peak of hurricane season and thus the prices were more than reasonable at this mammoth resort.

The last time Walter had been to Grand Cayman had been decades ago. Back then, the nicest hotel had been the Hyatt and it had been across the street from the beach. The problem, if you could call it a problem at all, was that Grand Cayman attracted divers. Divers were notorious for trashing hotel rooms with the salt from their gear. They didn't mean to be destructive. It's just that their focus was on the next dive and the Cayman Islands provided lots of amazing seascapes. Walter chuckled recalling the only time he'd ever gone scuba diving and it happened to have been here. He had taken the resort course, at which resort he couldn't even remember, and did his dive. But for some reason, he'd ruptured his eardrum on the way back to the surface and for days he whispered because it sounded like he was shouting. No more diving for him!

Walter thought it really was a shame that he had to spend his day looking for Pierce. There was no one on the beach...he would have it to himself! But he knew that Rachel was waiting in Dallas for some kind of news from him.

His first stop of the day would be to their condo. Rachel had given him the key. Since Grand Cayman was only roughly seven miles long and because they drove on the "wrong" side of the road, Walter elected not to rent a car. He'd Uber.

Walter pulled out his phone and typed in Rachel's address. It was a condo property on the beach less than a mile from the Ritz. He could walk! He slipped on a pair of walking shorts and a collared shirt and grabbed his flip flops. Just as he was about to close the door to his suite, he remembered to apply sunscreen. Walter also put on his hat and sunglasses and then headed down the white sand beach.

Rachel and Pierce's condo was in a three-story yellow stucco building. There was a very small pool between the beach and the building. A few of the balconies were littered with towels and fins. But most appeared to have been abandoned for the season. Rachel and Pierce were among the few couples who lived in their condo all year and never rented it out.

Walter headed past the pool and up to the back door of the building. He swiped the fob against the lock panel as Rachel had instructed him to do. The panel buzzed and the door unlocked. Walter suddenly felt uneasy. What if Pierce was dead in their condo? How would Walter explain his presence to the authorities? And worse, how would he ever get that picture out of his head? "Stop thinking about you!" he said out loud. Then he looked around to see if anyone had heard him.

Feeling foolish, Walter found the single elevator and punched the button to the third floor. The air in the elevator smelled dank and the floor was dry and clean which told Walter that no one had used it today or maybe even yesterday. The elevator doors slowly parted down the middle when they opened up onto the third floor. Hesitantly, Walter stepped off. He looked for the numbers and turned right looking for apartment 306. As Rachel had said, it was at the very end of the open air hall.

Walter raised his hand and knocked on the door. He waited. Nothing. He knocked again. "Pierce?" he called. Again nothing. Walter inserted the key into the lock and turned it to the right freeing the bolt. Slowly, he turned the knob and entered the Hayden's home.

The first thing Walter noticed was that it was stuffy. "Pierce?" he called just to make sure that he didn't surprise Pierce. Everything seemed to be in place, not that Walter had ever seen the condo. But there was no overturned furniture or contents of drawers spilled out everywhere as might be the case if the place had been ransacked. Walter heard stories all the time about friends vacationing at rentals in the Caribbean and waking to find their valuables had been taken while they were asleep.

Walter walked through the short foyer and into the main living room. The shades were open, but the sliding glass door was locked. Rachel and Pierce had a few pieces of furniture on their balcony. Turning to his right, Walter walked down a short hall to what must be Pierce's lab. The wall between the bedroom and bathroom had been knocked out so that Pierce could use the sink. He'd added more counters as well. Test tubes were scattered on top of one of the counters. Boxes of chemicals were stacked in the corner. It was impossible to tell if anything was missing.

There were two bedrooms on the other side of the apartment. One was the master bedroom which had stunning views of the ocean. The other was used as an office. Walter decided to sit down at the desk which was dotted with several piles of paper and a short stack of mail. He looked at the postmark on the top envelope that had been opened. It was from two weeks ago.

Walter didn't feel right leafing through the papers on Pierce's desk, at least not yet. He headed back to the main living area and checked out the kitchen. Pierce appeared to be a very tidy guy, but then that didn't surprise Walter. A scientist would have to be on the anal side to be thorough in their experiments.

Fatal Race

He opened the fridge. There was a carton of milk that was a week past its expiration, some leafy green lettuce in the crisper that appeared a little wilted, a half empty bottle of Chardonnay and a small loaf of bread. The freezer didn't really supply any clues at all. Pierce or maybe Rachel liked to keep their vodka in there. There was no ice cream or frozen treats of any kind.

Maybe the pantry would give him more insight. Walter found an open box of cereal, some crackers and a half eaten jar of peanut butter. Interesting, but not profound. "Maybe I should call Rachel," he said out loud as if someone might tell him what to do. It was at that moment that Walter spotted the first piece of evidence that something was amiss. There, on the granite kitchen counter, was a phone. Walter stopped himself from picking up the phone immediately. Maybe he'd watched too many TV crime shows, but something told him to pick it up with a paper towel in case there were any fingerprints. He walked to the sink and unrolled a small sheet from the spindle of paper toweling. Carefully, he wrapped it around his hand and turned over the phone. He pushed the round button at its base. Pierce's screen saver came up followed by a prompt to enter the passcode. Walter went to retrieve the password Rachel had given him from his wallet when he noticed two words in the upper left corner of the phone: no service. Ah ha! Maybe Pierce had bought another phone which he had with him! That explained everything...well almost everything. Why hadn't Pierce Hayden been in touch with his wife?

Diane Cobalt

What to do now, thought Walter. Should I hang out here hoping Pierce comes back? Or is that wasting time? Should I start walking around town flashing his picture around to see if anyone's seen him? Or should I facetime Rachel? Let her look around the condo and see if she sees anything strange?

Yes! Definitely the latter! He'd feel much better if Rachel directed him on what to do next.

CHAPTER THIRTY-EIGHT

Beau's plane landed in Frankfurt at eight in the morning, Frankfurt time. Dr. Hunnicutt had been so happy with the orders Beau had taken at the conference that he had insisted on upgrading Beau's overseas flight to Business Class. Beau had been able to stretch out in his "pod" and get at least four hours of sleep.

As he waited in line to be processed through customs, Preston Hightower's parting words were on an endless playlist in Beau's head. "Look, Bro, I know you want to find your sister. But just let the professionals look for her and get her back safely. The dudes that may have her are beyond evil. Remember our initiation? Trust your brother? You've got to trust me on this one." Trust your brother. Beyond evil. Get her back safely. Preston had made excellent points, but they didn't trump bloodlines. His sister was his blood relative, not a fraternity brother. If nothing else, he owed it to Ryan to find the one living parent he had left.

Beau's first stop was at his hotel in Frankfurt. He'd decided to shower, change and head to the bombing site. After that he would grab some lunch, maybe take a power nap and drive down to Munich, the site where Preston said there had been a possible sighting of Meredith. He would see if his hotel in Frankfurt could book some place for him to spend the night in Munich. Then he'd drive back to Frankfurt tomorrow, spend the night back at this hotel and head home early the next day. He promised Jennifer and his mother that he would be back in three days.

The bar where Geoffrey and Meredith had been attending a party in their honor, before it had been decimated, was actually located in a small village outside of Frankfurt. The village was quaint with two-story buildings decorated with bright pink and red flowers overflowing from window boxes at every window. Various shops were on the first floor with their owners living above. Occasionally, Beau would see a side balcony with a clothing line stretched out and shirts blowing in the gentle breeze. It was hard to imagine that something so horrific could have happened in this peaceful mecca.

Beau found a place to park and got out of the rental car. His heart was pounding as he turned the corner. He stopped. There it was. A blackened hole at the end of the road with pieces of concrete and glass piled now in one corner. Two pillars remained at the back of the property. Beau forced himself to walk closer. He noted the building next to what was once the bar had a big hole in its stucco exterior. The windows were boarded up. A sign that said "Konditorei" hung askew. Beau checked his phone for the translation. It had been a bakery. He was surprised there was no yellow crime scene tape around the property. Maybe they didn't do that here or maybe it had been too long since the bombing.

Beau walked to the corner and stopped. His shoe was actually touching the rubble from the remains of the bar. He tried hard to picture what it might have looked like. The building had been on a corner. It probably had two entrances, one facing the main street and another facing the side street. Beau's mom had told him that Meredith couldn't hear her in the bar because it was too noisy. So his sister had insisted that she would call their mother back in a few minutes. She just needed to walk outside where it was quieter. Martha Baldwin had waited phone in hand, for a call that never came. Beau now walked onto the site itself, sidestepping piles of debris. Toward the back he found part of what had likely been the bar. Lots of broken glass lay behind it. He looked to the side street. Meredith had probably exited the building towards that side. Beau crossed the property and stepped onto a sidewalk that now had a crater in the middle of it. Had she been standing here? Beau shuddered. He hoped not. Judging by the looks of the concrete and scattered debris, there was no way she could have survived had she been standing at the spot when the bomb went off.

Beau stooped down and picked up a hand of dirt, sifting through it for any evidence of his sister. It was mostly ash. Had he expected to find scraps of clothing or her purse or her ID? Drops of water hit his clenched hand. They were Beau's tears.

Disappointed, but on some level relieved that he hadn't found a trace of Meredith, Beau placed a bouquet of yellow roses he was holding in his left hand on the ground. "Rest in peace, Geoffrey. I promise I will always look after your son."

So far, driving on the autobahn had been the scariest part of Beau's trip. Just to keep up with the flow of traffic, he'd been driving over one hundred miles per hour. If you had an accident on that highway, it would certainly be your last. There had been a few places where he had to slow down due to road construction which meant the trip had taken a little longer than he'd expected. But even so, he was able to get to Munich in less than four hours and check into his hotel well before the dinner hour.

Ordinarily, Beau would be eager to get out and sightsee. But because of the stress of this morning and being cramped in a car, what he really wanted to do was to find a gym. When he checked in, he asked about the hotel's health club.

"What floor is your health club on?" he asked politely as the clerk handed him the key to his room.

Fatal Race

"I am very sorry, sir; but we don't have a health club on site. However, I can direct you to a gym just a short walk from here. Simply show them your room key and admission is complimentary." The clerk spoke perfect English albeit with a British accent. She handed him a pamphlet for the health club.

"Thanks," Beau said and headed to his room.

After making a quick call to Jennifer to let her know he would be staying in Munich tonight instead of Frankfurt, Beau changed into his gym shorts and t-shirt. Sitting on the edge of his bed, he looked at the pamphlet. The name of the club was Hart Guter Gesundheit. He leafed through the brochure which featured several pictures of what looked like a state-of-the-art gym, complete with rock climbing wall and outdoor sports courts for baseball, soccer and tennis. The back page featured a picture of the staff surrounding the owner, Alex Hart. Beau closed his eyes. It couldn't be…could it? Alex Hart had opened a club over here? What were the odds? That's just what he needed today—a confrontation with Mr. Romeo, the man who just several months ago had the audacity to take his wife on a romantic dinner? This was the man who had broken Jennifer's heart in college, prior to her meeting Beau. This guy had the balls to come waltzing back into his wife's life! If Alex Hart even thought for one moment that he could steal Jennifer back, he was sadly mistaken. It was time to set this asshole straight! Beau tied the laces on his sneakers and headed to the gym.

Diane Cobalt

The front desk staff at HGG was very welcoming and professional. In fact, Beau had to admit that he was impressed with Alex's place. The woman who checked him in got a man to show him to the locker room, but Beau didn't need to change so he went directly to a treadmill and programmed in a twenty minute workout. Fox news was on one of the six TV monitors. He grabbed the earplugs and tuned into the channel.

As the next phase on the treadmill kicked in, Beau slowly surveyed the room. He was looking for Alex. He hoped he hadn't gone back to Texas, but it looked like this facility had been open for several months. Why would the owner need to stay if things were running smoothly? Beau realized the one thing missing in Mr. Hart's gym was a punching bag. Had there been one, he would have ditched the treadmill for a quick round or two to get his anger for Alex out on an object he wouldn't go to jail for hitting.

What Beau couldn't see was the figure standing in the hallway outside the second story offices that overlooked the main floor of the health club. From his vantage point, Alex Hart could see Beau Baldwin. Alex had purchased a sophisticated check-in software program that alerted him as to who was in his gym. When he sold a pass to the hotels in the area, they were required to encode their keys with the guest's name. When Beau's name popped up a few minutes ago, Alex had been stunned. Surely it couldn't be Jennifer's husband! But then why should he be surprised that Beau was away from his wife...again?

Fatal Race

It seemed like a lifetime ago that Alex had been having dinner with Jennifer at one of their old "haunts," but in actuality it had been less than six months. Beau had been out of town—which irked Alex to no end. Jennifer had been busy working and taking care of Beau's nephew while her husband went on a seemingly endless string of business trips with his sexy boss. Alex had to rescue Jennifer one night when their house had been vandalized and she was being stalked by some lunatic who was obsessed with the Baldwins' house! What kind of man leaves his wife alone with all that going on? Evidently Beau Baldwin! So it hadn't bothered Alex one bit to protect Jennifer and let her know that he would always be there for her. Their last evening together which had been the last time he had seen Jennifer, Alex had toasted their future together. And that's when his sweet Jennifer had told him that she would always love him. "But I love Beau more. We are having a child together and they are my life now. Without Beau, I couldn't go on." That last sentence replayed in his head like an ear worm every single day.

It was difficult to really tell if the man Jennifer couldn't live without was actually standing in his gym. So Alex decided to take a stroll down to the main floor. Casually he walked past Beau to the trainers' desk where he could look back at the members using the treadmills. Yep, it was Jennifer's husband! As much as he would like to pretend Mr. Baldwin didn't exist, Alex's desperate need for information about Jennifer prevailed. He decided to approach Beau.

"Excuse me, but I think I know who you are," Alex said as he stood next to Beau. Beau removed his ear plugs, but continued walking on the treadmill. "I'm Alex Hart." Alex didn't offer to shake Beau's hands because Beau was holding on to the treadmill's handles.

"Beau Baldwin," was all Beau could think to say.

Alex smiled as he nodded. "You're a long way from home. What brings you to Munich?"

Beau punched a few buttons on the treadmill to end his exercise. He stepped down and shook Alex's hand. "My brother-in-law was killed in the bombing of a bar up in Frankfurt earlier this year. Unfortunately, my sister was also at the bar, but she hasn't been found." Beau spoke very matter-of-factly. He exuded no emotion.

Alex could tell that Beau disliked him and quite frankly he didn't blame him. If he were in Beau's shoes, he would hate Alex. "I remember hearing about it on the news. I had no idea it was your brother-in-law. I'm sorry. That's awful."

Beau seemed to soften. "Yeah. It really sucks for my nephew. Jennifer and I have been taking care of him."

Just when Alex was trying to like Beau, he had gone and said her name. Jennifer. Alex told himself to shake it off. "Hey, let's grab a smoothie and head to my office where we can talk...that is unless you want to finish your workout first."

Beau shook his head. "I'm done working out. The smoothie actually sounds good."

Once the two men got past their animosity towards each other, they actually seemed to get along. Alex led

Beau upstairs to his office. The pair sat down in adjacent chairs on the same side of Alex's desk.

"So I assume you came to Germany to look for your sister," Alex began.

"Yes. I went to the site this morning looking for any clues, but there were none."

"That had to have been tough," Alex commented.

Beau nodded, unable to speak.

"Is there anything I can to do help?"

Beau pulled out his phone. "A friend of mine in Washington said his sources tell him that Meredith was last spotted in Munich." Beau brought up a picture of Meredith on his phone. "By any chance have you seen her?'

Alex took Beau's phone. He studied it closely. It was the woman who'd given him the note several weeks ago. She had a different hairstyle and color, but the face...yeah he was sure it was her. "I have. She was here a few times with a couple of other women."

Beau was beyond elated. His face brightened. "When was the last time you saw her?"

Alex handed Beau's phone back to him trying to decide if he should tell Beau about the note. "It's been several weeks now."

Beau hung his head, disappointed. "She's probably moved on."

"Maybe."

"Did you talk to her?"

"I tried, but I got the feeling the women with her were watching her." Oh hell, Alex thought, I've got to tell him about the note. "Look, Beau, she gave me a note. Actually she found a way to get it into my pocket without me realizing it."

"What did the note say?" Beau's face brightened again.

"Her last name's Matthews, right?"

Beau nodded. "Yes. Meredith Matthews."

"That's what the note said—she was being held against her will and to call the CIA. She also said she was traveling under the name Gretchen Bruckmann and she gave her German passport number."

Beau stood up, unable to contain his excitement. "And? Did you call the CIA?"

Alex nodded. "I passed on the information. They are looking into it. I'm supposed to call them if she returns."

"That's great news! I never thought I'd say this to you, but thank you! Thank you from the bottom of my heart."

Alex stood as well. He shook Beau's hand. "Now would you mind answering a question for me?"

"Anything!"

"How's Jennifer?"

Beau smiled. "She's fine. We're...expecting a child. I don't know if you knew that or not."

Alex nodded. "I'd heard."

Beau didn't stop to wonder how Alex knew. "I really do understand why you love her, you know?"

"Of course. And I respect your marriage...as long as you promise to always take care of her."

"That's an easy promise to keep."

"Then you better get your ass back to Texas. If the CIA is involved, then the folks that may have your sister are not nice."

"But how can I leave when Meredith may be right around the corner?"

"Let me look for her. I don't have a family to take care of...you do. If something were to happen to me, I wouldn't be letting anybody down."

Beau sat back down as did Alex. "You know, Alex Hart, you're a decent guy."

"I'd like to think so. When's your flight back?"

"Not until the day after tomorrow. I leave out of Frankfurt."

Alex punched a number into his phone. "Hey, it's Alex. I need to get a friend of mine on the next flight out of Munich going back to Dallas. Great! Yes, he's right here. I'll let him give you his information."

Beau was in luck. There was a flight leaving later that evening. He'd have to connect through New York, but he'd be back in Dallas by tomorrow morning. Jennifer would be surprised!

"I can't thank you enough, Alex." Beau said. "Here's my number. Please keep in touch."

Alex smiled sadly. "You're a good guy. But if I ever find out you're not taking care of Jennifer, I'll personally hunt you down. In the meantime, I'll do my best to find your sister."

Beau decided not to let Jennifer know that he was on his way home. He would surprise her at her office in person.

Diane Cobalt

The ever faithful, but sometimes foolish, Fadwa Atwa had contacted Alan Smith a few weeks ago when she spotted two men entering Alex Hart's gym. Fadwa, who had been one of Gretchen's handlers, had gone to the gym several weeks ago with Daria and Vicki and the woman. From the beginning, Fadwa had had her suspicions that their unknown woman might be the missing CIA agent from their Frankfurt bombing. But for the longest time, the woman had given no indication of being that person. Until that day in the gym when Fadwa had caught her talking to the owner. And even then, she hadn't been sure. So she told Daria and Vicki that she had been reassigned and had moved into an empty second floor office space across the street from the health club so she could monitor Alex Hart. Fadwa had researched him and found nothing terribly interesting about the man. But hoping to rise in the ranks of the MOA, she needed to impress their leader, Alan Smith. So when she spotted two men dressed in sweats meeting with Alex Hart before the club opened one morning, she followed them and recognized one as a CIA agent. Fadwa had been only too happy to let Mr. Smith know.

Alan Smith had initially directed her to take care of things...immediately. But then he contacted her and told her to wait until he could personally oversee the mission.

Everything was in place. It was about five in the morning. Alan Smith stood next to Fadwa at their perch down the block looking out the window at the health club. The street was usually empty this time of day and today was no exception.

Fifteen minutes later, Alex arrived at HGG to get in his own workout before the staff showed up. He thought about Beau Baldwin flying across the Atlantic, heading back to the only woman Alex had ever loved. Alex inserted his key into the door of his health club. The bolt moved to the right. He entered the club and heard a click. Alex turned toward the noise. Before he could determine where the noise had come from, his health club exploded.

"Excellent. That's one less infidel," Alan said to Fadwa.

CHAPTER THIRTY-NINE

Jennifer woke up to the smell of bacon and smiled. It was so nice having Martha Baldwin stay with her while Beau was gone. And it was especially kind of Martha to fly back so soon after she'd just been here. Jennifer's parents had been due back from their trip and would have been around to help out with Ryan, but at the last minute the Monroes had changed their plans in order to meet up with some old friends. Martha had insisted she would return. And even better than the smell of breakfast was knowing that Beau would be home tomorrow.

After showering and getting dressed for work, Jennifer headed out to the kitchen. "Good morning, dear," Martha greeted her. "I hope you don't mind my making Ryan some breakfast. What can I get you?"

Jennifer gave her mother-in-law a hug. "Whatever you have on the griddle smells delicious and if there's enough, I'll have some too."

Ryan sat perched at the island, his favorite eating spot. "Grandma made me scrambled eggs and bacon and blueberry muffins."

"Wow! I'll bet they were yummy." Jennifer tousled Ryan's hair before sitting down next to him.

Ryan nodded. "And she's going to drive carpool this morning."

"Really, Martha, I can do that."

Martha set a plate of eggs and bacon garnished with a muffin in front of Jennifer. "Now, hon, you just take it easy. Let me take care of things around here. I absolutely adore spending time with Ryan and his friend. I'll pick them up from school too."

Jennifer smiled while she finished chewing a bite of muffin. "You're the best and these muffins are truly amazing. I'd love to have the recipe."

Martha practically beamed. Her baby blue eyes danced. "I'd be happy to share it with you. Now Ryan, what do you usually take in your lunchbox?"

While Ryan listed his favorite lunch items, Jennifer checked her phone. There was a text from Gordon. All it said was "Panera." Jennifer frowned. That was their meeting place lately. But usually they contacted her on her "third" cell phone. Jennifer wiped her mouth and stood. "Excuse me a minute. I need to make a call."

She headed back to her bedroom where her briefcase was. She unzipped the interior pocket where she kept the third phone and checked it for messages. There it was: another text from Gordon about thirty minutes ago when she had been in the shower. "Urgent. Please meet us at Panera at 8:15 or as soon as you drop off Ryan at school."

Uh oh, Jennifer thought. I wonder what Alan did to upset them now. She glanced at the clock on her nightstand. It was seven forty. Time for Martha to leave to drive the boys to school. Jennifer texted Gordon back: "Will be there at eight."

Twenty minutes later, Jennifer pulled open the door to Panera Bread and ordered a cup of decaf coffee. She selected a hazelnut roast, added a little milk and then headed to look for Jack and Gordon. They were both seated in their usual meeting spot: a round booth in the corner near the side entrance.

"Hi, Guys! What's up?" Jennifer slid in beside them. Both of them looked like someone had died.

"She hasn't seen the news," Jack commented.

Jennifer froze. "No. I haven't. What's going on?"

Jack and Gordon looked at each other, waiting for the other to update Jennifer.

Gordon cleared his throat and looked at her. "There was a bombing early this morning." He stopped.

"In Munich," Jack added.

Jennifer took a swift breath. "What? Was anyone hurt?" She assumed that Beau hadn't called her this morning because he was heading back to Frankfurt and sometimes couldn't get a good cell connection while driving on the autobahn. Jennifer grabbed her phone out of her purse and called Beau. It went right to voice mail.

"Probably. They're sifting through the rubble looking for bodies," Jack explained.

Gordon hit him on the sleeve. "You idiot!"

"What?"

"You didn't have to say bodies! You could have just said they don't know."

Jack hung his head. "Sorry, Jennifer."

"Look, just because Beau is there, doesn't mean he was anywhere near that explosion. Munich's a big place. What time did this happen?" Jennifer responded.

"They said about five a.m. Munich time," Gordon answered.

"Did it happen at a hotel?" Jennifer wanted to know.

Jack shook his head. "They haven't said."

"I appreciate you two worrying about Beau."

"Has he called you?" Gordon asked.

"Well, no. But he was going to head back to Frankfurt today so that he can catch his flight out tomorrow."

"Maybe you could call the hotel and see if he checked out," Jack suggested.

"Oh, okay." Jennifer looked up the name of the hotel Beau had given her and punched in the number.

"Grand Hotel Munich. How may I direct your call?"

"Beau Baldwin's room, please." Jennifer could hear the operator typing.

"I'm sorry. Mr. Baldwin checked out last night."

Jennifer felt her stomach drop. "Last night? Are you sure about that?"

"Yes. Is there anything else I can help you with?"

"No, thank you." Jennifer swallowed. Why wouldn't Beau have let her know he was changing hotels? Did someone abduct him?

"Hey, Jen, are you okay?" Gordon asked her.

"I will be once I find out where my husband is."

"In the meantime, we will keep checking the news reports…see if there are any updates," Jack offered.

"Thank you. You two are very kind," Jennifer said. She didn't know whether to be furious with Beau or worried. But she did know someone who could get an answer for her…Manuel.

"We should probably get to the office," suggested Gordon. "I'm not sure what time Alan is showing up today."

Jennifer nodded. She would see if she could reach Manuel on her short drive over. But on the way, Jennifer decided that was foolish. If something had happened to Beau, Manuel would have contacted her. Gordon had said the bombing occurred about five in the morning in Munich. That would have meant it happened around midnight their time. Manuel would have had plenty of time to contact her. There was no point in airing their marital issues with him.

Five minutes later, Jennifer pulled into the office parking lot. There was a man standing outside. His back was to her and he was peering inside the glass door.

"What the…?" Then she realized who it was and threw open her car door. "Beau!"

Beau spun around revealing a bouquet of peach colored roses. "Surprise! I'm home early!"

Jennifer burst into tears. "Hey I know you're happy to see me, but I didn't mean to make you cry." Beau folded her into his arms.

"I…" Jennifer sniffed. "I thought you were dead."

Beau leaned back. "Dead? Why?"

"There was an explosion in Munich earlier today. I thought you were there spending the night."

"I decided it was more important to get home than to keep looking for my sister. I found a flight out of Munich last night and changed my plans so I could surprise you. I didn't mean to worry you."

Jennifer took a deep breath. "As much as I love a good surprise, you did worry me! That's why we have that agreement to let each other know when we have a change in plans."

Beau smiled at her. "I understand. But who would have thought there would be an explosion in the town I was in. Did they say where specifically? Was anyone hurt?"

"I don't know. I haven't had the news on. Jack and Gordon are the ones who told me. You know, you better get home. Your mom is apt to turn on the TV and see what's going on in the world!"

Beau nodded. "Yes. That's a good idea." He wiped a tear off of his wife's cheek. "No more tears, Mrs. Baldwin."

"No more tears. I'm so thankful you are home safe and sound."

"Lunch? I've got lots to tell you about what I found out in Germany."

Jennifer nodded. "That should be fine. I just need to see how much Alan needs me to do today."

Beau smiled. "Just text me when you want me to pick you up."

"We probably should include your mom."

"Good idea." Beau kissed Jennifer and headed to his car.

Jennifer opened the door into the office. "Crisis averted," she announced to Jack and Gordon who were seated at their desks.

Gordon put his hands together as if praying. "Thank God."

Jennifer went on back to her office. It appeared that Alan was not in yet. She was sitting down at her desk when her phone rang. It was Kate.

"Jen, I'm glad I caught you."

"What's up? Are the boys okay?" Kate almost never called her while she was at work unless it was school related.

"You haven't heard." Kate's voice was somber.

"About the bombing in Munich? Yes. I have. And Beau's fine. In fact he took an earlier flight back and just showed up here at the office to surprise me. Of course I was furious with him for not letting me know that he had changed his plans! But all is well."

"Let me repeat myself. You haven't heard."

Jennifer was losing her patience with her best friend. "Haven't heard what?"

"A bomb went off at a health club in Munich."

"And?"

"And the owner was Alex Hart."

Jennifer was glad she was sitting down because all of a sudden the room began spinning. "Alex has a health club in Munich?"

"It was his reaction to your rejection. He didn't want to live in the same community where he might run into you. So he opened a chain of health clubs in Europe."

The spinning room seemed to be slowing down, but Jennifer felt sick to her stomach. "Are you sure it was his health club that exploded?"

"That's what they are reporting on all of the networks."

Jennifer took a deep breath. "But it happened at like five this morning. The club wouldn't have been open yet, right?"

"That's right. It hadn't opened yet."

"Wait a minute. You said the owner *was* Alex Hart. Was, as in past tense?"

"I'm sorry to tell you this, Jen. But they are reporting that Alex was killed in the blast."

Jennifer felt hot. Her vision was blurred. "No. That can't be right. Why would they have killed Alex?" It was a rhetorical question. Jennifer knew Kate didn't have the answer. But Manuel better have it.

Diane Cobalt

Manuel handed Jennifer another tissue as she sat weeping at the Eagle's Nest conference room table. "I repeat. Alex Hart's death is not your fault."

Jennifer sniffed. Anger was slowly replacing her sadness. "Then whose fault is it? Terrorists don't just target an American gym that recently opened in Munich. If their goal was to kill a bunch of people, why did they bomb it when no one was supposed to be there?"

"Like I said. We're looking into it. Unfortunately, there is no security footage available of the health club. Everything was destroyed."

"Then how do the authorities know Alex was even there?"

Manuel looked down at the table. "The German police were able to identify his body along with his car which had been blown across the street. It appears that the explosive device or devices were planted in the gym, not outside of it. It is believed they were detonated as Mr. Hart opened the door. He died from internal bleeding and head wounds."

Jennifer started crying again. "Beau was over there. It could have been him."

"But it wasn't. Try to focus on that. Let us do our jobs. We will find who did this, Jennifer, and bring them to justice," Manuel said sympathetically.

Jennifer shook her head. "Great. It won't bring Alex back." She stood and grabbed her purse. "I realize it's too late for me to get out of this undercover operative role." She looked Manuel in the eyes. "But you all need to do your jobs and protect my friends and family."

Manuel knew he couldn't promise her that.

Fatal Race

Jennifer had been so upset that she'd taken the rest of the day off. Alan Smith had not made an appearance at the office. Jack and Gordon said they'd tell him she wasn't feeling well if he showed up.

After meeting with Manuel, she drove straight home. Beau's car was in the garage. Jennifer walked into the house and found her husband standing three feet from their TV watching the latest reports of the bombing. His back was to her.

Beau turned and faced his wife. "You've heard?"

Jennifer stood like a statue across the room. She nodded. "At least it wasn't you."

"And it very easily could have been."

Beau was wringing his hands. His eyes looked like road maps from lack of sleep.

"Did you know Alex had a health club in Munich? I didn't."

Beau nodded. "Yes. I was there."

Jennifer remained rooted to her spot. "What do you mean you were there? You talked to Alex? Is that why you went to Munich?"

"Why don't we sit down? Mom went to the grocery store. It will be at least a half hour before she's back."

"No, that's okay. I'd rather stand to hear this."

"As I told you before, I went to Munich because Preston Hightower's sources had spotted Meredith there. When I checked into my hotel, I asked where their fitness center was. I had been driving for a long time and wanted to work out. They didn't have a gym, but gave me a brochure of one that their guests could use free of charge."

"And that just happened to be Alex's gym," Jennifer concluded. "Wow, what a coincidence."

"That's exactly what it was. When I saw his picture in the pamphlet...I knew I had to confront him."

Jennifer's eyebrows shot up. "Confront him? About what?"

"About how he felt about you...about him trying to butt into our marriage," Beau tried to stifle his anger by reminding himself that this guy was now dead.

"I handled that," Jennifer said defiantly.

"But I am your husband and it's my responsibility to defend our marriage. It was never okay with me that he called you, let alone took you to dinner that night..." Beau's voice trailed off knowing that neither of them wanted to rehash the events of the night that Beau's boss had died in their pool.

Jennifer dejectedly walked over to the couch. Beau took his place next to her. "Of course it is," she said. "And I am honored that you value our relationship so much that you want to set someone straight who is trying to intrude."

Beau put his arm around her. "How many times do I have to tell you that you are my world? No one gets to have you, but me!"

Jennifer kissed her husband. "Thank you. And I'm so glad you weren't at the gym when it exploded." But she still felt devastated that Alex was dead.

Beau sat back and folded his hands in his lap. "I do need to tell you about how that confrontation turned out."

"You didn't threaten him, did you?"

Beau chuckled. "No. Quite the opposite. Once Alex and I realized that what we had in common...our love for you...bonded us together in a weird way, we got on the same page. It turns out that Meredith had been in his gym a few weeks ago. But Alex didn't know who she was or that she was even an American...at least not the first time he saw her."

"That's terrific! That means she is alive!"

"Or at least she was when he saw her. She somehow snuck a note into his pocket asking him to call the CIA and tell them Meredith Matthews was alive and needed help. When I showed Alex her picture and confirmed her name is Meredith, he said that she had a different hairstyle and color but it was definitely the woman he had seen."

"Did he call the CIA?"

Beau nodded. "Right away and they met with him."

Jennifer got a sick feeling in her stomach. Whoever blew up Alex's health club might have known he was helping Meredith.

"When I wanted to stay in Munich to look for Meredith, Alex convinced me not to. In fact, the last thing he said to me was to go home and take care of you. He'd look for her." Beau started crying. "I'm sorry he's gone, Jen. I truly am. And not just because he was going to look for my sister, but because I know he meant a lot to you."

Jennifer pulled Beau into her arms. "Thank you for saying for that," she whispered in his ear. "He was a good guy."

CHAPTER FORTY

Meredith was free to come and go to work and to her apartment where Vicki was still her roommate. But beyond that, she was a prisoner. She taught three sections of German a day and gave tours to prospective parents and students who thought this was truly an international academy, not a terrorist training camp. Of the three classes Meredith taught, only one was a true German class. The others were just going over basic German phrases and working on pronunciation. Of the many languages Meredith had learned at Quantico, she would not have ever envisioned teaching German, especially in the U.S.

As she crossed the parking lot and then the soccer field, Meredith looked up at the azure blue Texas sky. At least she was back in the states and ironically was living very close to her brother. She climbed the steps to her second floor apartment and swiped her key across the lock. The apartment was empty, but there was a bag of groceries sitting on the counter of the kitchenette. When Meredith moved the bag to unpack it, she saw a local paper. Vicki must have messed up, she thought. There was no TV or radio in their unit effectively blocking news from the outside world.

Meredith stared down at the front page of *The Dallas Morning News*. A color picture of a bombing site in Germany stared back. Above the picture was the headline: "Texan Dead in Bombing of Munich Health Club." The line that followed named the dead man as the owner of the gym, Alex Hart.

"Shit," Meredith said out loud. "I'm so sorry I got you involved, Mr. Hart." Meredith scanned the rest of the article. The authorities were still trying to determine if it was an act of terrorism and to what extent Alex Hart may or may not have been involved. He had to have found her note and contacted the agency. Meredith was thankful for that. She wondered if they knew she was back in the country.

Hearing footsteps outside, Meredith quickly replaced the shopping bag on top of the paper, pretending she hadn't seen it. She quickly walked over to her bunk and sat down.

Vicki opened the door to the apartment. "Hello, there! Did you see I got us some groceries? I didn't have time to put them all away."

"Yes, thanks. Do you want me to help?"

"No, I've got it," Vicki said. She put up the groceries, but left the paper there. "Good thing we're not in Deutschland anymore," she commented, pointing to the paper.

Meredith was shocked. Why would Vicki give her information from the outside world? "Why's that?"

"The gym we went to a few times was blown up!"

"Why?"

Vicki shrugged. "Your guess is as good as mine. But you might get some questions about it in your German classes, so I suggest you read the article."

That was why Vicki had let her see the paper! Meredith got up and took it off the counter. She had hoped that maybe Vicki was softening some towards her and that she'd be able to use some of the tactics she'd learned in her training at Quantico to get Vicki on her side. Then Vicki surprised her again.

"Hey, I'm tired of cooking. Do you want to go out to eat tonight?"

Meredith wasn't sure what to say. How did Vicki know she wouldn't make a run for it? "Sure. That sounds nice."

"Good. Amy actually approved a dinner out. She's very pleased with your teaching abilities. You're doing a good job, Gretchen."

Was it Meredith's imagination, or did Vicki place an emphasis on the word, "Gretchen"?

After Meredith's first German class the next morning, perky Amy stuck her head in the classroom. "How was dinner out last night?"

"It was delicious," Meredith responded.

Fatal Race

"Vicki said you went out for Tex-Mex. Have you ever had that before?"

Meredith thought not too many Germans had had that cuisine. "No. I found it to be quite unusual, but tasty."

"There are a lot of fun places to eat nearby. You're actually earning a lot of good behavior awards, Gretchen. Keep up the good work."

"Gretchen" nodded. "I will."

"And one other thing. I need you to give a tour in about an hour."

"But that conflicts with my next class."

"I'll sub for you," Amy giggled. "They won't learn much from me though."

Meredith couldn't figure Amy out. She seemed so normal, so American. What the hell was she doing helping terrorists? It must be the money, Meredith thought.

An hour later, Meredith waited in the conference room for the parent who was coming to tour the school. Amy had said it was a private tour, one adult, no kids. It should be a piece of cake.

Alan Smith was already in his office when Jennifer got to work the next morning. There was a note on her desk to see him when she got in. "Hi, Alan. What can I do for you?"

"Jennifer, have a seat." He motioned for her to sit down. "I understand your nephew attends Grandview Elementary with some of my friends' children. I believe they played on the soccer team that your husband coaches?"

Alan's British accent was always a shock to Jennifer. "Maybe. What's their name?"

Alan smiled at her. "Well it really doesn't matter now, because they have moved out of the school."

"But why? It's supposed to be an excellent elementary school—one of the best in the district."

"Well, you see, we expect a little more from our schools. For example, we teach our children multiple languages at a young age. I was thinking that your nephew might benefit from a better school that my friends have found. In fact, I was able to get you a tour of the school this morning. I know you'll want to take advantage of my connections to get into this school. It's becoming very popular as many are not as infatuated with your little Grandview Elementary as you are."

Jennifer had to work hard not to get angry and not to roll her eyes. "Why thank you, Alan. Since you insist, I'll take that tour." There, that should appease him. Jennifer had no intention of moving Ryan to another school. "What's the name of this school?"

"Here. I've written it down for you. The address is on there as well," Alan said handing Jennifer a yellow sticky note.

Jennifer noted the tour time started in less than thirty minutes, but the school was only about ten minutes away. "Again, thank you for looking out for my nephew."

"I'll expect a report when you return. Oh and Jennifer, if you are interested, you can take your nephew on a separate tour that's geared more for the potential student."

Jennifer did her best to smile. "I will report back to you this afternoon."

Twenty minutes later, Jennifer sat waiting in the outer office of the principal of the International Academy. A secretary had offered to get her coffee, but Jennifer declined. She was already uncomfortable enough and she didn't need any caffeine to rattle her further. She tucked her wavy brown hair behind her ears and took a deep breath.

"Mrs. Baldwin?" A perky red-haired woman with an abundance of freckles stepped into the waiting area. "I'm Amy, the principal here." She offered her hand to Jennifer.

Jennifer stood and shook the principal's hand. "Nice to meet you, Amy."

"I understand you are considering moving your nephew here? And it looks like we may have another student from you in five years?" Amy pointed to Jennifer's stomach.

Jennifer smiled. "Yes. I'm expecting. We really hadn't thought about moving our nephew, but my boss suggested I come tour your school."

"You're going to love it," Amy said enthusiastically. "I think the best way to show off our school is for you to have an actual teacher give you a tour. Follow me."

Amy pushed through a set of double doors that separated the office area from the school. She looked over her shoulder to make sure Jennifer was following behind. "Here at IA, we believe in a global education for each and every one of our students. Therefore, languages are at the heart of our curriculum. I was able to snag one of our newer German teachers to lead you on a tour. She's waiting for us in the conference room."

Jennifer tagged closely behind Amy as she opened the conference room door. "Mrs. Baldwin, I'd like you to meet Fraulein Bruckmann, our German teacher."

"Hi, Mrs. Baldwin. I'm Gretchen," the German teacher said as she shook Jennifer's hand.

Jennifer smiled and shook Gretchen's hand. "Please, call me Jennifer." Jennifer congratulated herself for acting like she'd never met the woman whose hand was now in hers. She was face-to-face with her sister-in-law!

CHAPTER FORTY-ONE

The gleaming white tiled hallway where the trio now stood only amplified Jennifer's single thought. What do I do now? The thought was almost crowding out her ability to act as if she had never met Gretchen. Gretchen had shown absolutely no sign of recognition. Could Jennifer be mistaken?

"Right now our students are in class which is why the halls are empty," said Amy. The fluorescent lights reflected off her red hair. Red hair! Freckles! Jennifer shifted her focus from Gretchen to Amy, studying her face. This was the woman Manuel was looking for! That solved the question of Mari the soccer mom being the one. What were the odds that both women they were looking for would appear at the same time?

Jennifer realized Amy was waiting for some kind of response from her. "I'm sorry. Could you repeat your question?"

"Sure. I just wondered the age of your nephew."

The answer to her question was Jennifer's chance to seal the one percent doubt that Gretchen was Meredith. "Ryan is five. He's in kindergarten." Jennifer looked at Gretchen to see if there was any flicker of recognition at the mention of her son's name, but Gretchen had already turned her back to continue walking down the hall.

"Perfect," smiled Amy. "We prefer to get our students at a young age because it is much easier for them to learn languages. Isn't that right, Gretchen?"

Gretchen stopped walking and turned to face Jennifer and Amy. "Definitely. Would you like to see my classroom?"

Jennifer nodded. It was all she could do to keep from hugging her sister-in-law.

Amy's cell phone vibrated. She glanced down at it and frowned. "Ladies, I'm sorry, but I'm going to have to take this call. Gretchen, would you please finish the tour for Mrs. Baldwin?"

"Of course. I'd be happy to."

"Thanks," said Amy who scurried off down the hall.

Gretchen led Jennifer into her classroom closing the door behind them. *What do I do?* Jennifer surveyed the room for hidden cameras. She spotted one overhead and one over the door. She'd have to be careful with what she said or did. Maybe the best thing was to wait for Gretchen's cue.

"How long have you been teaching here?" Jennifer thought that was a good question, one a prospective parent would ask.

"I've only been here a few weeks," Gretchen replied while looking Jennifer directly in the eye. Jennifer felt she was begging her to ask more questions.

"My husband and I are taking care of his sister's son while she is...absent."

Gretchen's smile lit up her eyes. "How very kind of you! I'm sure she appreciates that."

It's her! Think, Jennifer! What would Manuel need to know?
"We're not sure how long she will be gone. Right now Ryan is going to Grandview Elementary. My best friend from college's son also goes there and they have become good friends. It's an excellent school."

"But you're looking here because...?" Gretchen questioned.

"Because my boss, Alan Smith, suggested that I look here. Several of his friends' children have recently transferred out of our school and over to here. I haven't told my husband yet that I'm even looking at transferring Ryan. I don't want to bring it up if I don't think this is the right thing to do. Ryan's had a lot of change in his life." Jennifer paused. Should she say that Ryan's father had died? What if Meredith didn't know? But Meredith would have to know that Geoffrey would be taking care of Ryan if he was okay. She decided to stop just in case.

Meredith nodded. "That's a good thought process. You might not want to separate him from his new friend at this point."

Was Meredith trying to tell her something?

"But of course, his friend could transfer here as well," Meredith said as an afterthought. "Please, have a seat." Meredith pointed to a chair adjacent to her desk. "What kinds of questions do you have?"

Think, Jennifer. What would a parent be asking her? "How many kindergarten students do you have?"

Meredith sat down at her desk and opened a drawer, pulling out a pad of paper. "Right now, we don't have any. But we actually don't believe in the grade level concept here. We group by ability. I'm sure your nephew...what did you say his name is?"

"It's Ryan," Jennifer had to swallow hard to keep from crying. "Ryan Matthews."

Meredith's nod was so slight, Jennifer almost missed it. "I'm sure Ryan is an exceptional student and he would do well in our program. But I would recommend you bring your best friend for a tour first, to make sure she would be on board with her son transferring here as well."

"Yes. That sounds like a great idea. Are there certain days and times that you give tours?"

"Amy schedules those. But you can always request me. Again, I wouldn't bring the boys until you are sure you want them to transfer. We almost always meet with the parents alone for the initial visit."

Jennifer was getting the message loud and clear: don't bring Ryan. He might recognize his mother. But should she bring Beau? Could she even tell him? Meredith must be forced into this for some reason. Otherwise, why wouldn't she have come to their house?

"That makes sense. We live not too far from here."

Meredith smiled. "That makes it convenient for you. How far away from Ryan's current school do you live?"

"He can't walk. And he couldn't walk here either. It's about a ten minute drive from our house. We carpool with his friend."

"Sounds like you have a great system. If you don't have any other questions for me, I should continue our tour."

"Sure. That's fine." Jennifer stood and followed Meredith out of her classroom. The next stop on the tour was the gym where about ten students were shooting arrows. "The students are studying archery right now."

"Even the young ones?" Jennifer sounded concerned.

"No. They have to be at least twelve to participate in that activity. The younger students will be focusing on some other hand-eye coordinating activity to prepare them down the road."

"I see. Do they have music classes?"

"Not at this time. Music doesn't quite fit into our philosophy of preparing students to survive and thrive in an international setting."

"Interesting." Jennifer was not sure she agreed with that, but didn't want to create any waves. She wanted to spend more time with Meredith in hopes that she might give her some kind of clues as to what was going on. Yet every minute she stayed in this school was one more minute her sister-in-law was perhaps being held captive.

"Would you like to see our lunchroom?" Meredith asked.

"How about if we save that for when I come back with my best friend? I know she'll have a ton of questions and I don't want to waste your time."

Meredith nodded. "So you'll be back?"

Jennifer thought she looked hopeful. "Yes. I'm not sure when. I'll have to check her schedule."

"Great! Just don't wait too long. They have a limited number of spaces here and they are adding more students every week. I'll walk you to the front door."

Had she made the right choice to leave before the tour was finished? Jennifer liked that Meredith knew she would be back. As they reached the front door, Jennifer hesitated, unsure of what to say. "Thank you for your time, Gretchen. It's been nice...meeting you."

"Likewise," Meredith replied holding out her hand. "I look forward to seeing you again."

As Jennifer shook her hand, she felt Meredith pressing a small piece of folded paper into her hand. Jennifer subtly took it and forced herself to walk at a normal pace back to her car.

Jennifer drove away, the note still pressed into the palm of her right hand. She pulled into the parking lot of the grocery store which was just a block away. Her hand was shaking as she unfolded the slip of paper.

I'm here against my will. Please let the CIA know.
Meredith Matthews

When had Meredith written that? Jennifer racked her brain, replaying the tour in her head. It had to have been when they were sitting at the desk in her class room. She'd been so fixated on what to do; she hadn't seen her even pick up a pen.

Maybe she should drive directly to the Eagle's Nest headquarters. Jennifer thought about that idea for a minute. No! What if she was being followed? Jennifer decided her best plan of action was to do a little grocery shopping. If someone had followed her from the school here, they wouldn't be suspicious. She grabbed her green phone out of her console and put it in her purse then nonchalantly walked into the store.

After she walked through the automatic doors, Jennifer dialed Manuel. "It's urgent."

"I'm at the Starbucks around the corner from you. Buy a newspaper and meet me there."

At least Jennifer was being followed by the good guys! She took a deep breath, bought a paper and headed down to the coffee shop.

Manuel was seated in the corner nursing a latte. Jennifer walked to the counter and ordered a shaken peach tea. When it was ready, she sat down next to Manuel.

"You've had a big morning," he stated.

All Jennifer could do was nod. "Here," she said handing him the folded note. Manuel read it.

"Thanks for the confirmation."

"You mean you knew?" Jennifer was shocked. For once she thought she had one-upped the organization.

"Yes. But we needed to establish a means for her to communicate with us...one that wouldn't seem suspicious."

"A heads up would have been nice," Jennifer countered.

"If we'd told you, you might not have acted as normally as you did. Our goal is to extract Meredith as soon and as safely as possible."

"And why can't that be today?"

"We need her on the inside for a little bit longer. What did she say? I take it she knows you have her son?"

Jennifer nodded. "Yes. I mentioned Ryan by name. I'm pretty sure she recognized me, but she didn't act like she did. I told her that I wouldn't consider transferring Ryan there unless his best friend came too. She suggested I bring my friend for a tour without the boys."

"That's excellent. Now we have a way to get information to her. But we'll only have one shot at that. So don't schedule that tour until you hear from me." Manuel drained the last of his latte and stood.

"Wait! Can I tell Beau...please?"

Manuel sat back down. "Not yet. Remember our goal. You don't want to compromise her safety...or yours."

"I was afraid you'd say that," Jennifer looked sad. "I almost forgot!"

"What?"

"I found the red-haired woman...the one you told me to look for!"

"And where is she?"

"She's the principal at the International Academy. Her name is Amy!"

Manuel smiled. "That's excellent work, Jennifer. You can pat yourself on the back. We didn't know she was working there."

Ha! Maybe I'm not such a bad undercover operative after all! Jennifer would have to remind herself of that over and over to keep the secret from Beau that his sister was living nearby.

CHAPTER FORTY-TWO

Meredith realized she was trembling as she watched Jennifer drive off. Had Jennifer read the note she'd placed in the palm of her hand yet? Would she know how to contact the CIA? For now, Meredith comforted herself with the news that Ryan was safe! And he was living with his aunt and uncle nearby! What wonderful news! Meredith put her hands in her pockets in hopes they would quit shaking. She turned and headed back to her classroom. Why hadn't she thought to ask Jennifer to see a picture of him? Surely Jennifer had recognized her. Meredith ducked into the restroom and checked her appearance in the mirror. Granted, her hair was blond and extremely short now and she was going by Gretchen, but Jennifer was a smart cookie and Meredith was sure she had seen recognition in her eyes. She also knew Jennifer couldn't bring Ryan here.

Opening the door, she stepped back out into the hallway and almost literally ran into Amy. "Hi, Gretchen! How did the rest of the tour go with Mrs. Baldwin?"

"It went well. She's going to try to get her best friend to come in for a tour so that her son would have a friend here." The pair started heading back to Meredith's classroom.

Amy clapped her hands together. "That would be wonderful! You two must have made a connection! Good job! I'll give Mrs. Baldwin a few days to talk to her friend and then I'll reach out to her to schedule another tour."

"I'd be happy to conduct the tour if that would be of help," Meredith suggested.

"Absolutely you will. I have the feeling if those two transfer their children, more will follow." As they got to Meredith's classroom, Amy stopped. "Why don't you take the afternoon off? Your students can have a well-deserved break and you can too. I'll be sure to let our leaders know what an excellent ambassador you are. I'm sure they'll be giving you some credits."

Meredith smiled. "Thank you. That is very nice of you." She went into her classroom and grabbed her clear clutch... the only purse she was allowed to have. When she closed the door to her room and walked into the hall, Amy was gone. It was all Meredith could do to keep herself from skipping back to her apartment.

She bounded up the two flights of stairs and swiped her key fob to open the door. Vicki was at their small kitchen table eating a sandwich. "Hi! I thought you had classes this afternoon," she greeted Meredith.

"Amy cancelled them. She was so pleased with the tour I gave today that she gave me the afternoon off."

"Wow, that's very uncharacteristic of her! You must have really blown her away."

Meredith thought that was a poor choice of words. But then Vicki didn't know what had happened to her. Geoffrey! Jennifer had not mentioned Ryan's father. If he were alive, wouldn't he be taking care of Ryan? Or maybe he was being held captive like Meredith was. "I didn't really do anything out of the ordinary. I guess I just made a connection with the parent of a potential student."

Vicki shrugged. "Well anytime you impress the leaders, it's a good thing not only for you, but for me as well. I've been invited to one of their parties tomorrow night."

"Parties? What kind of party?"

"Don't know much about them, except they are late at night. It doesn't really matter as long as I get out of here. No offense, Gretchen, but babysitting you is not my favorite thing to do."

"Are you trying to tell me I should make a run for it while you're out?"

"Hardly! I'm sure they will send someone to take my place and even if they don't, those fences give a pretty nasty zing to whoever dares to climb them."

"Thanks for reminding me," Meredith said as she plopped down on her bunk bed.

Fatal Race

Alan Smith's car was not in the parking lot when Jennifer returned to the office. It was lunch time, but she'd been too excited to eat. Not eating was not good for the baby, she reminded herself. Fortunately, she had a stash of granola bars in her desk drawer that would tie her over until later this afternoon.

She yanked open the glass front door. Both Jack and Gordon were at their desks. "Hi, guys!"

"Hey Jennifer," Gordon greeted her.

Jennifer noticed Gordon was not wearing his usual smile. "What's the matter?"

"His boyfriend died," Jack muttered while staring at his computer screen.

"What?" Jennifer was confused. She sat down in a spare chair.

"Maybe you haven't heard on the news. An American was a victim in that bombing in Munich. It was Alex Hart... the owner of the gym where you and I work out. I...I just can't believe that guy is gone."

Jennifer nodded. "I heard. I knew him...knew him well, actually."

Jack perked up when he heard the last statement. "Oh dandy, you two had the same boyfriend?"

"Jack, this is nothing to joke about! For once can't you offer a little sympathy to someone?" Gordon glared at his coworker.

"Sorry! Sorry!" Jack put his hands up in the air signifying a truce.

"Actually he was my boyfriend…back when I was in college," Jennifer said softly.

"Aw shit! I didn't know that, Jennifer. You must be crushed," Gordon said.

"It's quite a shock. Have they said who's responsible?"

"Damned terrorists most likely," said Jack.

"I can't imagine why they would have been after Alex," Jennifer added.

"You know, I hadn't seen him for quite some time, like maybe three or four months," Gordon said. "I guess he must have been spending his time opening that health club over there."

Jennifer stood. "I better get back to work. Alan will probably be back soon." She headed down the hall just as another tear escaped down her cheek.

An hour later Alan Smith returned. He stopped by Jennifer's office. "So how was the tour of the International Academy?"

"I was very impressed with their philosophy."

Alan nodded, smiling. "But of course you were! It's a very different take from the public school system," he added placing a derogatory emphasis on "public school system."

"I don't have a lot of experience with any school system other than the ones I have attended. The language aspect is very intriguing."

"It's an essential component. Americans think English should be the international language," Alan's tone turned stern.

Fatal Race

He said Americans like he's not one of us. "With all due respect, it is the international language," Jennifer countered.

Alan snorted. His eyes grew hard. "For now, maybe. Anyway, you can't argue that the more languages one knows, the more versatile he can be."

Jennifer realized there was no purpose in debating with Alan. "Absolutely!"

Alan seemed pleased, as if he'd won her over. "So what is your next step? Have you decided to transfer your nephew?"

"Well, first, I need to discuss it with my husband. My concern is that Ryan has had a lot of change in his life in the past few months. He seems really happy where he is. However, I did tell them at the school that I would let my best friend know. Her son is Ryan's best friend. Maybe if we transfer them together, it would be fine."

Alan bent over and placed both hands on Jennifer's desk. "That sounds like an excellent plan. Trust me, you don't want to wait too long to get your nephew out of that school." He stood and exited her office.

Or what? Jennifer thought Alan's last statement sounded like a threat. She knew Beau would never in a million years agree to transfer Ryan to another school. Both she and Beau had been raised going to public school systems and were big proponents of them. They'd selected their neighborhood because it was part of an excellent school district. On the other hand, she'd have to play the game with Alan. Step one would be to convince Kate to go take a look at it. That wouldn't be too hard. Jennifer could guise it as a way to see where all the soccer players on their team were going to school now.

Jennifer wondered how long it would be before Manuel needed her to return to the academy to give Meredith a message. It couldn't be too long or Alan might get suspicious. He certainly was applying pressure for her to transfer Ryan.

Jennifer felt a knot in her stomach. Was Alan trying to help recruit more students to the school? Or did he want Ryan and his family out of Grandview Elementary?

Well what mattered most was that Ryan and his mother would be reunited soon. She snapped her fingers. Yes, she would be sure to show Meredith the picture of Ryan on his first day of kindergarten!

One thing Jennifer felt sure of: Meredith would be accompanying her son to the first day of first grade.

CHAPTER FORTY-THREE

Soccer practice was in full swing when Jennifer arrived at the practice field after work. Beau was leading a drill on passing while Drew was working with the team's goalies. It felt good to be outside in the fresh air which finally wasn't so hot. Jennifer parked and approached the bleachers. Kate was sitting alone.

"Well there you are!" Kate greeted her friend. "Beau said you might stop by."

Jennifer hugged her. "You look fabulous! How are you feeling?"

Kate tilted her head to the side. "Better. Yes, definitely better. Dr. Morrison got the pathology back today and said that there was nothing to indicate the miscarriage was my fault and that we can try again in about six weeks!" Kate lowered her voice. "And how are you doing with the news about Alex?"

Jennifer looked away. "In shock is the best way to describe it. I just can't imagine why he would have been targeted. I'm glad no one else was hurt. He could have had a gym full of members...including my husband."

"What?" Kate's well-manicured eyebrows shot up. "Beau was there?"

At that very moment, Beau looked over at Jennifer and waved. "Yes. He even confronted Alex. It's a long story and no longer matters."

Kate rolled her eyes. "You can tell me some other time. Here comes your husband."

"Hey!" Beau said as he kissed Jennifer on the cheek. "We should be done here in about ten minutes. It's been short-attention-span theater with these guys today. Mom said she would babysit tonight so I can take you out for dinner...if you feel like it that is."

Jennifer felt so wound up from her day that going out with her husband seemed like a wonderful idea. "That sounds perfect! I'll head home and change."

As Beau walked back toward the field he looked at Jennifer over his shoulder and winked.

"Okay, I probably shouldn't say this..." Kate began.

"But you will anyway..."

"What's he so happy about? Surely it's not because Alex is once and for all out of the picture."

"No. I'm sure that's not it." Jennifer decided not to share with Kate that Alex was going to help look for Meredith.

"He is definitely happy about something. I guess I'll find out soon."

"You better go get changed. Find your sexiest maternity outfit!"

Jennifer knew Kate was feeling happier since she was joking. "Well that will narrow down my choices for sure. Before I run off, I need to ask you something."

"Ask away!"

"My boss is pressuring me to transfer Ryan to this international academy. Evidently some of the former players on our team have left our school to go there." Jennifer put up her hand to stop Kate from interrupting. "Now before you say no, I just want to tell you that I have absolutely no intention of transferring Ryan anywhere. In fact, I'm not even going to tell Beau about it. I just need to appease my boss."

"And what do I have to do with this?" Kate asked hesitantly.

"I may need you to go look at the school with me. That way there'd be safety in numbers when I decline the transfer. Plus, maybe we'll see what's so great about it."

Kate thought about it for a few minutes. "Well, okay, but under one condition."

"What's that?"

"Drew can't find out. He'd hit the roof."

Jennifer stuck out her hand for Kate to shake. "Deal."

Bistro 31, located in the chic Highland Park Village in Dallas, was busy even for a week night. The restaurant had several tables for two along the windows that faced the sidewalk where well-heeled shoppers passed by. It was a great people watching place that had outstanding food and impeccable service. Jennifer wore a black chiffon sleeveless maternity dress. And despite the flattering style, she felt fat.

"You know you look stunning in that dress," Beau whispered in her ear as he helped her out of the car.

"That's sweet of you," Jennifer acquiesced.

Beau held open the restaurant door for her. "Ah, Mr. and Mrs. Baldwin. It's good to see you this evening," said Cameron, the manager. He hugged Jennifer. "You look beautiful."

"Thank you," Jennifer replied.

"I have your table ready. Follow me." Cameron escorted them to one of the window tables. "Philip will be right with you. Enjoy your dinners."

"This is so nice of you, Beau. I love this place. So good for people watching."

Beau sat down across from Jennifer. "We've had a lot going on and I just thought it was time for us to have a date."

"Hello, hello!" Philip said as he approached the table. "It's good to see you again. What can I get to start you off with? Wine, bubbles..." Philip trailed off as he noticed Jennifer's belly. "Or something non-alcoholic perhaps?"

Jennifer laughed. "Yes, I'm pregnant."

"Okay, I thought so but that's never a comment that I want to get wrong! How about Topo Chico with a twist of lime?"

"That sounds perfect."

"And for you, Mr. Dad-to-be?"

"I'll have the same."

"No, Beau, have a glass of wine. It won't bother me."

"A glass of bubbles, then."

"Before I go get those, let me tell you the specials. We have the shrimp with squid ink pasta. And we also have the halibut..."

"One of each," said Beau knowing that the squid ink pasta was Jennifer's favorite. "And we'll split a salad as well."

"Very good. I'll be back."

"I can't wait for them to put the Christmas lights up," said Jennifer. "It's so pretty when they are on."

"Almost as pretty as you are," replied Beau. Jennifer's radiant smile and perfect teeth were what had first caught his attention back when they were in college.

"Okay. What are you so happy about?"

Philip delivered their drinks and a basket of bread.

Beau took his flute of champagne in his hand. "I wrote over a million dollars in orders at the conference and another half a million came in today! Dr. Hunnicutt is ecstatic! He told me to take you out tonight...on him!"

Jennifer lifted her flute of Topo Chico. "Sweetheart, that's incredible! Congratulations!"

"It gets better. Dr. Hunnicutt wants me to start hiring more sales reps as soon as possible and while I'll still be selling and making commission, I'll also be running the sales force."

"Wow! You deserve it! It looks like the third time's a charm!"

The Baldwins clinked their flutes together. "To you, Mr. Sales Superstar," Jennifer said.

"And one more better piece of news," Beau said.

Jennifer waited.

"You can quit your job anytime."

Jennifer froze. She wasn't sure how to react. At least she was still smiling. "I don't know what to say. I'm totally caught off-guard."

"You don't have to quit tomorrow or anything. I just don't want you to get worn out playing mom to Ryan while carrying our little one! Just think about it!"

Jennifer relaxed. She would be able to postpone her "retirement" until her project for Eagle's Nest was complete. "I will. I am so very proud of you, Beau. You will make this company take off. I'm so glad you found someone nice to work for. Please thank him for this dinner."

"I will. Now Mom is heading back to New York tomorrow unless you want her to stay longer."

Jennifer took a sip of her drink. "She should go back or stay here longer...it's her call. She was a big help to me while you were gone."

"Well that's the bad news. I may have to be gone some in order to conduct these interviews. So if you want her to stay..."

"No, it's okay. Mom and Dad are supposed to be back the end of this week and I can always rely on Kate until then. When do you have to go?"

"Probably not until next week at the earliest. I have to get things set up."

Jennifer was actually happy that Beau would be out of town. It would give her a chance to meet with Manuel when she needed to and do some more investigating on her own. But part of her felt bad that Martha Baldwin's missing daughter was in the same town as she was. Maybe she should have her mother-in-law stay. Jennifer thought about it while she enjoyed her salad. No, Martha was tired. And it could take weeks or even months before all of this was resolved and Meredith could be reunited with her family.

Tonight was about Beau and his success. Jennifer decided to focus on that, wishing that she could give him the best piece of news...that his sister was alive and well and living just blocks from their house.

CHAPTER FORTY-FOUR

The stark lab was quiet except for the occasional rustle of newspaper caused by the five mice that were running around in their cage. Rachel unlocked the lab door and flicked on the fluorescent lights. It was only seven in the morning and at this hour no one was in the medical office. She hadn't been able to sleep since her last phone call with Walter. Walter...her one hope of finding Pierce... had let her down. Admitting he was at a dead-end in his investigation of Pierce's disappearance, he had informed her last night that he would be returning home today.

Rachel placed her purse and backpack on the small desk in the corner of the lab. She had no idea what her next step should be. Out of habit, she approached the counter in the far end of the lab and looked down at the mice as if they might tell her what she should do or where her husband was. Was Pierce even alive?

Seeing the mice were alive, Rachel turned and went back to her desk. She decided a review of the events leading up to Pierce's vanishing might help. There was a dry-erase board hanging on the wall next to her desk. Rachel grabbed one of the markers and wrote down the facts leading up to the last time she spoke with him.

- Pierce tried to dissuade her from going after Jennifer Baldwin.
- The formula was working but had also killed a few mice.
- Pierce needed to modify the elements so that the mice lived, but was concerned it could alter the taste of the compound.
- Pierce had actually tasted the compound, laughing that he wasn't pregnant so it wouldn't hurt him and he would have to ingest hundreds of doses to endanger his life.
- Pierce dictated the changes to the formula.
- Mr. Smith contacted her because Pierce hadn't returned her calls. Needed her to finalize the formula and mass produce it for him ASAP.
- Mr. Smith promised to obtain FDA approval of Cardiovax.

Rachel stepped back from the dry-erase board and studied her notes. She erased the first point. Pierce's inane comment regarding Jennifer Baldwin couldn't possibly have anything to do with his going AWOL. They had barely discussed it. She also erased the second bullet point. So now she was getting to the crux of the experiment. Pierce had been concerned about the compound having any flavor to it. He had actually tasted it and had been fine. But had he tasted too much and died? But if he had died, wouldn't someone have found his body? It wasn't that big of an island. And how far could he have gone? They didn't have a car so he would either have used his moped or Ubered to go anywhere and chances are someone would have seen him. Rachel drew a question mark next to the bullet points relating to Pierce's concern about the taste of the formula.

That left Rachel with Pierce dictating to her his changes for the formula and Mr. Smith's urgent call about not being able to contact Pierce and his needing the formula mass produced. Something didn't seem right. She and Pierce were about to make a very large chunk of money. Rachel paced around the lab, circling the counter where she had concocted the formula and mass produced it.

Mr. Smith had not been in touch with her again so maybe she was free to return to Grand Cayman and search for Pierce herself. Rachel made a second circle around the counter looking at the test tubes, microscope and pipettes lined up perfectly, waiting to be used in another experiment. If she returned now, though, she wouldn't have accomplished her main goal of coming back to Texas: offing Jennifer Baldwin. While not an easy task, it was certainly easier now that she knew the components from their other compound that could cause death. Rachel wasn't exactly sure she could eliminate all the taste though and that would be difficult to test.

After her fourth "lap" around the counter, Rachel came up with a plan. She had five mice left. That meant she could easily make five iterations of what she now liked to think of as Jennifer's special water. She'd offer one mouse both regular water and Jennifer's concoction and see if the mouse refused to drink it. Ha! She was more of a scientist than she gave herself credit for! Pierce had also given her the formula for translating his compound from mice to men so she could use that same calculation...only just to be on the safe side, she'd up it a little bit. She only had one shot with this special water. It had to work after only a few swallows.

As soon as Rachel completed formulating Jennifer's water, she would approach Amy and ask her to make bottles for her new water brand. Since she wouldn't need a lot of bottles, she thought Amy could get them done in a matter of days. If she started right away, she could potentially be done by the end of the week. Rachel's plan was to deliver a gift basket to Jennifer at her office soon. Jennifer would drink the water, die and then Rachel could get on the next flight back to Grand Cayman. She was getting more confident that she would be able to find Pierce. She never should have left such an important task to Walter. He had no detective experience.

Diane Cobalt

Rachel stopped her pacing and opened the drawer in the counter where she kept Pierce's formula. She ran down the list of ingredients and then walked to the closet where the chemicals were stored. Yes! She had plenty of the fatal elements. Rachel gingerly plucked the bottle off the shelf and placed it on the counter next to a beaker. Carefully, she measured out the dose Pierce had prescribed. Next, she poured in the chemical that would neutralize the taste of the poison. She considered adding extra, but was afraid to dilute the effect of the first. Rachel poured the duo into a test tube, capped it and shook it to blend the two together. There! This was so quick and easy! She took a pipette and extracted enough to place in the mouse's "water bowl" and marked it "P" with a Sharpie. She filled a second bowl with regular tap water.

Crossing the room to the mouse hotel, she carefully placed each bowl in an isolated section. Rachel then slid open one of the doors allowing one mouse to access this part of the glassed-in cage.

She noted the time: five after eight. She'd check on the mouse in fifteen minutes. "It's happy hour, little guy," she said aloud. The mouse seemed to ignore both bowls. "Hmm, not thirsty yet?" Rachel asked. He would be soon.

Fifteen minutes later, the mouse had not drunk out of either bowl. Rachel was losing what little patience she had. Maybe a little salty cheese would help. She went to the lab cooler and extracted a small chunk of Swiss cheese and placed it in the special section of the cage. Instantly, the mouse nibbled at it. Rachel smiled.

Fatal Race

A ringing noise across the room jolted her back to reality. It was her cell. She ran to grab it out of her purse, hoping it would be Pierce. She looked at the caller ID. It was Walter.

"Hi, Walter," Rachel answered.

"Hi. My flight leaves here in about an hour. I fly through Miami, change planes and get back to Dallas about four this afternoon. I was wondering if you wanted to meet for dinner tonight."

Rachel considered Walter's invitation for a few minutes. What else did she have to do this evening? She'd need to talk to Amy at some point, but that wouldn't take long. "Sure. What time and where?"

"Let's say seven so I have time to battle rush hour traffic, get home and change. Would you mind meeting me closer to my place?"

"No. That's fine. How about Mi Cocina?"

"Perfect. I'll see you at seven unless you hear from me otherwise."

"Okay. Have a safe trip." Rachel suddenly realized that Walter was her only living relative; the only person who cared about her.

When mouse number one was still alive at ten o'clock, Rachel decided to make a second, stronger batch of the compound. She switched out the "mouse bowl" marked with a "P" and replaced it with one marked "P2". She picked the current mouse up by its tail and put it back in with its four other buddies. Then she extracted a different mouse, again by the tail, and placed it in the separated section.

The Swiss cheese she'd put in the cage had been eaten by mouse number one, so she went to the fridge and got a chunk for mouse number two.

Mouse number two ignored the cheese and went right for the "P2" concoction. He sniffed it and immediately went to the plain water which he lapped up. Damn! The taste was too strong. Rachel went back to Pierce's formula and modified it again.

By three that afternoon, Rachel was mixing her fourth batch of the compound. She was getting worried that she would never get it right. Then what would she do? Jennifer Baldwin had no right to still be on this earth after killing her sister.

While she waited for mouse number four to hopefully lap up the fourth version of the compound, Rachel decided to erase her bullet points, just in case the cleaning crew could actually read! She approached the board and studied what remained.

The last two bullet points had to do with Mr. Smith. He wanted the formula mass produced. Okay, nothing wrong with that. Rachel had even offered to give him the formula...which he didn't want! She remembered at the time thinking that was strange. He'd paid for it and could reproduce it anytime he wanted. So why didn't he?

Rachel looked at the last point. Mr. Smith had promised to obtain FDA approval for Cardiovax for them. Oh God! She froze. That was it! They would make millions of dollars off the sale of the Cardiovax formula. Pierce was the only one who had the correct formula. And Mr. Smith knew that.

CHAPTER FORTY-FIVE

Mi Cocina was packed. Walter had already texted Rachel that he was running about half an hour late so she knew he hadn't already turned his name in. Rachel approached the hostess stand. "How long for a table for two?" she asked.

The woman looked at her computer screen. "Thirty to forty minutes."

Rachel nodded. "Okay. The name's...put it under Walter."

"Okay, Ms. Walter. Here's a pager. It will vibrate when your table is ready. You're welcome to wait in the bar."

The bar was two-deep with people waiting to be served. Rachel had opted not to Uber so she shouldn't drink anyway— not that she couldn't use a frozen margarita! On her drive to the restaurant she debated with herself on whether or not to enlist Walter's help with Mr. Smith. Walter would probably chastise her for dealing with someone who was less than ethical. Maybe she didn't need to share with Walter what Mr. Smith had asked them to do. Yes! That was the answer—just tell Walter about Mr. Smith's promise to get FDA approval for Cardiovax. One thing was for sure, Rachel could not deal with Mr. Smith alone. She'd only met Alan Smith once for dinner and he'd definitely given her the creeps. She wondered if Pierce had ever met him in person.

"Hi, Rachel," Walter came up behind her. "Thank heavens I Ubered here. I would never have found a parking place. It's crazy busy!"

Rachel gave Walter a hug. "I know. I feel like I had to park in Fort Worth."

"Come on. Our table's ready," Walter said.

"But my pager hasn't gone off yet," Rachel responded.

Walter smiled. "I know the owners. I never wait for a table here."

"Well thanks for telling me that ahead of time, Cousin!" Rachel followed Walter to a corner booth. The two sat down and looked at the menu.

"What are we drinking tonight?" asked the server.

"I guess I'll have a frozen house margarita," Rachel said. "But only one. I'm driving."

"Make mine on the rocks," added Walter.

The server nodded and walked away.

"Walter, I want to thank you for taking the time to look for Pierce," Rachel began. "I know how busy you are and that you did your best..."

"I'm just sorry I wasn't successful."

"Look, I have a very bad feeling that Pierce met with foul play."

"What do you mean?" Walter sounded surprised. In his mind, he'd chalked up Pierce's disappearance as his way of leaving his wife. Walter felt that sooner or later Pierce would turn up with someone else on his arm.

Rachel took a sip of her water. "I think our client may have had him killed."

Walter's eyes widened. "That's ridiculous! What motive would your client have?"

"Money. Our client promised us that once Pierce perfected this formula he ordered he would get the FDA to approve Cardiovax."

"Who is this client? He must have a lot of powerful connections to be able to promise FDA approval."

"His name is Mr. Smith."

Walter laughed. "You're joking."

"Do you know him?"

Walter couldn't believe how naïve his cousin could be. "Rachel, Smith is one of the most common surnames in the United States. I'm sure I know quite a few Smiths. What's his first name?"

"Alan. I met with him once, right after I got here." Rachel started feeling really stupid. "And I don't think he's from the U.S. He has a strange British accent."

The server brought them their drinks. "Can I bring you an appetizer? Some queso perhaps?"

"Just bring us a Cocina Platter," Walter practically barked. He wanted the waiter gone.

"Yes, very good, sir."

Walter put his hand up to his forehead. "What have you gotten yourself into?"

"I didn't get us into anything. Pierce is the one who agreed to work for Mr. Smith. I don't think he ever even met him in person. All I know is that we agreed on a sum of money for this project. Mr. Smith transferred a portion of the amount into our bank."

"Into your bank account in Grand Cayman?"

Rachel nodded. "Isn't that what I said?"

"That means the funds are untraceable. It's not like our banks here in the states."

"Okay. I know that. I'm not a complete idiot." Rachel took a long sip of her margarita.

"Let me think. Do you have an address for him?"

"No."

"And we're not sure what country he's from or lives in?"

"No."

"Phone number?"

"Yes! He's called me twice. Let me look it up on my recent calls." Rachel dug her phone out of her purse and punched in her code. She scrolled through her list of recent calls. "Here it is." Rachel handed her phone to Walter.

He tilted his head. "Well, that's a positive thing. It's a local number."

"So that means he probably lives around here." Rachel tried to sound enthused.

"Yes and that means we've narrowed it down to several million people." Walter said sarcastically.

Rachel hung her head. She received a bit of a respite while the waiter brought their appetizer. After he left, she made a suggestion. "Can't we do one of those reverse number checks?"

"Yes, but most cell phone numbers don't give you any info. I think your best plan of attack is to call Mr. Smith. Ask him how soon he expects approval from the FDA. See if you can meet with him…of course I'll go with you to that meeting. There's no way you're dealing with this character by yourself, especially if he's done harm to Pierce."

Rachel nodded somberly. "I know you videoed our condo and it looked normal. If Mr. Smith or one of his associates had kidnapped Pierce, something would have looked out of place."

"If they abducted him from your condo…"

"This is a nightmare."

Walter felt bad for his cousin. Granted, she wasn't the most ethical, upstanding person he knew. Who was he kidding? This was the woman who wanted to kill Jennifer Baldwin. So why did he so desperately want to help her?

"I'll make a deal with you. I have several acquaintances that specialize in this sort of thing."

"That sounds cryptic."

"Do you want to hear the deal or not?" Walter was losing his patience.

Rachel nodded.

"Okay, then. I'll help you track down Mr. Smith and find out what he knows."

"If I...?"

"If you agree to leave Jennifer Baldwin and her family alone."

Rachel picked at the quesadilla in front of her with her fork. "You drive a hard bargain, Cousin. But I have to find Pierce."

"Deal?" asked Walter holding out his hand.

"Deal," echoed Rachel as she took his hand knowing full well she had no intention of upholding her part of the bargain.

It was almost eleven o'clock when Rachel finally turned off onto the street where she and Jennifer Baldwin lived. The Baldwin's home was two houses down from hers and on the opposite side of the street. The street gently curved so Rachel couldn't see the entire house from her bedroom window. As she inched her car by, she noted that all their lights were off. It made sense that the little family would be all tucked into bed by now.

Rachel brought her attention back to the road in front of her. One house down from the Baldwins, cars lined both sides of the street. "What the hell?" Rachel said out loud. "Now I'll never find a place to park." She turned down the side street just past where she lived in hopes of finding a spot there...nothing. Mercedes, Porsches, BMWs, and even a Maserati took up all the available parking. There were even cars parked in the driveway. Rachel went around the block in hopes that someone might be leaving. After her second loop around, a couple came walking down the sidewalk, put a large looking cylinder in the backseat of their Porsche Carrera and sped off. The gap left by their car was small, but then so was the car Rachel was driving. She expertly squeezed her car into the spot and headed to the front door.

Before she could turn the knob, the door swung open. "Name?" grunted a very tall and large man.

"It's Paige. And I live here."

"Sorry," the giant grunted as he checked a list of names. "You're right."

Rachel huffed by him and stood at the edge of the living room looking for her landlord. There were several couples milling around and speaking to men dressed in white long-sleeved dress shirts and black pants. Could they be Jehovah's witnesses? Rachel laughed. Hardly, not one of them was Caucasian.

Although she was exhausted, Rachel decided it was time for her to join the party. At a minimum, she needed to find Amy. Everyone seemed to have a drink in their hand. Wondering where the bar was set up, Rachel headed toward the kitchen. She could use a glass of wine. But when she turned the corner, the kitchen was empty.

Wait a minute! The other night she heard someone say something about the wine cellar which had to be in the basement. Rachel cut through the kitchen and headed to the laundry room. The door was open and she could hear voices coming from the other side of the door that led to the basement. She twisted the knob, opened the door and found herself face-to-face with a large, menacing man.

"Name tag or bottle of wine?" he asked.

Rachel looked down at her shirt. "Shoot, it must have fallen off. Do I need to get another one?"

"Sorry, I'm not supposed to let anyone down here who isn't wearing one."

Just as Rachel tried peering around the man, a couple came up the stairs behind him forcing the man to turn sideways and giving Rachel a partial view of the wine cellar.

During her brief view, Rachel concluded that the wine cellar was really just a private meeting room. She saw no wine bottles. It appeared that the room hadn't ever been finished out. There was a long folding table with metal folding chairs surrounding it. Several of the men wearing long sleeved white shirts were sitting at the table. One of the men unrolled what looked like blueprints and was pointing out something to the others.

The couple reached the top of the stairs, causing Rachel to back up into the small laundry room. They now stood between her and the gate keeper. Rachel decided to give up on gaining entry and resumed her search for Amy.

She spotted a friendly looking woman and approached her. "Excuse me, two questions. First, where did you get the drink? I'm parched. And second, have you seen Amy?" Rachel asked the woman whose name tag said "Vicki".

Vicki turned to face Rachel. "The bar's out by the pool. And yes, I have seen Amy. Do you know her?"

"I do. She's actually my landlady. How do you know Amy?"

Vicki nodded "I work with her at her school. It's called International Academy. They've been very successful recruiting top students for their program. I think she went into her room to look for something"

Amy was part of a school? Rachel was confused. She thought Amy worked for a bottled water company. "I didn't know she did that. I've been pretty busy since I moved in and haven't had a chance to talk to her." Okay this really didn't make any sense. "So all of these people here are part of the school?"

Vicki shrugged. "I'm not sure. I teach there. My name is Vicki." Vicki held out her hand. "And you are...?"

"Paige," Rachel felt her blouse where a name tag would have been. "My name tag fell off somewhere," she laughed. "Who are the dudes in the white shirts?"

Vicki looked around the room. "They're the founders of the school."

"So they're foreign?"

Vicki looked away. "Hey, someone across the room is waving me over. Nice meeting you."

Hmm, Rachel thought, Vicki didn't want to answer that question. This party was getting weirder and Rachel had had enough. She needed to ask Amy about creating the special water bottles and she really wanted to get to bed. Crossing the room, Rachel walked down a short hallway to the master bedroom. The door was closed. Rachel knocked and hearing a noise, took it to be an invitation to enter.

But when she opened the door, she immediately realized her mistake. A middle aged man with a bad blond toupee was naked and thrusting away on top of Amy who was moaning. The two were so into the throws of passion that they didn't hear her open or close the bedroom door. Rachel's question would have to wait. But even with her limited view of Amy's lover, she was fairly sure the man was Alan Smith.

CHAPTER FORTY-SIX

There were only two cars in the parking lot outside of the Eagle's Nest. Jennifer recognized one as Manuel's and the other as the receptionist's. Fortunately EN's headquarters were very close to Ryan's elementary school. So it had been easy this morning to drop off the boys and to meet Manuel without being too late for work. As always, Jennifer checked her rearview mirror to make sure she wasn't being watched before exiting her car.

The coast looked as clear as the autumn sky so Jennifer got out of her car and entered the building. Fall was finally trying to blow into Richardson. Jennifer appreciated the cooler weather because she was always hot carrying their baby.

Manuel was waiting for her in the lobby. "Good morning," he greeted her.

Jennifer shook his hand. "Hi."

"Do you have just a few minutes so I can update you?"

Jennifer nodded, smiling at the receptionist.

"Great. Let's head to the conference room." Manuel escorted Jennifer so she didn't need to check in. The conference room door rolled up as soon as Manuel placed his hand on the picture hanging to its right. He motioned for Jennifer to walk in ahead of him and take a seat.

Vincent was sitting in his usual spot at the end of the conference room table. "Jennifer! Welcome. Please, have a seat."

Jennifer sat down near Vincent. Manuel sat across from her. She hadn't expected Vincent to be present. Was this good news? "Are we getting close to freeing Meredith?" It was the first thing on her mind today. Ryan had nightmares last night, calling out for his mother several times. Both Beau and Jennifer had been up and down the stairs all night. Jennifer remembered that she needed to tell Manuel about the cars on her street that were coming and going during the wee hours of the morning. It was the second time this week there had been what looked like a party of wealthy adults.

Vincent nodded. "Actually, we are. But, there's been a lot of 'chatter' amongst those in the cell that we are watching. We must proceed with extreme caution right now. And we need your help."

"Jennifer, we suspect that the terrorists are about to execute...a small scale attack. Our intelligence tells us that if successful, this attack will be replicated across the country," Manuel added.

"What kind of attack?" Jennifer asked. Up until now everything she had observed only hinted at money laundering.

"We're not sure," Vincent replied. "We do know it's something they can easily copy."

"So they're not going to fly planes into buildings again?"

"We've had no indication of that. Nor have we heard anything related to our transportation system. We think Meredith can get us the final pieces of information we need to avert this attack or attacks," Vincent reported.

Jennifer felt sick to her stomach. This was scaring her. "Does this have something to do with the International Academy?"

"The IA is most definitely a training ground for future terrorists. Their goal is to radicalize young adults, especially American citizens, so they can achieve their ultimate objective."

"Which is...?" Jennifer asked.

"To destroy the United States from within," Manuel answered.

"We're a huge country. That's going to be impossible," Jennifer suggested.

"We are large both geographically and in population," Vincent agreed. "That's why it's necessary for them to recruit our own citizens. Despite recent incidents across the nation that have been carried out by different races, most Americans are only suspicious of Middle Easterners and Muslims. There are training compounds scattered throughout our country...some even here in Texas. They are being used to radicalize ex-cons. Then they are transporting them to 'schools' where they learn languages and the necessary strategies of that particular terrorist cell."

"Wow! I didn't notice anything like that going on in the school," Jennifer commented.

"And you wouldn't have seen it there. Down the street is their 'high school' where the actual training is going on," Manuel added.

Vincent checked his watch. "Look, I know you need to get to work soon so let me get to your assignment. We need you to get this phone to Meredith." Vincent slid a very small, black iPhone to Jennifer. And we need you to get it to her ASAP."

Jennifer took the phone which fit in the palm of her hand. It was thin and sleek, very high tech looking. "Okay. I don't know if I can accomplish that today. My idea is to take my best friend with me on the guise that she's interested in the school for her son."

Vincent smiled. "Tomorrow will be fine; but today would be better."

"That's it? That's all you want me to do?"

"Yes. Without you, we can't accomplish this very important part of our plan."

Jennifer nodded. "Okay. I'll see if I can get there today."

"Great," Vincent said. "Do you have any questions?"

Jennifer remembered the party across the street. It seemed insignificant in comparison to the potential attack, but she decided to tell them anyway. "No questions, just an observation. You may want to look into the late night soirees they are having two houses down and across the street from us. There are very fancy cars parked up and down our street with people coming and going until about two or three in the morning. Maybe it's a drug house?"

"Manuel, call Charles and have his guys get on that. Jennifer, if you can get any pictures of the party guests, please forward them to Manuel," Vincent instructed. Jennifer was surprised he was taking so much interest in her report.

Jennifer stood. "I will. Actually I do have one question and you probably know what it is."

Vincent nodded, knowingly. "Our intel is indicating the attack will occur within the week. Until then, Meredith has to remain with her captors."

Jennifer took a deep breath and nodded. "Okay, then. The race is on."

On her way to work, Jennifer called Kate. "Hey friend, I need your help today."

"Sure. What do you need?" Kate replied.

"Could you swing a visit to the International Academy with me if I can get an appointment this afternoon? I know it's short notice, but the rest of my week is a little crazy at work and I can spare an hour then."

"As long as we are done in time to pick up the boys from school, I can do it," Kate replied.

Just the sound of her best friend's voice soothed Jennifer's anxiety of the events to come.

"Thanks, Kate. You're the best! I'll see if I can get a tour at one. Meet me there?"

"Sounds like a plan."

Jennifer immediately called Amy at the International Academy to set up an appointment. She didn't know what she would do if Meredith weren't available. "Hello, Amy? Hi, it's Jennifer Baldwin. I took a tour the other day..."

"Yes. Hi, Jennifer. I'm sorry I didn't get to see you before you left. Is there a question I can answer for you?" Amy didn't sound quite as perky this morning.

"Would it be possible for me to bring my friend by for a tour about one o'clock this afternoon? She's interested in seeing if your school might be a match for her son. And she's intrigued by your language philosophy." Jennifer stopped herself. She almost said Meredith's name. "Would Gretchen be available then?"

"Let me check today's schedule," Amy replied. Jennifer could hear typing in the background. "Yes, actually that time would be perfect. Gretchen does have a class at two so she would need to be done with your tour by then, but I can always take over and answer any remaining questions."

"Great! We will see Gretchen at one."

Jennifer pulled into the parking lot in front of Data Shield. She texted Kate to confirm the appointment then headed inside. The lights were off. Jack and Gordon weren't there and neither was Alan. That was unusual, but fortuitous. She would be able to get most of her work done prior to the tour.

Kate and Jennifer entered the International Academy promptly at one o'clock that afternoon. The receptionist had them take a seat in the lobby while she paged Gretchen.

Gretchen, Gretchen, Gretchen. I must remember to use that name. Jennifer was nervous that she would say Meredith. For what seemed like the hundredth time, Jennifer gently felt the outline of the black phone in her jacket pocket. She must remember to somehow get the phone in the hands of her sister-in-law.

Within five minutes, Gretchen opened the door to the lobby. "Hi there! I'm Gretchen," she introduced herself to Kate. "And welcome back," she smiled at Jennifer. "If you two ladies are ready, follow me and we'll start the tour."

Kate, who always stood very straight and was five foot nine without heels, towered over Gretchen who was only five foot three. "You have a lovely facility here."

"Thank you. They've put a lot of money and effort into developing this school. Do you also have a son who might be interested in attending here?"

"Yes. My son, Chris, is a kindergartner. Jennifer probably told you that he is best buddies with her nephew, Ryan."

Was it just Jennifer or did it seem like Meredith was more relaxed today? Her face lit up when Kate said Ryan. Now might be a good time to show her a picture of the boys.

Diane Cobalt

"Actually I have a picture of them on my phone," Jennifer said, handing her phone to Gretchen. "Ryan's on the left and Chris is on the right," she added hastily realizing "Gretchen" wouldn't know what Ryan looked like.

Gretchen studied the picture closely. "They look like very nice young boys. Chris looks a lot like you," she said to Kate.

Kate couldn't help herself. She beamed. "I hear that a lot."

Gretchen repeated the same tour she had given Jennifer just a few days earlier. They ended in Gretchen's classroom. Jennifer had to figure out a way to hand her the phone without the cameras seeing. She looked around. There was no way she could do anything in this classroom. She'd have to hold out until they ended in the lobby and hope that Amy didn't show up.

"If you two ladies don't have any further questions, we'll swing by the science presentation before I take you back to the lobby. My class begins in about ten minutes. I can always grab Amy to answer any more questions you might have, though."

"No! I mean I think you've answered all our questions. Right, Kate?"

Kate took the hint from Jennifer. "Right. You were very thorough, Gretchen."

The trio entered the hall. Gretchen walked them to the gym. They stood in the doorway. A group of two teenagers were demonstrating gases and their flammability to a class of younger students. The kids squealed with delight as the older students flicked a lighter causing a small bang. "Sometimes our students from the high school practice their presentations on the younger students here," Gretchen whispered.

Kate and Jennifer nodded and then followed her past the lobby and into the foyer by the front door. "Well then. I hope we get the privilege of educating your sons."

Kate turned to leave and Jennifer looked at Meredith directly in the eyes as she held out her hand. "Thank you for your time, Gretchen."

Meredith shook Jennifer's hand which held the phone. She unobtrusively extracted it from Jennifer's palm into her own. "You're quite welcome, Mrs. Baldwin. You two take good care of those boys."

Jennifer exited the building. Kate was waiting in the parking lot for her. "There's no way in hell I'd transfer Chris here," she said. "Although Gretchen seemed very nice."

"I agree."

"In fact, every time I looked at Gretchen, Beau's face popped into my mind." Kate shrugged.

Jennifer frowned. She hadn't considered Kate might notice a resemblance. "Huh, I didn't see any similarities. Well, thanks for going today. I'll see you at soccer practice?"

Kate hugged her friend. "My pleasure and I'll see you then."

Jennifer got in her car. She'd accomplished her assignment.

CHAPTER FORTY-SEVEN

The small black iPhone, a model made only for the CIA, lived in Meredith's pocket during the two German classes she taught that afternoon. She didn't dare take it out. There were too many cameras positioned in strategic locations throughout the school. Meredith would have to wait until she was alone in the apartment. As thrilled as she was to receive a means of contact with the outside world, Meredith was ecstatic to have seen a recent picture of her son. Ryan looked happy. She was thankful that Beau and Jennifer had taken him under their wing. Jennifer seemed like an excellent mother as did her friend Kate. At night when she was alone with her thoughts, Meredith wondered if Ryan had forgotten about her.

In just a few minutes, the bell would ring indicating school was out for the day and she could head back to her apartment. Vicki had still been asleep this morning when Meredith left for school which wasn't surprising since Vicki hadn't returned to their apartment until three this morning. It must have been quite a party, Meredith thought. Vicki hadn't left until almost eleven to go to the shindig. She'd taken Meredith's key, essentially locking her in their unit until her return. The only way in or out of the apartment was via a key swipe. Meredith thought that was preferable to having a "babysitter" while Vicki was away.

The ringing of the bell startled her. "Auf Wiedersehen," she said to her class as they filed out of the room. Next week she would be teaching a class at the high school. That might allow her some more freedom. After the last student left, Meredith grabbed her clear tote and headed into the hallway. Hopefully she would make it to the door without being stopped. Occasionally, one of the guards searched her tote.

She was only three steps away from the door to the back of the school when she heard her name being called. "Gretchen! Wait!"

"Gretchen" turned around. It was Amy.

"Hi, Amy."

"I'm glad I caught you before you left for the day," Amy sounded out of breath.

"What can I do for you?"

"I need you to come to my office. Now."

"Gretchen" turned around as nonchalantly as she could and followed Amy to her office. Once inside, Amy motioned for her to close the door.

Oh no, thought Meredith. They saw Jennifer give me the phone.

"Have a seat," ordered Amy.

Meredith sat down, but said nothing.

"This is about Jennifer Baldwin."

"What about her?" Meredith asked, waiting for her to ask for the phone.

"I'm getting a lot of...pressure from the founders to process her little boy into our school as quickly as possible," Amy explained.

It seemed Meredith had dodged a bullet. "He's not *her* little boy. He is her nephew."

"Nephew, son, it doesn't matter," Amy literally waved away Meredith's comment. "Although, I have yet to hear the story about how the Baldwins came to have custody of Ryan."

"They have custody of him?"

"Well, yeah, or they couldn't enroll him in school," Amy said as if Meredith was stupid.

"I wouldn't know. I don't have kids," she lied.

"Anyway, I wanted your assessment of Mrs. Baldwin and her friend, Mrs. Lange."

Meredith lifted her shoulders. "They seem fine, but I'm not really sure if they fit in with our...culture here." She had to say something to prevent them from transferring Ryan here where he might see his mother.

"My thoughts exactly. As eager as we are to share our view of the world with others, we have to keep in mind that not all of them will agree with us. And what do we call those who don't agree with us, Gretchen?" Amy was testing her.

Dead? "Infidels."

Amy nodded. "That's correct. Unfortunately, that's not what our founders want to hear. One founder in particular, Mr. Smith, thinks Jennifer Baldwin will be an easy target to get on our side."

"What about her husband? Do you know anything about him?"

"Exactly! We know very little. Until we do, I will recommend to Mr. Smith that Ryan Baldwin and his little friend stay where they are."

Meredith nodded in agreement. "Do you think Mr. Smith will accept your recommendation?"

Amy's eyes glimmered. Her lips curved upward. "Oh yeah. He will if he wants to continue receiving my favors!"

Meredith was pretty sure she didn't want to know the details of Amy's last comment. "Is there anything else?" she asked.

"No. That's all. Thank you for your input, Gretchen. You're free to go."

Free to go! Not exactly, thought Meredith. She stood carefully so Amy wouldn't notice the bulge in her pocket. Carefully, Meredith walked down the hall once again toward the back of the school. She pushed open the door and walked steadily across the parking lot and soccer field. She fought the urge to run up the stairs, knowing there were outside cameras as well. Pulling the key fob out of her other pocket, Meredith unlocked the door. The apartment was empty!

She kicked off her shoes and crawled under the covers of her bunk bed. There, she took the phone out of her pocket and turned it on. Three text messages appeared. She knew from her training in Quantico that these messages would be visible for no more than ten seconds and then would disappear from her phone.

The first two messages were from her boss. He was glad to hear she was alive and back stateside. His second message informed her that Geoffrey had indeed died in the bombing. Meredith hurried to read the third message before the meaning of the second text sunk in. The final text was from a local number, a man named Manuel Garcia. He was working with local and federal authorities to take down a terrorist cell. There had been an increase in chatter indicating an attack within their community was imminent. If she learned of any details, she was to call or text him using the phone.

Shit! That meant Ryan was in danger. Meredith would have to figure out a way to get more information. And that source would have to be Vicki. Just as Meredith quietly slipped the phone inside her pillow case, Vicki burst into the room.

"Hey there! I hope I didn't wake you when I came in early this morning," she greeted Meredith.

"Nope, I was totally out," Meredith lied. "How was the party?"

Vicki put the bag of groceries she'd been holding on the counter. "Well if I told you, I'd have to kill you," she laughed.

Meredith did not laugh. "Then don't tell me."

"I'm just shittin' you. You know that's what people in the FBI slash CIA say."

Meredith simply nodded. "Yes, I've heard the phrase a time or two."

"Well, Meredith, this party was actually a clandestine meeting of some of the school's founders and students."

Meredith froze. Had Vicki called her Meredith? "My name is Gretchen."

"No it's not," said Vicki. "It's Meredith Matthews."

Meredith's training had taught her never to admit her identity. "Where'd you get that name?"

Vicki smiled. "You were in the Frankfurt bombing. Your husband, Geoffrey, died in it. Jennifer Baldwin is your sister-in-law and their nephew, Ryan, is your son."

Meredith chuckled. "And just where did you come up with that story?"

"From your CIA dossier."

Meredith got out of her bed and stood face-to-face with Vicki. "I don't know what you're talking about."

Vicki smiled. "Yes you do. The reason I've read your dossier is because I'm an agent too."

"What?" Meredith frantically looked around the room for the cameras and microphones she knew were there.

"Not to worry, friend. I wiped this place clean about an hour ago. No one's been in since. I'll have to replace it all in a few minutes or they'll come looking to see what happened to all their espionage equipment. So listen up. Jennifer Baldwin is working as an undercover operative to help take down this terrorist group. She was supposed to give you a phone today. It's how we are to communicate with them."

"I've got it. You're really CIA?" Meredith was incredulous. "You fooled me."

"Hopefully I've fooled everyone. Anyway, my condolences about your husband. I didn't know him personally, but heard about all his accolades. And I've heard about yours as well. But now the stakes are high. Your son is living in this community so we've got to stop these bastards once and for all."

Meredith choked back her tears for her dearly departed husband. There would be time for those later. "Agreed. What's the plan?"

"We keep our ears and eyes open. The party I went to last night was loaded with founders who were holding strategy sessions in the basement. I wasn't allowed to go down to the 'wine cellar' as they called it. I was only able to mix and mingle with some of the students who are in my class. We need to find out what they are planning. There's another party Thursday night and I'll be there. Your sister-in-law is working for the head founder, a man by the name of Alan Smith. Mr. Smith was bopping our principal Amy last night at the party. I want to see if he shows up there again."

"So is she part of this scheme? She seems too..."

"Perky and American?" Vicki finished.

"Yes. Exactly."

"Well yes she's part of their scheme and in reality she's neither perky nor American. Amy has had countless surgeries to make her look more like one of us. The trouble is these days, race can't be a consideration used to determine the good guys from the bad ones. Just like they told us in spy school: be careful who you trust."

"Agreed. I'll see if I can start teaching my class at the high school sooner. I'm scheduled to be there next week."

"Good. Now help me replace these recon devices before they realize they're not working. I made a map on the counter of where each one attaches."

Meredith nodded. "But first, one thing."

"What's that?" asked Vicki.

"Thank you for having my back…you're a saint!"

CHAPTER FORTY-EIGHT

Dr. Hunnicutt's office was empty. It was seven fifteen on Wednesday morning when Beau unlocked the front door and made his way to his office. It would only take him a few minutes to grab some additional marketing materials that he'd left on his desk before he flew to Houston for the day; so he didn't bother locking the door behind him or turning on any lobby lights. While he was there, he also needed to put a few more RPPMDs in his bag. A cardiovascular surgeon was implanting one of the new devices this morning during a procedure. Dr. Hunnicutt was already in Houston and would assist during the surgery. The doctor was hoping that a colleague of the surgeon performing today's surgery would want to try out his device tomorrow on another patient and he'd asked Beau to bring some extra units to have on hand.

Fatal Race

It didn't take Beau more than two minutes to unlock the cabinet that held the devices and collect more marketing pamphlets. He zipped them into his bag and hurriedly headed back to the front door. He had just over an hour to make his flight.

As Beau stepped into the dark hallway, he collided with someone. "Sorry I didn't see you," was the first thing that came to his mind. Judging by the white coat the woman wore, he assumed she was one of Dr. Hunnicutt's PA's. "I didn't know anyone was here."

Rachel picked up her bag which had fallen to the floor and tried not to look directly at Beau. "No worries. I work in the lab here."

"Okay. Well, nice meeting you. I've got to run," Beau said looking directly at her.

"Yes. Have a nice day," Rachel said turning her back to Beau and heading to her lab.

Beau exited the office through the front door and got in his car not giving the lab tech another thought.

It took Rachel an extra few seconds to unlock the door to her lab because she was shaking. What were the odds she'd literally run into Beau Baldwin? There weren't any cars in the parking lot behind their building when she arrived so she'd been totally caught off guard when he came out of his office. She flicked on the overhead lights and set down her backpack and purse on her desk.

She took a deep breath to steady herself. It was time to check on the last living mouse she'd named Alan Smith.

Diane Cobalt

Alan the mouse was happily running around his spacious home, spacious because his friends had all died.

Yesterday, Rachel had finally been able to meet with Amy about producing the special water bottles. Someone from Amy's company was due here any minute to get the "water" to fill the six bottles Rachel had ordered. They would add the labels, seal them up and get them to her by noon. Amy had proven to be a valuable resource.

But something was still bothering Rachel, something in the back of her mind. She just couldn't put her finger on it. Her thoughts were interrupted by a slight tap on the lab door. Cautiously, Rachel cracked it open. It was Amy.

"Good morning, roomie. I'm here to pick up your 'water'," she said making air quotes with her fingers.

Rachel nodded. "It's not a lot, so I'll help you to your car with it."

"Don't be silly. One of my guys will be here in a minute to get it. I popped in to have you approve the bottle color and label." Amy pulled out a folder and opened it to show Rachel several designs. "Which do you like best?"

"Baby Baldwin...that's perfect. Let's do three each of pink and blue bottles."

"Perfect. I should have these ready by lunch time. Do you want me to deliver them here or to the house?"

Rachel thought about it for a moment. "To the house. I need to go home for lunch anyway."

Amy nodded. "By the way, there will be another party tomorrow night. You're invited. Just make sure you put on a name tag. See you later."

Fatal Race

And with that, Amy exited the lab. Within a minute, a bulky man who looked very similar to the "wine cellar" gate keeper entered the lab and took the compound from Rachel. He wasn't the same man who'd picked up the order for Mr. Smith. Rachel snapped her fingers. That's what had bothered her. Did Amy also work for Alan Smith? And the party! Rachel squeezed her eyes shut picturing the woman she'd spoken to the other night. Her name tag said Vicki. Hadn't Vicki said that Amy ran an international school? That would be a full time job. So why was Amy doing this bottled water thing on the side?

More images from the party began flooding Rachel's brain. The man who was "riding" Amy in her bedroom the night of the party had to have been Alan Smith. She'd seen all of half of him; unfortunately it had been his backside. But she had noticed a blond toupee which had been shifting from side to side as he thrusted away. Rachel's glimpse of the man had lasted less than ten seconds, just long enough for her to register what was going on.

Alan Smith had to know where Pierce was...or what had happened to him. Amy might be her best way to get in touch with him. While she concocted her plan to reach Mr. Smith, Rachel decided it was time for the mouse version to die. She would be done with this lab after today.

Rachel withdrew a pipette from the drawer underneath the counter. She went to her lab refrigerator and selected the small vial of the poisonous compound. She added two drops to the mouse's water bowl, added water, and then placed the bowl in the mouse's house. Alan Smith, the mouse, was thirsty. He immediately lapped up the water.

It took less than five minutes for Alan Smith, the mouse, to go belly up.

There really had been no reason for Rachel to go back to the lab after today. She spent the rest of the morning clearing out her belongings and wiping it down for "prints." Dr. Hunnicutt and Beau were not in the office, so Rachel left the doctor a two week notice on his desk.

When she arrived back at Amy's house at noon, she found the six water bottles on the kitchen table. They looked professional. Rachel held one of the pink labeled ones up to the light and shook it. The liquid was totally clear. The compound had mixed in seamlessly.

Rachel took the bottles upstairs to her room where she had stored a bag of "goodies" along with a basket she'd bought yesterday at a craft store. After placing the bottles in the basket, she filled it with rattles, burp cloths and a stuffed teddy bear. Rachel stepped back to admire her work. The final item was a card that said "For Your Special Delivery." Of course she left it unsigned.

It had been easy finding out the address where Jennifer worked. She'd simply followed her one morning, driving on while Jennifer pulled into her parking space. Rachel had noted the address and the street number on the building and the location of the door Jennifer had entered. Because it was still the lunch hour, Rachel decided to make her "special delivery." Alan Smith, the mouse, might not be the only casualty of the day.

As she pulled into the parking lot outside Jennifer's office, she noticed Jennifer's car was not in the lot. Perfect! She just hoped that the door was unlocked. Rachel parked, and then gently lifted the large basket from her back seat. She was able to juggle it and still open the unlocked glass door by feeling for its handle.

"Hello? Is anybody here?" she called.

"Can I help you?" asked Gordon. "That looks heavy."

"Why yes, sir. This is a delivery for Jennifer Baldwin."

Gordon took the basket from her. "Why isn't that cute? Jennifer's gonna love it. Do you want me to put it on her desk?"

Rachel smiled at him. "That would be great. Thank you!"

Gordon smiled. "Should I tell her who it's from?"

"There's a card inside. I'm just the delivery lady." Rachel turned and headed out the door. She couldn't have asked for a better hand off. As she started her car, she noticed the company name on the door: Data Shield. Where had she heard that before?

She was pulling out of the parking lot when it hit her as to why the name sounded familiar. Data Shield was Alan Smith's company. That meant Jennifer Baldwin worked for the man who most likely knew what had happened to Pierce! She needed to contact Walter immediately.

CHAPTER FORTY-NINE

The late September Texas sun heated up the concrete, mimicking a frying pan. Rachel was growing more uncomfortable by the minute sitting in her car across the street from Data Shield. She alternated from keeping the engine running, to turning if off and putting down the windows, to keeping the air on and just running the battery. How long would it take for Jennifer Baldwin to return from lunch? And what was taking Walter so long to return her voice mail? Rachel shook her head. Patience had never been her virtue.

It wasn't as if she really had anything to do this afternoon. Her work at the lab was finished. She'd delivered the basket. The only thing left was to make "Paige's" airline reservation. Bingo! Perusing American's flight schedule would give her something to do for the next fifteen minutes or so. Rachel pulled up the airline's website on her phone. There was only one direct flight this time of year out of Dallas to Grand Cayman and it left at eleven in the morning. Today was Thursday. How soon could she be ready to leave? She guessed it would depend on what Walter was able to find out about Alan Smith. Crap! The direct flight only left on Saturdays so if she missed this week's she'd have to wait until the next Saturday or take an early morning flight which went through Miami. Since "Paige" needed to keep as low of a profile as possible, Rachel decided the direct flight would be the safest. She'd be paying top dollar for the flight on this short notice, but it would be worth it to get the hell out of here. She entered in the required information, including Paige's passport number and credit card and booked the flight for this Saturday. As she finished, her cell rang. It was Walter...finally!

"I've been researching Data Shield for the past half an hour and have come up with nothing," Walter said without even saying hello.

"What do you mean nothing? I'm looking right at its front door as we speak."

"It's as if it doesn't exist. I've checked Google, LinkedIn, White Pages Premium, and Corporation Wiki...nada! And Alan Smith is way too generic of a name to track down."

"So what do we do now?" Rachel asked.

"I don't know. Short of posing as a potential client and entering their business, I have no suggestions. The problem with that is that I don't know what the hell their business does…if anything. This could be a shell company used for money laundering."

"And Jennifer Baldwin would work for an unethical company? Hardly!" Rachel scoffed.

"I can hire a detective. But that will take time."

"Yeah and I don't have time. I want to get back home so I can look for Pierce myself. In fact, I've booked a flight on Saturday."

"This Saturday? As in the day after tomorrow?"

"One and the same, Cousin."

Walter took a deep breath. "Okay. I respect that. I can continue looking here if you want me to."

"Of course I want you to."

"Then that will be our plan. What about your work?" Walter was relieved that his cousin had apparently given up her vendetta against Jennifer Baldwin. She was staying true to her word.

"Pierce finished the project before he went AWOL."

"Okay then. Do you need me to take you to the airport on Saturday?"

"Nope. I'll just turn in my rental car there."

"Well, I guess this is goodbye, then."

"Yes. And Walter, I do appreciate all you've done to help me. Come visit me sometime."

"Oh I will. You don't have to ask me twice for that. You live on a beautiful island."

Rachel pressed the round red button on her phone to disconnect. Sweat was rolling down her back. She was tired of waiting around to see if Jennifer Baldwin would return to work this afternoon. Hopefully, she'd be dead before Saturday. Rachel restarted her car, pulled out of the parking lot and headed back to Amy's home trying to figure out a plan B, if necessary, to get rid of Jennifer.

When Meredith returned to their apartment shortly after school was out on Thursday afternoon, she was surprised that Vicki wasn't there. Since receiving the phone from Jennifer, she'd made taking an afternoon nap part of her routine. That way, she had a reason to lie down and surreptitiously remove the phone from the lining of her pillowcase and check it for messages. Today as she lay with her back to any cameras, she saw a text from Vicki. "Things are heating up. Will be back around five. I have approval to take you to dinner. Will discuss details then."

Meredith glanced at her watch. She'd have to wait for almost an hour. Taking a nap would actually be a good way to pass the time.

Thirty minutes later, Vicki came bursting through the door. "Gretchen? Time to get some food," she announced.

"Gretchen" pretended to be surprised. She'd worked the phone up her shirt sleeve so that it now was pressed into her armpit. "Okay," she said as unenthusiastically as she could.

Vicki bounded down the stairs. Meredith followed. Vicki drove like a crazy woman for the next ten minutes. Meredith wondered what the rush was. Finally, Vicki pulled into a parking garage near several restaurants. As soon as they got out of the car, Vicki started talking.

"We don't have more than an hour. I don't want them to get too suspicious," she said to Meredith as they crossed the street and went into Fernando's, a local Tex-Mex restaurant. "We're early and service is usually pretty prompt. Let's order right away so I can start filling you in."

Meredith nodded as she quickened her steps in order to keep up with Vicki. There was no wait inside the restaurant and they were seated at a booth in the far corner. The waiter took their orders.

"What's up?" Meredith asked.

"We're not a hundred percent sure what is up. But we are pretty certain of a timeline."

"And that is?"

"Tomorrow. Probably in the afternoon. And we're also fairly sure that the event will be catastrophic."

Meredith looked at her fellow agent in the eyes. "Is there any way I can be armed? Can you get me out of that school so I can be of some help?"

"I'm working on it. But everything will have to go like clockwork in order for us to pull this off."

"I'm listening."

Vicki leaned forward slightly. "Tomorrow will be your first day at the high school. I will clear it with Amy in the morning. At eight a.m. you will be called into her office and given your new assignment. The buses will be en route to the schools so you will have to walk. We will drive by it on the way back to our humble abode tonight. It's about four blocks south of where we are now. You will walk three blocks along the street in front of our school and then make an immediate right onto a side street called..." Vicki paused accessing the notes on her phone, "called Casper. There will be a silver Ford sedan with two men in front waiting for you. Get in on the passenger side. It hasn't been determined yet which two agents will be in the car so I can't give you those names. Quite possibly one will be named Manuel. They will give you further instructions. I'm telling Amy that I am taking you to get some school supplies before your first class which isn't until eleven. You'll walk out into the front parking lot with me. The buses will be blocking Amy's view of my car. I will leave... without you. You will be on foot. I will drive by the high school and pretend to drop you off around ten thirty. That will give you over a two hour head-start on your escape."

Vicki stopped talking as she saw the waiter approaching with their dinners.

"Can I get you anything else?" he asked.

Meredith shook her head. "Nope. Looks like we have everything."

"Great. Enjoy."

Vicki took a bite of her taco salad. "Okay. Repeat your instructions to me."

Meredith swallowed a bite of her enchilada. "I will be summoned to Amy's office at eight where she will tell me to report to the high school. You will be waiting for me in the parking lot on the other side of the buses to take me to get some school supplies. But I won't get in the car with you. I am to walk three blocks south down the street and turn right onto a side street named Casper. There will be a silver Ford sedan with two men in the front waiting for me. One may be named Manuel."

Vicki smiled. "That's perfect."

"Are you going to that party tonight?" Meredith asked.

Vicki broke off a piece of her taco salad shell and dipped it in one of the hot sauces. She shook her head. "As far as I know, it's been cancelled. We're taking that as another indicator that some of those who attend the party are involved in whatever is being planned for tomorrow."

"So, not good that the party's not happening?"

"Not good. But we are looking forward to circumventing whatever attack they may have planned. It will simply be one of those nonevents the public never hears about."

Meredith looked pleased. "That's our job! It feels good to be back."

Jennifer was exhausted. Her big brown eyes were unusually bloodshot and her wavy hair was starting to frizz. She'd decided to go home for lunch and take the afternoon off. Beau was coming back from Houston and would be home in time for dinner. Jennifer wanted to make him his favorite: lasagna and chocolate chip cookies. So after a nice nap, she began making cookies. Cookies! She'd make a double batch: one for the new "partying" neighbors across the street and one for the Baldwins.

Fatal Race

Beau planned on swinging by soccer practice to help out Drew if his plane from Houston was on time. Jennifer looked at the clock. She had time to drop off the cookies at the house down the street. She arranged them on a pretty plastic plate and headed out the door.

As she walked up their steep driveway, she noticed two men loading what looked like helium cylinders into the back of a van parked in the garage. When Jennifer smiled at them, they looked as if they'd been caught doing something wrong. Arriving at the front door, she pushed the doorbell.

A woman yanked open the door. "What do you guys need now?" she said not realizing that she had a visitor.

Jennifer's eyes widened. "Amy! I didn't know you lived here!"

Amy appeared startled, but quickly recovered. "Mrs. Baldwin! What a surprise!"

Jennifer handed the plate to Amy. "Please, call me Jennifer. I baked cookies today and thought I'd bring some to welcome my new neighbor! I had no idea it would be you!" Jennifer hoped Amy would invite her inside.

Amy smiled. "What a coincidence! How thoughtful! I'd invite you inside but we just had the carpets cleaned."

"No problem. I need to get back to start our dinner." Jennifer turned to head down the driveway.

"Thank you! Don't be a stranger!" Amy called after her.

Strange is a good word for what's going on, thought Jennifer.

CHAPTER FIFTY

When the Baldwin's alarm went off at six forty-five Friday morning, Jennifer groaned. The baby had pressed on her bladder several times during the night causing her to get up to go to the bathroom. Exhausted, she rolled over to kiss her husband.

"Tough night?" he asked.

Jennifer nodded. "I'm afraid it will be getting worse now that I am officially in the third trimester. I can sleep upstairs if I'm keeping you awake."

Beau hugged his wife. "Oh no you're not. You'll be sleeping next to me tonight and for all the remaining nights of your pregnancy. Let me take Ryan to school so you can have a little extra time this morning."

Jennifer sat up slowly and swung her legs over the side of the bed. "I'll take you up on that offer."

Ryan had been excited at breakfast about show-and-tell. He had spent an hour last night debating on what to take before finally deciding on a picture of him and his mother. It had been all Jennifer could to do to keep from crying.

"Okay, Ryan, do you have everything you need for school today?" Beau asked. "Lunch, homework, show-and-tell?"

"Yes, Uncle Beau. They are in my backpack which is on my back."

"Good job. Then we'll head off to school." Beau crossed the kitchen to say goodbye to his wife. "We have soccer practice right after school today so you don't need to pick him up." He bent over and gave Jennifer a kiss.

"Great! Have a wonderful day, you guys!"

As soon as Beau left to drive Ryan to school, Jennifer checked both of her extra phones. She was hoping to hear something from Manuel, but that phone showed no messages. However, there was a text from Gordon. "Meet us at the usual spot as soon as you drop off your nephew. We will be there at eight."

Jennifer sighed. Great! Something was up. She just wasn't up to doing battle with Alan Smith today. Promptly at eight, Jennifer pulled into the parking lot at Panera Bread and headed to get a cup of hazelnut decaf coffee before going to their usual table.

"You look tired," Gordon greeted her.

Jennifer nodded. "That's because I am. This baby is already keeping me up at night and it hasn't even been born."

"Have a seat," said Jack.

"We've 'perfected' the app Alan asked for," Gordon began. "And by 'perfected' I mean it will look that way to him when we demo it this morning using your phone."

"Yeah. But don't worry," added Jack. "It only appears to block all communications."

"You're sure about that?"

"Positive," Gordon answered. "We've been testing it for over two weeks. We just needed to give you a heads up before our meeting with him this morning."

Jennifer did her best to smile. "Wonderful. I knew you two would find a way around his request."

Jack and Gordon were silent. Simultaneously they looked at each other and started to speak.

"You first," Jack snarled.

"Uh, there's something else we need to tell you," Gordon said to Jennifer. "Go ahead, Jack."

Jack cleared his throat. "You know the other day when we were in Alan's office and he closed the door?"

Jennifer nodded.

"Aw you tell her..." Jack said to Gordon.

"Alan asked us to start transferring large sums of money," Gordon almost whispered.

Jennifer did her best not to react. "To whom?"

Jack shrugged.

"It's not to whom so much as to where," Gordon answered.

Jennifer looked at them questioningly.

"Syria," said Jack. "The rat bastard has us transferring money to Syria."

"That's illegal, guys. You've got to stop."

Gordon shook his head. "Can't. If we do, he'll kill our families."

"And probably will do something worse than that to us," added Jack.

"Oh...that's..." Jennifer didn't know what to say.

"We probably shouldn't have shared this with you, but someone needs to know," said Gordon.

Jennifer nodded. *And that someone is Manuel Garcia.*

A short time later when Jennifer entered her office, she saw the big basket filled with baby items and water bottles. She walked back towards the front door to find Jack and Gordon. "Is that basket from you?" she asked.

"No, I wish we could just lie and say it was," said Gordon. "Some woman stopped by yesterday and dropped it off. She said there was a card inside."

"There is, but it is blank."

Jack frowned. "That's strange. It's probably from Alan."

Jennifer shrugged and returned to her desk. There was a pile of new folders on her chair. The basket probably was from Alan. Jennifer quickly flipped through the manila folders. The first one was labeled BWP. This was one of the first companies she had set up for Alan. There were several customers to bill. One was for Grandview Elementary. Jennifer looked at the paperwork closely. It was for the water bottles they sold at the fundraiser. She frowned. BWP? Did that stand for bottled water something? What did the P stand for? Jennifer got a bad feeling. Did P stand for poison? Then it hit her: all of the miscarriages at the school...Kate's miscarriage...had it been from the bottled water?

"Jennifer, would you please come to my office?" Alan startled her. He was standing in her doorway. "And bring your phone."

"Sure!" She left the folder open on her desk.

Gordon and Jack were already standing in Alan's office. "Hey! Can I see your phone?" Gordon asked.

Jennifer handed him her cell. The pair ran through the jamming device they had developed, proving it worked on Jennifer's cell by calling it from theirs. Alan was ecstatic. "Good job! Please send me a copy of the code you used."

Gordon and Jack looked at each other. "Now?" Jack asked.

"When you get a minute. I'd like it today."

Jack and Gordon looked deflated. "Sure Boss," said Gordon.

"Will you two please stay? Jennifer, you are free to get back to your work." Alan's tone turned ominous.

Jennifer shot Jack and Gordon a concerned look before taking back her phone and returning to her desk.

After several minutes of entering data into QuickBooks, Jennifer was getting thirsty. She should have picked up a tea instead of drinking coffee which dehydrated her. Jennifer eyed the bottled water in the basket before looking at the file she had left open. She reached for one of the bottles and looked at it closely. There, on the bottom, were the initials BWP. This bottle had come from Alan's company!

Fatal Race

Precisely at eight o'clock, Amy summoned "Gretchen" to her office to inform her of her new assignment at the high school. "Gretchen" appropriately appeared enthused. She left Amy's office, headed to the other side of the school buses where Vicki was getting into her car. Meredith then walked south for three blocks and turned right onto a road marked Casper. There she found a silver Ford sedan with two men sitting in front. She opened the back door on the passenger side and got in.

The man on the passenger side turned to face her. "Vincent!" Meredith said, shaking his hand. "It's so good to see you again!"

"I can't tell you how good it is to see you," he replied. "Our driver is Manuel Garcia. He's with Border Patrol and part of our group here in Richardson. We're heading downtown this morning to check out a potential target."

"So I'm done being Gretchen?"

"You're done, Fraulein," Vincent confirmed.

"And what about Vicki?"

"She's not quite done, but almost. She's got to cover for you."

"How's my son? Is Geoffrey really dead?"

Vincent looked at her. "Yes, Geoffrey did not survive the bombing. But your son is safe and well and living with your brother and his wife. We hope to reunite you with him soon."

Meredith knew better than to ask what soon meant.

Shortly after eight on Friday morning, Rachel's cell rang. She didn't recognize the number but decided to answer it anyway. "Hello?"

"Rachel?" came a hoarse whisper.

"Yes? Who is this?"

"It's..." there was a cough, "Pierce."

"Oh my God! Pierce! You sound so strange. Are you okay? Where in the hell are you?"

"They...I'm at Grandview Elementary. Please...come..."

The call was disconnected. The blueprints! The ones she'd seen rolled out at the party! Could they have been of the elementary school? Rachel grabbed her purse and put the name of the school in her phone for directions. She ran downstairs and got in her car.

Alan Smith's big day had arrived. Today was the day he had spent years planning. If his attack succeeded, it would be replicated across the country within days. And more importantly, Alan, who was better known in his circles as Abdul Al-Serwan, would be elevated to a higher status in the MOA.

His cell phone vibrated on his desk. It was Amy.

"Yes!" he answered somewhat gruffly.

"It's urgent I speak with you."

"I am about to leave my office. I will call you on the way to my...appointment."

Fatal Race

≖╬╬≖

Jennifer had always been good at solving different kinds of word puzzles. In fact, Beau used to make fun of her love for solving cryptograms. BWP was her most important cryptic solution to date. She needed to get out of the office and call Manuel and tell him what she'd learned from Gordon and Jack this morning.

She heard Alan end his call and headed to his office. "Alan, I'm going to go make these deposits," Jennifer said as she stood in Alan's doorway holding one of the bottles of water. "I should be back in about half an hour. Did you leave the gift basket on my desk?" She handed him the bottle.

"No I didn't. That's fine, Jennifer," Alan replied in his strange British accent taking the water. "Thank you. What a cute little bottle. I'll drink this on my way to the meeting I have to go to. I may not be back for a while."

Jennifer got into her car and immediately texted Gordon. She watched Alan get into his car and speed off. She waited two minutes before both Jack and Gordon walked to her car. Both looked like they were about to vomit.

"He gave us our next assignment," Gordon started.

"Yeah, he wants us to essentially find a way to hack into the city's water supply," Jack finished.

"We're quitting. Today." Gordon announced.

"Come on," Jack said to Gordon. "Now's our chance to get our stuff and leave before the bastard returns."

"But wait..." Jennifer said too late. The pair had headed inside.

She had no time to chase after them. As Jennifer started her car, she called Beau from her regular phone. She could no longer keep the truth from him. He answered on the second ring. "Hey Sweetheart! How's..."

Jennifer cut him off. "Meet me at the school. There's going to be some kind of attack. They're executing their plan today!"

"Slow down," Beau said calmly. "Who are 'they'?"

"The terrorist cell. Beau, I'm so sorry. I've had to keep this secret from you. I've been working with a government group to try to prevent a terrorist attack. They've been looking for Meredith. She's alive!" Jennifer talked faster than she ever had before.

"You're working for whom?"

"Don't worry about who they are. Meredith's not only alive, but she's here in town. She's been working undercover at that International Academy down the street. I've been there twice...I've seen her! Please forgive me for not telling you this before. They said it would protect her if you didn't know." Jennifer started crying.

"Okay. You're just upset. Take a deep breath. I'll meet you at the school, out front in the parking lot. We'll handle this together. Everything will be okay."

Jennifer's other cell phone was ringing. "I've got to go. Please forgive me! I love you!"

"Talk to me," the voice on the green phone said.

"He's trying to poison the water," Jennifer said. "He owns the bottled water company our school used for a fundraiser. He poisoned the water or something so pregnant women would miscarry. Now he's asked Jack and Gordon to hack into the city's water supply."

"Hang on a second, Jen. I've got another call coming in. Don't hang up."

But somehow the call dropped. Jennifer tried frantically calling Manuel back but couldn't get through.

While idling at the first stoplight, Alan Smith put the bottle of water in his cup holder and punched in Amy's number. "What's so urgent?"

"Jennifer Baldwin is a spy! She brought me cookies last night."

Alan laughed. "That doesn't make her a spy."

"Well I'd never met her as a neighbor, but when I came to the door she recognized me as Amy from the International Academy."

"Okay. No harm done."

"Except they were loading the cylinders into the van in my garage. She probably saw them."

"So?"

"So I went back and reviewed all the video of her last tour with Gretchen. She slipped her something. I can't make out what it is, but somehow they know each other."

Alan pulled his car into a lot two blocks from Grandview Elementary. He grabbed the water bottle and exited the car. "Thanks for letting me know. I will take care of her." He disconnected before Amy could answer. Then he pulled up the app on his phone that the two imbeciles he'd hired had coded for him. It had taken only one of his comrades fifteen minutes to circumvent the lock they had put on it so that it wouldn't work. And it had only taken a few more hours for his comrade to download a version onto every Grandview Elementary school parent's and teacher's cell phone through the school's website. Alan hit the button marked "jam" on his control panel and began walking to his "perch" to watch the chaos that was about to occur.

The city of Richardson's traffic lights were notorious for not being in sync. Jennifer ran through the events of the past few days while she waited at the second red light. Something didn't seem right. Lots of children and men had consumed the bottled water and were fine. In fact, no one had died. So how could there be an attack at the elementary school using water?

By the third light, Jennifer had thrown out that possibility. And then it hit her. The water was a diversion. She remembered the boom in the science lab at the International Academy the other day. The metal cylinders being loaded into a van at Amy's house yesterday when she'd taken cookies over to her flashed into her brain. They were going to blow up the school.

She tried again to call Manuel. Nothing. Then she tried to dial 911. Nothing. She looked down at the corner of her phone. "No Service" it read.

Fatal Race

Jennifer raced down the street and parked in front of Grandview Elementary. Everything was quiet. There were a few classes on the playground for recess. Jennifer ran up the steps as fast as she could at seven months pregnant. She entered the first set of double doors and pressed the buzzer for someone in the office to let her in.

"Hello, Mrs. Baldwin," said Karen who was one of the secretaries.

"They're going to blow up the school. They've got cylinders of some kind of gas...please evacuate the school now!"

Karen frowned. "Let me buzz you in. I'll get the principal."

Jennifer yanked open the second set of double doors and entered the school office. "We don't have time!" Jennifer could see from Karen's face that she was coming across like a crazy woman. "Look, there's a terrorist cell that's been planning an attack. They've jammed our cell phones!"

Karen walked to her desk and picked up her cell phone. She tried calling the principal with it. Nothing happened. "Huh. It says no service!"

"Yes! On everyone's. That's part of their plan. Please call 911 from the landline. Have them tell Charles Connor, the Chief of Police, that Jennifer Baldwin said they are going to blow up the school!"

Karen walked over to the fire handle and pulled it. Nothing happened. "Get on the loud speaker and tell them we have been notified to evacuate the building!" Karen yelled across the office as she picked up the landline phone to dial 911.

Jennifer didn't wait to see what happened. She had to find Ryan.

As the announcement was made, students and teachers began pouring out of the school's front and side doors. "Ryan? Chris?" Jennifer called. She ran through the halls, ducking her head into their classroom but it was empty. She paused to catch her breath. She shouldn't be here, but she had to find her nephew.

"Ryan!" she screamed as she ran by the janitor's closet.

Inside the closet, Rachel was frantically trying to free Pierce from the chains that shackled him to the janitor's sink. Strapped to his chest was the timer for the ignitor that would create an explosion with the gas that had by now filled the school. She'd used every tool she could get her hands on in order to cut through the metal rope. None had worked.

"Just go," Pierce whispered. "Save yourself. Please tell them I didn't want to develop this gas...they said if I didn't, they would hurt you."

Rachel ignored the tears that were racing down her cheeks. While she had been busy designing the water to kill Jennifer Baldwin, her husband had been forced to use a similar formula to develop an odorless, highly flammable gas made from easy to obtain elements. The gas would be used to destroy schools across the country.

"Ryan!" Rachel heard a woman scream on the other side of the door.

"Ryan, that's the name of Jennifer's nephew," she said to Pierce. "I'll be right back."

Rachel threw open the door to the closet and raced into the hallway. "He's in here," she said to Jennifer.

"Oh thank God," Jennifer said, not realizing who she was talking to. But as she peered around the open door and saw Pierce tied to the janitor's sink she realized Ryan was not there. "Who are you?"

"Get out of here! Both of you," Pierce said as loudly as he was able to.

Rachel ignored him. "I'm Christina LaRue's sister...the woman you killed in your pool?" Rachel pulled Jennifer into the closet. "Now it's your turn to die."

Jennifer paused to look at the woman. She did resemble Christina. "I didn't kill your sister. She was electrocuted in our pool. It was an accident."

"A matter of semantics, wouldn't you say? I guess you didn't drink the water I left for you on your desk. Too bad. Oh well. At least Plan B's been designed for me."

Rachel had one hand on Jennifer's arm. As she stooped to pick up a coil of rope on the floor next to Pierce, Jennifer used her free hand to grab a large bottle of bleach propped up next to the wall. She hit Rachel in the back of the head as hard as she could.

Jennifer stepped over Rachel's limp body and ran into the hallway making her way to the front of the school. She pushed open the first set of glass doors and then the second set. The kids were all across the street in front! They must have been outside at recess. She stood at the top of the steps that led to the doors searching for Ryan in the crowd. "Ryan!" she yelled. There was a lot of commotion and she could hear sirens in the distance.

Alan Smith observed the mayhem from his vantage point on a small hill hidden by the maple trees across the creek from the front of the school. There was really nothing that gave him a bigger thrill than watching so many infidels die at one time. And today he was even getting a bonus: he had seen Jennifer Baldwin race into the building, most likely looking for her nephew. So far, she hadn't come out. He checked his watch. The timer was set to cause a spark in just under a minute. Alan opened the bottle of water Jennifer Baldwin had given him earlier. "Goodbye, Jennifer Baldwin!" he said. As he guzzled the last drop from the bottle, he realized he couldn't breathe. His whole body went rigid and he fell down. Alan Smith was dead before he hit the ground.

Jennifer used her vantage point at the top of the steps to look for Ryan. "Aunt Jennifer!" she thought she heard to her left. She turned in time to see Ryan waving to her, holding Meredith's hand. Kate and Chris were standing next to them.

Meredith was motioning frantically for Jennifer to join them. Just as she was about to start down the steps, Jennifer heard her name being called again, this time from her right side. It was Beau's voice.

"Jennifer! Get away from there!"

Before Jennifer started down the stairs, she smiled at Beau. She motioned him to where Ryan was standing.

Fatal Race

The blast from behind her was deafening. Jennifer felt herself being propelled forward. Something hit her head and then her world went dark.

EPILOGUE

One week later

Two men sat in an idling, silver Ford sedan. The maple trees lining the quiet street had provided them shade on the very hot day they had first driven by. But today there was a thick layer of clouds. Their eyes which once followed the children frolicking on the Grandview Elementary playground across the street, now surveyed the rubble where the school once stood. The street which ended just past the front was riddled with debris from the blast. There now was a clear view of the playground; its slides, swings and jungle gyms had been toppled.

Fatal Race

"Wow, you'd never guess there had been a grade school tucked away back here," commented the passenger. "Was it really just over a year ago when we first drove by?"

The driver nodded. "I believe on our first visit we had commented about how it was so quiet and protected."

"Isolated...and a potential target was what we had concluded," added the passenger. "Sometimes it sucks to be right."

The driver's eyes shifted focus from the twisted steel of the playground equipment to the metal bleachers adjacent to the soccer field. A lone figure sat hunched over on its top tier. "Who's that sitting over there?"

The passenger looked to where the driver was pointing. "I can't tell without seeing a face. Guess we better investigate."

Manuel Garcia and Vincent O'Donley exited the car and headed toward the figure, carefully stepping around chunks of concrete, brick and glass.

"It looks like a war zone," Vincent commented.

Manuel nodded. "A war without the mass casualties. I should be happy about that...but I'm not."

Vincent patted Manuel's back. "Me neither."

As the pair approached the bleachers they split. Vincent walked around the risers to the left and Manuel to the right. Both men had their right hands on their guns as they had been trained to do.

The figure on the bench looked up at the men facing him. A large, rounded heap of gauze covered his left cheek and stitches zigzagged along his left arm. The man's eyes were red and bloodshot. His face was wet with tears.

"Beau," Manuel said simply as he climbed up to the top row and sat down next to him. Vincent climbed up on the other side. The three sat in silence.

Beau looked straight ahead. "You know it was just last week that I was coaching Ryan's soccer team here. Jennifer came by after work. She sat right there," he pointed to a spot on the first row, "next to Kate."

Manuel and Vincent remained silent, allowing Beau to continue.

"I remember walking up to Jennifer and telling her to go home and put on a dress because I was taking her to dinner. We went to one of her favorite restaurants, Bistro 31. My boss sent us there to celebrate my success in selling my first million dollars of his new medical device. She was so happy and proud of me." Beau paused to wipe his nose with the back of his hand. He continued to look straight ahead. "We toasted to my achievement. And then I told her my other piece of good news: that she could quit her job. I knew I had caught her off guard by her reaction. I told her to think about it. She had been doing so much—taking care of my nephew while working full-time and being pregnant..." Beau couldn't continue. Vincent and Manuel looked at each other as if willing the other not to break down. "You know what I wish now?"

"No, Beau, what do you wish?" Manuel asked.

Fatal Race

"I wish I hadn't wasted those precious moments with her celebrating *my* success when *she's* the one who was quietly working to save us all. I should have been toasting her."

Manuel had to turn away so Beau wouldn't see his anguish.

Vincent nodded.

"But I didn't know. She kept it all a secret from me...that she was helping you. How could you have let an innocent woman work for such a heinous terrorist? My God, she had no training in how to deal with that."

Beau sat up from his hunched over position. He put his good arm on Manuel's. "I remember when I first met you. I was on the plane heading to Harlingen and then on to Mexico to track down a piece of missing medical equipment. You asked me if I had a family and I asked you about yours. You said you had been married once to a Mexican girl but that it had a very sad ending. Then you warned me not to go to Mexico, but gave me your card in case I needed help—which of course I did. You saved my life, but now I have a very sad story to tell about *my* wife. I wonder if I'd heeded your advice that day in the plane if none of this would have happened. Jennifer would never have met you...any of you," he said referring to Vincent. "She'd be alive right now. Our baby would be alive right now. I wouldn't be alone." Beau laughed a hollow laugh. "During our last conversation, she asked me to forgive her for keeping this a secret. I should have asked her to forgive me for not heeding your advice that day on the plane."

Manuel attempted to speak. "You can't go there, my amigo. You can't blame yourself for any of this. I know how you feel. I blamed myself for years about what happened to my wife and you know where that got me?"

Beau shook his head.

"Nowhere. It didn't bring her back. You can't undo anything now. If anyone's to blame it's us."

"And the damn terrorists who are infiltrating our country," added Vincent.

"Okay, them too," agreed Manuel. "But you need to remember that your wife wanted to help us. She wanted to save her community. Without Jennifer, Abdul Al-Serwan, aka Alan Smith, one of America's most-wanted and most nefarious terrorists would not be dead. Without your wife, we would have been unable to apprehend the leaders of the terrorist cell who had been plotting to mimic this type of attack on elementary schools all across the country. We wouldn't have been able to shut down that international academy and arrest the students they had radicalized. That makes her extra special, my friend. Jennifer saved the lives of every single child, teacher and administrator of this school. And she saved your sister. So your nephew has his mother back."

"And don't forget she also saved Richardson's water supply. She's the one who figured out the water was being tainted to cause miscarriages. The terrorists were just steps away from introducing it into the water going to that tower over there," added Vincent.

Beau nodded. "Every time I close my eyes I see myself running up that street," he pointed towards the front of the school. I was looking for Ryan and for Jennifer. I spotted Ryan first, holding my sister's hand, standing across the street. They were pointing to the front door and yelling Jennifer's name. I shouted at her too. I told her to run. I'll never forget how beautiful she looked standing there. She saw me and smiled—and then—and then her life ended."

Manuel hugged Beau gently. "Here's another piece of unsolicited advice from me. Certainly you need to take time to grieve. But don't waste too much time wallowing in self-pity. Jennifer wouldn't want that. Decide you're going to do something that would have made her proud...turn a horrific event into something good. No terrorist can stop you from doing that."

Beau sat silently for several minutes. A very small area of blue sky finally broke through the heavy cloud layer. Beau looked up. Jennifer had always told him all you needed was a patch of blue sky the size of your knee to allow the sun to break through. He had been up all night trying to decide what his next step should be, where his life should go. Suddenly he knew. "We have to stop them," he said quietly but with conviction. "Put me on your team."

ACKNOWLEDGEMENTS

I am fortunate to have a magnificent group of friends who volunteered to read *Fatal Race* and provided valuable feedback. Thank you to Donna Friedel, Bonni Garrison, Melissa Glanton, Kathy Haddox, Marikka Law, Pat Shaw, Nancy Wiginton and Rob Woessner. You all made the final installment of the *Fatal Trilogy* much better. As always, any remaining errors are mine.

Congratulations to Bonni, winner of the Fatal Race contest! Bonni named the character, Vicki in honor of her sister, Vicki Beveridge, whom Bonni claims really is a saint! Also, congratulations to "Maui" Mike, winner of the "On the Move" contest! "Maui" Mike submitted a picture of himself reading *Fatal Move* on the beach in Maui.

Ending the *Fatal Trilogy* was challenging and emotional. My two sons, Chad and Gage, once again provided thoughtful comments pertaining to the story. They have encouraged me to pursue my dream. Thank you!

Finally, I could not have finished this novel without my husband's encouragement. He had the unenviable task of being the first person to read *Fatal Race* as I cranked out each chapter. While I sometimes took his criticism of my work personally, he made me revisit parts of the plot and facets of my characters which made them stronger and more believable. Thank you, Chip, for pushing me to continually hone my writing skills and cheering me on to never give up.

To all who have read the *Fatal Trilogy*, I give you my deepest, heartfelt thanks.

Cheers!

DC

Made in the USA
Columbia, SC
26 October 2021